WILLIAM SYDNEY PORTER (1862–1910), pseudonymously famous as O. HENRY, was one of the finest American short story writers. His writings were famously marked by ironic humour and surprise endings. Some of his major works are *The Four Million* (1906), *The Trimmed Lamp* (1907), *Heart of the West* (1907) and *Whirligigs* (1910).

Porter began his writing career with the setting up of *The Rolling Stone* in 1894, a humorous weekly which did not do well. This was followed by a short stint at *The Houston Post* as a reporter, columnist and cartoonist. However, Porter was imprisoned for embezzlement of bank funds and served a sentence, eventually getting early release for good behaviour. While in jail, he started writing short stories under the pseudonym O. Henry to support his daughter, and became renowned.

O. Henry died on June 5, 1910, aged 47.

The Skylight Room and Other Stories

O. Henry

Om Books International

This edition first published in 2020 by

Om Books International

Corporate & Editorial Office
A-12, Sector 64, Noida 201 301
Uttar Pradesh, India
Phone: +91 120 477 4100
Email: editorial@ombooks.com
Website: www.ombooksinternational.com

Sales Office
107, Ansari Road, Darya Ganj,
New Delhi 110 002, India
Phone: +91 11 4000 9000
Fax: +91 11 2327 8091
Email: sales@ombooks.com
Website: www.ombooks.com

Compiled by: Anukriti Singh

ISBN: 978-93-53763-67-1

Printed in India

10 9 8 7 6 5 4 3 2 1

Contents

1

The Duplicity of Hargraves

When Major Pendleton Talbot, of Mobile, sir, and his daughter, Miss Lydia Talbot, came to Washington to reside, they selected for a boarding place a house that stood fifty yards back from one of the quietest avenues. It was an old-fashioned brick building, with a portico upheld by tall white pillars. The yard was shaded by stately locusts and elms, and a catalpa tree in season rained its pink and white blossoms upon the grass. Rows of high box bushes lined the fence and walks. It was the Southern style and aspect of the place that pleased the eyes of the Talbots.

In this pleasant, private boarding house they engaged rooms, including a study for Major Talbot, who was adding the finishing chapters to his book, "Anecdotes and Reminiscences of the Alabama Army, Bench, and Bar."

Major Talbot was of the old, old South. The present day had little interest or excellence in his eyes. His mind lived in that period before the Civil War, when the Talbots owned thousands of acres of fine cotton land and the slaves to till them; when the family mansion was the scene of princely hospitality, and drew its guests from the aristocracy of the South. Out of that period he had brought all its old pride and scruples of honor, an antiquated and punctilious politeness, and (you would think) its wardrobe.

Such clothes were surely never made within fifty years. The major was tall, but whenever he made that wonderful, archaic genuflexion he called a bow, the corners of his frock coat swept the floor. That garment was a surprise even to Washington, which has long ago ceased to shy at the frocks and broad-brimmed hats of Southern congressmen. One of the boarders christened it a "Father Hubbard," and it certainly was high in the waist and full in the skirt.

But the major, with all his queer clothes, his immense area of plaited, raveling shirt bosom, and the little black string tie with the bow always slipping on one side, both was smiled at and liked in Mrs. Vardeman' s select boarding house. Some of the young department clerks would often "string him," as they called it, getting him started upon the subject dearest to him—the traditions and history of his beloved Southland. During his talks he would quote freely from the "Anecdotes and Reminiscences." But they were very careful not to let him see their designs, for in spite of his sixty-eight years, he could make the boldest of them uncomfortable under the steady regard of his piercing gray eyes.

Miss Lydia was a plump, little old maid of thirty-five, with smoothly drawn, tightly twisted hair that made her look still older. Old fashioned, too, she was; but antebellum glory did not radiate from her as it did from the major. She possessed a thrifty common sense; and it was she who handled the finances of the family, and met all comers when there were bills to pay. The major regarded board bills and wash bills as contemptible nuisances. They kept coming in so persistently and so often. Why, the major wanted to know, could they not be filed and paid in a lump sum at some convenient period—say when the "Anecdotes and Reminiscences" had been published and paid for? Miss Lydia would calmly go on with her sewing and say, "We'll pay as we go as long as the money lasts, and then perhaps they'll have to lump it."

Most of Mrs. Vardeman's boarders were away during the day, being nearly all department clerks and business men; but there was one of them who was about the house a great deal from morning to night. This was a young man named Henry Hopkins Hargraves—every one in the house addressed him by his full name—who was engaged at one of the popular vaudeville theaters. Vaudeville has risen to such a respectable plane in the last few years, and Mr. Hargraves was such a modest and well-mannered person, that Mrs. Vardeman could find no objection to enrolling him upon her list of boarders.

At the theatre Hargraves was known as an all-round dialect comedian, having a large repertoire of German, Irish, Swede, and black-face specialties. But Mr. Hargraves was ambitious, and often spoke of his great desire to succeed in legitimate comedy.

This young man appeared to conceive a strong fancy for Major Talbot. Whenever that gentleman would begin his Southern reminiscences, or repeat some of the liveliest of the anecdotes, Hargraves could always be found, the most attentive among his listeners.

For a time the major showed an inclination to discourage the advances of the "play actor," as he privately termed him; but soon the young man's agreeable manner and indubitable appreciation of the old gentleman's stories completely won him over.

It was not long before the two were like old chums. The major set apart each afternoon to read to him the manuscript of his book. During the anecdotes Hargraves never failed to laugh at exactly the right point. The major was moved to declare to Miss Lydia one day that young Hargraves possessed remarkable perception and a gratifying respect for the old regime. And when it came to talking of those old days—if Major Talbot liked to talk, Mr. Hargraves was entranced to listen.

Like almost all old people who talk of the past, the major loved to linger over details. In describing the splendid, almost royal, days of the old planters, he would hesitate until he had recalled the name of the Negro who held his horse, or the exact date of certain minor happenings, or the number of bales of cotton raised in such a year; but Hargraves never grew impatient or lost interest. On the contrary, he would advance questions on a variety of subjects connected with the life of that time, and he never failed to extract ready replies.

The fox hunts, the 'possum suppers, the hoe downs and jubilees in the Negro quarters, the banquets in the plantation-house hall, when invitations went for fifty miles around; the occasional feuds with the neighboring gentry; the major's duel with Rathbone Culbertson about Kitty Chalmers, who afterward married a Thwaite of South Carolina; and private yacht races for fabulous sums on Mobile Bay; the quaint beliefs, improvident habits, and loyal virtues of the old slaves—all these were subjects that held both the major and Hargraves absorbed for hours at a time.

Sometimes, at night, when the young man would be coming upstairs to his room after his turn at the theatre was over, the major would appear at the door of his study and beckon archly to him. Going in, Hargraves would find a little table set with a decanter, sugar bowl, fruit, and a big bunch of fresh green mint.

"It occurred to me," the major would begin—he was always ceremonious—"that perhaps you might have found your duties at the—at your place of occupation—sufficiently arduous to enable you, Mr. Hargraves, to appreciate what the poet might well have had in his mind when he wrote, 'tired Nature's sweet restorer,'—one of our Southern juleps."

It was a fascination to Hargraves to watch him make it. He took rank among artists when he began, and he never varied the process. With what delicacy he bruised the mint; with what exquisite nicety he estimated the ingredients; with what solicitous care he capped the compound with the scarlet fruit glowing against the dark green fringe! And then the hospitality and grace with which he offered it, after the selected oat straws had been plunged into its tinkling depths!

After about four months in Washington, Miss Lydia discovered one morning that they were almost without money. The "Anecdotes and Reminiscences" was completed, but publishers had not jumped at the collected gems of Alabama sense and wit. The rental of a small house which they still owned in Mobile was two months in arrears. Their board money for the month would be due in three days. Miss Lydia called her father to a consultation.

"No money?" said he with a surprised look. "It is quite annoying to be called on so frequently for these petty sums. Really, I—"

The major searched his pockets. He found only a two-dollar bill, which he returned to his vest pocket.

"I must attend to this at once, Lydia," he said. "Kindly get me my umbrella and I will go down town immediately. The congressman from our district, General Fulghum, assured me some days ago that he would use his influence to get my book published at an early date. I will go to his hotel at once and see what arrangement has been made."

With a sad little smile Miss Lydia watched him button his "Father Hubbard" and depart, pausing at the door, as he always did, to bow profoundly.

That evening, at dark, he returned. It seemed that Congressman Fulghum had seen the publisher who had the major's manuscript for reading. That person had said that if the anecdotes, etc., were carefully pruned down about one half, in order to eliminate the sectional and class prejudice with which the book was dyed from end to end, he might consider its publication.

The major was in a white heat of anger, but regained his equanimity, according to his code of manners, as soon as he was in Miss Lydia's presence.

"We must have money," said Miss Lydia, with a little wrinkle above her nose. "Give me the two dollars, and I will telegraph to Uncle Ralph for some tonight."

The major drew a small envelope from his upper vest pocket and tossed it on the table.

"Perhaps it was injudicious," he said mildly, "but the sum was so merely nominal that I bought tickets to the theatre tonight. It's a new war drama, Lydia. I thought you would be pleased to witness its first production in Washington. I am told that the South has very fair treatment in the play. I confess I should like to see the performance myself."

Miss Lydia threw up her hands in silent despair.

Still, as the tickets were bought, they might as well be used. So that evening, as they sat in the theatre listening to the lively overture, even Miss Lydia was minded to relegate their troubles, for the hour, to second place. The major, in spotless linen, with his extraordinary coat showing only where it was closely buttoned, and his white hair smoothly roached, looked really fine and distinguished. The curtain went up on the first act of "A Magnolia Flower," revealing a typical Southern plantation scene. Major Talbot betrayed some interest.

"Oh, see!" exclaimed Miss Lydia, nudging his arm, and pointing to her program.

The major put on his glasses and read the line in the cast of characters that her finger indicated.

Col. Webster Calhoun . . . . H. Hopkins Hargraves.

"It's our Mr. Hargraves," said Miss Lydia. "It must be his first appearance in what he calls 'the legitimate.' I'm so glad for him."

Not until the second act did Col. Webster Calhoun appear upon the stage. When he made his entry Major Talbot gave an audible sniff, glared at him, and seemed to freeze solid. Miss Lydia uttered a little, ambiguous squeak and crumpled her program in her hand. For Colonel Calhoun was made up as nearly resembling Major Talbot as one pea does another. The long, thin white hair, curly at the ends, the aristocratic beak of a nose, the crumpled, wide, raveling shirt front, the string tie, with the bow nearly under one ear, were almost exactly duplicated. And then, to clinch the imitation, he wore the twin to the major's supposed to be unparalleled coat. High-collared, baggy, empire-waisted, ample-skirted, hanging a foot lower in front than behind, the garment could have been designed from no other pattern. From then on, the major and Miss Lydia sat bewitched, and saw the counterfeit presentment of a haughty Talbot "dragged," as the major afterward expressed it, "through the slanderous mire of a corrupt stage."

Mr. Hargraves had used his opportunities well. He had caught the major's little idiosyncrasies of speech, accent, and intonation and his pompous courtliness to perfection—exaggerating all to the purposes of the stage. When he performed that marvelous bow that the major fondly imagined to be the pink of all salutations, the audience sent forth a sudden round of hearty applause.

Miss Lydia sat immovable, not daring to glance toward her father. Sometimes her hand next to him would be laid against her cheek, as if to conceal the smile which, in spite of her disapproval, she could not entirely suppress.

The culmination of Hargraves's audacious imitation took place in the third act. The scene is where Colonel Calhoun entertains a few of the neighboring planters in his "den."

Standing at a table in the center of the stage, with his friends grouped about him, he delivers that inimitable, rambling, character monologue so famous in "A Magnolia Flower," at the same time that he deftly makes juleps for the party.

Major Talbot, sitting quietly, but white with indignation, heard his best stories retold, his pet theories and hobbies advanced and expanded, and the dream of the "Anecdotes and Reminiscences" served, exaggerated and garbled. His favorite narrative—that of his duel with Rathbone Culbertson—was not omitted, and it was delivered with more fire, egotism, and gusto than the major himself put into it.

The monologue concluded with a quaint, delicious, witty little lecture on the art of concocting a julep, illustrated by the act. Here Major Talbot's delicate but showy science was reproduced to a hair's breadth—from his dainty handling of the fragrant weed—"the one-thousandth part of a grain too much pressure, gentlemen, and you extract the bitterness, instead of the aroma, of this heaven-bestowed plant"—to his solicitous selection of the oaten straws.

At the close of the scene the audience raised a tumultuous roar of appreciation. The portrayal of the type was so exact, so sure and thorough, that the leading characters in the play were forgotten. After repeated calls, Hargraves came before the curtain and bowed, his rather boyish face bright and flushed with the knowledge of success.

At last Miss Lydia turned and looked at the major. His thin nostrils were working like the gills of a fish. He laid both shaking hands upon the arms of his chair to rise.

"We will go, Lydia," he said chokingly. "This is an abominable—desecration."

Before he could rise, she pulled him back into his seat. "We will stay it out," she declared. "Do you want to advertise the copy by exhibiting the original coat?" So they remained to the end.

Hargraves's success must have kept him up late that night, for neither at the breakfast nor at the dinner table did he appear.

About three in the afternoon he tapped at the door of Major Talbot's study. The major opened it, and Hargraves walked in with his hands full of the morning papers—too full of his triumph to notice anything unusual in the major's demeanor.

"I put it all over 'em last night, major," he began exultantly. "I had my inning, and, I think, scored. Here's what the *Post* says:

His conception and portrayal of the old-time Southern colonel, with his absurd grandiloquence, his eccentric garb, his quaint idioms and phrases, his moth-eaten pride of family, and his really kind heart, fastidious sense of honor, and lovable simplicity, is the best delineation of a character role on the boards today. The coat worn by Colonel Calhoun is itself nothing less than an evolution of genius. Mr. Hargraves has captured his public.

"How does that sound, major, for a first nighter?"

"I had the honor"—the major's voice sounded ominously frigid—"of witnessing your very remarkable performance, sir, last night."

Hargraves looked disconcerted.

"You were there? I didn't know you ever—I didn't know you cared for the theatre. Oh, I say, Major Talbot," he exclaimed frankly, "don't you be offended. I admit I did get a lot of pointers from you that helped me out wonderfully in the part. But it's a type, you know—not individual. The way the audience caught on shows that. Half the patrons of that theatre are Southerners. They recognized it."

"Mr. Hargraves," said the major, who had remained standing, "you have put upon me an unpardonable insult. You have burlesqued my person, grossly betrayed my confidence, and misused my hospitality. If I thought you possessed the faintest conception of what is the sign manual of a gentleman, or what is due one, I would call you out, sir, old as I am. I will ask you to leave the room, sir."

The actor appeared to be slightly bewildered, and seemed hardly to take in the full meaning of the old gentleman's words.

"I am truly sorry you took offence," he said regretfully. "Up here we don't look at things just as you people do. I know men who would buy out half the house to have their personality put on the stage so the public would recognize it."

"They are not from Alabama, sir," said the major haughtily.

"Perhaps not. I have a pretty good memory, major; let me quote a few lines from your book. In response to a toast at a banquet given in—Milledgeville, I believe—you uttered, and intend to have printed, these words:

The Northern man is utterly without sentiment or warmth except in so far as the feelings may be turned to his own commercial profit. He will suffer without resentment any imputation cast upon the honor of himself or his loved ones that does not bear with it the consequence of pecuniary loss. In his charity, he gives with a liberal hand; but it must be heralded with the trumpet and chronicled in brass.

"Do you think that picture is fairer than the one you saw of Colonel Calhoun last night?"

"The description," said the major frowning, "is—not without grounds. Some exag—latitude must be allowed in public speaking."

"And in public acting," replied Hargraves.

"That is not the point," persisted the major, unrelenting. "It was a personal caricature. I positively decline to overlook it, sir."

"Major Talbot," said Hargraves, with a winning smile, "I wish you would understand me. I want you to know that I never dreamed of insulting you. In my profession, all life belongs to me. I take what I want, and what I can, and return it over the footlights. Now, if you will, let's let it go at that. I came in to see you about something else. We've been pretty good friends for some months, and I'm going to take the risk of offending you again. I know you are hard up for money—never mind how I found out; a boarding house is no place to keep such matters secret—and I want you to let me help you out of the pinch. I've been there often enough myself. I've been getting a fair salary all the season, and I've saved some money. You're welcome to a couple hundred—or even more—until you get—"

"Stop!" commanded the major, with his arm outstretched. "It seems that my book didn't lie, after all. You think your money salve will heal all the hurts of honor. Under no circumstances would I accept a loan from a casual acquaintance; and as to you, sir, I would starve before I would consider your insulting offer of a financial adjustment of the circumstances we have discussed. I beg to repeat my request relative to your quitting the apartment."

Hargraves took his departure without another word. He also left the house the same day, moving, as Mrs. Vardeman explained at the supper table, nearer the vicinity of the down-town theatre, where "A Magnolia Flower" was booked for a week's run.

Critical was the situation with Major Talbot and Miss Lydia. There was no one in Washington to whom the major's scruples allowed him to apply for a loan. Miss Lydia wrote a letter to Uncle Ralph, but it was doubtful whether that relative's constricted affairs would permit him to furnish help. The major was forced to make an apologetic address to Mrs. Vardeman regarding the delayed payment for board, referring to "delinquent rentals" and "delayed remittances" in a rather confused strain.

Deliverance came from an entirely unexpected source.

Late one afternoon the door maid came up and announced an old colored man who wanted to see Major Talbot. The major asked that he be sent up to his study. Soon an old darkey appeared in the doorway, with his hat in hand, bowing, and scraping with one clumsy foot. He was quite decently dressed in a baggy suit of black. His big, coarse shoes shone with a metallic luster suggestive of stove polish. His bushy wool was gray—almost white. After middle life, it is difficult to estimate the age of a Negro. This one might have seen as many years as had Major Talbot.

"I be bound you don't know me, Mars' Pendleton," were his first words.

The major rose and came forward at the old, familiar style of address. It was one of the old plantation darkeys without a doubt; but they had been widely scattered, and he could not recall the voice or face.

"I don't believe I do," he said kindly—"unless you will assist my memory."

"Don't you 'member Cindy's Mose, Mars' Pendleton, what 'migrated 'mediately after de war?"

"Wait a moment," said the major, rubbing his forehead with the tips of his fingers. He loved to recall everything connected with those beloved days. "Cindy's Mose," he reflected. "You worked among the horses—breaking the colts. Yes, I remember now. After the surrender, you took the name of—don't prompt me—Mitchell, and went to the West—to Nebraska."

"Yassir, yassir,"—the old man's face stretched with a delighted grin—"dat's him, dat's it. Newbraska. Dat's me—Mose Mitchell. Old Uncle Mose Mitchell, dey calls me now. Old mars', your pa, gimme a pah of dem mule colts when I lef' fur to staht me goin' with. You 'member dem colts, Mars' Pendleton?"

"I don't seem to recall the colts," said the major. "You know I was married the first year of the war and living at the old Follinsbee place. But sit down, sit down, Uncle Mose. I'm glad to see you. I hope you have prospered."

Uncle Mose took a chair and laid his hat carefully on the floor beside it.

"Yassir; of late I done mouty famous. When I first got to Newbraska, dey folks come all roun' me to see dem mule colts. Dey ain't see no mules like dem in Newbraska. I sold dem mules for three hundred dollars. Yassir—three hundred.

"Den I open a blacksmith shop, suh, and made some money and bought some lan'. Me and my old 'oman done raised up seb'm chillun, and all doin' well 'cept two of 'em what died. Fo' year ago a railroad come along and staht a town slam ag'inst my lan', and, suh, Mars' Pendleton, Uncle Mose am worth leb'm thousand dollars in money, property, and lan'."

"I'm glad to hear it," said the major heartily. "Glad to hear it."

"And dat little baby of yo'n, Mars' Pendleton—one what you name Miss Lyddy—I be bound dat little tad done growed up tell nobody wouldn't know her."

The major stepped to the door and called: "Lydia, dear, will you come?"

Miss Lydia, looking quite grown up and a little worried, came in from her room.

"Dar, now! What'd I tell you? I knowed dat baby done be plum growed up. You don't 'member Uncle Mose, child?"

"This is Aunt Cindy's Mose, Lydia," explained the major. "He left Sunnymead for the West when you were two years old."

"Well," said Miss Lydia, "I can hardly be expected to remember you, Uncle Mose, at that age. And, as you say, I'm 'plum growed up,' and was a blessed long time ago. But I'm glad to see you, even if I can't remember you."

And she was. And so was the major. Something alive and tangible had come to link them with the happy past. The three sat and talked over the olden times, the major and Uncle Mose correcting or prompting each other as they reviewed the plantation scenes and days.

The major inquired what the old man was doing so far from his home.

"Uncle Mose am a delicate," he explained, "to de grand Baptis' convention in dis city. I never preached none, but bein' a residin' elder in de church, and able fur to pay my own expenses, dey sent me along."

"And how did you know we were in Washington?" inquired Miss Lydia.

"Dey's a cullud man works in de hotel whar I stops, what comes from Mobile. He told me he seen Mars' Pendleton comin' outen dish here house one mawnin'.

"What I come fur," continued Uncle Mose, reaching into his pocket—"besides de sight of home folks—was to pay Mars' Pendleton what I owes him."

"Owe me?" said the major, in surprise.

"Yassir—three hundred dollars." He handed the major a roll of bills. "When I lef' old mars' says: 'Take dem mule colts, Mose, and, if it be so you gits able, pay fur 'em'. Yassir—dem was his words. De war had done lef' old mars' po' hisself. Old mars' bein' 'long ago dead, de debt descends to Mars' Pendleton. Three hundred dollars. Uncle Mose is plenty able to pay now. When dat railroad buy my lan' I laid off to pay fur dem mules. Count de money, Mars' Pendleton. Dat's what I sold dem mules fur. Yassir."

Tears were in Major Talbot's eyes. He took Uncle Mose's hand and laid his other upon his shoulder.

"Dear, faithful, old servitor," he said in an unsteady voice, "I don't mind saying to you that 'Mars' Pendleton' spent his last dollar in the world a week ago. We will accept this money, Uncle Mose, since, in a way, it is a sort of payment, as well as a token of the loyalty and devotion of the old regime. Lydia, my dear, take the money. You are better fitted than I to manage its expenditure."

"Take it, honey," said Uncle Mose. "Hit belongs to you. Hit's Talbot money."

After Uncle Mose had gone, Miss Lydia had a good cry—for joy; and the major turned his face to a corner, and smoked his clay pipe volcanically.

The succeeding days saw the Talbots restored to peace and ease. Miss Lydia's face lost its worried look. The major appeared in a new frock coat, in which he looked like a wax figure personifying the memory of his golden age. Another publisher who read the manuscript of the "Anecdotes and Reminiscences" thought that, with a little retouching and toning down of the high lights, he could make a really bright and salable volume of it. Altogether, the situation was comfortable, and not without the touch of hope that is often sweeter than arrived blessings.

One day, about a week after their piece of good luck, a maid brought a letter for Miss Lydia to her room. The postmark showed that it was from New York. Not knowing any one there, Miss Lydia, in a mild flutter of wonder, sat down by her table and opened the letter with her scissors. This was what she read:

> Dear Miss Talbot:
> I thought you might be glad to learn of my good fortune. I have received and accepted an offer of two hundred dollars per week by a New York stock company to play Colonel Calhoun in "A Magnolia Flower."
>
> There is something else I wanted you to know. I guess you'd better not tell Major Talbot. I was anxious to make him some amends for the great help he was to me in studying the part, and for the bad humor he was in about it. He refused to let me, so I did it anyhow. I could easily spare the three hundred.
> Sincerely yours,
> H. Hopkins Hargraves,
>
> P.S. How did I play Uncle Mose?

Major Talbot, passing through the hall, saw Miss Lydia's door open and stopped.

"Any mail for us this morning, Lydia, dear?" he asked.

Miss Lydia slid the letter beneath a fold of her dress.

"The *Mobile Chronicle* came," she said promptly. "It's on the table in your study."

2

A Retrieved Reformation

A guard came to the prison shoe-shop, where Jimmy Valentine was assiduously stitching uppers, and escorted him to the front office. There the warden handed Jimmy his pardon, which had been signed that morning by the governor. Jimmy took it in a tired kind of way. He had served nearly ten months of a four year sentence. He had expected to stay only about three months, at the longest. When a man with as many friends on the outside as Jimmy Valentine had is received in the "stir" it is hardly worth while to cut his hair.

"Now, Valentine," said the warden, "you'll go out in the morning. Brace up, and make a man of yourself. You're not a bad fellow at heart. Stop cracking safes, and live straight."

"Me?" said Jimmy, in surprise. "Why, I never cracked a safe in my life."

"Oh, no," laughed the warden. "Of course not. Let's see, now. How was it you happened to get sent up on that Springfield job? Was it because you wouldn't prove an alibi for fear of compromising somebody in extremely high-toned society? Or was it simply a case of a mean old jury that had it in for you? It's always one or the other with you innocent victims."

"Me?" said Jimmy, still blankly virtuous. "Why, warden, I never was in Springfield in my life!"

"Take him back, Cronin!" said the warden, "and fix him up with outgoing clothes. Unlock him at seven in the morning, and let him come to the bull-pen. Better think over my advice, Valentine."

At a quarter past seven on the next morning Jimmy stood in the warden's outer office. He had on a suit of the villainously fitting, ready-made clothes and a pair of the stiff, squeaky shoes that the state furnishes to its discharged compulsory guests.

The clerk handed him a railroad ticket and the five-dollar bill with which the law expected him to rehabilitate himself into good citizenship and prosperity. The warden gave him a cigar, and shook hands. Valentine, 9762, was chronicled on the books, "Pardoned by Governor," and Mr. James Valentine walked out into the sunshine.

Disregarding the song of the birds, the waving green trees, and the smell of the flowers, Jimmy headed straight for a restaurant. There he tasted the first sweet joys of liberty in the shape of a broiled chicken and a bottle of white wine—followed by a cigar a grade better than the one the warden had given him. From there he proceeded leisurely to the depot. He tossed a quarter into the hat of a blind man sitting by the door, and boarded his train. Three hours set him down in a little town near the state line. He went to the café of one Mike Dolan and shook hands with Mike, who was alone behind the bar.

"Sorry we couldn't make it sooner, Jimmy, me boy," said Mike. "But we had that protest from Springfield to buck against, and the governor nearly balked. Feeling all right?"

"Fine," said Jimmy. "Got my key?"

He got his key and went upstairs, unlocking the door of a room at the rear. Everything was just as he had left it. There on the floor was still Ben Price's collar-button that had been torn from that eminent detective's shirt-band when they had overpowered Jimmy to arrest him.

Pulling out from the wall a folding-bed, Jimmy slid back a panel in the wall and dragged out a dust-covered suit-case. He opened this and gazed fondly at the finest set of burglar's tools in the East. It was a complete set, made of specially tempered steel, the latest designs in drills, punches, braces and bits, jimmies, clamps, and augers, with two or three novelties, invented by Jimmy himself, in which he took pride. Over nine hundred dollars they had cost him to have made at ——, a place where they make such things for the profession.

In half an hour Jimmy went down stairs and through the café. He was now dressed in tasteful and well-fitting clothes, and carried his dusted and cleaned suit-case in his hand.

"Got anything on?" asked Mike Dolan, genially.

"Me?" said Jimmy, in a puzzled tone. "I don't understand. I'm representing the New York Amalgamated Short Snap Biscuit Cracker and Frazzled Wheat Company."

This statement delighted Mike to such an extent that Jimmy had to take a seltzer-and-milk on the spot. He never touched "hard" drinks.

A week after the release of Valentine, 9762, there was a neat job of safe-burglary done in Richmond, Indiana, with no clue to the author. A scant eight hundred dollars was all that was secured. Two weeks after that a patented, improved, burglar-proof safe in Logansport was opened like a cheese to the tune of fifteen hundred dollars, currency; securities and silver untouched. That began to interest the rogue-catchers. Then an old-fashioned bank-safe in Jefferson City became active and threw out of its crater an eruption of bank-notes amounting to five thousand dollars. The losses were now high enough to bring the matter up into Ben Price's class of work. By comparing notes, a remarkable similarity in the methods of the burglaries was noticed. Ben Price investigated the scenes of the robberies, and was heard to remark:

"That's Dandy Jim Valentine's autograph. He's resumed business. Look at that combination knob—jerked out as easy as pulling up a radish in wet weather. He's got the only clamps that can do it. And look how clean those tumblers were punched out! Jimmy never has to drill but one hole. Yes, I guess I want Mr. Valentine. He'll do his bit next time without any short-time or clemency foolishness."

Ben Price knew Jimmy's habits. He had learned them while working up the Springfield case. Long jumps, quick get-aways, no confederates, and a taste for good society—these ways had helped Mr. Valentine to become noted as a successful dodger of retribution. It was given out that Ben Price had taken up the trail of the elusive cracksman, and other people with burglar-proof safes felt more at ease.

One afternoon Jimmy Valentine and his suit-case climbed out of the mail-hack in Elmore, a little town five miles off the railroad down in the black-jack country of Arkansas. Jimmy, looking like an athletic young senior just home from college, went down the board side-walk toward the hotel.

A young lady crossed the street, passed him at the corner and entered a door over which was the sign, "The Elmore Bank." Jimmy Valentine looked into her eyes, forgot what he was, and became another man. She lowered her eyes and colored slightly. Young men of Jimmy's style and looks were scarce in Elmore.

Jimmy collared a boy that was loafing on the steps of the bank as if he were one of the stockholders, and began to ask him questions about the town, feeding him dimes at intervals. By and by the young lady came out, looking royally unconscious of the young man with the suit-case, and went her way.

"Isn't that young lady Polly Simpson?" asked Jimmy, with specious guile.

"Naw," said the boy. "She's Annabel Adams. Her pa owns this bank. What'd you come to Elmore for? Is that a gold watch-chain? I'm going to get a bulldog. Got any more dimes?"

Jimmy went to the Planters' Hotel, registered as Ralph D. Spencer, and engaged a room. He leaned on the desk and declared his platform to the clerk. He said he had come to Elmore to look for a location to go into business. How was the shoe business, now, in the town? He had thought of the shoe business. Was there an opening?

The clerk was impressed by the clothes and manner of Jimmy. He, himself, was something of a pattern of fashion to the thinly gilded youth of Elmore, but he now perceived his shortcomings. While trying to figure out Jimmy's manner of tying his four-in-hand he cordially gave information.

Yes, there ought to be a good opening in the shoe line. There wasn't an exclusive shoe-store in the place. The dry-goods and general stores handled them. Business in all lines was fairly good. Hoped Mr. Spencer would decide to locate in Elmore. He would find it a pleasant town to live in, and the people very sociable.

Mr. Spencer thought he would stop over in the town a few days and look over the situation. No, the clerk needn't call the boy. He would carry up his suit-case, himself; it was rather heavy.

Mr. Ralph Spencer, the phoenix that arose from Jimmy Valentine's ashes—ashes left by the flame of a sudden and alternative attack of love—remained in Elmore, and prospered. He opened a shoe-store and secured a good run of trade.

Socially he was also a success, and made many friends. And he accomplished the wish of his heart. He met Miss Annabel Adams, and became more and more captivated by her charms.

At the end of a year the situation of Mr. Ralph Spencer was this: he had won the respect of the community, his shoe-store was flourishing, and he and Annabel were engaged to be married in two weeks. Mr. Adams, the typical, plodding, country banker, approved of Spencer. Annabel's pride in him almost equaled her affection. He was as much at home in the family of Mr. Adams and that of Annabel's married sister as if he were already a member.

One day Jimmy sat down in his room and wrote this letter, which he mailed to the safe address of one of his old friends in St. Louis:

> DEAR OLD PAL:
>
> I want you to be at Sullivan's place, in Little Rock, next Wednesday night, at nine o'clock. I want you to wind up some little matters for me. And, also, I want to make you a present of my kit of tools. I know you'll be glad to get them—you couldn't duplicate the lot for a thousand dollars. Say, Billy, I've quit the old business—a year ago. I've got a nice store. I'm making an honest living, and I'm going to marry the finest girl on earth two weeks from now. It's the only life, Billy—the straight one. I wouldn't touch a dollar of another man's money now for a million. After I get married I'm going to sell out and go West, where there won't be so much danger of having old scores brought up against me. I tell you, Billy, she's an angel. She believes in

me; and I wouldn't do another crooked thing for the whole world. Be sure to be at Sully's, for I must see you. I'll bring along the tools with me.

Your old friend,

JIMMY.

On the Monday night after Jimmy wrote this letter, Ben Price jogged unobtrusively into Elmore in a livery buggy. He lounged about town in his quiet way until he found out what he wanted to know. From the drug-store across the street from Spencer's shoe-store he got a good look at Ralph D. Spencer.

"Going to marry the banker's daughter are you, Jimmy?" said Ben to himself, softly. "Well, I don't know!"

The next morning Jimmy took breakfast at the Adamses. He was going to Little Rock that day to order his wedding-suit and buy something nice for Annabel. That would be the first time he had left town since he came to Elmore. It had been more than a year now since those last professional "jobs," and he thought he could safely venture out.

After breakfast quite a family party went downtown together—Mr. Adams, Annabel, Jimmy, and Annabel's married sister with her two little girls, aged five and nine. They came by the hotel where Jimmy still boarded, and he ran up to his room and brought along his suit-case. Then they went on to the bank. There stood Jimmy's horse and buggy and Dolph Gibson, who was going to drive him over to the railroad station.

All went inside the high, carved oak railings into the banking-room—Jimmy included, for Mr. Adams's future son-in-law was welcome anywhere. The clerks were pleased to be greeted by the good-looking, agreeable young man who was going to marry Miss Annabel. Jimmy set his suit-case down. Annabel, whose heart was bubbling with happiness and lively youth, put on Jimmy's hat, and picked up the suit-case. "Wouldn't I make a nice drummer?" said Annabel. "My! Ralph, how heavy it is? Feels like it was full of gold bricks."

"Lot of nickel-plated shoe-horns in there," said Jimmy, coolly, "that I'm going to return. Thought I'd save express charges by taking them up. I'm getting awfully economical."

The Elmore Bank had just put in a new safe and vault. Mr. Adams was very proud of it, and insisted on an inspection by every one. The vault was a small one, but it had a new, patented door. It fastened with three solid steel bolts thrown simultaneously with a single handle, and had a time-lock. Mr. Adams beamingly explained its workings to Mr. Spencer, who showed a courteous but not too intelligent interest. The two children, May and Agatha, were delighted by the shining metal and funny clock and knobs.

While they were thus engaged Ben Price sauntered in and leaned on his elbow, looking casually inside between the railings. He told the teller that he didn't want anything; he was just waiting for a man he knew.

Suddenly there was a scream or two from the women, and a commotion. Unperceived by the elders, May, the nine-year-old girl, in a spirit of play, had shut Agatha in the vault. She had then shot the bolts and turned the knob of the combination as she had seen Mr. Adams do.

The old banker sprang to the handle and tugged at it for a moment. "The door can't be opened," he groaned. "The clock hasn't been wound nor the combination set."

Agatha's mother screamed again, hysterically.

"Hush!" said Mr. Adams, raising his trembling hand. "All be quite for a moment. Agatha!" he called as loudly as he could. "Listen to me." During the following silence they could just hear the faint sound of the child wildly shrieking in the dark vault in a panic of terror.

"My precious darling!" wailed the mother. "She will die of fright! Open the door! Oh, break it open! Can't you men do something?"

"There isn't a man nearer than Little Rock who can open that door," said Mr. Adams, in a shaky voice. "My God! Spencer, what shall we do? That child—she can't stand it long in there. There isn't enough air, and, besides, she'll go into convulsions from fright."

Agatha's mother, frantic now, beat the door of the vault with her hands. Somebody wildly suggested dynamite. Annabel turned to Jimmy, her large eyes full of anguish, but not yet despairing. To a woman nothing seems quite impossible to the powers of the man she worships.

"Can't you do something, Ralph—*try*, won't you?"

He looked at her with a queer, soft smile on his lips and in his keen eyes.

"Annabel," he said, "give me that rose you are wearing, will you?"

Hardly believing that she heard him aright, she unpinned the bud from the bosom of her dress, and placed it in his hand. Jimmy stuffed it into his vest-pocket, threw off his coat and pulled up his shirt-sleeves. With that act Ralph D. Spencer passed away and Jimmy Valentine took his place.

"Get away from the door, all of you," he commanded, shortly.

He set his suit-case on the table, and opened it out flat. From that time on he seemed to be unconscious of the presence of any one else. He laid out the shining, queer implements swiftly and orderly, whistling softly to himself as he always did when at work. In a deep silence and immovable, the others watched him as if under a spell.

In a minute Jimmy's pet drill was biting smoothly into the steel door. In ten minutes—breaking his own burglarious record—he threw back the bolts and opened the door.

Agatha, almost collapsed, but safe, was gathered into her mother's arms.

Jimmy Valentine put on his coat, and walked outside the railings towards the front door. As he went he thought he heard a far-away voice that he once knew call "Ralph!" But he never hesitated.

At the door a big man stood somewhat in his way.

"Hello, Ben!" said Jimmy, still with his strange smile. "Got around at last, have you? Well, let's go. I don't know that it makes much difference, now."

And then Ben Price acted rather strangely.

"Guess you're mistaken, Mr. Spencer," he said. "Don't believe I recognize you. Your buggy's waiting for you, ain't it?"

And Ben Price turned and strolled down the street.

3

The Cop and the Anthem

On his bench in Madison Square Soapy moved uneasily. When wild geese honk high of nights, and when women without sealskin coats grow kind to their husbands, and when Soapy moves uneasily on his bench in the park, you may know that winter is near at hand.

A dead leaf fell in Soapy's lap. That was Jack Frost's card. Jack is kind to the regular denizens of Madison Square, and gives fair warning of his annual call. At the corners of four streets he hands his pasteboard to the North Wind, footman of the mansion of All Outdoors, so that the inhabitants thereof may make ready.

Soapy's mind became cognizant of the fact that the time had come for him to resolve himself into a singular Committee of Ways and Means to provide against the coming rigor. And therefore he moved uneasily on his bench.

The hibernatorial ambitions of Soapy were not of the highest. In them there were no considerations of Mediterranean cruises, of soporific Southern skies drifting in the Vesuvian Bay. Three months on the Island was what his soul craved. Three months of assured board and bed and congenial company, safe from Boreas and bluecoats, seemed to Soapy the essence of things desirable.

For years the hospitable Blackwell's had been his winter quarters. Just as his more fortunate fellow New Yorkers had bought their tickets to Palm Beach and the Riviera each winter, so Soapy had made his humble arrangements for his annual hegira to the Island. And now the time was come. On the previous night three Sabbath newspapers, distributed beneath his coat, about his ankles and over his lap, had failed to repulse the cold as he slept on his bench near the spurting fountain in the ancient square. So the Island loomed big and timely in Soapy's mind. He scorned the provisions made in the name of charity for the city's dependents. In Soapy's opinion the Law was more benign than Philanthropy. There was an endless round of institutions, municipal and eleemosynary, on which he might set out and receive lodging and food accordant with the simple life. But to one of Soapy's proud spirit the gifts of charity are encumbered. If not in coin you must pay in humiliation of spirit for every benefit received at the hands of philanthropy. As Caesar had his Brutus, every bed of charity must have its toll of a bath, every loaf of bread its compensation of a private and personal inquisition. Wherefore it is better to be a guest of the law, which though conducted by rules, does not meddle unduly with a gentleman's private affairs.

Soapy, having decided to go to the Island, at once set about accomplishing his desire. There were many easy ways of doing this. The pleasantest was to dine luxuriously at some expensive restaurant; and then, after declaring insolvency, be handed over quietly and without uproar to a policeman. An accommodating magistrate would do the rest.

Soapy left his bench and strolled out of the square and across the level sea of asphalt, where Broadway and Fifth Avenue flow together. Up Broadway he turned, and halted at a glittering café, where are gathered together nightly the choicest products of the grape, the silkworm and the protoplasm.

Soapy had confidence in himself from the lowest button of his vest upward. He was shaven, and his coat was decent and his neat black, ready-tied four-in-hand had been presented to him by a lady missionary on Thanksgiving Day. If he could reach a table in the restaurant unsuspected success would be his. The portion of him that would show above the table would raise no doubt in the waiter's mind. A roasted mallard duck, thought Soapy, would be about the thing—with a bottle of Chablis, and then Camembert, a demi-tasse and a cigar. One dollar for the cigar would be enough. The total would not be so high as to call forth any supreme manifestation of revenge from the café management; and yet the meat would leave him filled and happy for the journey to his winter refuge.

But as Soapy set foot inside the restaurant door the head waiter's eye fell upon his frayed trousers and decadent shoes. Strong and ready hands turned him about and conveyed him in silence and haste to the sidewalk and averted the ignoble fate of the menaced mallard.

Soapy turned off Broadway. It seemed that his route to the coveted island was not to be an epicurean one. Some other way of entering limbo must be thought of.

At a corner of Sixth Avenue electric lights and cunningly displayed wares behind plate-glass made a shop window conspicuous. Soapy took a cobblestone and dashed it through the glass. People came running around the corner, a policeman in the lead. Soapy stood still, with his hands in his pockets, and smiled at the sight of brass buttons.

"Where's the man that done that?" inquired the officer excitedly.

"Don't you figure out that I might have had something to do with it?" said Soapy, not without sarcasm, but friendly, as one greets good fortune.

The policeman's mind refused to accept Soapy even as a clue. Men who smash windows do not remain to parley with the law's minions. They take to their heels. The policeman saw a man half way down the block running to catch a car. With drawn club he joined in the pursuit. Soapy, with disgust in his heart, loafed along, twice unsuccessful.

On the opposite side of the street was a restaurant of no great pretensions. It catered to large appetites and modest purses. Its crockery and atmosphere were thick; its soup and napery thin. Into this place Soapy took his accusive shoes and telltale trousers without challenge. At a table he sat and consumed beefsteak, flapjacks, doughnuts and pie. And then to the waiter be betrayed the fact that the minutest coin and himself were strangers.

"Now, get busy and call a cop," said Soapy. "And don't keep a gentleman waiting."

"No cop for youse," said the waiter, with a voice like butter cakes and an eye like the cherry in a Manhattan cocktail. "Hey, Con!"

Neatly upon his left ear on the callous pavement two waiters pitched Soapy. He arose, joint by joint, as a carpenter's rule opens, and beat the dust from his clothes. Arrest seemed but a rosy dream. The Island seemed very far away. A policeman who stood before a drug store two doors away laughed and walked down the street.

Five blocks Soapy traveled before his courage permitted him to woo capture again. This time the opportunity presented what he fatuously termed to himself a "cinch." A young woman of a modest and pleasing guise was standing before a show window gazing with sprightly interest at its display of shaving mugs and inkstands, and two yards from the window a large policeman of severe demeanor leaned against a water plug.

It was Soapy's design to assume the role of the despicable and execrated "masher." The refined and elegant appearance of his victim and the contiguity of the conscientious cop encouraged him to believe that he would soon feel the pleasant official clutch upon his arm that would insure his winter quarters on the right little, tight little isle.

Soapy straightened the lady missionary's ready-made tie, dragged his shrinking cuffs into the open, set his hat at a killing cant and sidled toward the young woman. He made eyes at her, was taken with sudden coughs and "hems," smiled, smirked and went brazenly through the impudent and contemptible litany of the "masher." With half an eye Soapy saw that the policeman was watching him fixedly. The young woman moved away a few steps, and again bestowed her absorbed attention upon the shaving mugs. Soapy followed, boldly stepping to her side, raised his hat and said:

"Ah there, Bedelia! Don't you want to come and play in my yard?"

The policeman was still looking. The persecuted young woman had but to beckon a finger and Soapy would be practically en route for his insular haven. Already he imagined he could feel the cozy warmth of the station-house. The young woman faced him and, stretching out a hand, caught Soapy's coat sleeve.

"Sure, Mike," she said joyfully, "if you'll blow me to a pail of suds. I'd have spoke to you sooner, but the cop was watching."

With the young woman playing the clinging ivy to his oak Soapy walked past the policeman overcome with gloom. He seemed doomed to liberty.

At the next corner he shook off his companion and ran. He halted in the district where by night are found the lightest streets, hearts, vows and librettos. Women in furs and men in greatcoats moved gaily in the wintry air. A sudden fear seized Soapy that some dreadful enchantment had rendered him immune to arrest. The thought brought a little of panic upon it, and when he came upon another policeman lounging grandly in front of a transplendent theatre he caught at the immediate straw of "disorderly conduct."

On the sidewalk Soapy began to yell drunken gibberish at the top of his harsh voice. He danced, howled, raved and otherwise disturbed the welkin.

The policeman twirled his club, turned his back to Soapy and remarked to a citizen.

"'Tis one of them Yale lads celebratin' the goose egg they give to the Hartford College. Noisy; but no harm. We've instructions to lave them be."

Disconsolate, Soapy ceased his unavailing racket. Would never a policeman lay hands on him? In his fancy the Island seemed an unattainable Arcadia. He buttoned his thin coat against the chilling wind.

In a cigar store he saw a well-dressed man lighting a cigar at a swinging light. His silk umbrella he had set by the door on entering. Soapy stepped inside, secured the umbrella and sauntered off with it slowly. The man at the cigar light followed hastily.

"My umbrella," he said, sternly.

"Oh, is it?" sneered Soapy, adding insult to petit larceny. "Well, why don't you call a policeman? I took it. Your umbrella! Why don't you call a cop? There stands one on the corner."

The umbrella owner slowed his steps. Soapy did likewise, with a presentiment that luck would again run against him. The policeman looked at the two curiously.

"Of course," said the umbrella man—"that is—well, you know how these mistakes occur—I—if it's your umbrella I hope you'll excuse me—I picked it up this morning in a restaurant—If you recognize it as yours, why—I hope you'll—"

"Of course it's mine," said Soapy, viciously.

The ex-umbrella man retreated. The policeman hurried to assist a tall blonde in an opera cloak across the street in front of a street car that was approaching two blocks away.

Soapy walked eastward through a street damaged by improvements. He hurled the umbrella wrathfully into an excavation. He muttered against the men who wear helmets and carry clubs. Because he wanted to fall into their clutches, they seemed to regard him as a king who could do no wrong.

At length Soapy reached one of the avenues to the east where the glitter and turmoil was but faint. He set his face down this toward Madison Square, for the homing instinct survives even when the home is a park bench.

But on an unusually quiet corner Soapy came to a standstill. Here was an old church, quaint and rambling and gabled. Through one violet-stained window a soft light glowed, where, no doubt, the organist loitered over the keys, making sure of his mastery of the coming Sabbath anthem. For there drifted out to Soapy's ears sweet music that caught and held him transfixed against the convolutions of the iron fence.

The moon was above, lustrous and serene; vehicles and pedestrians were few; sparrows twittered sleepily in the eaves—for a little while the scene might have been a country churchyard. And the anthem that the organist played cemented Soapy to the iron fence, for he had known it well in the days when his life contained such things as mothers and roses and ambitions and friends and immaculate thoughts and collars.

The conjunction of Soapy's receptive state of mind and the influences about the old church wrought a sudden and wonderful change in his soul. He viewed with swift horror the pit into which he had tumbled, the degraded days, unworthy desires, dead hopes, wrecked faculties and base motives that made up his existence.

And also in a moment his heart responded thrillingly to this novel mood. An instantaneous and strong impulse moved him to battle with his desperate fate. He would pull himself out of the mire; he would make a man of himself again; he would conquer the evil that had taken possession of him. There was time; he was comparatively young yet; he would resurrect his old eager ambitions and pursue them without faltering. Those solemn but sweet organ notes had set up a revolution in him. Tomorrow he would go into the roaring downtown district and find work. A fur importer had once offered him a place as driver. He would find him tomorrow and ask for the position. He would be somebody in the world. He would—

Soapy felt a hand laid on his arm. He looked quickly around into the broad face of a policeman.

"What are you doin' here?" asked the officer.

"Nothin'," said Soapy.

"Then come along," said the policeman.

"Three months on the Island," said the Magistrate in the Police Court the next morning.

4

The Furnished Room

Restless, shifting, fugacious as time itself is a certain vast bulk of the population of the red brick district of the lower West Side. Homeless, they have a hundred homes. They flit from furnished room to furnished room, transients forever—transients in abode, transients in heart and mind. They sing "Home, Sweet Home" in ragtime; they carry their *lares et penates* in a bandbox; their vine is entwined about a picture hat; a rubber plant is their fig tree.

Hence the houses of this district, having had a thousand dwellers, should have a thousand tales to tell, mostly dull ones, no doubt; but it would be strange if there could not be found a ghost or two in the wake of all these vagrant guests.

One evening after dark a young man prowled among these crumbling red mansions, ringing their bells. At the twelfth he rested his lean hand-baggage upon the step and wiped the dust from his hat-band and forehead. The bell sounded faint and far away in some remote, hollow depths.

To the door of this, the twelfth house whose bell he had rung, came a housekeeper who made him think of an unwholesome, surfeited worm that had eaten its nut to a hollow shell and now sought to fill the vacancy with edible lodgers.

He asked if there was a room to let.

"Come in," said the housekeeper. Her voice came from her throat; her throat seemed lined with fur. "I have the third floor back, vacant since a week back. Should you wish to look at it?"

The young man followed her up the stairs. A faint light from no particular source mitigated the shadows of the halls. They trod noiselessly upon a stair carpet that its own loom would have forsworn. It seemed to have become vegetable; to have degenerated in that rank, sunless air to lush lichen or spreading moss that grew in patches to the staircase and was viscid under the foot like organic matter. At each turn of the stairs were vacant niches in the wall. Perhaps plants had once been set within them. If so they had died in that foul and tainted air. It may be that statues of the saints had stood there, but it was not difficult to conceive that imps and devils had dragged them forth in the darkness and down to the unholy depths of some furnished pit below.

"This is the room," said the housekeeper, from her furry throat. "It's a nice room. It ain't often vacant. I had some most elegant people in it last summer—no trouble at all, and paid in advance to the minute. The water's at the end of the hall. Sprowls and Mooney kept it three months. They done a vaudeville sketch. Miss B'retta Sprowls—you may have heard of her—Oh, that was just the stage names—right there over the dresser is where the marriage certificate hung, framed. The gas is here, and you see there is plenty of closet room. It's a room everybody likes. It never stays idle long."

"Do you have many theatrical people rooming here?" asked the young man.

"They comes and goes. A good proportion of my lodgers is connected with the theaters. Yes, sir, this is the theatrical district. Actor people never stays long anywhere. I get my share. Yes, they comes and they goes."

He engaged the room, paying for a week in advance. He was tired, he said, and would take possession at once. He counted out the money. The room had been made ready, she said, even to towels and water. As the housekeeper moved away he put, for the thousandth time, the question that he carried at the end of his tongue.

"A young girl—Miss Vashner—Miss Eloise Vashner—do you remember such a one among your lodgers? She would be singing on the stage, most likely. A fair girl, of medium height and slender, with reddish, gold hair and a dark mole near her left eyebrow."

"No, I don't remember the name. Them stage people has names they change as often as their rooms. They comes and they goes. No, I don't call that one to mind."

No. Always no. Five months of ceaseless interrogation and the inevitable negative. So much time spent by day in questioning managers, agents, schools and choruses; by night among the audiences of theaters from all-star casts down to music halls so low that he dreaded to find what he most hoped for. He who had loved her best had tried to find her. He was sure that since her disappearance from home this great, water-girt city held her somewhere, but it was like a monstrous quicksand, shifting its particles constantly, with no foundation, its upper granules of today buried tomorrow in ooze and slime.

The furnished room received its latest guest with a first glow of pseudo-hospitality, a hectic, haggard, perfunctory welcome like the specious smile of a demirep. The sophistical comfort came in reflected gleams from the decayed furniture, the ragged brocade upholstery of a couch and two chairs, a foot-wide cheap pier glass between the two windows, from one or two gilt picture frames and a brass bedstead in a corner.

The guest reclined, inert, upon a chair, while the room, confused in speech as though it were an apartment in Babel, tried to discourse to him of its divers tenantry.

A polychromatic rug like some brilliant-flowered rectangular, tropical islet lay surrounded by a billowy sea of soiled matting. Upon the gay-papered wall were those pictures that pursue the homeless one from house to house—The Huguenot Lovers, The First Quarrel, The Wedding Breakfast, Psyche at the Fountain. The mantel's chastely severe outline was ingloriously veiled behind some pert drapery drawn rakishly askew like the sashes of the Amazonian ballet. Upon it was some desolate flotsam cast aside by the room's marooned when a lucky sail had borne them to a fresh port—a trifling vase or two, pictures of actresses, a medicine bottle, some stray cards out of a deck.

One by one, as the characters of a cryptograph become explicit, the little signs left by the furnished room's procession of guests developed a significance. The threadbare space in the rug in front of the dresser told that lovely woman had marched in the throng. Tiny finger prints on the wall spoke of little prisoners trying to feel their way to sun and air. A splattered stain, raying like the shadow of a bursting bomb, witnessed where a hurled glass or bottle had splintered with its contents against the wall. Across the pier glass had been scrawled with a diamond in staggering letters the name "Marie." It seemed that the succession of dwellers in the furnished room had turned in fury—perhaps tempted beyond forbearance by its garish coldness—and wreaked upon it their passions. The furniture was chipped and bruised; the couch, distorted by bursting springs, seemed a horrible monster that had been slain during the stress of some grotesque convulsion. Some more potent upheaval had cloven a great slice from the marble mantel. Each plank in the floor owned its particular cant and shriek as from a separate and individual agony. It seemed incredible that all this malice and injury had been wrought upon the room by those who had called it for a time their home; and yet it may have been the cheated home instinct surviving blindly, the resentful rage at false household gods that had kindled their wrath. A hut that is our own we can sweep and adorn and cherish.

The young tenant in the chair allowed these thoughts to file, soft-shod, through his mind, while there drifted into the room furnished sounds and furnished scents. He heard in one room a tittering and incontinent, slack laughter; in others the monologue of a scold, the rattling of dice, a lullaby, and one crying dully; above him a banjo tinkled with spirit. Doors banged somewhere; the elevated trains roared intermittently; a cat yowled miserably upon a back fence. And he breathed the breath of the house—a dank savor rather than a smell—a cold, musty effluvium as from underground vaults mingled with the reeking exhalations of linoleum and mildewed and rotten woodwork.

Then, suddenly, as he rested there, the room was filled with the strong, sweet odor of mignonette. It came as upon a single buffet of wind with such sureness and fragrance and emphasis that it almost seemed a living visitant. And the man cried aloud: "What, dear?" as if he had been called, and sprang up and faced about. The rich odor clung to him and wrapped him around. He reached out his arms for it, all his senses for the time confused and commingled. How could one be peremptorily called by an odor? Surely it must have been a sound. But, was it not the sound that had touched, that had caressed him?

"She has been in this room," he cried, and he sprang to wrest from it a token, for he knew he would recognize the smallest thing that had belonged to her or that she had touched. This enveloping scent of mignonette, the odor that she had loved and made her own—whence came it?

The room had been but carelessly set in order. Scattered upon the flimsy dresser scarf were half a dozen hairpins—those discreet, indistinguishable friends of womankind, feminine of gender, infinite of mood and uncommunicative of tense. These he ignored, conscious of their triumphant lack of identity. Ransacking the drawers of the dresser he came upon a discarded, tiny, ragged handkerchief. He pressed it to his face. It was racy and insolent with heliotrope; he hurled it to the floor. In another drawer he found odd buttons, a theatre program, a pawnbroker's card, two lost marshmallows, a book on the divination of dreams. In the last was a woman's black satin hair bow, which halted him, poised between ice and fire. But the black satin hair-bow also is femininity's demure, impersonal, common ornament, and tells no tales.

And then he traversed the room like a hound on the scent, skimming the walls, considering the corners of the bulging matting on his hands and knees, rummaging mantel and tables, the curtains and hangings, the drunken cabinet in the corner, for a visible sign, unable to perceive that she was there beside, around, against, within, above him, clinging to him, wooing him, calling him so poignantly through the finer senses that even his grosser ones became cognizant of the call. Once again he answered loudly: "Yes, dear!" and turned, wild-eyed, to gaze on vacancy, for he could not yet discern form and color and love and outstretched arms in the odour of mignonette. Oh, God!

Whence that odor, and since when have odors had a voice to call? Thus he groped.

He burrowed in crevices and corners, and found corks and cigarettes. These he passed in passive contempt. But once he found in a fold of the matting a half-smoked cigar, and this he ground beneath his heel with a green and trenchant oath. He sifted the room from end to end. He found dreary and ignoble small records of many a peripatetic tenant; but of her whom he sought, and who may have lodged there, and whose spirit seemed to hover there, he found no trace.

And then he thought of the housekeeper.

He ran from the haunted room downstairs and to a door that showed a crack of light. She came out to his knock. He smothered his excitement as best he could.

"Will you tell me, madam," he besought her, "who occupied the room I have before I came?"

"Yes, sir. I can tell you again. 'Twas Sprowls and Mooney, as I said. Miss B'retta Sprowls it was in the theatres, but Missis Mooney she was. My house is well known for respectability. The marriage certificate hung, framed, on a nail over—"

"What kind of a lady was Miss Sprowls—in looks, I mean?"

"Why, black-haired, sir, short, and stout, with a comical face. They left a week ago Tuesday."

"And before they occupied it?"

"Why, there was a single gentleman connected with the draying business. He left owing me a week. Before him was Missis Crowder and her two children, that stayed four months; and back of them was old Mr. Doyle, whose sons paid for him. He kept the room six months. That goes back a year, sir, and further I do not remember."

He thanked her and crept back to his room. The room was dead. The essence that had vivified it was gone. The perfume of mignonette had departed. In its place was the old, stale odor of moldy house furniture, of atmosphere in storage.

The ebbing of his hope drained his faith. He sat staring at the yellow, singing gaslight. Soon he walked to the bed and began to tear the sheets into strips. With the blade of his knife he drove them tightly into every crevice around windows and door. When all was snug and taut he turned out the light, turned the gas full on again and laid himself gratefully upon the bed.

~

It was Mrs. McCool's night to go with the can for beer. So she fetched it and sat with Mrs. Purdy in one of those subterranean retreats where house-keepers foregather and the worm dieth seldom.

"I rented out my third floor, back, this evening," said Mrs. Purdy, across a fine circle of foam. "A young man took it. He went up to bed two hours ago."

"Now, did ye, Mrs. Purdy, ma'am?" said Mrs. McCool, with intense admiration. "You do be a wonder for rentin' rooms of that kind. And did ye tell him, then?" she concluded in a husky whisper, laden with mystery.

"Rooms," said Mrs. Purdy, in her furriest tones, "are furnished for to rent. I did not tell him, Mrs. McCool."

"'Tis right ye are, ma'am; 'tis by renting rooms we kape alive. Ye have the rale sense for business, ma'am. There be many people will rayjict the rentin' of a room if they be tould a suicide has been after dyin' in the bed of it."

"As you say, we has our living to be making," remarked Mrs. Purdy.

"Yis, ma'am; 'tis true. 'Tis just one wake ago this day I helped ye lay out the third floor, back. A pretty slip of a colleen she was to be killin' herself wid the gas—a swate little face she had, Mrs. Purdy, ma'am."

"She'd a-been called handsome, as you say," said Mrs. Purdy, assenting but critical, "but for that mole she had a-growin' by her left eyebrow. Do fill up your glass again, Mrs. McCool."

5

The Gift of the Magi

One dollar and eighty-seven cents. That was all. And sixty cents of it was in pennies. Pennies saved one and two at a time by bulldozing the grocer and the vegetable man and the butcher until one's cheeks burned with the silent imputation of parsimony that such close dealing implied. Three times Della counted it. One dollar and eighty-seven cents. And the next day would be Christmas.

There was clearly nothing to do but flop down on the shabby little couch and howl. So Della did it. Which instigates the moral reflection that life is made up of sobs, sniffles, and smiles, with sniffles predominating.

While the mistress of the home is gradually subsiding from the first stage to the second, take a look at the home. A furnished flat at $8 per week. It did not exactly beggar description, but it certainly had that word on the lookout for the mendicancy squad.

In the vestibule below was a letter-box into which no letter would go, and an electric button from which no mortal finger could coax a ring. Also appertaining thereunto was a card bearing the name "Mr. James Dillingham Young."

The "Dillingham" had been flung to the breeze during a former period of prosperity when its possessor was being paid $30 per week. Now, when the income was shrunk to $20, though, they were thinking seriously of contracting to a modest and unassuming D. But whenever Mr. James Dillingham Young came home and reached his flat above he was called "Jim" and greatly hugged by Mrs. James Dillingham Young, already introduced to you as Della. Which is all very good.

Della finished her cry and attended to her cheeks with the powder rag. She stood by the window and looked out dully at a gray cat walking a gray fence in a gray backyard. Tomorrow would be Christmas Day, and she had only $1.87 with which to buy Jim a present. She had been saving every penny she could for months, with this result. Twenty dollars a week doesn't go far. Expenses had been greater than she had calculated. They always are. Only $1.87 to buy a present for Jim. Her Jim. Many a happy hour she had spent planning for something nice for him. Something fine and rare and sterling—something just a little bit near to being worthy of the honor of being owned by Jim.

There was a pier glass between the windows of the room. Perhaps you have seen a pier glass in an $8 flat. A very thin and very agile person may, by observing his reflection in a rapid sequence of longitudinal strips, obtain a fairly accurate conception of his looks. Della, being slender, had mastered the art.

Suddenly she whirled from the window and stood before the glass. Her eyes were shining brilliantly, but her face had lost its color within twenty seconds. Rapidly she pulled down her hair and let it fall to its full length.

Now, there were two possessions of the James Dillingham Youngs in which they both took a mighty pride. One was Jim's gold watch that had been his father's and his grandfather's. The other was Della's hair. Had the queen of Sheba lived in the flat across the air-shaft, Della would have let her hair hang out the window some day to dry just to depreciate Her Majesty's jewels and gifts. Had King Solomon been the janitor, with all his treasures piled up in the basement, Jim would have pulled out his watch every time he passed, just to see him pluck at his beard from envy.

So now Della's beautiful hair fell about her rippling and shining like a cascade of brown waters. It reached below her knee and made itself almost a garment for her. And then she did it up again nervously and quickly. Once she faltered for a minute and stood still while a tear or two splashed on the worn red carpet.

On went her old brown jacket; on went her old brown hat. With a whirl of skirts and with the brilliant sparkle still in her eyes, she fluttered out the door and down the stairs to the street.

Where she stopped the sign read: "Mme. Sofronie. Hair Goods of All Kinds." One flight up Della ran, and collected herself, panting. Madame, large, too white, chilly, hardly looked the "Sofronie."

"Will you buy my hair?" asked Della.

"I buy hair," said Madame. "Take yer hat off and let's have a sight at the looks of it."

Down rippled the brown cascade.

"Twenty dollars," said Madame, lifting the mass with a practiced hand.

"Give it to me quick," said Della.

Oh, and the next two hours tripped by on rosy wings. Forget the hashed metaphor. She was ransacking the stores for Jim's present.

She found it at last. It surely had been made for Jim and no one else. There was no other like it in any of the stores, and she had turned all of them inside out. It was a platinum fob chain simple and chaste in design, properly proclaiming its value by substance alone and not by meretricious ornamentation—as all good things should do. It was even worthy of The Watch. As soon as she saw it she knew that it must be Jim's. It was like him. Quietness and value—the description applied to both. Twenty-one dollars they took from her for it, and she hurried home with the 87 cents. With that chain on his watch Jim might be properly anxious about the time in any company. Grand as the watch was, he sometimes looked at it on the sly on account of the old leather strap that he used in place of a chain.

When Della reached home her intoxication gave way a little to prudence and reason. She got out her curling irons and lighted the gas and went to work repairing the ravages made by generosity added to love. Which is always a tremendous task, dear friends—a mammoth task.

Within forty minutes her head was covered with tiny, close-lying curls that made her look wonderfully like a truant schoolboy. She looked at her reflection in the mirror long, carefully, and critically.

"If Jim doesn't kill me," she said to herself, "before he takes a second look at me, he'll say I look like a Coney Island chorus girl. But what could I do—oh! What could I do with a dollar and eighty-seven cents?"

At 7 o'clock the coffee was made and the frying-pan was on the back of the stove hot and ready to cook the chops.

Jim was never late. Della doubled the fob chain in her hand and sat on the corner of the table near the door that he always entered. Then she heard his step on the stair away down on the first flight, and she turned white for just a moment. She had a habit of saying a little silent prayer about the simplest everyday things, and now she whispered: "Please God, make him think I am still pretty."

The door opened and Jim stepped in and closed it. He looked thin and very serious. Poor fellow, he was only twenty-two—and to be burdened with a family! He needed a new overcoat and he was without gloves.

Jim stopped inside the door, as immovable as a setter at the scent of quail. His eyes were fixed upon Della, and there was an expression in them that she could not read, and it terrified her. It was not anger, nor surprise, nor disapproval, nor horror, nor any of the sentiments that she had been prepared for. He simply stared at her fixedly with that peculiar expression on his face.

Della wriggled off the table and went for him.

"Jim, darling," she cried, "don't look at me that way. I had my hair cut off and sold because I couldn't have lived through Christmas without giving you a present. It'll grow out again—you won't mind, will you? I just had to do it. My hair grows awfully fast. Say 'Merry Christmas!' Jim, and let's be happy. You don't know what a nice—what a beautiful, nice gift I've got for you."

"You've cut off your hair?" asked Jim, laboriously, as if he had not arrived at that patent fact yet even after the hardest mental labor.

"Cut it off and sold it," said Della. "Don't you like me just as well, anyhow? I'm me without my hair, ain't I?"

Jim looked about the room curiously.

"You say your hair is gone?" he said, with an air almost of idiocy.

"You needn't look for it," said Della. "It's sold, I tell you—sold and gone, too. It's Christmas Eve, boy. Be good to me, for it went for you. Maybe the hairs of my head were numbered," she went on with sudden serious sweetness, "but nobody could ever count my love for you. Shall I put the chops on, Jim?"

Out of his trance Jim seemed quickly to wake. He enfolded his Della. For ten seconds let us regard with discreet scrutiny some inconsequential object in the other direction. Eight dollars a week or a million a year—what is the difference? A mathematician or a wit would give you the wrong answer. The magi brought valuable gifts, but that was not among them. This dark assertion will be illuminated later on.

Jim drew a package from his overcoat pocket and threw it upon the table.

"Don't make any mistake, Dell," he said, "about me. I don't think there's anything in the way of a haircut or a shave or a shampoo that could make me like my girl any less. But if you'll unwrap that package you may see why you had me going a while at first."

White fingers and nimble tore at the string and paper. And then an ecstatic scream of joy; and then, alas! a quick feminine change to hysterical tears and wails, necessitating the immediate employment of all the comforting powers of the lord of the flat.

For there lay The Combs—the set of combs, side and back, that Della had worshiped long in a Broadway window. Beautiful combs, pure tortoise shell, with jeweled rims—just the shade to wear in the beautiful vanished hair. They were expensive combs, she knew, and her heart had simply craved and yearned over them without the least hope of possession. And now, they were hers, but the tresses that should have adorned the coveted adornments were gone.

But she hugged them to her bosom, and at length she was able to look up with dim eyes and a smile and say: "My hair grows so fast, Jim!"

And then Della leaped up like a little singed cat and cried, "Oh, oh!"

Jim had not yet seen his beautiful present. She held it out to him eagerly upon her open palm. The dull precious metal seemed to flash with a reflection of her bright and ardent spirit.

"Isn't it a dandy, Jim? I hunted all over town to find it. You'll have to look at the time a hundred times a day now. Give me your watch. I want to see how it looks on it."

Instead of obeying, Jim tumbled down on the couch and put his hands under the back of his head and smiled.

"Dell," said he, "let's put our Christmas presents away and keep 'em a while. They're too nice to use just at present. I sold the watch to get the money to buy your combs. And now suppose you put the chops on."

The magi, as you know, were wise men—wonderfully wise men—who brought gifts to the Babe in the manger. They invented the art of giving Christmas presents. Being wise, their gifts were no doubt wise ones, possibly bearing the privilege of exchange in case of duplication. And here I have lamely related to you the uneventful chronicle of two foolish children in a flat who most unwisely sacrificed for each other the greatest treasures of their house. But in a last word to the wise of these days let it be said that of all who give gifts these two were the wisest. Of all who give and receive gifts, such as they are wisest. Everywhere they are wisest. They are the magi.

6

A Cosmopolite in a Café

At midnight the café was crowded. By some chance the little table at which I sat had escaped the eye of incomers, and two vacant chairs at it extended their arms with venal hospitality to the influx of patrons.

And then a cosmopolite sat in one of them, and I was glad, for I held a theory that since Adam no true citizen of the world has existed. We hear of them, and we see foreign labels on much luggage, but we find travelers instead of cosmopolites.

I invoke your consideration of the scene—the marble-topped tables, the range of leather-upholstered wall seats, the gay company, the ladies dressed in demi-state toilets, speaking in an exquisite visible chorus of taste, economy, opulence or art; the sedulous and largess-loving *garçons*, the music wisely catering to all with its raids upon the composers; the *mélange* of talk and laughter—and, if you will, the Würzburger in the tall glass cones that bend to your lips as a ripe cherry sways on its branch to the beak of a robber jay. I was told by a sculptor from Mauch Chunk that the scene was truly Parisian.

My cosmopolite was named E. Rushmore Coglan, and he will be heard from next summer at Coney Island. He is to establish a new "attraction" there, he informed me, offering kingly diversion. And then his conversation rang along parallels of latitude and longitude. He took the great, round world in his hand, so to speak, familiarly, contemptuously, and it seemed no larger than the seed of a Maraschino cherry in a *table d'hôte* grape fruit. He spoke disrespectfully of the equator, he skipped from continent to continent, he derided the zones, he mopped up the high seas with his napkin. With a wave of his hand he would speak of a certain bazaar in Hyderabad. Whiff! He would have you on skis in Lapland. Zip! Now you rode the breakers with the Kanakas at Kealaikahiki. Presto! He dragged you through an Arkansas post-oak swamp, let you dry for a moment on the alkali plains of his Idaho ranch, then whirled you into the society of Viennese archdukes. Anon he would be telling you of a cold he acquired in a Chicago lake breeze and how old Escamila cured it in Buenos Ayres with a hot infusion of the *chuchula* weed. You would have addressed a letter to "E. Rushmore Coglan, Esq., the Earth, Solar System, the Universe," and have mailed it, feeling confident that it would be delivered to him.

I was sure that I had found at last the one true cosmopolite since Adam, and I listened to his worldwide discourse fearful lest I should discover in it the local note of the mere globe-trotter. But his opinions never fluttered or drooped; he was as impartial to cities, countries and continents as the winds or gravitation.

And as E. Rushmore Coglan prattled of this little planet I thought with glee of a great almost-cosmopolite who wrote for the whole world and dedicated himself to Bombay. In a poem he has to say that there is pride and rivalry between the cities of the earth, and that "the men that breed from them, they traffic up and down, but cling to their cities' hem as a child to the mother's gown." And whenever they walk "by roaring streets unknown" they remember their native city "most faithful, foolish, fond; making her mere-breathed name their bond upon their bond." And my glee was roused because I had caught Mr. Kipling napping. Here I had found a man not made from dust; one who had no narrow boasts of birthplace or country, one who, if he bragged at all, would brag of his whole round globe against the Martians and the inhabitants of the Moon.

Expression on these subjects was precipitated from E. Rushmore Coglan by the third corner to our table. While Coglan was describing to me the topography along the Siberian Railway the orchestra glided into a medley. The concluding air was "Dixie," and as the exhilarating notes tumbled forth they were almost overpowered by a great clapping of hands from almost every table.

It is worth a paragraph to say that this remarkable scene can be witnessed every evening in numerous cafés in the City of New York. Tons of brew have been consumed over theories to account for it. Some have conjectured hastily that all Southerners in town hie themselves to cafés at nightfall. This applause of the "rebel" air in a Northern city does puzzle a little; but it is not insolvable. The war with Spain, many years' generous mint and watermelon crops, a few long-shot winners at the New Orleans race-track, and the brilliant banquets given by the Indiana and Kansas citizens who compose the North Carolina Society have made the South rather a "fad" in Manhattan. Your manicure will lisp softly that your left forefinger reminds her so much of a gentleman's in Richmond, Va. Oh, certainly; but many a lady has to work now—the war, you know.

When "Dixie" was being played a dark-haired young man sprang up from somewhere with a Mosby guerrilla yell and waved frantically his soft-brimmed hat. Then he strayed through the smoke, dropped into the vacant chair at our table and pulled out cigarettes.

The evening was at the period when reserve is thawed. One of us mentioned three Würzburgers to the waiter; the dark-haired young man acknowledged his inclusion in the order by a smile and a nod. I hastened to ask him a question because I wanted to try out a theory I had.

"Would you mind telling me," I began, "whether you are from—"

The fist of E. Rushmore Coglan banged the table and I was jarred into silence.

"Excuse me," said he, "but that's a question I never like to hear asked. What does it matter where a man is from? Is it fair to judge a man by his post-office address? Why, I've seen Kentuckians who hated whiskey, Virginians who weren't descended from Pocahontas, Indianians who hadn't written a novel, Mexicans who didn't wear velvet trousers with silver dollars sewed along the seams, funny Englishmen, spendthrift Yankees, cold-blooded Southerners, narrow-minded Westerners, and New Yorkers who were too busy to stop for an hour on the street to watch a one-armed grocer's clerk do up cranberries in paper bags. Let a man be a man and don't handicap him with the label of any section."

"Pardon me," I said, "but my curiosity was not altogether an idle one. I know the South, and when the band plays 'Dixie' I like to observe. I have formed the belief that the man who applauds that air with special violence and ostensible sectional loyalty is invariably a native of either Secaucus, N.J., or the district between Murray Hill Lyceum and the Harlem River, this city. I was about to put my opinion to the test by inquiring of this gentleman when you interrupted with your own—larger theory, I must confess."

And now the dark-haired young man spoke to me, and it became evident that his mind also moved along its own set of grooves.

"I should like to be a periwinkle," said he, mysteriously, "on the top of a valley, and sing tooralloo-ralloo."

This was clearly too obscure, so I turned again to Coglan.

"I've been around the world twelve times," said he. "I know an Esquimau in Upernavik who sends to Cincinnati for his neckties, and I saw a goat-herder in Uruguay who won a prize in a Battle Creek breakfast food puzzle competition. I pay rent on a room in Cairo, Egypt, and another in Yokohama all the year around. I've got slippers waiting for me in a tea-house in Shanghai, and I don't have to tell 'em how to cook my eggs in Rio de Janeiro or Seattle. It's a mighty little old world. What's the use of bragging about being from the North, or the South, or the old manor house in the dale, or Euclid avenue, Cleveland, or Pike's Peak, or Fairfax County, Va., or Hooligan's Flats or any place? It'll be a better world when we quit being fools about some mildewed town or ten acres of swampland just because we happened to be born there."

"You seem to be a genuine cosmopolite," I said admiringly. "But it also seems that you would decry patriotism."

"A relic of the stone age," declared Coglan, warmly. "We are all brothers—Chinamen, Englishmen, Zulus, Patagonians and the people in the bend of the Kaw River. Some day all this petty pride in one's city or State or section or country will be wiped out, and we'll all be citizens of the world, as we ought to be."

"But while you are wandering in foreign lands," I persisted, "do not your thoughts revert to some spot—some dear and—"

"Nary a spot," interrupted E. R. Coglan, flippantly. "The terrestrial, globular, planetary hunk of matter, slightly flattened at the poles, and known as the Earth, is my abode. I've met a good many object-bound citizens of this country abroad. I've seen men from Chicago sit in a gondola in Venice on a moonlight night and brag about their drainage canal. I've seen a Southerner on being introduced to the King of England hand that monarch, without batting his eyes, the information that his grand-aunt on his mother's side was related by marriage to the Perkinses, of Charleston. I knew a New Yorker who was kidnapped for ransom by some Afghanistan bandits. His people sent over the money and he came back to Kabul with the agent. 'Afghanistan?' the natives said to him through an interpreter. 'Well, not so slow, do you think?' 'Oh, I don't know,' says he, and he begins to tell them about a cab driver at Sixth avenue and Broadway. Those ideas don't suit me. I'm not tied down to anything that isn't 8,000 miles in diameter. Just put me down as E. Rushmore Coglan, citizen of the terrestrial sphere."

My cosmopolite made a large adieu and left me, for he thought he saw some one through the chatter and smoke whom he knew. So I was left with the would-be periwinkle, who was reduced to Würzburger without further ability to voice his aspirations to perch, melodious, upon the summit of a valley.

I sat reflecting upon my evident cosmopolite and wondering how the poet had managed to miss him. He was my discovery and I believed in him. How was it? "The men that breed from them they traffic up and down, but cling to their cities' hem as a child to the mother's gown."

Not so E. Rushmore Coglan. With the whole world for his—

My meditations were interrupted by a tremendous noise and conflict in another part of the café. I saw above the heads of the seated patrons E. Rushmore Coglan and a stranger to me engaged in terrific battle. They fought between the tables like Titans, and glasses crashed, and men caught their hats up and were knocked down, and a brunette screamed, and a blonde began to sing "Teasing."

My cosmopolite was sustaining the pride and reputation of the Earth when the waiters closed in on both combatants with their famous flying wedge formation and bore them outside, still resisting.

I called McCarthy, one of the French *garçons*, and asked him the cause of the conflict.

"The man with the red tie" (that was my cosmopolite), said he, "got hot on account of things said about the bum sidewalks and water supply of the place he come from by the other guy."

"Why," said I, bewildered, "that man is a citizen of the world—a cosmopolite. He—"

"Originally from Mattawamkeag, Maine, he said," continued McCarthy, "and he wouldn't stand for no knockin' the place."

7

After Twenty Years

The policeman on the beat moved up the avenue impressively. The impressiveness was habitual and not for show, for spectators were few. The time was barely 10 o'clock at night, but chilly gusts of wind with a taste of rain in them had well nigh de-peopled the streets.

Trying doors as he went, twirling his club with many intricate and artful movements, turning now and then to cast his watchful eye adown the pacific thoroughfare, the officer, with his stalwart form and slight swagger, made a fine picture of a guardian of the peace. The vicinity was one that kept early hours. Now and then you might see the lights of a cigar store or of an all-night lunch counter; but the majority of the doors belonged to business places that had long since been closed.

When about midway of a certain block the policeman suddenly slowed his walk. In the doorway of a darkened hardware store a man leaned, with an unlighted cigar in his mouth. As the policeman walked up to him the man spoke up quickly.

"It's all right, officer," he said, reassuringly. "I'm just waiting for a friend. It's an appointment made twenty years ago. Sounds a little funny to you, doesn't it? Well, I'll explain if you'd like to make certain it's all straight. About that long ago there used to be a restaurant where this store stands—'Big Joe' Brady's restaurant."

"Until five years ago," said the policeman. "It was torn down then."

The man in the doorway struck a match and lit his cigar. The light showed a pale, square-jawed face with keen eyes, and a little white scar near his right eyebrow. His scarf-pin was a large diamond, oddly set.

"Twenty years ago tonight," said the man, "I dined here at 'Big Joe' Brady's with Jimmy Wells, my best chum, and the finest chap in the world. He and I were raised here in New York, just like two brothers, together. I was eighteen and Jimmy was twenty. The next morning I was to start for the West to make my fortune. You couldn't have dragged Jimmy out of New York; he thought it was the only place on earth. Well, we agreed that night that we would meet here again exactly twenty years from that date and time, no matter what our conditions might be or from what distance we might have to come. We figured that in twenty years each of us ought to have our destiny worked out and our fortunes made, whatever they were going to be."

"It sounds pretty interesting," said the policeman. "Rather a long time between meets, though, it seems to me. Haven't you heard from your friend since you left?"

"Well, yes, for a time we corresponded," said the other. "But after a year or two we lost track of each other. You see, the West is a pretty big proposition, and I kept hustling around over it pretty lively. But I know Jimmy will meet me here if he's alive, for he always was the truest, stanchest old chap in the world. He'll never forget. I came a thousand miles to stand in this door tonight, and it's worth it if my old partner turns up."

The waiting man pulled out a handsome watch, the lids of it set with small diamonds.

"Three minutes to ten," he announced. "It was exactly ten o'clock when we parted here at the restaurant door."

"Did pretty well out West, didn't you?" asked the policeman.

"You bet! I hope Jimmy has done half as well. He was a kind of plodder, though, good fellow as he was. I've had to compete with some of the sharpest wits going to get my pile. A man gets in a groove in New York. It takes the West to put a razor-edge on him."

The policeman twirled his club and took a step or two.

"I'll be on my way. Hope your friend comes around all right. Going to call time on him sharp?"

"I should say not!" said the other. "I'll give him half an hour at least. If Jimmy is alive on earth he'll be here by that time. So long, officer."

"Good-night, sir," said the policeman, passing on along his beat, trying doors as he went.

There was now a fine, cold drizzle falling, and the wind had risen from its uncertain puffs into a steady blow. The few foot passengers astir in that quarter hurried dismally and silently along with coat collars turned high and pocketed hands. And in the door of the hardware store the man who had come a thousand miles to fill an appointment, uncertain almost to absurdity, with the friend of his youth, smoked his cigar and waited.

About twenty minutes he waited, and then a tall man in a long overcoat, with collar turned up to his ears, hurried across from the opposite side of the street. He went directly to the waiting man.

"Is that you, Bob?" he asked, doubtfully.

"Is that you, Jimmy Wells?" cried the man in the door.

"Bless my heart!" exclaimed the new arrival, grasping both the other's hands with his own. "It's Bob, sure as fate. I was certain I'd find you here if you were still in existence. Well, well, well!—Twenty years is a long time. The old restaurant's gone, Bob; I wish it had lasted, so we could have had another dinner there. How has the West treated you, old man?"

"Bully; it has given me everything I asked it for. You've changed lots, Jimmy. I never thought you were so tall by two or three inches."

"Oh, I grew a bit after I was twenty."

"Doing well in New York, Jimmy?"

"Moderately. I have a position in one of the city departments. Come on, Bob; we'll go around to a place I know of, and have a good long talk about old times."

The two men started up the street, arm in arm. The man from the West, his egotism enlarged by success, was beginning to outline the history of his career. The other, submerged in his overcoat, listened with interest.

At the corner stood a drug store, brilliant with electric lights. When they came into this glare each of them turned simultaneously to gaze upon the other's face.

The man from the West stopped suddenly and released his arm.

"You're not Jimmy Wells," he snapped. "Twenty years is a long time, but not long enough to change a man's nose from a Roman to a pug."

"It sometimes changes a good man into a bad one," said the tall man. "You've been under arrest for ten minutes, 'Silky' Bob. Chicago thinks you may have dropped over our way and wires us she wants to have a chat with you. Going quietly, are you? That's sensible. Now, before we go on to the station here's a note I was asked to hand you. You may read it here at the window. It's from Patrolman Wells."

The man from the West unfolded the little piece of paper handed him. His hand was steady when he began to read, but it trembled a little by the time he had finished. The note was rather short.

Bob: I was at the appointed place on time. When you struck the match to light your cigar I saw it was the face of the man wanted in Chicago. Somehow I couldn't do it myself, so I went around and got a plain clothes man to do the job.

JIMMY.

8

An Adjustment of Nature

In an art exhibition the other day I saw a painting that had been sold for $5,000. The painter was a young scrub out of the West named Kraft, who had a favorite food and a pet theory. His pabulum was an unquenchable belief in the Unerring Artistic Adjustment of Nature. His theory was fixed around corned-beef hash with poached egg. There was a story behind the picture, so I went home and let it drip out of a fountain-pen. The idea of Kraft—but that is not the beginning of the story.

Three years ago Kraft, Bill Judkins (a poet), and I took our meals at Cypher's, on Eighth Avenue. I say "took." When we had money, Cypher got it "off of" us, as he expressed it. We had no credit; we went in, called for food and ate it. We paid or we did not pay. We had confidence in Cypher's sullenness and smoldering ferocity. Deep down in his sunless soul he was either a prince, a fool or an artist. He sat at a worm-eaten desk, covered with files of waiters' checks so old that I was sure the bottomest one was for clams that Hendrik Hudson had eaten and paid for. Cypher had the power, in common with Napoleon III, and the goggle-eyed perch, of throwing a film over his eyes, rendering opaque the windows of his soul. Once when we left him unpaid, with egregious excuses, I looked back and saw him shaking with inaudible laughter behind his film. Now and then we paid up back scores.

But the chief thing at Cypher's was Milly. Milly was a waitress. She was a grand example of Kraft's theory of the artistic adjustment of nature. She belonged, largely, to waiting, as Minerva did to the art of scrapping, or Venus to the science of serious flirtation. Pedestaled and in bronze she might have stood with the noblest of her heroic sisters as "Liver-and-Bacon Enlivening the World." She belonged to Cypher's. You expected to see her colossal figure loom through that reeking blue cloud of smoke from frying fat just as you expect the Palisades to appear through a drifting Hudson River fog. There amid the steam of vegetables and the vapors of acres of "ham and," the crash of crockery, the clatter of steel, the screaming of "short orders," the cries of the hungering and all the horrid tumult of feeding man, surrounded by swarms of the buzzing winged beasts bequeathed us by Pharaoh, Milly steered her magnificent way like some great liner cleaving among the canoes of howling savages.

Our Goddess of Grub was built on lines so majestic that they could be followed only with awe. Her sleeves were always rolled above her elbows. She could have taken us three musketeers in her two hands and dropped us out of the window. She had seen fewer years than any of us, but she was of such superb Evehood and simplicity that she mothered us from the beginning. Cypher's store of eatables she poured out upon us with royal indifference to price and quantity, as from a cornucopia that knew no exhaustion. Her voice rang like a great silver bell; her smile was many-toothed and frequent; she seemed like a yellow sunrise on mountain tops. I never saw her but I thought of the Yosemite. And yet, somehow, I could never think of her as existing outside of Cypher's. There nature had placed her, and she had taken root and grown mightily. She seemed happy, and took her few poor dollars on Saturday nights with the flushed pleasure of a child that receives an unexpected donation.

It was Kraft who first voiced the fear that each of us must have held latently. It came up apropos, of course, of certain questions of art at which we were hammering. One of us compared the harmony existing between a Haydn symphony and pistache ice cream to the exquisite congruity between Milly and Cypher's.

"There is a certain fate hanging over Milly," said Kraft, "and if it overtakes her she is lost to Cypher's and to us."

"She will grow fat?" asked Judkins, fearsomely.

"She will go to night school and become refined?" I ventured anxiously.

"It is this," said Kraft, punctuating in a puddle of spilled coffee with a stiff forefinger. "Caesar had his Brutus—the cotton has its bollworm, the chorus girl has her Pittsburger, the summer boarder has his poison ivy, the hero has his Carnegie medal, art has its Morgan, the rose has its—"

"Speak," I interrupted, much perturbed. "You do not think that Milly will begin to lace?"

"One day," concluded Kraft, solemnly, "there will come to Cypher's for a plate of beans a millionaire lumberman from Wisconsin, and he will marry Milly."

"Never!" exclaimed Judkins and I, in horror.

"A lumberman," repeated Kraft, hoarsely.

"And a millionaire lumberman!" I sighed, despairingly.

"From Wisconsin!" groaned Judkins.

We agreed that the awful fate seemed to menace her. Few things were less improbable. Milly, like some vast virgin stretch of pine woods, was made to catch the lumberman's eye. And well we knew the habits of the Badgers, once fortune smiled upon them. Straight to New York they hie, and lay their goods at the feet of the girl who serves them beans in a beanery. Why, the alphabet itself connives. The Sunday newspaper's headliner's work is cut for him.

"Winsome Waitress Wins Wealthy Wisconsin Woodsman."

For a while we felt that Milly was on the verge of being lost to us.

It was our love of the Unerring Artistic Adjustment of Nature that inspired us. We could not give her over to a lumberman, doubly accursed by wealth and provincialism. We shuddered to think of Milly, with her voice modulated and her elbows covered, pouring tea in the marble teepee of a tree murderer. No! In Cypher's she belonged—in the bacon smoke, the cabbage perfume, the grand, Wagnerian chorus of hurled ironstone china and rattling casters.

Our fears must have been prophetic, for on that same evening the wild-wood discharged upon us Milly's preordained confiscator—our fee to adjustment and order. But Alaska and not Wisconsin bore the burden of the visitation.

We were at our supper of beef stew and dried apples when he trotted in as if on the heels of a dog team, and made one of the mess at our table. With the freedom of the camps he assaulted our ears and claimed the fellowship of men lost in the wilds of a hash house. We embraced him as a specimen, and in three minutes we had all but died for one another as friends.

He was rugged and bearded and wind-dried. He had just come off the "trail," he said, at one of the North River ferries. I fancied I could see the snow dust of Chilcoot yet powdering his shoulders. And then he strewed the table with the nuggets, stuffed ptarmigans, bead work and seal pelts of the returned Klondiker, and began to prate to us of his millions.

"Bank drafts for two millions," was his summing up, "and a thousand a day piling up from my claims. And now I want some beef stew and canned peaches. I never got off the train since I mushed out of Seattle, and I'm hungry. The stuff the niggers feed you on Pullmans don't count. You gentlemen order what you want."

And then Milly loomed up with a thousand dishes on her bare arm—loomed up big and white and pink and awful as Mount Saint Elias—with a smile like day breaking in a gulch. And the Klondiker threw down his pelts and nuggets as dross, and let his jaw fall half-way, and stared at her. You could almost see the diamond tiaras on Milly's brow and the hand-embroidered silk Paris gowns that he meant to buy for her.

At last the bollworm had attacked the cotton—the poison ivy was reaching out its tendrils to entwine the summer boarder—the millionaire lumberman, thinly disguised as the Alaskan miner, was about to engulf our Milly and upset Nature's adjustment.

Kraft was the first to act. He leaped up and pounded the Klondiker's back. "Come out and drink," he shouted. "Drink first and eat afterward." Judkins seized one arm and I the other.

Gaily, roaringly, irresistibly, in jolly-good-fellow style, we dragged him from the restaurant to a café, stuffing his pockets with his embalmed birds and indigestible nuggets.

There he rumbled a roughly good-humored protest. "That's the girl for my money," he declared. "She can eat out of my skillet the rest of her life. Why, I never see such a fine girl. I'm going back there and ask her to marry me. I guess she won't want to sling hash any more when she sees the pile of dust I've got."

"You'll take another whiskey and milk now," Kraft persuaded, with Satan's smile. "I thought you up-country fellows were better sports."

Kraft spent his puny store of coin at the bar and then gave Judkins and me such an appealing look that we went down to the last dime we had in toasting our guest.

Then, when our ammunition was gone and the Klondiker, still somewhat sober, began to babble again of Milly, Kraft whispered into his ear such a polite, barbed insult relating to people who were miserly with their funds, that the miner crashed down handful after handful of silver and notes, calling for all the fluids in the world to drown the imputation.

Thus the work was accomplished. With his own guns we drove him from the field. And then we had him carted to a distant small hotel and put to bed with his nuggets and baby seal-skins stuffed around him.

"He will never find Cypher's again," said Kraft. "He will propose to the first white apron he sees in a dairy restaurant tomorrow. And Milly—I mean the Natural Adjustment—is saved!"

And back to Cypher's went we three, and, finding customers scarce, we joined hands and did an Indian dance with Milly in the center.

This, I say, happened three years ago. And about that time a little luck descended upon us three, and we were enabled to buy costlier and less wholesome food than Cypher's. Our paths separated, and I saw Kraft no more and Judkins seldom.

But, as I said, I saw a painting the other day that was sold for $5,000. The title was "Boadicea," and the figure seemed to fill all out-of-doors. But of all the picture's admirers who stood before it, I believe I was the only one who longed for Boadicea to stalk from her frame, bringing me corned-beef hash with poached egg.

I hurried away to see Kraft. His satanic eyes were the same, his hair was worse tangled, but his clothes had been made by a tailor.

"I didn't know," I said to him.

"We've bought a cottage in the Bronx with the money," said he. "Any evening at 7."

"Then," said I, "when you led us against the lumberman—the—Klondiker—it wasn't altogether on account of the Unerring Artistic Adjustment of Nature?"

"Well, not altogether," said Kraft, with a grin.

9

An Unfinished Story

We no longer groan and heap ashes upon our heads when the flames of Tophet are mentioned. For, even the preachers have begun to tell us that God is radium, or ether or some scientific compound, and that the worst we wicked ones may expect is a chemical reaction. This is a pleasing hypothesis; but there lingers yet some of the old, goodly terror of orthodoxy.

There are but two subjects upon which one may discourse with a free imagination, and without the possibility of being controverted. You may talk of your dreams; and you may tell what you heard a parrot say. Both Morpheus and the bird are incompetent witnesses; and your listener dare not attack your recital. The baseless fabric of a vision, then, shall furnish my theme—chosen with apologies and regrets instead of the more limited field of pretty Polly's small talk.

I had a dream that was so far removed from the higher criticism that it had to do with the ancient, respectable, and lamented bar-of-judgment theory.

Gabriel had played his trump; and those of us who could not follow suit were arraigned for examination. I noticed at one side a gathering of professional bondsmen in solemn black and collars that buttoned behind; but it seemed there was some trouble about their real estate titles; and they did not appear to be getting any of us out.

A fly cop—an angel policeman—flew over to me and took me by the left wing. Near at hand was a group of very prosperous-looking spirits arraigned for judgment.

"Do you belong with that bunch?" the policeman asked.

"Who are they?" was my answer.

"Why," said he, "they are—"

But this irrelevant stuff is taking up space that the story should occupy.

Dulcie worked in a department store. She sold Hamburg edging, or stuffed peppers, or automobiles, or other little trinkets such as they keep in department stores. Of what she earned, Dulcie received six dollars per week. The remainder was credited to her and debited to somebody else's account in the ledger kept by G—— Oh, primal energy, you say, Reverend Doctor—Well then, in the Ledger of Primal Energy.

During her first year in the store, Dulcie was paid five dollars per week. It would be instructive to know how she lived on that amount. Don't care? Very well; probably you are interested in larger amounts. Six dollars is a larger amount. I will tell you how she lived on six dollars per week.

One afternoon at six, when Dulcie was sticking her hat-pin within an eighth of an inch of her *medulla oblongata*, she said to her chum, Sadie—the girl that waits on you with her left side:

"Say, Sade, I made a date for dinner this evening with Piggy."

"You never did!" exclaimed Sadie admiringly. "Well, ain't you the lucky one? Piggy's an awful swell; and he always takes a girl to swell places. He took Blanche up to the Hoffman House one evening, where they have swell music, and you see a lot of swells. You'll have a swell time, Dulce."

Dulcie hurried homeward. Her eyes were shining, and her cheeks showed the delicate pink of life's—real life's—approaching dawn. It was Friday; and she had fifty cents left of her last week's wages.

The streets were filled with the rush-hour floods of people. The electric lights of Broadway were glowing—calling moths from miles, from leagues, from hundreds of leagues out of darkness around to come in and attend the singeing school. Men in accurate clothes, with faces like those carved on cherry stones by the old salts in sailors' homes, turned and stared at Dulcie as she sped, unheeding, past them. Manhattan, the night-blooming cereus, was beginning to unfold its dead-white, heavy-odored petals.

Dulcie stopped in a store where goods were cheap and bought an imitation lace collar with her fifty cents. That money was to have been spent otherwise—fifteen cents for supper, ten cents for breakfast, ten cents for lunch. Another dime was to be added to her small store of savings; and five cents was to be squandered for licorice drops—the kind that made your cheek look like the toothache, and last as long. The licorice was an extravagance—almost a carouse—but what is life without pleasures?

Dulcie lived in a furnished room. There is this difference between a furnished room and a boarding-house. In a furnished room, other people do not know it when you go hungry.

Dulcie went up to her room—the third floor back in a West Side brownstone-front. She lit the gas. Scientists tell us that the diamond is the hardest substance known. Their mistake. Landladies know of a compound beside which the diamond is as putty. They pack it in the tips of gas-burners; and one may stand on a chair and dig at it in vain until one's fingers are pink and bruised. A hairpin will not remove it; therefore let us call it immovable.

So Dulcie lit the gas. In its one-fourth-candlepower glow we will observe the room.

Couch-bed, dresser, table, washstand, chair—of this much the landlady was guilty. The rest was Dulcie's. On the dresser were her treasures—a gilt china vase presented to her by Sadie, a calendar issued by a pickle works, a book on the divination of dreams, some rice powder in a glass dish, and a cluster of artificial cherries tied with a pink ribbon.

Against the wrinkly mirror stood pictures of General Kitchener, William Muldoon, the Duchess of Marlborough, and Benvenuto Cellini. Against one wall was a plaster of Paris plaque of an O'Callahan in a Roman helmet. Near it was a violent oleograph of a lemon-colored child assaulting an inflammatory butterfly. This was Dulcie's final judgment in art; but it had never been upset. Her rest had never been disturbed by whispers of stolen copes; no critic had elevated his eyebrows at her infantile entomologist.

Piggy was to call for her at seven. While she swiftly makes ready, let us discreetly face the other way and gossip.

For the room, Dulcie paid two dollars per week. On week-days her breakfast cost ten cents; she made coffee and cooked an egg over the gaslight while she was dressing. On Sunday mornings she feasted royally on veal chops and pineapple fritters at "Billy's" restaurant, at a cost of twenty-five cents—and tipped the waitress ten cents. New York presents so many temptations for one to run into extravagance. She had her lunches in the department-store restaurant at a cost of sixty cents for the week; dinners were $1.05. The evening papers—show me a New Yorker going without his daily paper!—came to six cents; and two Sunday papers—one for the personal column and the other to read—were ten cents. The total amounts to $4.76. Now, one has to buy clothes, and—

I give it up. I hear of wonderful bargains in fabrics, and of miracles performed with needle and thread; but I am in doubt. I hold my pen poised in vain when I would add to Dulcie's life some of those joys that belong to woman by virtue of all the unwritten, sacred, natural, inactive ordinances of the equity of heaven. Twice she had been to Coney Island and had ridden the hobby-horses. 'Tis a weary thing to count your pleasures by summers instead of by hours.

Piggy needs but a word. When the girls named him, an undeserving stigma was cast upon the noble family of swine. The words-of-three-letters lesson in the old blue spelling book begins with Piggy's biography. He was fat; he had the soul of a rat, the habits of a bat, and the magnanimity of a cat . . . He wore expensive clothes; and was a connoisseur in starvation. He could look at a shop-girl and tell you to an hour how long it had been since she had eaten anything more nourishing than marshmallows and tea. He hung about the shopping districts, and prowled around in department stores with his invitations to dinner. Men who escort dogs upon the streets at the end of a string look down upon him. He is a type; I can dwell upon him no longer; my pen is not the kind intended for him; I am no carpenter.

At ten minutes to seven Dulcie was ready. She looked at herself in the wrinkly mirror. The reflection was satisfactory. The dark blue dress, fitting without a wrinkle, the hat with its jaunty black feather, the but-slightly-soiled gloves—all representing self-denial, even of food itself—were vastly becoming.

Dulcie forgot everything else for a moment except that she was beautiful, and that life was about to lift a corner of its mysterious veil for her to observe its wonders. No gentleman had ever asked her out before. Now she was going for a brief moment into the glitter and exalted show.

The girls said that Piggy was a "spender." There would be a grand dinner, and music, and splendidly dressed ladies to look at, and things to eat that strangely twisted the girls' jaws when they tried to tell about them. No doubt she would be asked out again. There was a blue pongee suit in a window that she knew—by saving twenty cents a week instead of ten, in—let's see—Oh, it would run into years! But there was a second-hand store in Seventh Avenue where—

Somebody knocked at the door. Dulcie opened it. The landlady stood there with a spurious smile, sniffing for cooking by stolen gas.

"A gentleman's downstairs to see you," she said. "Name is Mr. Wiggins."

By such epithet was Piggy known to unfortunate ones who had to take him seriously.

Dulcie turned to the dresser to get her handkerchief; and then she stopped still, and bit her underlip hard. While looking in her mirror she had seen fairyland and herself, a princess, just awakening from a long slumber. She had forgotten one that was watching her with sad, beautiful, stern eyes—the only one there was to approve or condemn what she did. Straight and slender and tall, with a look of sorrowful reproach on his handsome, melancholy face, General Kitchener fixed his wonderful eyes on her out of his gilt photograph frame on the dresser.

Dulcie turned like an automatic doll to the landlady.

"Tell him I can't go," she said dully. "Tell him I'm sick, or something. Tell him I'm not going out."

After the door was closed and locked, Dulcie fell upon her bed, crushing her black tip, and cried for ten minutes. General Kitchener was her only friend. He was Dulcie's ideal of a gallant knight. He looked as if he might have a secret sorrow, and his wonderful mustache was a dream, and she was a little afraid of that stern yet tender look in his eyes. She used to have little fancies that he would call at the house sometime, and ask for her, with his sword clanking against his high boots. Once, when a boy was rattling a piece of chain against a lamp-post she had opened the window and looked out. But there was no use. She knew that General Kitchener was away over in Japan, leading his army against the savage Turks; and he would never step out of his gilt frame for her. Yet one look from him had vanquished Piggy that night. Yes, for that night.

When her cry was over Dulcie got up and took off her best dress, and put on her old blue kimono. She wanted no dinner. She sang two verses of "Sammy." Then she became intensely interested in a little red speck on the side of her nose. And after that was attended to, she drew up a chair to the rickety table, and told her fortune with an old deck of cards.

"The horrid, impudent thing!" she said aloud. "And I never gave him a word or a look to make him think it!"

At nine o'clock Dulcie took a tin box of crackers and a little pot of raspberry jam out of her trunk, and had a feast. She offered General Kitchener some jam on a cracker; but he only looked at her as the sphinx would have looked at a butterfly—if there are butterflies in the desert.

"Don't eat it if you don't want to," said Dulcie. "And don't put on so many airs and scold so with your eyes. I wonder if you'd be so superior and snippy if you had to live on six dollars a week."

It was not a good sign for Dulcie to be rude to General Kitchener. And then she turned Benvenuto Cellini face downward with a severe gesture. But that was not inexcusable; for she had always thought he was Henry VIII, and she did not approve of him.

At half-past nine Dulcie took a last look at the pictures on the dresser, turned out the light, and skipped into bed. It's an awful thing to go to bed with a good-night look at General Kitchener, William Muldoon, the Duchess of Marlborough, and Benvenuto Cellini. This story really doesn't get anywhere at all. The rest of it comes later—sometime when Piggy asks Dulcie again to dine with him, and she is feeling lonelier than usual, and General Kitchener happens to be looking the other way; and then—

As I said before, I dreamed that I was standing near a crowd of prosperous-looking angels, and a policeman took me by the wing and asked if I belonged with them.

"Who are they?" I asked.

"Why," said he, "they are the men who hired working-girls, and paid 'em five or six dollars a week to live on. Are you one of the bunch?"

"Not on your immortality," said I. "I'm only the fellow that set fire to an orphan asylum, and murdered a blind man for his pennies."

10. The May moon shone bright upon the private boarding-house of Mrs. Murphy. By reference to the almanac a large amount of territory will be discovered upon which its rays also fell. Spring was in its heyday, with hay fever soon to follow. The parks were green with new leaves and buyers for the Western and Southern trade. Flowers and summer-resort agents were blowing; the air and answers to Lawson were growing milder; hand-organs, fountains and pinochle were playing everywhere.

The windows of Mrs. Murphy's boarding-house were open. A group of boarders were seated on the high stoop upon round, flat mats like German pancakes.

In one of the second-floor front windows Mrs. McCaskey awaited her husband. Supper was cooling on the table. Its heat went into Mrs. McCaskey.

At nine Mr. McCaskey came. He carried his coat on his arm and his pipe in his teeth; and he apologized for disturbing the boarders on the steps as he selected spots of stone between them on which to set his size 9, width Ds.

As he opened the door of his room he received a surprise. Instead of the usual stove-lid or potato-masher for him to dodge, came only words.

Mr. McCaskey reckoned that the benign May moon had softened the breast of his spouse.

"I heard ye," came the oral substitutes for kitchenware. "Ye can apollygise to riff-raff of the streets for settin' yer unhandy feet on the tails of their frocks, but ye'd walk on the neck of yer wife the length of a clothes-line without so much as a 'Kiss me fut,' and I'm sure it's that long from rubberin' out the windy for ye and the victuals cold such as there's money to buy after drinkin' up yer wages at Gallegher's every Saturday evenin', and the gas man here twice today for his."

"Woman!" said Mr. McCaskey, dashing his coat and hat upon a chair, "the noise of ye is an insult to me appetite. When ye run down politeness ye take the mortar from between the bricks of the foundations of society. 'Tis no more than exercisin' the acrimony of a gentleman when ye ask the dissent of ladies blockin' the way for steppin' between them. Will ye bring the pig's face of ye out of the windy and see to the food?"

Mrs. McCaskey arose heavily and went to the stove. There was something in her manner that warned Mr. McCaskey. When the corners of her mouth went down suddenly like a barometer it usually foretold a fall of crockery and tinware.

"Pig's face, is it?" said Mrs. McCaskey, and hurled a stewpan full of bacon and turnips at her lord.

Mr. McCaskey was no novice at repartee. He knew what should follow the entrée. On the table was a roast sirloin of pork, garnished with shamrocks. He retorted with this, and drew the appropriate return of a bread pudding in an earthen dish. A hunk of Swiss cheese accurately thrown by her husband struck Mrs. McCaskey below one eye. When she replied with a well-aimed coffee-pot full of a hot, black, semi-fragrant liquid the battle, according to courses, should have ended.

But Mr. McCaskey was no 50-cent *table d'hôter*. Let cheap Bohemians consider coffee the end, if they would. Let them make that *faux pas*. He was foxier still. Finger-bowls were not beyond the compass of his experience. They were not to be had in the Pension Murphy; but their equivalent was at hand. Triumphantly he sent the granite-ware wash basin at the head of his matrimonial adversary. Mrs. McCaskey dodged in time. She reached for a flatiron, with which, as a sort of cordial, she hoped to bring the gastronomical duel to a close. But a loud, wailing scream downstairs caused both her and Mr. McCaskey to pause in a sort of involuntary armistice.

On the sidewalk at the corner of the house Policeman Cleary was standing with one ear upturned, listening to the crash of household utensils.

"'Tis Jawn McCaskey and his missis at it again," meditated the policeman. "I wonder shall I go up and stop the row. I will not. Married folks they are; and few pleasures they have. 'Twill not last long. Sure, they'll have to borrow more dishes to keep it up with."

And just then came the loud scream below-stairs, betokening fear or dire extremity. "'Tis probably the cat," said Policeman Cleary, and walked hastily in the other direction.

The boarders on the steps were fluttered. Mr. Toomey, an insurance solicitor by birth and an investigator by profession, went inside to analyze the scream. He returned with the news that Mrs. Murphy's little boy, Mike, was lost. Following the messenger, out bounced Mrs. Murphy—two hundred pounds in tears and hysterics, clutching the air and howling to the sky for the loss of thirty pounds of freckles and mischief. Bathos, truly; but Mr. Toomey sat down at the side of Miss Purdy, millinery, and their hands came together in sympathy. The two old maids, Misses Walsh, who complained every day about the noise in the halls, inquired immediately if anybody had looked behind the clock.

Major Grigg, who sat by his fat wife on the top step, arose and buttoned his coat. "The little one lost?" he exclaimed. "I will scour the city." His wife never allowed him out after dark. But now she said: "Go, Ludovic!" in a baritone voice. "Whoever can look upon that mother's grief without springing to her relief has a heart of stone." "Give me some thirty or—sixty cents, my love," said the Major. "Lost children sometimes stray far. I may need carfares."

Old man Denny, hall room, fourth floor back, who sat on the lowest step, trying to read a paper by the street lamp, turned over a page to follow up the article about the carpenters' strike. Mrs.

Murphy shrieked to the moon: "Oh, ar-r-Mike, f'r Gawd's sake, where is me little bit av a boy?"

"When'd ye see him last?" asked old man Denny, with one eye on the report of the Building Trades League.

"Oh," wailed Mrs. Murphy, "'twas yisterday, or maybe four hours ago! I dunno. But it's lost he is, me little boy Mike. He was playin' on the sidewalk only this mornin'—or was it Wednesday? I'm that busy with work, 'tis hard to keep up with dates. But I've looked the house over from top to cellar, and it's gone he is. Oh, for the love av Hiven—"

Silent, grim, colossal, the big city has ever stood against its revilers. They call it hard as iron; they say that no pulse of pity beats in its bosom; they compare its streets with lonely forests and deserts of lava. But beneath the hard crust of the lobster is found a delectable and luscious food. Perhaps a different simile would have been wiser. Still, nobody should take offence. We would call no one a lobster without good and sufficient claws.

No calamity so touches the common heart of humanity as does the straying of a little child. Their feet are so uncertain and feeble; the ways are so steep and strange.

Major Griggs hurried down to the corner, and up the avenue into Billy's place. "Gimme a rye-high," he said to the servitor. "Haven't seen a bow-legged, dirty-faced little devil of a six-year-old lost kid around here anywhere, have you?"

Mr. Toomey retained Miss Purdy's hand on the steps. "Think of that dear little babe," said Miss Purdy, "lost from his mother's side—perhaps already fallen beneath the iron hoofs of galloping steeds—oh, isn't it dreadful?"

"Ain't that right?" agreed Mr. Toomey, squeezing her hand. "Say I start out and help look for um!"

"Perhaps," said Miss Purdy, "you should. But, oh, Mr. Toomey, you are so dashing—so reckless—suppose in your enthusiasm some accident should befall you, then what—"

Old man Denny read on about the arbitration agreement, with one finger on the lines.

In the second floor front Mr. and Mrs. McCaskey came to the window to recover their second wind. Mr. McCaskey was scooping turnips out of his vest with a crooked forefinger, and his lady was wiping an eye that the salt of the roast pork had not benefited. They heard the outcry below, and thrust their heads out of the window.

"'Tis little Mike is lost," said Mrs. McCaskey, in a hushed voice, "the beautiful, little, trouble-making angel of a gossoon!"

"The bit of a boy mislaid?" said Mr. McCaskey, leaning out of the window. "Why, now, that's bad enough, entirely. The childer, they be different. If 'twas a woman I'd be willin', for they leave peace behind 'em when they go."

Disregarding the thrust, Mrs. McCaskey caught her husband's arm.

"Jawn," she said, sentimentally, "Missis Murphy's little bye is lost. 'Tis a great city for losing little boys. Six years old he was. Jawn, 'tis the same age our little bye would have been if we had had one six years ago."

"We never did," said Mr. McCaskey, lingering with the fact.

"But if we had, Jawn, think what sorrow would be in our hearts this night, with our little Phelan run away and stolen in the city nowheres at all."

"Ye talk foolishness," said Mr. McCaskey. "'Tis Pat he would be named, after me old father in Cantrim."

"Ye lie!" said Mrs. McCaskey, without anger. "Me brother was worth tin dozen bog-trotting McCaskeys. After him would the bye be named." She leaned over the window-sill and looked down at the hurrying and bustle below.

"Jawn," said Mrs. McCaskey, softly, "I'm sorry I was hasty wid ye."

"'Twas hasty puddin', as ye say," said her husband, "and hurry-up turnips and get-a-move-on-ye coffee. 'Twas what ye could call a quick lunch, all right, and tell no lie."

Mrs. McCaskey slipped her arm inside her husband's and took his rough hand in hers.

"Listen at the cryin' of poor Mrs. Murphy," she said. "'Tis an awful thing for a bit of a bye to be lost in this great big city. If 'twas our little Phelan, Jawn, I'd be breakin' me heart."

Awkwardly Mr. McCaskey withdrew his hand. But he laid it around the nearing shoulder of his wife.

"'Tis foolishness, of course," said he, roughly, "but I'd be cut up some meself if our little Pat was kidnapped or anything. But there never was any childer for us. Sometimes I've been ugly and hard with ye, Judy. Forget it."

They leaned together, and looked down at the heart-drama being acted below.

Long they sat thus. People surged along the sidewalk, crowding, questioning, filling the air with rumors, and inconsequent surmises. Mrs. Murphy ploughed back and forth in their midst, like a soft mountain down which plunged an audible cataract of tears. Couriers came and went.

Loud voices and a renewed uproar were raised in front of the boarding-house.

"What's up now, Judy?" asked Mr. McCaskey.

"'Tis Missis Murphy's voice," said Mrs. McCaskey, harking. "She says she's after finding little Mike asleep behind the roll of old linoleum under the bed in her room."

Mr. McCaskey laughed loudly.

"That's yer Phelan," he shouted, sardonically. "Divil a bit would a Pat have done that trick. If the bye we never had is strayed and stole, by the powers, call him Phelan, and see him hide out under the bed like a mangy pup."

Mrs. McCaskey arose heavily, and went toward the dish closet, with the corners of her mouth drawn down.

Policeman Cleary came back around the corner as the crowd dispersed. Surprised, he upturned an ear toward the McCaskey apartment, where the crash of irons and china-ware and the ring of hurled kitchen utensils seemed as loud as before. Policeman Cleary took out his timepiece.

"By the deported snakes!" he exclaimed, "Jawn McCaskey and his lady have been fightin' for an hour and a quarter by the watch. The missis could give him forty pounds weight. Strength to his arm."

Policeman Cleary strolled back around the corner.

Old man Denny folded his paper and hurried up the steps just as Mrs. Murphy was about to lock the door for the night.

10

Mammon and the Archer

Old Anthony Rockwall, retired manufacturer and proprietor of Rockwall's Eureka Soap, looked out the library window of his Fifth Avenue mansion and grinned. His neighbor to the right—the aristocratic clubman, G. Van Schuylight Suffolk-Jones—came out to his waiting motor-car, wrinkling a contumelious nostril, as usual, at the Italian renaissance sculpture of the soap palace's front elevation.

"Stuck-up old statuette of nothing doing!" commented the ex-Soap King. "The Eden Musee'll get that old frozen Nesselrode yet if he don't watch out. I'll have this house painted red, white, and blue next summer and see if that'll make his Dutch nose turn up any higher."

And then Anthony Rockwall, who never cared for bells, went to the door of his library and shouted "Mike!" in the same voice that had once chipped off pieces of the welkin on the Kansas prairies.

"Tell my son," said Anthony to the answering menial, "to come in here before he leaves the house."

When young Rockwall entered the library the old man laid aside his newspaper, looked at him with a kindly grimness on his big, smooth, ruddy countenance, rumpled his mop of white hair with one hand and rattled the keys in his pocket with the other.

"Richard," said Anthony Rockwall, "what do you pay for the soap that you use?"

Richard, only six months home from college, was startled a little. He had not yet taken the measure of this sire of his, who was as full of unexpectednesses as a girl at her first party.

"Six dollars a dozen, I think, dad."

"And your clothes?"

"I suppose about sixty dollars, as a rule."

"You're a gentleman," said Anthony, decidedly. "I've heard of these young bloods spending $24 a dozen for soap, and going over the hundred mark for clothes. You've got as much money to waste as any of 'em, and yet you stick to what's decent and moderate. Now I use the old Eureka—not only for sentiment, but it's the purest soap made. Whenever you pay more than 10 cents a cake for soap you buy bad perfumes and labels. But 50 cents is doing very well for a young man in your generation, position and condition. As I said, you're a gentleman. They say it takes three generations to make one. They're off. Money'll do it as slick as soap grease. It's made you one. By hokey! It's almost made one of me. I'm nearly as impolite and disagreeable and ill-mannered as these two old Knickerbocker gents on each side of me that can't sleep of nights because I bought in between 'em."

"There are some things that money can't accomplish," remarked young Rockwall, rather gloomily.

"Now, don't say that," said old Anthony, shocked. "I bet my money on money every time. I've been through the encyclopedia down to Y looking for something you can't buy with it; and I expect to have to take up the appendix next week. I'm for money against the field. Tell me something money won't buy."

"For one thing," answered Richard, rankling a little, "it won't buy one into the exclusive circles of society."

"Oho! Won't it?" thundered the champion of the root of evil. "You tell me where your exclusive circles would be if the first Astor hadn't had the money to pay for his steerage passage over?"

Richard sighed.

"And that's what I was coming to," said the old man, less boisterously. "That's why I asked you to come in. There's something going wrong with you, boy. I've been noticing it for two weeks. Out with it. I guess I could lay my hands on eleven millions within twenty-four hours, besides the real estate. If it's your liver, there's the *Rambler* down in the bay, coaled, and ready to steam down to the Bahamas in two days."

"Not a bad guess, dad; you haven't missed it far."

"Ah," said Anthony, keenly; "what's her name?"

Richard began to walk up and down the library floor. There was enough comradeship and sympathy in this crude old father of his to draw his confidence.

"Why don't you ask her?" demanded old Anthony. "She'll jump at you. You've got the money and the looks, and you're a decent boy. Your hands are clean. You've got no Eureka soap on 'em. You've been to college, but she'll overlook that."

"I haven't had a chance," said Richard.

"Make one," said Anthony. "Take her for a walk in the park, or a straw ride, or walk home with her from church. Chance! Pshaw!"

"You don't know the social mill, dad. She's part of the stream that turns it. Every hour and minute of her time is arranged for days in advance. I must have that girl, dad, or this town is a blackjack swamp forevermore. And I can't write it—I can't do that."

"Tut!" said the old man. "Do you mean to tell me that with all the money I've got you can't get an hour or two of a girl's time for yourself?"

"I've put it off too late. She's going to sail for Europe at noon day after tomorrow for a two years' stay. I'm to see her alone tomorrow evening for a few minutes. She's at Larchmont now at her aunt's. I can't go there. But I'm allowed to meet her with a cab at the Grand Central Station tomorrow evening at the 8.30 train. We drive down Broadway to Wallack's at a gallop, where her mother and a box party will be waiting for us in the lobby. Do you think she would listen to a declaration from me during that six or eight minutes under those circumstances? No. And what chance would I have in the theatre or afterward? None. No, dad, this is one tangle that your money can't unravel. We can't buy one minute of time with cash; if we could, rich people would live longer. There's no hope of getting a talk with Miss Lantry before she sails."

"All right, Richard, my boy," said old Anthony, cheerfully. "You may run along down to your club now. I'm glad it ain't your liver. But don't forget to burn a few punk sticks in the joss house to the great god Mazuma from time to time. You say money won't buy time? Well, of course, you can't order eternity wrapped up and delivered at your residence for a price, but I've seen Father Time get pretty bad stone bruises on his heels when he walked through the gold diggings."

That night came Aunt Ellen, gentle, sentimental, wrinkled, sighing, oppressed by wealth, in to Brother Anthony at his evening paper, and began discourse on the subject of lovers' woes.

"He told me all about it," said brother Anthony, yawning. "I told him my bank account was at his service. And then he began to knock money. Said money couldn't help. Said the rules of society couldn't be bucked for a yard by a team of ten-millionaires."

"Oh, Anthony," sighed Aunt Ellen, "I wish you would not think so much of money. Wealth is nothing where a true affection is concerned. Love is all-powerful. If he only had spoken earlier! She could not have refused our Richard. But now I fear it is too late. He will have no opportunity to address her. All your gold cannot bring happiness to your son."

At eight o'clock the next evening Aunt Ellen took a quaint old gold ring from a moth-eaten case and gave it to Richard.

"Wear it tonight, nephew," she begged. "Your mother gave it to me. Good luck in love she said it brought. She asked me to give it to you when you had found the one you loved."

Young Rockwall took the ring reverently and tried it on his smallest finger. It slipped as far as the second joint and stopped. He took it off and stuffed it into his vest pocket, after the manner of man. And then he 'phoned for his cab.

At the station he captured Miss Lantry out of the gadding mob at eight thirty-two.

"We mustn't keep mamma and the others waiting," said she.

"To Wallack's Theatre as fast as you can drive!" said Richard loyally.

They whirled up Forty-second to Broadway, and then down the white-starred lane that leads from the soft meadows of sunset to the rocky hills of morning.

At Thirty-fourth Street young Richard quickly thrust up the trap and ordered the cab-man to stop.

"I've dropped a ring," he apologized, as he climbed out. "It was my mother's, and I'd hate to lose it. I won't detain you a minute—I saw where it fell."

In less than a minute he was back in the cab with the ring.

But within that minute a crosstown car had stopped directly in front of the cab. The cab-man tried to pass to the left, but a heavy express wagon cut him off. He tried the right, and had to back away from a furniture van that had no business to be there. He tried to back out, but dropped his reins and swore dutifully. He was blockaded in a tangled mess of vehicles and horses.

One of those street blockades had occurred that sometimes tie up commerce and movement quite suddenly in the big city.

"Why don't you drive on?" said Miss Lantry, impatiently. "We'll be late."

Richard stood up in the cab and looked around. He saw a congested flood of wagons, trucks, cabs, vans and street cars filling the vast space where Broadway, Sixth Avenue and Thirty-fourth street cross one another as a twenty-six inch maiden fills her twenty-two inch girdle. And still from all the cross streets they were hurrying and rattling toward the converging point at full speed, and hurling themselves into the struggling mass, locking wheels and adding their drivers' imprecations to the clamor. The entire traffic of Manhattan seemed to have jammed itself around them. The oldest New Yorker among the thousands of spectators that lined the sidewalks had not witnessed a street blockade of the proportions of this one.

"I'm very sorry," said Richard, as he resumed his seat, "but it looks as if we are stuck. They won't get this jumble loosened up in an hour. It was my fault. If I hadn't dropped the ring we—"

"Let me see the ring," said Miss Lantry. "Now that it can't be helped, I don't care. I think theaters are stupid, anyway."

At 11 o'clock that night somebody tapped lightly on Anthony Rockwall's door.

"Come in," shouted Anthony, who was in a red dressing-gown, reading a book of piratical adventures.

Somebody was Aunt Ellen, looking like a gray-haired angel that had been left on earth by mistake.

"They're engaged, Anthony," she said, softly. "She has promised to marry our Richard. On their way to the theatre there was a street blockade, and it was two hours before their cab could get out of it.

"And oh, brother Anthony, don't ever boast of the power of money again. A little emblem of true love—a little ring that symbolized unending and unmercenary affection—was the cause of our Richard finding his happiness. He dropped it in the street, and got out to recover it. And before they could continue the blockade occurred. He spoke to his love and won her there while the cab was hemmed in. Money is dross compared with true love, Anthony."

"All right," said old Anthony. "I'm glad the boy has got what he wanted. I told him I wouldn't spare any expense in the matter if—"

"But, brother Anthony, what good could your money have done?"

"Sister," said Anthony Rockwall. "I've got my pirate in a devil of a scrape. His ship has just been scuttled, and he's too good a judge of the value of money to let drown. I wish you would let me go on with this chapter."

The story should end here. I wish it would as heartily as you who read it wish it did. But we must go to the bottom of the well for truth.

The next day a person with red hands and a blue polka-dot necktie, who called himself Kelly, called at Anthony Rockwall's house, and was at once received in the library.

"Well," said Anthony, reaching for his chequebook, "it was a good bilin' of soap. Let's see—you had $5,000 in cash."

"I paid out $300 more of my own," said Kelly. "I had to go a little above the estimate. I got the express wagons and cabs mostly for $5; but the trucks and two-horse teams mostly raised me to $10. The motormen wanted $10, and some of the loaded teams $20. The cops struck me hardest—$50 I paid two, and the rest $20 and $25. But didn't it work beautiful, Mr. Rockwall? I'm glad William A. Brady wasn't onto that little outdoor vehicle mob scene. I wouldn't want William to break his heart with jealousy. And never a rehearsal, either! The boys was on time to the fraction of a second. It was two hours before a snake could get below Greeley's statue."

"Thirteen hundred—there you are, Kelly," said Anthony, tearing off a check. "Your thousand, and the $300 you were out. You don't despise money, do you, Kelly?"

"Me?" said Kelly. "I can lick the man that invented poverty."

Anthony called Kelly when he was at the door.

"You didn't notice," said he, "anywhere in the tie-up, a kind of a fat boy without any clothes on shooting arrows around with a bow, did you?"

"Why, no," said Kelly, mystified. "I didn't. If he was like you say, maybe the cops pinched him before I got there."

"I thought the little rascal wouldn't be on hand," chuckled Anthony. "Goodbye, Kelly."

11

Memoirs of a Yellow Dog

I don't suppose it will knock any of you people off your perch to read a contribution from an animal. Mr. Kipling and a good many others have demonstrated the fact that animals can express themselves in remunerative English, and no magazine goes to press nowadays without an animal story in it, except the old-style monthlies that are still running pictures of Bryan and the Mont Pélee horror.

But you needn't look for any stuck-up literature in my piece, such as Bearoo, the bear, and Snakoo, the snake, and Tammanoo, the tiger, talk in the jungle books. A yellow dog that's spent most of his life in a cheap New York flat, sleeping in a corner on an old sateen underskirt (the one she spilled port wine on at the Lady Longshoremen's banquet), mustn't be expected to perform any tricks with the art of speech.

I was born a yellow pup; date, locality, pedigree and weight unknown. The first thing I can recollect, an old woman had me in a basket at Broadway and Twenty-third trying to sell me to a fat lady. Old Mother Hubbard was boosting me to beat the band as a genuine Pomeranian-Hambletonian-Red-Irish-Cochin-China-Stoke-Pogis fox terrier. The fat lady chased a V around among the samples of gros grain flannelette in her shopping bag till she cornered it, and gave up. From that moment I was a pet—a mamma's own wootsey squidlums. Say, gentle reader, did you ever have a 200-pound woman breathing a flavour of Camembert cheese and Peau d'Espagne pick you up and wallop her nose all over you, remarking all the time in an Emma Eames tone of voice: "Oh, oo's um oodlum, doodlum, woodlum, toodlum, bitsy-witsy skoodlums?"

From a pedigreed yellow pup I grew up to be an anonymous yellow cur looking like a cross between an Angora cat and a box of lemons. But my mistress never tumbled. She thought that the two primeval pups that Noah chased into the ark were but a collateral branch of my ancestors. It took two policemen to keep her from entering me at the Madison Square Garden for the Siberian bloodhound prize.

I'll tell you about that flat. The house was the ordinary thing in New York, paved with parian marble in the entrance hall and cobblestones above the first floor. Our fiat was three—well, not flights—climbs up. My mistress rented it unfurnished, and put in the regular things—1903 antique unholstered parlor set, oil chromo of geishas in a Harlem tea house, rubber plant and husband.

By Sirius! There was a biped I felt sorry for. He was a little man with sandy hair and whiskers a good deal like mine. Henpecked?—Well, toucans and flamingoes and pelicans all had their bills in him. He wiped the dishes and listened to my mistress tell about the cheap, ragged things the lady with the squirrel-skin coat on the second floor hung out on her line to dry. And every evening while she was getting supper she made him take me out on the end of a string for a walk.

If men knew how women pass the time when they are alone they'd never marry. Laura Lean Jibbey, peanut brittle, a little almond cream on the neck muscles, dishes unwashed, half an hour's talk with the iceman, reading a package of old letters, a couple of pickles and two bottles of malt extract, one hour peeking through a hole in the window shade into the flat across the air-shaft—that's about all there is to it. Twenty minutes before time for him to come home from work she straightens up the house, fixes her rat so it won't show, and gets out a lot of sewing for a ten-minute bluff.

I led a dog's life in that flat. 'Most all day I lay there in my corner watching that fat woman kill time. I slept sometimes and had pipe dreams about being out chasing cats into basements and growling at old ladies with black mittens, as a dog was intended to do. Then she would pounce upon me with a lot of that driveling poodle palaver and kiss me on the nose—but what could I do? A dog can't chew cloves.

I began to feel sorry for Hubby, dog my cats if I didn't. We looked so much alike that people noticed it when we went out; so we shook the streets that Morgan's cab drives down, and took to climbing the piles of last December's snow on the streets where cheap people live.

One evening when we were thus promenading, and I was trying to look like a prize St. Bernard, and the old man was trying to look like he wouldn't have murdered the first organ-grinder he heard play Mendelssohn's wedding-march, I looked up at him and said, in my way:

"What are you looking so sour about, you oakum trimmed lobster? She don't kiss you. You don't have to sit on her lap and listen to talk that would make the book of a musical comedy sound like the maxims of Epictetus. You ought to be thankful you're not a dog. Brace up, Benedick, and bid the blues begone."

The matrimonial mishap looked down at me with almost canine intelligence in his face.

"Why, doggie," says he, "good doggie. You almost look like you could speak. What is it, doggie—Cats?"

Cats! Could speak!

But, of course, he couldn't understand. Humans were denied the speech of animals. The only common ground of communication upon which dogs and men can get together is in fiction.

In the flat across the hall from us lived a lady with a black-and-tan terrier. Her husband strung it and took it out every evening, but he always came home cheerful and whistling. One day I touched noses with the black-and-tan in the hall, and I struck him for an elucidation.

"See, here, Wiggle-and-Skip," I says, "you know that it ain't the nature of a real man to play dry nurse to a dog in public. I never saw one leashed to a bow-wow yet that didn't look like he'd like to lick every other man that looked at him. But your boss comes in every day as perky and set up as an amateur prestidigitator doing the egg trick. How does he do it? Don't tell me he likes it."

"Him?" says the black-and-tan. "Why, he uses Nature's Own Remedy. He gets spifflicated. At first when we go out he's as shy as the man on the steamer who would rather play pedro when they make 'em all jackpots. By the time we've been in eight saloons he don't care whether the thing on the end of his line is a dog or a catfish. I've lost two inches of my tail trying to sidestep those swinging doors."

The pointer I got from that terrier—vaudeville please copy—set me to thinking.

One evening about 6 o'clock my mistress ordered him to get busy and do the ozone act for Lovey. I have concealed it until now, but that is what she called me. The black-and-tan was called "Tweetness." I consider that I have the bulge on him as far as you could chase a rabbit. Still "Lovey" is something of a nomenclatural tin can on the tail of one's self respect.

At a quiet place on a safe street I tightened the line of my custodian in front of an attractive, refined saloon. I made a dead-ahead scramble for the doors, whining like a dog in the press dispatches that lets the family know that little Alice is bogged while gathering lilies in the brook.

"Why, darn my eyes," says the old man, with a grin; "darn my eyes if the saffron-coloured son of a seltzer lemonade ain't asking me in to take a drink. Lemme see—how long's it been since I saved shoe leather by keeping one foot on the foot-rest? I believe I'll—"

I knew I had him. Hot Scotches he took, sitting at a table. For an hour he kept the Campbells coming. I sat by his side rapping for the waiter with my tail, and eating free lunch such as mamma in her flat never equaled with her homemade truck bought at a delicatessen store eight minutes before papa comes home.

When the products of Scotland were all exhausted except the rye bread the old man unwound me from the table leg and played me outside like a fisherman plays a salmon. Out there he took off my collar and threw it into the street.

"Poor doggie," says he; "good doggie. She shan't kiss you any more. 'S a darned shame. Good doggie, go away and get run over by a street car and be happy."

I refused to leave. I leaped and frisked around the old man's legs happy as a pug on a rug.

"You old flea-headed woodchuck-chaser," I said to him—"you moon-baying, rabbit-pointing, egg-stealing old beagle, can't you see that I don't want to leave you? Can't you see that we're both Pups in the Wood and the missis is the cruel uncle after you with the dish towel and me with the flea liniment and a pink bow to tie on my tail. Why not cut that all out and be pards forever more?"

Maybe you'll say he didn't understand—maybe he didn't. But he kind of got a grip on the Hot Scotches, and stood still for a minute, thinking.

"Doggie," says he, finally, "we don't live more than a dozen lives on this earth, and very few of us live to be more than 300. If I ever see that flat any more I'm a flat, and if you do you're flatter; and that's no flattery. I'm offering 60 to 1 that Westward Ho wins out by the length of a dachshund."

There was no string, but I frolicked along with my master to the Twenty-third street ferry. And the cats on the route saw reason to give thanks that prehensile claws had been given them.

On the Jersey side my master said to a stranger who stood eating a currant bun:

"Me and my doggie, we are bound for the Rocky Mountains."

But what pleased me most was when my old man pulled both of my ears until I howled, and said: "You common, monkey-headed, rat-tailed, sulphur-colored son of a door mat, do you know what I'm going to call you?"

I thought of "Lovey," and I whined dolefully.

"I'm going to call you 'Pete,'" says my master; and if I'd had five tails I couldn't have done enough wagging to do justice to the occasion.

12

Springtime a la Carte

It was a day in March.

Never, never begin a story this way when you write one. No opening could possibly be worse. It is unimaginative, flat, dry and likely to consist of mere wind. But in this instance it is allowable. For the following paragraph, which should have inaugurated the narrative, is too wildly extravagant and preposterous to be flaunted in the face of the reader without preparation.

Sarah was crying over her bill of fare.

Think of a New York girl shedding tears on the menu card!

To account for this you will be allowed to guess that the lobsters were all out, or that she had sworn ice-cream off during Lent, or that she had ordered onions, or that she had just come from a Hackett matinée. And then, all these theories being wrong, you will please let the story proceed.

The gentleman who announced that the world was an oyster which he with his sword would open made a larger hit than he deserved. It is not difficult to open an oyster with a sword. But did you ever notice any one try to open the terrestrial bivalve with a typewriter? Like to wait for a dozen raw opened that way?

Sarah had managed to pry apart the shells with her unhandy weapon far enough to nibble a wee bit at the cold and clammy world within. She knew no more shorthand than if she had been a graduate in stenography just let slip upon the world by a business college. So, not being able to stenog, she could not enter that bright galaxy of office talent. She was a free-lance typewriter and canvassed for odd jobs of copying.

The most brilliant and crowning feat of Sarah's battle with the world was the deal she made with Schulenberg's Home Restaurant. The restaurant was next door to the old red brick in which she hall-roomed. One evening after dining at Schulenberg's 40-cent, five-course *table d'hôte* (served as fast as you throw the five baseballs at the coloured gentleman's head) Sarah took away with her the bill of fare. It was written in an almost unreadable script neither English nor German, and so arranged that if you were not careful you began with a toothpick and rice pudding and ended with soup and the day of the week.

The next day Sarah showed Schulenberg a neat card on which the menu was beautifully typewritten with the viands temptingly marshalled under their right and proper heads from "hors d'oeuvre" to "not responsible for overcoats and umbrellas."

Schulenberg became a naturalized citizen on the spot. Before Sarah left him she had him willingly committed to an agreement. She was to furnish typewritten bills of fare for the twenty-one tables in the restaurant—a new bill for each day's dinner, and new ones for breakfast and lunch as often as changes occurred in the food or as neatness required.

In return for this Schulenberg was to send three meals per diem to Sarah's hall room by a waiter—an obsequious one if possible—and furnish her each afternoon with a pencil draft of what Fate had in store for Schulenberg's customers on the morrow.

Mutual satisfaction resulted from the agreement. Schulenberg's patrons now knew what the food they ate was called even if its nature sometimes puzzled them. And Sarah had food during a cold, dull winter, which was the main thing with her.

And then the almanac lied, and said that spring had come. Spring comes when it comes. The frozen snows of January still lay like adamant in the crosstown streets. The hand-organs still played "In the Good Old Summertime," with their December vivacity and expression. Men began to make thirty-day notes to buy Easter dresses. Janitors shut off steam. And when these things happen one may know that the city is still in the clutches of winter.

One afternoon Sarah shivered in her elegant hall bedroom; "house heated; scrupulously clean; conveniences; seen to be appreciated." She had no work to do except Schulenberg's menu cards. Sarah sat in her squeaky willow rocker, and looked out the window. The calendar on the wall kept crying to her: "Springtime is here, Sarah—springtime is here, I tell you. Look at me, Sarah, my figures show it. You've got a neat figure yourself, Sarah—a—nice springtime figure—why do you look out the window so sadly?"

Sarah's room was at the back of the house. Looking out the window she could see the windowless rear brick wall of the box factory on the next street. But the wall was clearest crystal; and Sarah was looking down a grassy lane shaded with cherry trees and elms and bordered with raspberry bushes and Cherokee roses.

Spring's real harbingers are too subtle for the eye and ear. Some must have the flowering crocus, the wood-starring dogwood, the voice of bluebird—even so gross a reminder as the farewell handshake of the retiring buckwheat and oyster before they can welcome the Lady in Green to their dull bosoms. But to old earth's choicest kin there come straight, sweet messages from his newest bride, telling them they shall be no stepchildren unless they choose to be.

On the previous summer Sarah had gone into the country and loved a farmer.

(In writing your story never hark back thus. It is bad art, and cripples interest. Let it march, march.)

Sarah stayed two weeks at Sunnybrook Farm. There she learned to love old Farmer Franklin's son Walter. Farmers have been loved and wedded and turned out to grass in less time. But young Walter Franklin was a modern agriculturist. He had a telephone in his cow house, and he could figure up exactly what effect next year's Canada wheat crop would have on potatoes planted in the dark of the moon.

It was in this shaded and raspberried lane that Walter had wooed and won her. And together they had sat and woven a crown of dandelions for her hair. He had immoderately praised the effect of the yellow blossoms against her brown tresses; and she had left the chaplet there, and walked back to the house swinging her straw sailor in her hands.

They were to marry in the spring—at the very first signs of spring, Walter said. And Sarah came back to the city to pound her typewriter.

A knock at the door dispelled Sarah's visions of that happy day. A waiter had brought the rough pencil draft of the Home Restaurant's next day fare in old Schulenberg's angular hand.

Sarah sat down to her typewriter and slipped a card between the rollers. She was a nimble worker. Generally in an hour and a half the twenty-one menu cards were written and ready.

Today there were more changes on the bill of fare than usual. The soups were lighter; pork was eliminated from the entrées, figuring only with Russian turnips among the roasts. The gracious spirit of spring pervaded the entire menu. Lamb, that lately capered on the greening hillsides, was becoming exploited with the sauce that commemorated its gambols. The song of the oyster, though not silenced, was *dimuendo con amore*. The frying-pan seemed to be held, inactive, behind the beneficent bars of the broiler. The pie list swelled; the richer puddings had vanished; the sausage, with his drapery wrapped about him, barely lingered in a pleasant thanatopsis with the buckwheats and the sweet but doomed maple.

Sarah's fingers danced like midgets above a summer stream. Down through the courses she worked, giving each item its position according to its length with an accurate eye. Just above the desserts came the list of vegetables. Carrots and peas, asparagus on toast, the perennial tomatoes and corn and succotash, lima beans, cabbage—and then—

Sarah was crying over her bill of fare. Tears from the depths of some divine despair rose in her heart and gathered to her eyes. Down went her head on the little typewriter stand; and the keyboard rattled a dry accompaniment to her moist sobs.

For she had received no letter from Walter in two weeks, and the next item on the bill of fare was dandelions—dandelions with some kind of egg—but bother the egg!—dandelions, with whose golden blooms Walter had crowned her his queen of love and future bride—dandelions, the harbingers of spring, her sorrow's crown of sorrow—reminder of her happiest days.

Madam, I dare you to smile until you suffer this test: Let the Marechal Niel roses that Percy brought you on the night you gave him your heart be served as a salad with French dressing before your eyes at a Schulenberg *table d'hôte*. Had Juliet so seen her love tokens dishonoured the sooner would she have sought the lethean herbs of the good apothecary.

But what a witch is Spring! Into the great cold city of stone and iron a message had to be sent. There was none to convey it but the little hardy courier of the fields with his rough green coat and modest air. He is a true soldier of fortune, this *dent-de-lion*—this lion's tooth, as the French chefs call him. Flowered, he will assist at love-making, wreathed in my lady's nut-brown hair; young and callow and unblossomed, he goes into the boiling pot and delivers the word of his sovereign mistress.

By and by Sarah forced back her tears. The cards must be written. But, still in a faint, golden glow from her dandeleonine dream, she fingered the typewriter keys absently for a little while, with her mind and heart in the meadow lane with her young farmer. But soon she came swiftly back to the rock-bound lanes of Manhattan, and the typewriter began to rattle and jump like a strike-breaker's motor car.

At 6 o'clock the waiter brought her dinner and carried away the typewritten bill of fare. When Sarah ate she set aside, with a sigh, the dish of dandelions with its crowning ovarious accompaniment. As this dark mass had been transformed from a bright and love-indorsed flower to be an ignominious vegetable, so had her summer hopes wilted and perished. Love may, as Shakespeare said, feed on itself: but Sarah could not bring herself to eat the dandelions that had graced, as ornaments, the first spiritual banquet of her heart's true affection.

At 7:30 the couple in the next room began to quarrel: the man in the room above sought for A on his flute; the gas went a little lower; three coal wagons started to unload—the only sound of which the phonograph is jealous; cats on the back fences slowly retreated toward Mukden. By these signs Sarah knew that it was time for her to read. She got out "The Cloister and the Hearth," the best non-selling book of the month, settled her feet on her trunk, and began to wander with Gerard.

The front door bell rang. The landlady answered it. Sarah left Gerard and Denys treed by a bear and listened. Oh, yes; you would, just as she did!

And then a strong voice was heard in the hall below, and Sarah jumped for her door, leaving the book on the floor and the first round easily the bear's. You have guessed it. She reached the top of the stairs just as her farmer came up, three at a jump, and reaped and garnered her, with nothing left for the gleaners.

"Why haven't you written—oh, why?" cried Sarah.

"New York is a pretty large town," said Walter Franklin. "I came in a week ago to your old address. I found that you went away on a Thursday. That consoled some; it eliminated the possible Friday bad luck. But it didn't prevent my hunting for you with police and otherwise ever since!

"I wrote!" said Sarah, vehemently.

"Never got it!"

"Then how did you find me?"

The young farmer smiled a springtime smile.

"I dropped into that Home Restaurant next door this evening," said he. "I don't care who knows it; I like a dish of some kind of greens at this time of the year. I ran my eye down that nice typewritten bill of fare looking for something in that line. When I got below cabbage I turned my chair over and hollered for the proprietor. He told me where you lived."

"I remember," sighed Sarah, happily. "That was dandelions below cabbage."

"I'd know that cranky capital W 'way above the line that your typewriter makes anywhere in the world," said Franklin.

"Why, there's no W in dandelions," said Sarah, in surprise.

The young man drew the bill of fare from his pocket, and pointed to a line.

Sarah recognized the first card she had typewritten that afternoon. There was still the rayed splotch in the upper right-hand corner where a tear had fallen. But over the spot where one should have read the name of the meadow plant, the clinging memory of their golden blossoms had allowed her fingers to strike strange keys.

Between the red cabbage and the stuffed green peppers was the item:

"DEAREST WALTER, WITH HARD-BOILED EGG."

13

The Coming-Out of Maggie

Every Saturday night the Clover Leaf Social Club gave a hop in the hall of the Give and Take Athletic Association on the East Side. In order to attend one of these dances you must be a member of the Give and Take—or, if you belong to the division that starts off with the right foot in waltzing, you must work in Rhinegold's paper-box factory. Still, any Clover Leaf was privileged to escort or be escorted by an outsider to a single dance. But mostly each Give and Take brought the paper-box girl that he affected; and few strangers could boast of having shaken a foot at the regular hops.

Maggie Toole, on account of her dull eyes, broad mouth and left-handed style of footwork in the two-step, went to the dances with Anna McCarty and her "fellow." Anna and Maggie worked side by side in the factory, and were the greatest chums ever. So Anna always made Jimmy Burns take her by Maggie's house every Saturday night so that her friend could go to the dance with them.

The Give and Take Athletic Association lived up to its name. The hall of the association in Orchard street was fitted out with muscle-making inventions. With the fibres thus builded up the members were wont to engage the police and rival social and athletic organizations in joyous combat. Between these more serious occupations the Saturday night hop with the paper-box factory girls came as a refining influence and as an efficient screen. For sometimes the tip went 'round, and if you were among the elect that tiptoed up the dark back stairway you might see as neat and satisfying a little welter-weight affair to a finish as ever happened inside the ropes.

On Saturdays Rhinegold's paper-box factory closed at 3 P. M. On one such afternoon Anna and Maggie walked homeward together. At Maggie's door Anna said, as usual: "Be ready at seven, sharp, Mag; and Jimmy and me'll come by for you."

But what was this? Instead of the customary humble and grateful thanks from the non-escorted one there was to be perceived a high-poised head, a prideful dimpling at the corners of a broad mouth, and almost a sparkle in a dull brown eye.

"Thanks, Anna," said Maggie; "but you and Jimmy needn't bother tonight. I've a gentleman friend that's coming 'round to escort me to the hop."

The comely Anna pounced upon her friend, shook her, chided and beseeched her. Maggie Toole catch a fellow! Plain, dear, loyal, unattractive Maggie, so sweet as a chum, so unsought for a two-step or a moonlit bench in the little park. How was it? When did it happen? Who was it?

"You'll see tonight," said Maggie, flushed with the wine of the first grapes she had gathered in Cupid's vineyard. "He's swell all right. He's two inches taller than Jimmy, and an up-to-date dresser. I'll introduce him, Anna, just as soon as we get to the hall."

Anna and Jimmy were among the first Clover Leafs to arrive that evening. Anna's eyes were brightly fixed upon the door of the hall to catch the first glimpse of her friend's "catch."

At 8:30 Miss Toole swept into the hall with her escort. Quickly her triumphant eye discovered her chum under the wing of her faithful Jimmy.

"Oh, gee!" cried Anna, "Mag ain't made a hit—oh, no! Swell fellow? Well, I guess! Style? Look at 'um."

"Go as far as you like," said Jimmy, with sandpaper in his voice. "Cop him out if you want him. These new guys always win out with the push. Don't mind me. He don't squeeze all the limes, I guess. Huh!"

"Shut up, Jimmy. You know what I mean. I'm glad for Mag. First fellow she ever had. Oh, here they come."

Across the floor Maggie sailed like a coquettish yacht convoyed by a stately cruiser. And truly, her companion justified the encomiums of the faithful chum. He stood two inches taller than the average Give and Take athlete; his dark hair curled; his eyes and his teeth flashed whenever he bestowed his frequent smiles. The young men of the Clover Leaf Club pinned not their faith to the graces of person as much as they did to its prowess, its achievements in hand-to-hand conflicts, and its preservation from the legal duress that constantly menaced it. The member of the association who would bind a paper-box maiden to his conquering chariot scorned to employ Beau Brummel airs. They were not considered honorable methods of warfare. The swelling biceps, the coat straining at its buttons over the chest, the air of conscious conviction of the super-eminence of the male in the cosmogony of creation, even a calm display of bow legs as subduing and enchanting agents in the gentle tourneys of Cupid—these were the approved arms and ammunition of the Clover Leaf gallants. They viewed, then, genuflexions and alluring poses of this visitor with their chins at a new angle.

"A friend of mine, Mr. Terry O'Sullivan," was Maggie's formula of introduction. She led him around the room, presenting him to each new-arriving Clover Leaf. Almost was she pretty now, with the unique luminosity in her eyes that comes to a girl with her first suitor and a kitten with its first mouse.

"Maggie Toole's got a fellow at last," was the word that went round among the paper-box girls. "Pipe Mag's floor-walker"—thus the Give and Takes expressed their indifferent contempt.

Usually at the weekly hops Maggie kept a spot on the wall warm with her back. She felt and showed so much gratitude whenever a self-sacrificing partner invited her to dance that his pleasure was cheapened and diminished. She had even grown used to noticing Anna joggle the reluctant Jimmy with her elbow as a signal for him to invite her chum to walk over his feet through a two-step.

But tonight the pumpkin had turned to a coach and six. Terry O'Sullivan was a victorious Prince Charming, and Maggie Toole winged her first butterfly flight. And though our tropes of fairyland be mixed with those of entomology they shall not spill one drop of ambrosia from the rose-crowned melody of Maggie's one perfect night.

The girls besieged her for introductions to her "fellow." The Clover Leaf young men, after two years of blindness, suddenly perceived charms in Miss Toole. They flexed their compelling muscles before her and bespoke her for the dance.

Thus she scored; but to Terry O'Sullivan the honors of the evening fell thick and fast. He shook his curls; he smiled and went easily through the seven motions for acquiring grace in your own room before an open window ten minutes each day. He danced like a faun; he introduced manner and style and atmosphere; his words came trippingly upon his tongue, and—he waltzed twice in succession with the paper-box girl that Dempsey Donovan brought.

Dempsey was the leader of the association. He wore a dress suit, and could chin the bar twice with one hand. He was one of "Big Mike" O'Sullivan's lieutenants, and was never troubled by trouble. No cop dared to arrest him. Whenever he broke a pushcart man's head or shot a member of the Heinrick B. Sweeney Outing and Literary Association in the kneecap, an officer would drop around and say:

"The Cap'n 'd like to see ye a few minutes round to the office whin ye have time, Dempsey, me boy."

But there would be sundry gentlemen there with large gold fob chains and black cigars; and somebody would tell a funny story, and then Dempsey would go back and work half an hour with the six-pound dumbbells. So, doing a tight-rope act on a wire stretched across Niagara was a safe terpsichorean performance compared with waltzing twice with Dempsey Donovan's paper-box girl. At 10 o'clock the jolly round face of "Big Mike" O'Sullivan shone at the door for five minutes upon the scene. He always looked in for five minutes, smiled at the girls and handed out real perfectos to the delighted boys.

Dempsey Donovan was at his elbow instantly, talking rapidly. "Big Mike" looked carefully at the dancers, smiled, shook his head and departed.

The music stopped. The dancers scattered to the chairs along the walls. Terry O'Sullivan, with his entrancing bow, relinquished a pretty girl in blue to her partner and started back to find Maggie. Dempsey intercepted him in the middle of the floor.

Some fine instinct that Rome must have bequeathed to us caused nearly every one to turn and look at them—there was a subtle feeling that two gladiators had met in the arena. Two or three Give and Takes with tight coat sleeves drew nearer.

"One moment, Mr. O'Sullivan," said Dempsey. "I hope you're enjoying yourself. Where did you say you live?"

The two gladiators were well matched. Dempsey had, perhaps, ten pounds of weight to give away. The O'Sullivan had breadth with quickness. Dempsey had a glacial eye, a dominating slit of a mouth, an indestructible jaw, a complexion like a belle's and the coolness of a champion. The visitor showed more fire in his contempt and less control over his conspicuous sneer. They were enemies by the law written when the rocks were molten. They were each too splendid, too mighty, too incomparable to divide preeminence. One only must survive.

"I live on Grand," said O'Sullivan, insolently; "and no trouble to find me at home. Where do you live?"

Dempsey ignored the question.

"You say your name's O'Sullivan," he went on. "Well, 'Big Mike' says he never saw you before."

"Lots of things he never saw," said the favorite of the hop.

"As a rule," went on Dempsey, huskily sweet, "O'Sullivans in this district know one another. You escorted one of our lady members here, and we want a chance to make good. If you've got a family tree let's see a few historical O'Sullivan buds come out on it. Or do you want us to dig it out of you by the roots?"

"Suppose you mind your own business," suggested O'Sullivan, blandly.

Dempsey's eye brightened. He held up an inspired forefinger as though a brilliant idea had struck him.

"I've got it now," he said cordially. "It was just a little mistake. You ain't no O'Sullivan. You are a ring-tailed monkey. Excuse us for not recognizing you at first."

O'Sullivan's eye flashed. He made a quick movement, but Andy Geoghan was ready and caught his arm.

Dempsey nodded at Andy and William McMahan, the secretary of the club, and walked rapidly toward a door at the rear of the hall. Two other members of the Give and Take Association swiftly joined the little group. Terry O'Sullivan was now in the hands of the Board of Rules and Social Referees. They spoke to him briefly and softly, and conducted him out through the same door at the rear.

This movement on the part of the Clover Leaf members requires a word of elucidation. Back of the association hall was a smaller room rented by the club. In this room personal difficulties that arose on the ballroom floor were settled, man to man, with the weapons of nature, under the supervision of the board. No lady could say that she had witnessed a fight at a Clover Leaf hop in several years. Its gentlemen members guaranteed that.

So easily and smoothly had Dempsey and the board done their preliminary work that many in the hall had not noticed the checking of the fascinating O'Sullivan's social triumph. Among these was Maggie. She looked about for her escort.

"Smoke up!" said Rose Cassidy. "Wasn't you on? Demps Donovan picked a scrap with your Lizzie-boy, and they've waltzed out to the slaughter room with him. How's my hair look done up this way, Mag?"

Maggie laid a hand on the bosom of her cheesecloth waist.

"Gone to fight with Dempsey!" she said, breathlessly. "They've got to be stopped. Dempsey Donovan can't fight him. Why, he'll—he'll kill him!"

"Ah, what do you care?" said Rosa. "Don't some of 'em fight every hop?"

But Maggie was off, darting her zig-zag way through the maze of dancers. She burst through the rear door into the dark hall and then threw her solid shoulder against the door of the room of single combat. It gave way, and in the instant that she entered her eye caught the scene—the Board standing about with open watches; Dempsey Donovan in his shirt sleeves dancing, light-footed, with the wary grace of the modern pugilist, within easy reach of his adversary; Terry O'Sullivan standing with arms folded and a murderous look in his dark eyes. And without slacking the speed of her entrance she leaped forward with a scream—leaped in time to catch and hang upon the arm of O'Sullivan that was suddenly uplifted, and to whisk from it the long, bright stiletto that he had drawn from his bosom.

The knife fell and rang upon the floor. Cold steel drawn in the rooms of the Give and Take Association! Such a thing had never happened before. Every one stood motionless for a minute. Andy Geoghan kicked the stiletto with the toe of his shoe curiously, like an antiquarian who has come upon some ancient weapon unknown to his learning.

And then O'Sullivan hissed something unintelligible between his teeth. Dempsey and the board exchanged looks. And then Dempsey looked at O'Sullivan without anger, as one looks at a stray dog, and nodded his head in the direction of the door.

"The back stairs, Giuseppi," he said, briefly. "Somebody'll pitch your hat down after you."

Maggie walked up to Dempsey Donovan. There was a brilliant spot of red in her cheeks, down which slow tears were running. But she looked him bravely in the eye.

"I knew it, Dempsey," she said, as her eyes grew dull even in their tears. "I knew he was a Guinea. His name's Tony Spinelli. I hurried in when they told me you and him was scrappin'. Them Guineas always carries knives. But you don't understand, Dempsey. I never had a fellow in my life. I got tired of comin' with Anna and Jimmy every night, so I fixed it with him to call himself O'Sullivan, and brought him along. I knew there'd be nothin' doin' for him if he came as a Dago. I guess I'll resign from the club now."

Dempsey turned to Andy Geoghan.

"Chuck that cheese slicer out of the window," he said, "and tell 'em inside that Mr. O'Sullivan has had a telephone message to go down to Tammany Hall."

And then he turned back to Maggie.

"Say, Mag," he said, "I'll see you home. And how about next Saturday night? Will you come to the hop with me if I call around for you?"

It was remarkable how quickly Maggie's eyes could change from dull to a shining brown.

"With you, Dempsey?" she stammered. "Say—will a duck swim?"

14

The Green Door

Suppose you should be walking down Broadway after dinner, with ten minutes allotted to the consummation of your cigar while you are choosing between a diverting tragedy and something serious in the way of vaudeville. Suddenly a hand is laid upon your arm. You turn to look into the thrilling eyes of a beautiful woman, wonderful in diamonds and Russian sables. She thrusts hurriedly into your hand an extremely hot buttered roll, flashes out a tiny pair of scissors, snips off the second button of your overcoat, meaningly ejaculates the one word, "parallelogram!" and swiftly flies down a cross street, looking back fearfully over her shoulder.

That would be pure adventure. Would you accept it? Not you. You would flush with embarrassment; you would sheepishly drop the roll and continue down Broadway, fumbling feebly for the missing button. This you would do unless you are one of the blessed few in whom the pure spirit of adventure is not dead.

True adventurers have never been plentiful. They who are set down in print as such have been mostly business men with newly invented methods. They have been out after the things they wanted—golden fleeces, holy grails, lady loves, treasure, crowns and fame. The true adventurer goes forth aimless and uncalculating to meet and greet unknown fate. A fine example was the Prodigal Son—when he started back home.

Half-adventurers—brave and splendid figures—have been numerous. From the Crusades to the Palisades they have enriched the arts of history and fiction and the trade of historical fiction. But each of them had a prize to win, a goal to kick, an axe to grind, a race to run, a new thrust in tierce to deliver, a name to carve, a crow to pick—so they were not followers of true adventure.

In the big city the twin spirits Romance and Adventure are always abroad seeking worthy wooers. As we roam the streets they slyly peep at us and challenge us in twenty different guises. Without knowing why, we look up suddenly to see in a window a face that seems to belong to our gallery of intimate portraits; in a sleeping thoroughfare we hear a cry of agony and fear coming from an empty and shuttered house; instead of at our familiar curb, a cab-driver deposits us before a strange door, which one, with a smile, opens for us and bids us enter; a slip of paper, written upon, flutters down to our feet from the high lattices of Chance; we exchange glances of instantaneous hate, affection and fear with hurrying strangers in the passing crowds; a sudden douse of rain—and our umbrella may be sheltering the daughter of the Full Moon and first cousin of the Sidereal System; at every corner handkerchiefs drop, fingers beckon, eyes besiege, and the lost, the lonely, the rapturous, the mysterious, the perilous, changing clues of adventure are slipped into our fingers. But few of us are willing to hold and follow them. We are grown stiff with the ramrod of convention down our backs. We pass on; and some day we come, at the end of a very dull life, to reflect that our romance has been a pallid thing of a marriage or two, a satin rosette kept in a safe-deposit drawer, and a lifelong feud with a steam radiator.

Rudolf Steiner was a true adventurer. Few were the evenings on which he did not go forth from his hall bedchamber in search of the unexpected and the egregious. The most interesting thing in life seemed to him to be what might lie just around the next corner. Sometimes his willingness to tempt fate led him into strange paths. Twice he had spent the night in a station-house; again and again he had found himself the dupe of ingenious and mercenary tricksters; his watch and money had been the price of one flattering allurement. But with undiminished ardour he picked up every glove cast before him into the merry lists of adventure.

One evening Rudolf was strolling along a crosstown street in the older central part of the city. Two streams of people filled the sidewalks—the home-hurrying, and that restless contingent that abandons home for the specious welcome of the thousand-candle-power *table d'hôte*.

The young adventurer was of pleasing presence, and moved serenely and watchfully. By daylight he was a salesman in a piano store. He wore his tie drawn through a topaz ring instead of fastened with a stick pin; and once he had written to the editor of a magazine that "Junie's Love Test" by Miss Libbey, had been the book that had most influenced his life.

During his walk a violent chattering of teeth in a glass case on the sidewalk seemed at first to draw his attention (with a qualm), to a restaurant before which it was set; but a second glance revealed the electric letters of a dentist's sign high above the next door. A giant negro, fantastically dressed in a red embroidered coat, yellow trousers and a military cap, discreetly distributed cards to those of the passing crowd who consented to take them.

This mode of dentistic advertising was a common sight to Rudolf. Usually he passed the dispenser of the dentist's cards without reducing his store; but tonight the African slipped one into his hand so deftly that he retained it there smiling a little at the successful feat.

When he had traveled a few yards further he glanced at the card indifferently. Surprised, he turned it over and looked again with interest. One side of the card was blank; on the other was written in ink three words, "The Green Door." And then Rudolf saw, three steps in front of him, a man throw down the card the negro had given him as he passed. Rudolf picked it up. It was printed with the dentist's name and address and the usual schedule of "plate work" and "bridge work" and "crowns," and specious promises of "painless" operations.

The adventurous piano salesman halted at the corner and considered. Then he crossed the street, walked down a block, recrossed and joined the upward current of people again. Without seeming to notice the negro as he passed the second time, he carelessly took the card that was handed him. Ten steps away he inspected it. In the same handwriting that appeared on the first card "The Green Door" was inscribed upon it. Three or four cards were tossed to the pavement by pedestrians both following and leading him. These fell blank side up. Rudolf turned them over. Every one bore the printed legend of the dental "parlors."

Rarely did the arch sprite Adventure need to beckon twice to Rudolf Steiner, his true follower. But twice it had been done, and the quest was on.

Rudolf walked slowly back to where the giant negro stood by the case of rattling teeth. This time as he passed he received no card. In spite of his gaudy and ridiculous garb, the Ethiopian displayed a natural barbaric dignity as he stood, offering the cards suavely to some, allowing others to pass unmolested. Every half minute he chanted a harsh, unintelligible phrase akin to the jabber of car conductors and grand opera. And not only did he withhold a card this time, but it seemed to Rudolf that he received from the shining and massive black countenance a look of cold, almost contemptuous disdain.

The look stung the adventurer. He read in it a silent accusation that he had been found wanting. Whatever the mysterious written words on the cards might mean, the black had selected him twice from the throng for their recipient; and now seemed to have condemned him as deficient in the wit and spirit to engage the enigma.

Standing aside from the rush, the young man made a rapid estimate of the building in which he conceived that his adventure must lie. Five stories high it rose. A small restaurant occupied the basement.

The first floor, now closed, seemed to house millinery or furs. The second floor, by the winking electric letters, was the dentist's. Above this a polyglot babel of signs struggled to indicate the abodes of palmists, dressmakers, musicians and doctors. Still higher up draped curtains and milk bottles white on the window sills proclaimed the regions of domesticity.

After concluding his survey Rudolf walked briskly up the high flight of stone steps into the house. Up two flights of the carpeted stairway he continued; and at its top paused. The hallway there was dimly lighted by two pale jets of gas—one far to his right, the other nearer, to his left. He looked toward the nearer light and saw, within its wan halo, a green door. For one moment he hesitated; then he seemed to see the contumelious sneer of the African juggler of cards; and then he walked straight to the green door and knocked against it.

Moments like those that passed before his knock was answered measure the quick breath of true adventure. What might not be behind those green panels! Gamesters at play; cunning rogues baiting their traps with subtle skill; beauty in love with courage, and thus planning to be sought by it; danger, death, love, disappointment, ridicule—any of these might respond to that temerarious rap.

A faint rustle was heard inside, and the door slowly opened. A girl not yet twenty stood there, white-faced and tottering. She loosed the knob and swayed weakly, groping with one hand. Rudolf caught her and laid her on a faded couch that stood against the wall. He closed the door and took a swift glance around the room by the light of a flickering gas jet. Neat, but extreme poverty was the story that he read.

The girl lay still, as if in a faint. Rudolf looked around the room excitedly for a barrel. People must be rolled upon a barrel who—no, no; that was for drowned persons. He began to fan her with his hat. That was successful, for he struck her nose with the brim of his derby and she opened her eyes. And then the young man saw that hers, indeed, was the one missing face from his heart's gallery of intimate portraits. The frank, gray eyes, the little nose, turning pertly outward; the chestnut hair, curling like the tendrils of a pea vine, seemed the right end and reward of all his wonderful adventures. But the face was woefully thin and pale.

The girl looked at him calmly, and then smiled.

"Fainted, didn't I?" she asked, weakly. "Well, who wouldn't? You try going without anything to eat for three days and see!"

"Himmel!" exclaimed Rudolf, jumping up. "Wait till I come back."

He dashed out the green door and down the stairs. In twenty minutes he was back again, kicking at the door with his toe for her to open it. With both arms he hugged an array of wares from the grocery and the restaurant. On the table he laid them—bread and butter, cold meats, cakes, pies, pickles, oysters, a roasted chicken, a bottle of milk and one of red-hot tea.

"This is ridiculous," said Rudolf, blusteringly, "to go without eating. You must quit making election bets of this kind. Supper is ready." He helped her to a chair at the table and asked: "Is there a cup for the tea?" "On the shelf by the window," she answered. When he turned again with the cup he saw her, with eyes shining rapturously, beginning upon a huge Dill pickle that she had rooted out from the paper bags with a woman's unerring instinct. He took it from her, laughingly, and poured the cup full of milk. "Drink that first" he ordered, "and then you shall have some tea, and then a chicken wing. If you are very good you shall have a pickle tomorrow. And now, if you'll allow me to be your guest we'll have supper."

He drew up the other chair. The tea brightened the girl's eyes and brought back some of her color. She began to eat with a sort of dainty ferocity like some starved wild animal. She seemed to regard the young man's presence and the aid he had rendered her as a natural thing—not as though she undervalued the conventions; but as one whose great stress gave her the right to put aside the artificial for the human. But gradually, with the return of strength and comfort, came also a sense of the little conventions that belong; and she began to tell him her little story. It was one of a thousand such as the city yawns at every day—the shop girl's story of insufficient wages, further reduced by "fines" that go to swell the store's profits; of time lost through illness; and then of lost positions, lost hope, and—the knock of the adventurer upon the green door.

But to Rudolf the history sounded as big as the Iliad or the crisis in "Junie's Love Test."

"To think of you going through all that," he exclaimed.

"It was something fierce," said the girl, solemnly.

"And you have no relatives or friends in the city?"

"None whatever."

"I am all alone in the world, too," said Rudolf, after a pause.

"I am glad of that," said the girl, promptly; and somehow it pleased the young man to hear that she approved of his bereft condition.

Very suddenly her eyelids dropped and she sighed deeply.

"I'm awfully sleepy," she said, "and I feel so good."

Then Rudolf rose and took his hat. "I'll say good-night. A long night's sleep will be fine for you."

He held out his hand, and she took it and said "good-night." But her eyes asked a question so eloquently, so frankly and pathetically that he answered it with words.

"Oh, I'm coming back tomorrow to see how you are getting along. You can't get rid of me so easily."

Then, at the door, as though the way of his coming had been so much less important than the fact that he had come, she asked: "How did you come to knock at my door?"

He looked at her for a moment, remembering the cards, and felt a sudden jealous pain. What if they had fallen into other hands as adventurous as his? Quickly he decided that she must never know the truth. He would never let her know that he was aware of the strange expedient to which she had been driven by her great distress.

"One of our piano tuners lives in this house," he said. "I knocked at your door by mistake."

The last thing he saw in the room before the green door closed was her smile.

At the head of the stairway he paused and looked curiously about him. And then he went along the hallway to its other end; and, coming back, ascended to the floor above and continued his puzzled explorations. Every door that he found in the house was painted green.

Wondering, he descended to the sidewalk. The fantastic African was still there. Rudolf confronted him with his two cards in his hand.

"Will you tell me why you gave me these cards and what they mean?" he asked.

In a broad, good-natured grin the negro exhibited a splendid advertisement of his master's profession.

"Dar it is, boss," he said, pointing down the street. "But I 'spect you is a little late for de fust act."

Looking the way he pointed Rudolf saw above the entrance to a theatre the blazing electric sign of its new play, "The Green Door."

"I'm informed dat it's a fust-rate show, sah," said the negro. "De agent what represents it pussented me with a dollar, sah, to distribute a few of his cards along with de doctah's. May I offer you one of de doctah's cards, sah?"

At the corner of the block in which he lived Rudolf stopped for a glass of beer and a cigar. When he had come out with his lighted weed he buttoned his coat, pushed back his hat and said, stoutly, to the lamp post on the corner:

"All the same, I believe it was the hand of Fate that doped out the way for me to find her."

Which conclusion, under the circumstances, certainly admits Rudolf Steiner to the ranks of the true followers of Romance and Adventure.

15

The Romance of a Busy Broker

Pitcher, confidential clerk in the office of Harvey Maxwell, broker, allowed a look of mild interest and surprise to visit his usually expressionless countenance when his employer briskly entered at half past nine in company with his young lady stenographer. With a snappy "Good morning, Pitcher," Maxwell dashed at his desk as though he were intending to leap over it, and then plunged into the great heap of letters and telegrams waiting there for him.

The young lady had been Maxwell's stenographer for a year. She was beautiful in a way that was decidedly unstenographic. She forewent the pomp of the alluring pompadour. She wore no chains, bracelets or lockets. She had not the air of being about to accept an invitation to luncheon. Her dress was gray and plain, but it fitted her figure with fidelity and discretion. In her neat black turban hat was the gold-green wing of a macaw. On this morning she was softly and shyly radiant. Her eyes were dreamily bright, her cheeks genuine peachblow, her expression a happy one, tinged with reminiscence.

Pitcher, still mildly curious, noticed a difference in her ways this morning. Instead of going straight into the adjoining room, where her desk was, she lingered, slightly irresolute, in the outer office. Once she moved over by Maxwell's desk, near enough for him to be aware of her presence.

The machine sitting at that desk was no longer a man; it was a busy New York broker, moved by buzzing wheels and uncoiling springs.

"Well—what is it? Anything?" asked Maxwell sharply. His opened mail lay like a bank of stage snow on his crowded desk. His keen grey eye, impersonal and brusque, flashed upon her half impatiently.

"Nothing," answered the stenographer, moving away with a little smile.

"Mr. Pitcher," she said to the confidential clerk, "did Mr. Maxwell say anything yesterday about engaging another stenographer?"

"He did," answered Pitcher. "He told me to get another one. I notified the agency yesterday afternoon to send over a few samples this morning. It's 9.45 o'clock, and not a single picture hat or piece of pineapple chewing gum has showed up yet."

"I will do the work as usual, then," said the young lady, "until some one comes to fill the place." And she went to her desk at once and hung the black turban hat with the gold-green macaw wing in its accustomed place.

He who has been denied the spectacle of a busy Manhattan broker during a rush of business is handicapped for the profession of anthropology. The poet sings of the "crowded hour of glorious life." The broker's hour is not only crowded, but the minutes and seconds are hanging to all the straps and packing both front and rear platforms.

And this day was Harvey Maxwell's busy day. The ticker began to reel out jerkily its fitful coils of tape, the desk telephone had a chronic attack of buzzing. Men began to throng into the office and call at him over the railing, jovially, sharply, viciously, excitedly. Messenger boys ran in and out with messages and telegrams. The clerks in the office jumped about like sailors during a storm. Even Pitcher's face relaxed into something resembling animation.

On the Exchange there were hurricanes and landslides and snowstorms and glaciers and volcanoes, and those elemental disturbances were reproduced in miniature in the broker's offices. Maxwell shoved his chair against the wall and transacted business after the manner of a toe dancer. He jumped from ticker to 'phone, from desk to door with the trained agility of a harlequin.

In the midst of this growing and important stress the broker became suddenly aware of a high-rolled fringe of golden hair under a nodding canopy of velvet and ostrich tips, an imitation sealskin sacque and a string of beads as large as hickory nuts, ending near the floor with a silver heart. There was a self-possessed young lady connected with these accessories; and Pitcher was there to construe her.

"Lady from the Stenographer's Agency to see about the position," said Pitcher.

Maxwell turned half around, with his hands full of papers and ticker tape.

"What position?" he asked, with a frown.

"Position of stenographer," said Pitcher. "You told me yesterday to call them up and have one sent over this morning."

"You are losing your mind, Pitcher," said Maxwell. "Why should I have given you any such instructions? Miss Leslie has given perfect satisfaction during the year she has been here. The place is hers as long as she chooses to retain it. There's no place open here, madam. Countermand that order with the agency, Pitcher, and don't bring any more of 'em in here."

The silver heart left the office, swinging and banging itself independently against the office furniture as it indignantly departed. Pitcher seized a moment to remark to the bookkeeper that the "old man" seemed to get more absent-minded and forgetful every day of the world.

The rush and pace of business grew fiercer and faster. On the floor they were pounding half a dozen stocks in which Maxwell's customers were heavy investors. Orders to buy and sell were coming and going as swift as the flight of swallows. Some of his own holdings were imperiled, and the man was working like some high-geared, delicate, strong machine—strung to full tension, going at full speed, accurate, never hesitating, with the proper word and decision and act ready and prompt as clockwork. Stocks and bonds, loans and mortgages, margins and securities—here was a world of finance, and there was no room in it for the human world or the world of nature.

When the luncheon hour drew near there came a slight lull in the uproar.

Maxwell stood by his desk with his hands full of telegrams and memoranda, with a fountain pen over his right ear and his hair hanging in disorderly strings over his forehead. His window was open, for the beloved janitress Spring had turned on a little warmth through the waking registers of the earth.

And through the window came a wandering—perhaps a lost—odor—a delicate, sweet odor of lilac that fixed the broker for a moment immovable. For this odor belonged to Miss Leslie; it was her own, and hers only.

The odor brought her vividly, almost tangibly before him. The world of finance dwindled suddenly to a speck. And she was in the next room—twenty steps away.

"By George, I'll do it now," said Maxwell, half aloud. "I'll ask her now. I wonder I didn't do it long ago."

He dashed into the inner office with the haste of a short trying to cover. He charged upon the desk of the stenographer.

She looked up at him with a smile. A soft pink crept over her cheek, and her eyes were kind and frank. Maxwell leaned one elbow on her desk. He still clutched fluttering papers with both hands and the pen was above his ear.

"Miss Leslie," he began hurriedly, "I have but a moment to spare. I want to say something in that moment. Will you be my wife? I haven't had time to make love to you in the ordinary way, but I really do love you. Talk quick, please—those fellows are clubbing the stuffing out of Union Pacific."

"Oh, what are you talking about?" exclaimed the young lady. She rose to her feet and gazed upon him, round-eyed.

"Don't you understand?" said Maxwell, restively. "I want you to marry me. I love you, Miss Leslie. I wanted to tell you, and I snatched a minute when things had slackened up a bit.

They're calling me for the 'phone now. Tell 'em to wait a minute, Pitcher. Won't you, Miss Leslie?"

The stenographer acted very queerly. At first she seemed overcome with amazement; then tears flowed from her wondering eyes; and then she smiled sunnily through them, and one of her arms slid tenderly about the broker's neck.

"I know now," she said, softly. "It's this old business that has driven everything else out of your head for the time. I was frightened at first. Don't you remember, Harvey? We were married last evening at 8 o'clock in the Little Church Around the Corner."

16

The Skylight Room

First Mrs. Parker would show you the double parlors. You would not dare to interrupt her description of their advantages and of the merits of the gentleman who had occupied them for eight years. Then you would manage to stammer forth the confession that you were neither a doctor nor a dentist. Mrs. Parker's manner of receiving the admission was such that you could never afterward entertain the same feeling toward your parents, who had neglected to train you up in one of the professions that fitted Mrs. Parker's parlors.

Next you ascended one flight of stairs and looked at the second-floor-back at $8. Convinced by her second-floor manner that it was worth the $12 that Mr. Toosenberry always paid for it until he left to take charge of his brother's orange plantation in Florida near Palm Beach, where Mrs. McIntyre always spent the winters that had the double front room with private bath, you managed to babble that you wanted something still cheaper.

If you survived Mrs. Parker's scorn, you were taken to look at Mr. Skidder's large hall room on the third floor. Mr. Skidder's room was not vacant. He wrote plays and smoked cigarettes in it all day long. But every room-hunter was made to visit his room to admire the lambrequins. After each visit, Mr. Skidder, from the fright caused by possible eviction, would pay something on his rent.

Then—oh, then—if you still stood on one foot, with your hot hand clutching the three moist dollars in your pocket, and hoarsely proclaimed your hideous and culpable poverty, nevermore would Mrs. Parker be cicerone of yours. She would honk loudly the word "Clara," she would show you her back, and march downstairs. Then Clara, the colored maid, would escort you up the carpeted ladder that served for the fourth flight, and show you the Skylight Room. It occupied 7×8 feet of floor space at the middle of the hall. On each side of it was a dark lumber closet or storeroom.

In it was an iron cot, a washstand and a chair. A shelf was the dresser. Its four bare walls seemed to close in upon you like the sides of a coffin. Your hand crept to your throat, you gasped, you looked up as from a well—and breathed once more. Through the glass of the little skylight you saw a square of blue infinity.

"Two dollars, suh," Clara would say in her half-contemptuous, half-Tuskegeenial tones.

One day Miss Leeson came hunting for a room. She carried a typewriter made to be lugged around by a much larger lady. She was a very little girl, with eyes and hair that had kept on growing after she had stopped and that always looked as if they were saying: "Goodness me! Why didn't you keep up with us?"

Mrs. Parker showed her the double parlors. "In this closet," she said, "one could keep a skeleton or anesthetic or coal—"

"But I am neither a doctor nor a dentist," said Miss Leeson, with a shiver.

Mrs. Parker gave her the incredulous, pitying, sneering, icy stare that she kept for those who failed to qualify as doctors or dentists, and led the way to the second floor back.

"Eight dollars?" said Miss Leeson. "Dear me! I'm not Hetty if I do look green. I'm just a poor little working girl. Show me something higher and lower."

Mr. Skidder jumped and strewed the floor with cigarette stubs at the rap on his door.

"Excuse me, Mr. Skidder," said Mrs. Parker, with her demon's smile at his pale looks. "I didn't know you were in. I asked the lady to have a look at your lambrequins."

"They're too lovely for anything," said Miss Leeson, smiling in exactly the way the angels do.

After they had gone Mr. Skidder got very busy erasing the tall, black-haired heroine from his latest (unproduced) play and inserting a small, roguish one with heavy, bright hair and vivacious features.

"Anna Held'll jump at it," said Mr. Skidder to himself, putting his feet up against the lambrequins and disappearing in a cloud of smoke like an aerial cuttlefish.

Presently the tocsin call of "Clara!" sounded to the world the state of Miss Leeson's purse. A dark goblin seized her, mounted a Stygian stairway, thrust her into a vault with a glimmer of light in its top and muttered the menacing and cabalistic words "Two dollars!"

"I'll take it!" sighed Miss Leeson, sinking down upon the squeaky iron bed.

Every day Miss Leeson went out to work. At night she brought home papers with handwriting on them and made copies with her typewriter. Sometimes she had no work at night, and then she would sit on the steps of the high stoop with the other roomers. Miss Leeson was not intended for a sky-light room when the plans were drawn for her creation. She was gay-hearted and full of tender, whimsical fancies. Once she let Mr. Skidder read to her three acts of his great (unpublished) comedy, "It's No Kid; or, The Heir of the Subway."

There was rejoicing among the gentlemen roomers whenever Miss Leeson had time to sit on the steps for an hour or two. But Miss Longnecker, the tall blonde who taught in a public school and said, "Well, really!" to everything you said, sat on the top step and sniffed. And Miss Dorn, who shot at the moving ducks at Coney every Sunday and worked in a department store, sat on the bottom step and sniffed. Miss Leeson sat on the middle step and the men would quickly group around her.

Especially Mr. Skidder, who had cast her in his mind for the star part in a private, romantic (unspoken) drama in real life. And especially Mr. Hoover, who was forty-five, fat, flush and foolish. And especially very young Mr. Evans, who set up a hollow cough to induce her to ask him to leave off cigarettes. The men voted her "the funniest and jolliest ever," but the sniffs on the top step and the lower step were implacable.

~

I pray you let the drama halt while Chorus stalks to the footlights and drops an epicedian tear upon the fatness of Mr. Hoover. Tune the pipes to the tragedy of tallow, the bane of bulk, the calamity of corpulence. Tried out, Falstaff might have rendered more romance to the ton than would have Romeo's rickety ribs to the ounce. A lover may sigh, but he must not puff. To the train of Momus are the fat men remanded. In vain beats the faithfullest heart above a 52-inch belt. Avaunt, Hoover! Hoover, forty-five, flush and foolish, might carry off Helen herself; Hoover, forty-five, flush, foolish and fat is meat for perdition. There was never a chance for you, Hoover.

As Mrs. Parker's roomers sat thus one summer's evening, Miss Leeson looked up into the firmament and cried with her little gay laugh:

"Why, there's Billy Jackson! I can see him from down here, too."

All looked up—some at the windows of skyscrapers, some casting about for an airship, Jackson-guided.

"It's that star," explained Miss Leeson, pointing with a tiny finger. "Not the big one that twinkles—the steady blue one near it. I can see it every night through my skylight. I named it Billy Jackson."

"Well, really!" said Miss Longnecker. "I didn't know you were an astronomer, Miss Leeson."

"Oh, yes," said the small star gazer, "I know as much as any of them about the style of sleeves they're going to wear next fall in Mars."

"Well, really!" said Miss Longnecker. "The star you refer to is Gamma, of the constellation Cassiopeia. It is nearly of the second magnitude, and its meridian passage is—"

"Oh," said the very young Mr. Evans, "I think Billy Jackson is a much better name for it."

"Same here," said Mr. Hoover, loudly breathing defiance to Miss Longnecker. "I think Miss Leeson has just as much right to name stars as any of those old astrologers had."

"Well, really!" said Miss Longnecker.

"I wonder whether it's a shooting star," remarked Miss Dorn. "I hit nine ducks and a rabbit out of ten in the gallery at Coney Sunday."

"He doesn't show up very well from down here," said Miss Leeson. "You ought to see him from my room. You know you can see stars even in the daytime from the bottom of a well. At night my room is like the shaft of a coal mine, and it makes Billy Jackson look like the big diamond pin that Night fastens her kimono with."

There came a time after that when Miss Leeson brought no formidable papers home to copy. And when she went out in the morning, instead of working, she went from office to office and let her heart melt away in the drip of cold refusals transmitted through insolent office boys. This went on.

There came an evening when she wearily climbed Mrs. Parker's stoop at the hour when she always returned from her dinner at the restaurant. But she had had no dinner.

As she stepped into the hall Mr. Hoover met her and seized his chance. He asked her to marry him, and his fatness hovered above her like an avalanche. She dodged, and caught the balustrade. He tried for her hand, and she raised it and smote him weakly in the face. Step by step she went up, dragging herself by the railing. She passed Mr. Skidder's door as he was red-inking a stage direction for Myrtle Delorme (Miss Leeson) in his (unaccepted) comedy, to "pirouette across stage from L to the side of the Count." Up the carpeted ladder she crawled at last and opened the door of the skylight room.

She was too weak to light the lamp or to undress. She fell upon the iron cot, her fragile body scarcely hollowing the worn springs. And in that Erebus of the skylight room, she slowly raised her heavy eyelids, and smiled.

For Billy Jackson was shining down on her, calm and bright and constant through the skylight. There was no world about her. She was sunk in a pit of blackness, with but that small square of pallid light framing the star that she had so whimsically and oh, so ineffectually named. Miss Longnecker must be right; it was Gamma, of the constellation Cassiopeia, and not Billy Jackson. And yet she could not let it be Gamma.

As she lay on her back she tried twice to raise her arm. The third time she got two thin fingers to her lips and blew a kiss out of the black pit to Billy Jackson. Her arm fell back limply.

"Good-bye, Billy," she murmured faintly. "You're millions of miles away and you won't even twinkle once. But you kept where I could see you most of the time up there when there wasn't anything else but darkness to look at, didn't you? . . . Millions of miles . . . Good-bye, Billy Jackson."

Clara, the colored maid, found the door locked at 10 the next day, and they forced it open. Vinegar, and the slapping of wrists and burnt feathers proving of no avail, some one ran to 'phone for an ambulance.

In due time it backed up to the door with much gong-clanging, and the capable young medico, in his white linen coat, ready, active, confident, with his smooth face half debonair, half grim, danced up the steps.

"Ambulance call to 49," he said briefly. "What's the trouble?"

"Oh, yes, doctor," sniffed Mrs. Parker, as though her trouble that there should be trouble in the house was the greater. "I can't think what can be the matter with her. Nothing we could do would bring her to. It's a young woman, a Miss Elsie—yes, a Miss Elsie Leeson. Never before in my house—"

"What room?" cried the doctor in a terrible voice, to which Mrs. Parker was a stranger.

"The skylight room. It—"

Evidently the ambulance doctor was familiar with the location of skylight rooms. He was gone up the stairs, four at a time. Mrs. Parker followed slowly, as her dignity demanded.

On the first landing she met him coming back bearing the astronomer in his arms. He stopped and let loose the practiced scalpel of his tongue, not loudly. Gradually Mrs. Parker crumpled as a stiff garment that slips down from a nail. Ever afterward there remained crumples in her mind and body. Sometimes her curious roomers would ask her what the doctor said to her.

"Let that be," she would answer. "If I can get forgiveness for having heard it I will be satisfied."

The ambulance physician strode with his burden through the pack of hounds that follow the curiosity chase, and even they fell back along the sidewalk abashed, for his face was that of one who bears his own dead.

They noticed that he did not lay down upon the bed prepared for it in the ambulance the form that he carried, and all that he said was: "Drive like h——l, Wilson," to the driver.

That is all. Is it a story? In the next morning's paper I saw a little news item, and the last sentence of it may help you (as it helped me) to weld the incidents together.

It recounted the reception into Bellevue Hospital of a young woman who had been removed from No. 49 East —— street, suffering from debility induced by starvation. It concluded with these words:

"Dr. William Jackson, the ambulance physician who attended the case, says the patient will recover."

17

A Midsummer Knight's Dream

"The knights are dead;
Their swords are rust.
Except a few who have to hust-
Le all the time
To raise the dust."

Dear Reader: It was summertime. The sun glared down upon the city with pitiless ferocity. It is difficult for the sun to be ferocious and exhibit compunction simultaneously. The heat was—oh, bother thermometers!—who cares for standard measures, anyhow? It was so hot that—

The roof gardens put on so many extra waiters that you could hope to get your gin fizz now—as soon as all the other people got theirs. The hospitals were putting in extra cots for bystanders. For when little, woolly dogs loll their tongues out and say "woof, woof!" at the fleas that bite 'em, and nervous old black bombazine ladies screech "Mad dog!" and policemen begin to shoot, somebody is going to get hurt. The man from Pompton, N.J., who always wears an overcoat in July, had turned up in a Broadway hotel drinking hot Scotches and enjoying his annual ray from the calcium. Philanthropists were petitioning the Legislature to pass a bill requiring builders to make tenement fire-escapes more commodious, so that families might die all together of the heat instead of one or two at a time. So many men were telling you about the number of baths they took each day that you wondered how they got along after the real lessee of the apartment came back to town and thanked 'em for taking such good care of it. The young man who called loudly for cold beef and beer in the restaurant, protesting that roast pullet and Burgundy was really too heavy for such weather, blushed when he met your eye, for you had heard him all winter calling, in modest tones, for the same ascetic viands. Soup, pocketbooks, shirt waists, actors and baseball excuses grew thinner. Yes, it was summertime.

A man stood at Thirty-fourth street waiting for a downtown car. A man of forty, gray-haired, pink-faced, keen, nervous, plainly dressed, with a harassed look around the eyes. He wiped his forehead and laughed loudly when a fat man with an outing look stopped and spoke with him.

"No, siree," he shouted with defiance and scorn. "None of your old mosquito-haunted swamps and skyscraper mountains without elevators for me. When I want to get away from hot weather I know how to do it. New York, sir, is the finest summer resort in the country. Keep in the shade and watch your diet, and don't get too far away from an electric fan. Talk about your Adirondacks and your Catskills! There's more solid comfort in the borough of Manhattan than in all the rest of the country together. No, siree! No tramping up perpendicular cliffs and being waked up at 4 in the morning by a million flies, and eating canned goods straight from the city for me. Little old New York will take a few select summer boarders; comforts and conveniences of homes—that's the ad that I answer every time."

"You need a vacation," said the fat man, looking closely at the other. "You haven't been away from town in years. Better come with me for two weeks, anyhow. The trout in the Beaverkill are jumping at anything now that looks like a fly. Harding writes me that he landed a three-pound brown last week."

"Nonsense!" cried the other man. "Go ahead, if you like, and boggle around in rubber boots wearing yourself out trying to catch fish. When I want one I go to a cool restaurant and order it. I laugh at you fellows whenever I think of you hustling around in the heat in the country thinking you are having a good time. For me Father Knickerbocker's little improved farm with the big shady lane running through the middle of it."

The fat man sighed over his friend and went his way. The man who thought New York was the greatest summer resort in the country boarded a car and went buzzing down to his office. On the way he threw away his newspaper and looked up at a ragged patch of sky above the housetops.

"Three pounds!" he muttered, absently. "And Harding isn't a liar. I believe, if I could—but it's impossible—they've got to have another month—another month at least."

In his office the upholder of urban midsummer joys dived, headforemost, into the swimming pool of business. Adkins, his clerk, came and added a spray of letters, memoranda and telegrams.

At 5 o'clock in the afternoon the busy man leaned back in his office chair, put his feet on the desk and mused aloud:

"I wonder what kind of bait Harding used."

~

She was all in white that day; and thereby Compton lost a bet to Gaines. Compton had wagered she would wear light blue, for she knew that was his favorite color, and Compton was a millionaire's son, and that almost laid him open to the charge of betting on a sure thing. But white was her choice, and Gaines held up his head with twenty-five's lordly air.

The little summer hotel in the mountains had a lively crowd that year. There were two or three young college men and a couple of artists and a young naval officer on one side. On the other there were enough beauties among the young ladies for the correspondent of a society paper to refer to them as a "bevy." But the moon among the stars was Mary Sewell. Each one of the young men greatly desired to arrange matters so that he could pay her millinery bills, and fix the furnace, and have her do away with the "Sewell" part of her name forever. Those who could stay only a week or two went away hinting at pistols and blighted hearts. But Compton stayed like the mountains themselves, for he could afford it. And Gaines stayed because he was a fighter and wasn't afraid of millionaire's sons, and—well, he adored the country.

"What do you think, Miss Mary?" he said once. "I knew a duffer in New York who claimed to like it in the summer time. Said you could keep cooler there than you could in the woods. Wasn't he an awful silly? I don't think I could breathe on Broadway after the 1st of June."

"Mamma was thinking of going back week after next," said Miss Mary with a lovely frown.

"But when you think of it," said Gaines, "there are lots of jolly places in town in the summer. The roof gardens, you know, and the—er—the roof gardens."

Deepest blue was the lake that day—the day when they had the mock tournament, and the men rode clumsy farm horses around in a glade in the woods and caught curtain rings on the end of a lance. Such fun!

Cool and dry as the finest wine came the breath of the shadowed forest. The valley below was a vision seen through an opal haze. A white mist from hidden falls blurred the green of a hand's breadth of tree tops half-way down the gorge. Youth made merry hand-in-hand with young summer. Nothing on Broadway like that.

The villagers gathered to see the city folks pursue their mad drollery. The woods rang with the laughter of pixies and naiads and sprites. Gaines caught most of the rings. His was the privilege to crown the queen of the tournament. He was the conquering knight—as far as the rings went. On his arm he wore a white scarf. Compton wore light blue. She had declared her preference for blue, but she wore white that day.

Gaines looked about for the queen to crown her. He heard her merry laugh, as if from the clouds. She had slipped away and climbed Chimney Rock, a little granite bluff, and stood there, a white fairy among the laurels, fifty feet above their heads.

Instantly he and Compton accepted the implied challenge. The bluff was easily mounted at the rear, but the front offered small hold to hand or foot. Each man quickly selected his route and began to climb, A crevice, a bush, a slight projection, a vine or tree branch—all of these were aids that counted in the race. It was all foolery—there was no stake; but there was youth in it, cross reader, and light hearts, and something else that Miss Clay writes so charmingly about.

Gaines gave a great tug at the root of a laurel and pulled himself to Miss Mary's feet. On his arm he carried the wreath of roses; and while the villagers and summer boarders screamed and applauded below he placed it on the queen's brow.

"You are a gallant knight," said Miss Mary.

"If I could be your true knight always," began Gaines, but Miss Mary laughed him dumb, for Compton scrambled over the edge of the rock one minute behind time.

What a twilight that was when they drove back to the hotel! The opal of the valley turned slowly to purple, the dark woods framed the lake as a mirror, the tonic air stirred the very soul in one. The first pale stars came out over the mountain tops where yet a faint glow of—

~

"I beg your pardon, Mr. Gaines," said Adkins.

The man who believed New York to be the finest summer resort in the world opened his eyes and kicked over the mucilage bottle on his desk.

"I—I believe I was asleep," he said.

"It's the heat," said Adkins. "It's something awful in the city these"—

"Nonsense!" said the other. "The city beats the country ten to one in summer. Fools go out tramping in muddy brooks and wear themselves out trying to catch little fish as long as your finger. Stay in town and keep comfortable—that's my idea."

"Some letters just came," said Adkins. "I thought you might like to glance at them before you go."

Let us look over his shoulder and read just a few lines of one of them:

My Dear, Dear Husband: Just received your letter ordering us to stay another month. … Rita's cough is almost gone. … Johnny has simply gone wild like a little Indian … Will be the making of both children … work so hard, and I know that your business can hardly afford to keep us here so long … best man that ever … you always pretend that you like the city in summer … trout fishing that you used to be so fond of … and all to keep us well and happy … come to you if it were not doing the babies so much good. … I stood last evening on Chimney Rock in exactly the same spot where I was when you put the wreath of roses on my head … through all the world … when you said you would be my true knight … fifteen years ago, dear, just think! … have always been that to me … ever and ever,

Mary.

The man who said he thought New York the finest summer resort in the country dropped into a café on his way home and had a glass of beer under an electric fan.

"Wonder what kind of a fly old Harding used," he said to himself.

18

Conscience in Art

"I never could hold my partner, Andy Tucker, down to legitimate ethics of pure swindling," said Jeff Peters to me one day.

"Andy had too much imagination to be honest. He used to devise schemes of money-getting so fraudulent and high-financial that they wouldn't have been allowed in the bylaws of a railroad rebate system.

"Myself, I never believed in taking any man's dollars unless I gave him something for it—something in the way of rolled gold jewelry, garden seeds, lumbago lotion, stock certificates, stove polish or a crack on the head to show for his money. I guess I must have had New England ancestors away back and inherited some of their stanch and rugged fear of the police.

"But Andy's family tree was in different kind. I don't think he could have traced his descent any further back than a corporation.

"One summer while we was in the middle West, working down the Ohio valley with a line of family albums, headache powders and roach destroyer, Andy takes one of his notions of high and actionable financiering.

"'Jeff,' says he, 'I've been thinking that we ought to drop these rutabaga fanciers and give our attention to something more nourishing and prolific. If we keep on snapshooting these hinds for their egg money we'll be classed as nature fakers. How about plunging into the fastnesses of the skyscraper country and biting some big bull caribous in the chest?'

"'Well,' says I, 'you know my idiosyncrasies. I prefer a square, non-illegal style of business such as we are carrying on now. When I take money I want to leave some tangible object in the other fellow's hands for him to gaze at and to distract his attention from my spoor, even if it's only a Komical Kuss Trick Finger Ring for Squirting Perfume in a Friend's Eye. But if you've got a fresh idea, Andy,' says I, 'let's have a look at it. I'm not so wedded to petty graft that I would refuse something better in the way of a subsidy.'

"'I was thinking,' says Andy, 'of a little hunt without horn, hound or camera among the great herd of the Midas Americanus, commonly known as the Pittsburg millionaires.'

"'In New York?' I asks.

"'No, sir,' says Andy, 'in Pittsburg. That's their habitat. They don't like New York. They go there now and then just because it's expected of 'em.'

"'A Pittsburg millionaire in New York is like a fly in a cup of hot coffee—he attracts attention and comment, but he don't enjoy it. New York ridicules him for "blowing" so much money in that town of sneaks and snobs, and sneers. The truth is, he don't spend anything while he is there. I saw a memorandum of expenses for a ten days trip to Bunkum Town made by a Pittsburg man worth $15,000,000 once. Here's the way he set it down:

R.R. fare to and from	$ 21 00
Cab fare to and from hotel	2 00
Hotel bill @ $5 per day	50 00
Tips	5,750 00
Total	$5,823 00

"'That's the voice of New York,' goes on Andy. 'The town's nothing but a head waiter. If you tip it too much it'll go and stand by the door and make fun of you to the hat check boy. When a Pittsburger wants to spend money and have a good time he stays at home. That's where we'll go to catch him.'

"Well, to make a dense story more condensed, me and Andy cached our Paris green and antipyrine powders and albums in a friend's cellar, and took the trail to Pittsburg. Andy didn't have any especial prospectus of chicanery and violence drawn up, but he always had plenty of confidence that his immoral nature would rise to any occasion that presented itself.

"As a concession to my ideas of self-preservation and rectitude he promised that if I should take an active and incriminating part in any little business venture that we might work up there should be something actual and cognizant to the senses of touch, sight, taste or smell to transfer to the victim for the money so my conscience might rest easy. After that I felt better and entered more cheerfully into the foul play.

"'Andy,' says I, as we strayed through the smoke along the cinder-path they call Smithfield street, 'had you figured out how we are going to get acquainted with these coke kings and pig iron squeezers? Not that I would decry my own worth or system of drawing room deportment, and work with the olive fork and pie knife,' says I, 'but isn't the entree nous into the salons of the stogie smokers going to be harder than you imagined?'

"'If there's any handicap at all,' says Andy, 'it's our own refinement and inherent culture. Pittsburg millionaires are a fine body of plain, wholehearted, unassuming, democratic men.

"'They are rough but uncivil in their manners, and though their ways are boisterous and unpolished, under it all they have a great deal of impoliteness and discourtesy. Nearly every one of 'em rose from obscurity,' says Andy, 'and they'll live in it till the town gets to using smoke consumers. If we act simple and unaffected and don't go too far from the saloons and keep making a noise like an import duty on steel rails we won't have any trouble in meeting some of 'em socially.'

"Well Andy and me drifted about town three or four days getting our bearings. We got to knowing several millionaires by sight.

"One used to stop his automobile in front of our hotel and have a quart of champagne brought out to him. When the waiter opened it he'd turn it up to his mouth and drink it out of the bottle. That showed he used to be a glassblower before he made his money.

"One evening Andy failed to come to the hotel for dinner. About 11 o'clock he came into my room.

"'Landed one, Jeff,' says he. 'Twelve millions. Oil, rolling mills, real estate and natural gas. He's a fine man; no airs about him. Made all his money in the last five years. He's got professors posting him up now in education—art and literature and haberdashery and such things.

"'When I saw him he'd just won a bet of $10,000 with a Steel Corporation man that there'd be four suicides in the Allegheny rolling mills today. So everybody in sight had to walk up and have drinks on him. He took a fancy to me and asked me to dinner with him. We went to a restaurant in Diamond alley and sat on stools and had a sparkling Moselle and clam chowder and apple fritters.

"'Then he wanted to show me his bachelor apartment on Liberty street. He's got ten rooms over a fish market with privilege of the bath on the next floor above. He told me it cost him $18,000 to furnish his apartment, and I believe it.

"'He's got $40,000 worth of pictures in one room, and $20,000 worth of curios and antiques in another. His name's Scudder, and he's 45, and taking lessons on the piano and 15,000 barrels of oil a day out of his wells.'

"'All right,' says I. 'Preliminary canter satisfactory. But, kay vooly, voo? What good is the art junk to us? And the oil?'

"'Now, that man,' says Andy, sitting thoughtfully on the bed, 'ain't what you would call an ordinary scutt. When he was showing me his cabinet of art curios his face lighted up like the door of a coke oven. He says that if some of his big deals go through he'll make J. P. Morgan's collection of sweatshop tapestry and Augusta, Me, beadwork look like the contents of an ostrich's craw thrown on a screen by a magic lantern.

"'And then he showed me a little carving,' went on Andy, 'that anybody could see was a wonderful thing. It was something like 2,000 years old, he said. It was a lotus flower with a woman's face in it carved out of a solid piece of ivory.

"Scudder looks it up in a catalogue and describes it. An Egyptian carver named Khafra made two of 'em for King Rameses II about the year B.C. The other one can't be found. The junkshops and antique bugs have rubbered all Europe for it, but it seems to be out of stock. Scudder paid $2,000 for the one he has.'

"'Oh, well,' says I, 'this sounds like the purling of a rill to me. I thought we came here to teach the millionaires business, instead of learning art from 'em?'

"'Be patient,' says Andy, kindly. 'Maybe we will see a rift in the smoke ere long.'

"All the next morning Andy was out. I didn't see him until about noon. He came to the hotel and called me into his room across the hall. He pulled a roundish bundle about as big as a goose egg out of his pocket and unwrapped it. It was an ivory carving just as he had described the millionaire's to me.

"'I went in an old second hand store and pawnshop a while ago,' says Andy, 'and I see this half hidden under a lot of old daggers and truck. The pawnbroker said he'd had it several years and thinks it was soaked by some Arabs or Turks or some foreign dubs that used to live down by the river.

"'I offered him $2 for it, and I must have looked like I wanted it, for he said it would be taking the pumpernickel out of his children's mouths to hold any conversation that did not lead up to a price of $35. I finally got it for $25.

"'Jeff,' goes on Andy, 'this is the exact counterpart of Scudder's carving. It's absolutely a dead ringer for it. He'll pay $2,000 for it as quick as he'd tuck a napkin under his chin. And why shouldn't it be the genuine other one, anyhow, that the old gypsy whittled out?'

"'Why not, indeed?' says I. 'And how shall we go about compelling him to make a voluntary purchase of it?'

"Andy had his plan all ready, and I'll tell you how we carried it out.

"I got a pair of blue spectacles, put on my black frock coat, rumpled my hair up and became Prof. Pickleman. I went to another hotel, registered, and sent a telegram to Scudder to come to see me at once on important art business. The elevator dumped him on me in less than an hour. He was a foggy man with a clarion voice, smelling of Connecticut wrappers and naphtha.

"'Hello, Profess!' he shouts. 'How's your conduct?'

"I rumpled my hair some more and gave him a blue glass stare.

"'Sir,' says I, 'are you Cornelius T. Scudder? Of Pittsburg, Pennsylvania?'

"'I am,' says he. 'Come out and have a drink.'

"'I've neither the time nor the desire,' says I, 'for such harmful and deleterious amusements. I have come from New York,' says I, 'on a matter of busi—on a matter of art.

"'I learned there that you are the owner of an Egyptian ivory carving of the time of Rameses II, representing the head of Queen Isis in a lotus flower. There were only two of such carvings made. One has been lost for many years. I recently discovered and purchased the other in a pawn—in an obscure museum in Vienna. I wish to purchase yours. Name your price.'

"'Well, the great ice jams, Profess!' says Scudder. 'Have you found the other one? Me sell? No. I don't guess Cornelius Scudder needs to sell anything that he wants to keep. Have you got the carving with you, Profess?'

"I shows it to Scudder. He examines it careful all over.

"'It's the article,' says he. 'It's a duplicate of mine, every line and curve of it. Tell you what I'll do,' he says. 'I won't sell, but I'll buy. Give you $2,500 for yours.'

"'Since you won't sell, I will,' says I. 'Large bills, please. I'm a man of few words. I must return to New York tonight. I lecture tomorrow at the aquarium.'

"Scudder sends a check down and the hotel cashes it. He goes off with his piece of antiquity and I hurry back to Andy's hotel, according to arrangement.

"Andy is walking up and down the room looking at his watch.

"'Well?' he says.

"'Twenty-five hundred,' says I. 'Cash.'

"'We've got just eleven minutes,' says Andy, 'to catch the B. & O. westbound. Grab your baggage.'

"'What's the hurry,' says I. 'It was a square deal. And even if it was only an imitation of the original carving it'll take him some time to find it out. He seemed to be sure it was the genuine article.'

"'It was,' says Andy. 'It was his own. When I was looking at his curios yesterday he stepped out of the room for a moment and I pocketed it. Now, will you pick up your suit case and hurry?'

"'Then,' says I, 'why was that story about finding another one in the pawn—'

"'Oh,' says Andy, 'out of respect for that conscience of yours. Come on.'"

19

The Caballero's Way

The Cisco Kid had killed six men in more or less fair scrimmages, had murdered twice as many (mostly Mexicans), and had winged a larger number whom he modestly forbore to count. Therefore a woman loved him.

The Kid was twenty-five, looked twenty; and a careful insurance company would have estimated the probable time of his demise at, say, twenty-six. His habitat was anywhere between the Frio and the Rio Grande. He killed for the love of it—because he was quick-tempered— to avoid arrest—for his own amusement—any reason that came to his mind would suffice. He had escaped capture because he could shoot five-sixths of a second sooner than any sheriff or ranger in the service, and because he rode a speckled roan horse that knew every cow-path in the mesquite and pear thickets from San Antonio to Matamoras.

Tonia Perez, the girl who loved the Cisco Kid, was half Carmen, half Madonna, and the rest—oh, yes, a woman who is half Carmen and half Madonna can always be something more—the rest, let us say, was humming-bird. She lived in a grass-roofed *jacal* near a little Mexican settlement at the Lone

Wolf Crossing of the Frio. With her lived a father or grandfather, a lineal Aztec, somewhat less than a thousand years old, who herded a hundred goats and lived in a continuous drunken dream from drinking *mescal*. Back of the *jacal* a tremendous forest of bristling pear, twenty feet high at its worst, crowded almost to its door. It was along the bewildering maze of this spinous thicket that the speckled roan would bring the Kid to see his girl. And once, clinging like a lizard to the ridge-pole, high up under the peaked grass roof, he had heard Tonia, with her Madonna face and Carmen beauty and humming-bird soul, parley with the sheriff's posse, denying knowledge of her man in her soft *mélange* of Spanish and English.

One day the adjutant-general of the State, who is, *ex offico*, commander of the ranger forces, wrote some sarcastic lines to Captain Duval of Company X, stationed at Laredo, relative to the serene and undisturbed existence led by murderers and desperadoes in the said captain's territory.

The captain turned the color of brick dust under his tan, and forwarded the letter, after adding a few comments, per ranger Private Bill Adamson, to ranger Lieutenant Sandridge, camped at a water hole on the Nueces with a squad of five men in preservation of law and order.

Lieutenant Sandridge turned a beautiful *couleur de rose* through his ordinary strawberry complexion, tucked the letter in his hip pocket, and chewed off the ends of his gamboge mustache.

The next morning he saddled his horse and rode alone to the Mexican settlement at the Lone Wolf Crossing of the Frio, twenty miles away.

Six feet two, blond as a Viking, quiet as a deacon, dangerous as a machine gun, Sandridge moved among the *Jacales*, patiently seeking news of the Cisco Kid.

Far more than the law, the Mexicans dreaded the cold and certain vengeance of the lone rider that the ranger sought. It had been one of the Kid's pastimes to shoot Mexicans "to see them kick": if he demanded from them moribund Terpsichorean feats, simply that he might be entertained, what terrible and extreme penalties would be certain to follow should they anger him! One and all they lounged with upturned palms and shrugging shoulders, filling the air with "*quien sabes*" and denials of the Kid's acquaintance.

But there was a man named Fink who kept a store at the Crossing—a man of many nationalities, tongues, interests, and ways of thinking.

"No use to ask them Mexicans," he said to Sandridge. "They're afraid to tell. This *hombre* they call the Kid—Goodall is his name, ain't it?—he's been in my store once or twice. I have an idea you might run across him at—but I guess I don't keer to say, myself. I'm two seconds later in pulling a gun than I used to be, and the difference is worth thinking about. But this Kid's got a half-Mexican girl at the Crossing that he comes to see. She lives in that *jacal* a hundred yards down the arroyo at the edge of the pear. Maybe she—no, I don't suppose she would, but that *jacal* would be a good place to watch, anyway."

Sandridge rode down to the *jacal* of Perez. The sun was low, and the broad shade of the great pear thicket already covered the grass- thatched hut. The goats were enclosed for the night in a brush corral near by. A few kids walked the top of it, nibbling the chaparral leaves. The old Mexican lay upon a blanket on the grass, already in a stupor from his mescal, and dreaming, perhaps, of the nights when he and Pizarro touched glasses to their New World fortunes—so old his wrinkled face seemed to proclaim him to be. And in the door of the *jacal* stood Tonia. And Lieutenant Sandridge sat in his saddle staring at her like a gannet agape at a sailor-man.

The Cisco Kid was a vain person, as all eminent and successful assassins are, and his bosom would have been ruffled had he known that at a simple exchange of glances two persons, in whose minds he had been looming large, suddenly abandoned (at least for the time) all thought of him.

Never before had Tonia seen such a man as this. He seemed to be made of sunshine and blood-red tissue and clear weather. He seemed to illuminate the shadow of the pear when he smiled, as though the sun were rising again. The men she had known had been small and dark. Even the Kid, in spite of his achievements, was a stripling no larger than herself, with black, straight hair and a cold, marble face that chilled the noonday.

As for Tonia, though she sends description to the poorhouse, let her make a millionaire of your fancy. Her blue-black hair, smoothly divided in the middle and bound close to her head, and her large eyes full of the Latin melancholy, gave her the Madonna touch. Her motions and air spoke of the concealed fire and the desire to charm that she had inherited from the *gitanas* of the Basque province. As for the humming-bird part of her, that dwelt in her heart; you could not perceive it unless her bright red skirt and dark blue blouse gave you a symbolic hint of the vagarious bird.

The newly lighted sun-god asked for a drink of water. Tonia brought it from the red jar hanging under the brush shelter. Sandridge considered it necessary to dismount so as to lessen the trouble of her ministrations.

I play no spy; nor do I assume to master the thoughts of any human heart; but I assert, by the chronicler's right, that before a quarter of an hour had sped, Sandridge was teaching her how to plaint a six-strand rawhide stake-rope, and Tonia had explained to him that were it not for her little English book that the peripatetic *padre* had given her and the little crippled *chivo*, that she fed from a bottle, she would be very, very lonely indeed.

Which leads to a suspicion that the Kid's fences needed repairing, and that the adjutant-general's sarcasm had fallen upon unproductive soil.

In his camp by the water hole Lieutenant Sandridge announced and reiterated his intention of either causing the Cisco Kid to nibble the black loam of the Frio country prairies or of haling him before a judge and jury. That sounded business-like. Twice a week he rode over to the Lone Wolf Crossing of the Frio, and directed Tonia's slim, slightly lemon-tinted fingers among the intricacies of the slowly growing lariata. A six-strand plait is hard to learn and easy to teach.

The ranger knew that he might find the Kid there at any visit. He kept his armament ready, and had a frequent eye for the pear thicket at the rear of the *jacal*. Thus he might bring down the kite and the humming-bird with one stone.

While the sunny-haired ornithologist was pursuing his studies the Cisco Kid was also attending to his professional duties. He moodily shot up a saloon in a small cow village on Quintana Creek, killed the town marshal (plugging him neatly in the centre of his tin badge), and then rode away, morose and unsatisfied. No true artist is uplifted by shooting an aged man carrying an old-style .38 bulldog.

On his way the Kid suddenly experienced the yearning that all men feel when wrong-doing loses its keen edge of delight. He yearned for the woman he loved to reassure him that she was his in spite of it. He wanted her to call his bloodthirstiness bravery and his cruelty devotion. He wanted Tonia to bring him water from the red jar under the brush shelter, and tell him how the *chivo* was thriving on the bottle.

The Kid turned the speckled roan's head up the ten-mile pear flat that stretches along the Arroyo Hondo until it ends at the Lone Wolf Crossing of the Frio. The roan whickered; for he had a sense of locality and direction equal to that of a belt-line street-car horse; and he knew he would soon be nibbling the rich mesquite grass at the end of a forty-foot stake-rope while Ulysses rested his head in Circe's straw-roofed hut.

More weird and lonesome than the journey of an Amazonian explorer is the ride of one through a Texas pear flat. With dismal monotony and startling variety the uncanny and multiform shapes of the cacti lift their twisted trunks, and fat, bristly hands to encumber the way. The demon plant, appearing to live without soil or rain, seems to taunt the parched traveler with its lush grey greenness. It warps itself a thousand times about what look to be open and inviting paths, only to lure the rider into blind and impassable spine-defended "bottoms of the bag," leaving him to retreat, if he can, with the points of the compass whirling in his head.

To be lost in the pear is to die almost the death of the thief on the cross, pierced by nails and with grotesque shapes of all the fiends hovering about.

But it was not so with the Kid and his mount. Winding, twisting, circling, tracing the most fantastic and bewildering trail ever picked out, the good roan lessened the distance to the Lone Wolf Crossing with every coil and turn that he made.

While they fared the Kid sang. He knew but one tune and sang it, as he knew but one code and lived it, and but one girl and loved her. He was a single-minded man of conventional ideas. He had a voice like a coyote with bronchitis, but whenever he chose to sing his song he sang it. It was a conventional song of the camps and trail, running at its beginning as near as may be to these words:

Don't you monkey with my Lulu girl
Or I'll tell you what I'll do—

And so on. The roan was inured to it, and did not mind.

But even the poorest singer will, after a certain time, gain his own consent to refrain from contributing to the world's noises. So the Kid, by the time he was within a mile or two of Tonia's *jacal*, had reluctantly allowed his song to die away—not because his vocal performance had become less charming to his own ears, but because his laryngeal muscles were aweary.

As though he were in a circus ring the speckled roan wheeled and danced through the labyrinth of pear until at length his rider knew by certain landmarks that the Lone Wolf Crossing was close at hand. Then, where the pear was thinner, he caught sight of the grass roof of the *jacal* and the hackberry tree on the edge of the arroyo. A few yards farther the Kid stopped the roan and gazed intently through the prickly openings. Then he dismounted, dropped the roan's reins, and proceeded on foot, stooping and silent, like an Indian. The roan, knowing his part, stood still, making no sound.

The Kid crept noiselessly to the very edge of the pear thicket and reconnoitered between the leaves of a clump of cactus.

Ten yards from his hiding-place, in the shade of the *jacal*, sat his Tonia calmly plaiting a rawhide lariat. So far she might surely escape condemnation; women have been known, from time to time, to engage in more mischievous occupations. But if all must be told, there is to be added that her head reposed against the broad and comfortable chest of a tall red-and-yellow man, and that his arm was about her, guiding her nimble fingers that required so many lessons at the intricate six- strand plait.

Sandridge glanced quickly at the dark mass of pear when he heard a slight squeaking sound that was not altogether unfamiliar. A gun- scabbard will make that sound when one grasps the handle of a six- shooter suddenly. But the sound was not repeated; and Tonia's fingers needed close attention.

And then, in the shadow of death, they began to talk of their love; and in the still July afternoon every word they uttered reached the ears of the Kid.

"Remember, then," said Tonia, "you must not come again until I send for you. Soon he will be here. A *vaquero at the tienda* said today he saw him on the Guadalupe three days ago. When he is that near he always comes. If he comes and finds you here he will kill you. So, for my sake, you must come no more until I send you the word."

"All right," said the stranger. "And then what?"

"And then," said the girl, "you must bring your men here and kill him. If not, he will kill you."

"He ain't a man to surrender, that's sure," said Sandridge. "It's kill or be killed for the officer that goes up against Mr. Cisco Kid."

"He must die," said the girl. "Otherwise there will not be any peace in the world for thee and me. He has killed many. Let him so die. Bring your men, and give him no chance to escape."

"You used to think right much of him," said Sandridge.

Tonia dropped the lariat, twisted herself around, and curved a lemon- tinted arm over the ranger's shoulder.

"But then," she murmured in liquid Spanish, "I had not beheld thee, thou great, red mountain of a man! And thou art kind and good, as well as strong. Could one choose him, knowing thee? Let him die; for then I will not be filled with fear by day and night lest he hurt thee or me."

"How can I know when he comes?" asked Sandridge.

"When he comes," said Tonia, "he remains two days, sometimes three. Gregorio, the small son of old Luisa, the *lavendera*, has a swift pony. I will write a letter to thee and send it by him, saying how it will be best to come upon him. By Gregorio will the letter come. And bring many men with thee, and have much care, oh, dear red one, for the rattlesnake is not quicker to strike than is '*El Chivato*,' as they call him, to send a ball from his *pistola*."

"The Kid's handy with his gun, sure enough," admitted Sandridge, "but when I come for him I shall come alone. I'll get him by myself or not at all. The Cap wrote one or two things to me that make me want to do the trick without any help. You let me know when Mr. Kid arrives, and I'll do the rest."

"I will send you the message by the boy Gregorio," said the girl. "I knew you were braver than that small slayer of men who never smiles. How could I ever have thought I cared for him?"

It was time for the ranger to ride back to his camp on the water hole. Before he mounted his horse he raised the slight form of Tonia with one arm high from the earth for a parting salute. The drowsy stillness of the torpid summer air still lay thick upon the dreaming afternoon. The smoke from the fire in the *jacal*, where the *frijoles* blubbered in the iron pot, rose straight as a plumb-line above the clay-daubed chimney. No sound or movement disturbed the serenity of the dense pear thicket ten yards away.

When the form of Sandridge had disappeared, loping his big dun down the steep banks of the Frio crossing, the Kid crept back to his own horse, mounted him, and rode back along the tortuous trail he had come.

But not far. He stopped and waited in the silent depths of the pear until half an hour had passed. And then Tonia heard the high, untrue notes of his unmusical singing coming nearer and nearer; and she ran to the edge of the pear to meet him.

The Kid seldom smiled; but he smiled and waved his hat when he saw her. He dismounted, and his girl sprang into his arms. The Kid looked at her fondly. His thick, black hair clung to his head like a wrinkled mat. The meeting brought a slight ripple of some undercurrent of feeling to his smooth, dark face that was usually as motionless as a clay mask.

"How's my girl?" he asked, holding her close.

"Sick of waiting so long for you, dear one," she answered. "My eyes are dim with always gazing into that devil's pincushion through which you come. And I can see into it such a little way, too. But you are here, beloved one, and I will not scold. *Que mal muchacho*! Not to come to see your *alma* more often. Go in and rest, and let me water your horse and stake him with the long rope. There is cool water in the jar for you."

The Kid kissed her affectionately.

"Not if the court knows itself do I let a lady stake my horse for me," said he. "But if you'll run in, *chica,* and throw a pot of coffee together while I attend to the *caballo,* I'll be a good deal obliged."

Besides his marksmanship the Kid had another attribute for which he admired himself greatly. He was *muy caballero,* as the Mexicans express it, where the ladies were concerned. For them he had always gentle words and consideration. He could not have spoken a harsh word to a woman. He might ruthlessly slay their husbands and brothers, but he could not have laid the weight of a finger in anger upon a woman. Wherefore many of that interesting division of humanity who had come under the spell of his politeness declared their disbelief in the stories circulated about Mr. Kid. One shouldn't believe everything one heard, they said. When confronted by their indignant men folk with proof of the *caballero's* deeds of infamy, they said maybe he had been driven to it, and that he knew how to treat a lady, anyhow.

Considering this extremely courteous idiosyncrasy of the Kid and the pride he took in it, one can perceive that the solution of the problem that was presented to him by what he saw and heard from his hiding- place in the pear that afternoon (at least as to one of the actors) must have been obscured by difficulties. And yet one could not think of the Kid overlooking little matters of that kind.

At the end of the short twilight they gathered around a supper of *frijoles,* goat steaks, canned peaches, and coffee, by the light of a lantern in the *jacal.* Afterward, the ancestor, his flock corralled, smoked a cigarette and became a mummy in a grey blanket. Tonia washed the few dishes while the Kid dried them with the flour-sacking towel. Her eyes shone; she chatted volubly of the inconsequent happenings of her small world since the Kid's last visit; it was as all his other home-comings had been.

Then outside Tonia swung in a grass hammock with her guitar and sang sad *canciones de amor*.

"Do you love me just the same, old girl?" asked the Kid, hunting for his cigarette papers.

"Always the same, little one," said Tonia, her dark eyes lingering upon him.

"I must go over to Fink's," said the Kid, rising, "for some tobacco. I thought I had another sack in my coat. I'll be back in a quarter of an hour."

"Hasten," said Tonia, "and tell me—how long shall I call you my own this time? Will you be gone again tomorrow, leaving me to grieve, or will you be longer with your Tonia?"

"Oh, I might stay two or three days this trip," said the Kid, yawning. "I've been on the dodge for a month, and I'd like to rest up."

He was gone half an hour for his tobacco. When he returned Tonia was still lying in the hammock.

"It's funny," said the Kid, "how I feel. I feel like there was somebody lying behind every bush and tree waiting to shoot me. I never had mullygrubs like them before. Maybe it's one of them presumptions. I've got half a notion to light out in the morning before day. The Guadalupe country is burning up about that old Dutchman I plugged down there."

"You are not afraid—no one could make my brave little one fear."

"Well, I haven't been usually regarded as a jack-rabbit when it comes to scrapping; but I don't want a posse smoking me out when I'm in your *jacal*. Somebody might get hurt that oughtn't to."

"Remain with your Tonia; no one will find you here."

The Kid looked keenly into the shadows up and down the arroyo and toward the dim lights of the Mexican village.

"I'll see how it looks later on," was his decision.

~

At midnight a horseman rode into the rangers' camp, blazing his way by noisy "halloes" to indicate a pacific mission. Sandridge and one or two others turned out to investigate the row. The rider announced himself to be Domingo Sales, from the Lone Wolf Crossing. he bore a letter for Senor Sandridge. Old Luisa, the *lavendera*, had persuaded him to bring it, he said, her son Gregorio being too ill of a fever to ride.

Sandridge lighted the camp lantern and read the letter. These were its words:

Dear One: He has come. Hardly had you ridden away when he came out of the pear. When he first talked he said he would stay three days or more. Then as it grew later he was like a wolf or a fox, and walked about without rest, looking and listening. Soon he said he must leave before daylight when it is dark and stillest. And then he seemed to suspect that I be not true to him. He looked at me so strange that I am frightened. I swear to him that I love him, his own Tonia. Last of all he said I must prove to him I am true. He thinks that even now men are waiting to kill him as he rides from my house. To escape he says he will dress in my clothes, my red skirt and the blue waist I wear and the brown mantilla over the head, and thus ride away. But before that he says that I must put on his clothes, his *pantalones* and *camisa* and hat, and ride away on his horse from the *jacal* as far as the big road beyond the crossing and back again. This before he goes, so he can tell if I am true and if men are hidden to shoot him. It is a terrible thing. An hour before daybreak this is to be. Come, my dear one, and kill this man and take me for your Tonia. Do not try to take hold of him alive, but kill him quickly. Knowing all, you should do that. You must come long before the time and hide yourself in the little shed near the *jacal* where the wagon and saddles are kept. It is dark in there. He will wear my red skirt and blue waist and brown mantilla. I send you a hundred kisses.

Come surely and shoot quickly and straight.

Thine Own Tonia.

Sandridge quickly explained to his men the official part of the missive. The rangers protested against his going alone.

"I'll get him easy enough," said the lieutenant. "The girl's got him trapped. And don't even think he'll get the drop on me."

Sandridge saddled his horse and rode to the Lone Wolf Crossing. He tied his big dun in a clump of brush on the arroyo, took his Winchester from its scabbard, and carefully approached the Perez *jacal*. There was only the half of a high moon drifted over by ragged, milk-white gulf clouds.

The wagon-shed was an excellent place for ambush; and the ranger got inside it safely. In the black shadow of the brush shelter in front of the *jacal* he could see a horse tied and hear him impatiently pawing the hard-trodden earth.

He waited almost an hour before two figures came out of the *jacal*. One, in man's clothes, quickly mounted the horse and galloped past the wagon-shed toward the crossing and village. And then the other figure, in skirt, waist, and mantilla over its head, stepped out into the faint moonlight, gazing after the rider. Sandridge thought he would take his chance then before Tonia rode back. He fancied she might not care to see it.

"Throw up your hands," he ordered loudly, stepping out of the wagon- shed with his Winchester at his shoulder.

There was a quick turn of the figure, but no movement to obey, so the ranger pumped in the bullets—one—two—three—and then twice more; for you never could be too sure of bringing down the Cisco Kid. There was no danger of missing at ten paces, even in that half moonlight.

The old ancestor, asleep on his blanket, was awakened by the shots. Listening further, he heard a great cry from some man in mortal distress or anguish, and rose up grumbling at the disturbing ways of moderns.

The tall, red ghost of a man burst into the *jacal*, reaching one hand, shaking like a *tule* reed, for the lantern hanging on its nail. The other spread a letter on the table.

"Look at this letter, Perez," cried the man. "Who wrote it?"

"*Ah, Dios*! it is Senor Sandridge," mumbled the old man, approaching. "*Pues, senor*, that letter was written by '*El Chivato*,' as he is called—by the man of Tonia. They say he is a bad man; I do not know. While Tonia slept he wrote the letter and sent it by this old hand of mine to Domingo Sales to be brought to you. Is there anything wrong in the letter? I am very old; and I did not know. *Valgame Dios*! It is a very foolish world; and there is nothing in the house to drink— nothing to drink."

Just then all that Sandridge could think of to do was to go outside and throw himself face downward in the dust by the side of his humming-bird, of whom not a feather fluttered. He was not a *caballero* by instinct, and he could not understand the niceties of revenge.

A mile away the rider who had ridden past the wagon-shed struck up a harsh, untuneful song, the words of which began:

Don't you monkey with my Lulu girl
Or I'll tell you what I'll do—

20

The Last Leaf

In a little district west of Washington Square the streets have run crazy and broken themselves into small strips called "places." These "places" make strange angles and curves. One street crosses itself a time or two. An artist once discovered a valuable possibility in this street. Suppose a collector with a bill for paints, paper and canvas should, in traversing this route, suddenly meet himself coming back, without a cent having been paid on account!

So, to quaint old Greenwich Village the art people soon came prowling, hunting for north windows and eighteenth-century gables and Dutch attics and low rents. Then they imported some pewter mugs and a chafing dish or two from Sixth avenue, and became a "colony."

At the top of a squatty, three-story brick Sue and Johnsy had their studio. "Johnsy" was familiar for Joanna. One was from Maine; the other from California. They had met at the *table d'hôte* of an Eighth street "Delmonico's," and found their tastes in art, chicory salad and bishop sleeves so congenial that the joint studio resulted.

That was in May. In November a cold, unseen stranger, whom the doctors called Pneumonia, stalked about the colony, touching one here and there with his icy fingers. Over on the east side this ravager strode boldly, smiting his victims by scores, but his feet trod slowly through the maze of the narrow and moss-grown "places."

Mr. Pneumonia was not what you would call a chivalric old gentleman. A mite of a little woman with blood thinned by California zephyrs was hardly fair game for the red-fisted, short-breathed old duffer. But Johnsy he smote; and she lay, scarcely moving, on her painted iron bedstead, looking through the small Dutch window-panes at the blank side of the next brick house.

One morning the busy doctor invited Sue into the hallway with a shaggy, gray eyebrow.

"She has one chance in—let us say, ten," he said, as he shook down the mercury in his clinical thermometer. "And that chance is for her to want to live. This way people have of lining-up on the side of the undertaker makes the entire pharmacopoeia look silly. Your little lady has made up her mind that she's not going to get well. Has she anything on her mind?"

"She—she wanted to paint the Bay of Naples some day," said Sue.

"Paint?—Bosh! Has she anything on her mind worth thinking about twice—a man, for instance?"

"A man?" said Sue, with a jew's-harp twang in her voice. "Is a man worth—but, no, doctor; there is nothing of the kind."

"Well, it is the weakness, then," said the doctor. "I will do all that science, so far as it may filter through my efforts, can accomplish. But whenever my patient begins to count the carriages in her funeral procession I subtract 50 per cent from the curative power of medicines. If you will get her to ask one question about the new winter styles in cloak sleeves I will promise you a one-in-five chance for her, instead of one in ten."

After the doctor had gone Sue went into the workroom and cried a Japanese napkin to a pulp. Then she swaggered into Johnsy's room with her drawing board, whistling ragtime.

Johnsy lay, scarcely making a ripple under the bedclothes, with her face toward the window. Sue stopped whistling, thinking she was asleep.

She arranged her board and began a pen-and-ink drawing to illustrate a magazine story. Young artists must pave their way to Art by drawing pictures for magazine stories that young authors write to pave their way to Literature.

As Sue was sketching a pair of elegant horse-show riding trousers and a monocle on the figure of the hero, an Idaho cowboy, she heard a low sound, several times repeated. She went quickly to the bedside.

Johnsy's eyes were open wide. She was looking out the window and counting—counting backward.

"Twelve," she said, and a little later "eleven;" and then "ten," and "nine;" and then "eight" and "seven," almost together.

Sue looked solicitously out the window. What was there to count? There was only a bare, dreary yard to be seen, and the blank side of the brick house twenty feet away. An old, old ivy vine, gnarled and decayed at the roots, climbed half way up the brick wall. The cold breath of autumn had stricken its leaves from the vine until its skeleton branches clung, almost bare, to the crumbling bricks.

"What is it, dear?" asked Sue.

"Six," said Johnsy, in almost a whisper. "They're falling faster now. Three days ago there were almost a hundred. It made my head ache to count them. But now it's easy. There goes another one. There are only five left now."

"Five what, dear. Tell your Sudie."

"Leaves. On the ivy vine. When the last one falls I must go, too. I've known that for three days. Didn't the doctor tell you?"

"Oh, I never heard of such nonsense," complained Sue, with magnificent scorn. "What have old ivy leaves to do with your getting well? And you used to love that vine so, you naughty girl. Don't be a goosey. Why, the doctor told me this morning that your chances for getting well real soon were—let's see exactly what he said—he said the chances were ten to one! Why, that's almost as good a chance as we have in New York when we ride on the street cars or walk past a new building. Try to take some broth now, and let Sudie go back to her drawing, so she can sell the editor man with it, and buy port wine for her sick child, and pork chops for her greedy self."

"You needn't get any more wine," said Johnsy, keeping her eyes fixed out the window. "There goes another. No, I don't want any broth. That leaves just four. I want to see the last one fall before it gets dark. Then I'll go, too."

"Johnsy, dear," said Sue, bending over her, "will you promise me to keep your eyes closed, and not look out the window until I am done working? I must hand those drawings in by tomorrow. I need the light, or I would draw the shade down."

"Couldn't you draw in the other room?" asked Johnsy, coldly.

"I'd rather be here by you," said Sue. "Besides I don't want you to keep looking at those silly ivy leaves."

"Tell me as soon as you have finished," said Johnsy, closing her eyes, and lying white and still as a fallen statue, "because I want to see the last one fall. I'm tired of waiting. I'm tired of thinking. I want to turn loose my hold on everything, and go sailing down, down, just like one of those poor, tired leaves."

"Try to sleep," said Sue. "I must call Behrman up to be my model for the old hermit miner. I'll not be gone a minute. Don't try to move 'till I come back."

Old Behrman was a painter who lived on the ground floor beneath them. He was past sixty and had a Michael Angelo's Moses beard curling down from the head of a satyr along the body of an imp. Behrman was a failure in art. Forty years he had wielded the brush without getting near enough to touch the hem of his Mistress's robe. He had been always about to paint a masterpiece, but had never yet begun it. For several years he had painted nothing except now and then a daub in the line of commerce or advertising. He earned a little by serving as a model to those young artists in the colony who could not pay the price of a professional. He drank gin to excess, and still talked of his coming masterpiece. For the rest he was a fierce little old man, who scoffed terribly at softness in any one, and who regarded himself as especial mastiff-in-waiting to protect the two young artists in the studio above.

Sue found Behrman smelling strongly of juniper berries in his dimly lighted den below. In one corner was a blank canvas on an easel that had been waiting there for twenty-five years to receive the first line of the masterpiece. She told him of Johnsy's fancy, and how she feared she would, indeed, light and fragile as a leaf herself, float away when her slight hold upon the world grew weaker.

Old Behrman, with his red eyes, plainly streaming, shouted his contempt and derision for such idiotic imaginings.

"Vass!" he cried. "Is dere people in de world mit der foolishness to die because leafs dey drop off from a confounded vine? I haf not heard of such a thing. No, I will not bose as a model for your fool hermit-dunderhead. Vy do you allow dot silly pusiness to come in der prain of her? Ach, dot poor lettle Miss Johnsy."

"She is very ill and weak," said Sue, "and the fever has left her mind morbid and full of strange fancies. Very well, Mr. Behrman, if you do not care to pose for me, you needn't. But I think you are a horrid old—old flibbertigibbet."

"You are just like a woman!" yelled Behrman. "Who said I will not bose? Go on. I come mit you. For half an hour I haf peen trying to say dot I am ready to bose. Gott! Dis is not any blace in which one so goot as Miss Yohnsy shall lie sick. Some day I vill baint a masterpiece, and ve shall all go away. Gott! Yes."

Johnsy was sleeping when they went upstairs. Sue pulled the shade down to the window-sill, and motioned Behrman into the other room. In there they peered out the window fearfully at the ivy vine. Then they looked at each other for a moment without speaking. A persistent, cold rain was falling, mingled with snow. Behrman, in his old blue shirt, took his seat as the hermit-miner on an upturned kettle for a rock.

When Sue awoke from an hour's sleep the next morning she found Johnsy with dull, wide-open eyes staring at the drawn green shade.

"Pull it up; I want to see," she ordered, in a whisper.

Wearily Sue obeyed.

But, lo! After the beating rain and fierce gusts of wind that had endured through the livelong night, there yet stood out against the brick wall one ivy leaf. It was the last on the vine. Still dark green near its stem, but with its serrated edges tinted with the yellow of dissolution and decay, it hung bravely from a branch some twenty feet above the ground.

"It is the last one," said Johnsy. "I thought it would surely fall during the night. I heard the wind. It will fall today, and I shall die at the same time."

"Dear, dear!" said Sue, leaning her worn face down to the pillow, "think of me, if you won't think of yourself. What would I do?"

But Johnsy did not answer. The lonesomest thing in all the world is a soul when it is making ready to go on its mysterious, far journey. The fancy seemed to possess her more strongly as one by one the ties that bound her to friendship and to earth were loosed.

The day wore away, and even through the twilight they could see the lone ivy leaf clinging to its stem against the wall. And then, with the coming of the night the north wind was again loosed, while the rain still beat against the windows and pattered down from the low Dutch eaves.

When it was light enough Johnsy, the merciless, commanded that the shade be raised.

The ivy leaf was still there.

Johnsy lay for a long time looking at it. And then she called to Sue, who was stirring her chicken broth over the gas stove.

"I've been a bad girl, Sudie," said Johnsy. "Something has made that last leaf stay there to show me how wicked I was. It is a sin to want to die. You may bring me a little broth now, and some milk with a little port in it, and—no; bring me a hand-mirror first, and then pack some pillows about me, and I will sit up and watch you cook."

An hour later she said.

"Sudie, some day I hope to paint the Bay of Naples."

The doctor came in the afternoon, and Sue had an excuse to go into the hallway as he left.

"Even chances," said the doctor, taking Sue's thin, shaking hand in his. "With good nursing you'll win. And now I must see another case I have downstairs. Behrman, his name is—some kind of an artist, I believe. Pneumonia, too. He is an old, weak man, and the attack is acute. There is no hope for him; but he goes to the hospital today to be made more comfortable."

The next day the doctor said to Sue: "She's out of danger. You've won. Nutrition and care now—that's all."

And that afternoon Sue came to the bed where Johnsy lay, contentedly knitting a very blue and very useless woolen shoulder scarf, and put one arm around her, pillows and all.

"I have something to tell you, white mouse," she said. "Mr. Behrman died of pneumonia today in the hospital. He was ill only two days. The janitor found him on the morning of the first day in his room downstairs helpless with pain. His shoes and clothing were wet through and icy cold. They couldn't imagine where he had been on such a dreadful night. And then they found a lantern, still lighted, and a ladder that had been dragged from its place, and some scattered brushes, and a palette with green and yellow colors mixed on it, and—look out the window, dear, at the last ivy leaf on the wall. Didn't you wonder why it never fluttered or moved when the wind blew? Ah, darling, it's Behrman's masterpiece—he painted it there the night that the last leaf fell."

21

The Making of a New Yorker

Besides many other things, Raggles was a poet. He was called a tramp; but that was only an elliptical way of saying that he was a philosopher, an artist, a traveller, a naturalist and a discoverer. But most of all he was a poet. In all his life he never wrote a line of verse; he lived his poetry. His Odyssey would have been a Limerick, had it been written. But, to linger with the primary proposition, Raggles was a poet.

Raggles's specialty, had he been driven to ink and paper, would have been sonnets to the cities. He studied cities as women study their reflections in mirrors; as children study the glue and sawdust of a dislocated doll; as the men who write about wild animals study the cages in the zoo. A city to Raggles was not merely a pile of bricks and mortar, peopled by a certain number of inhabitants; it was a thing with a soul characteristic and distinct; an individual conglomeration of life, with its own peculiar essence, flavor and feeling. Two thousand miles to the north and south, east and west, Raggles wandered in poetic fervor, taking the cities to his breast. He footed it on dusty roads, or sped magnificently in freight cars, counting time as of no account. And when he had found the heart of a city and listened to its secret confession, he strayed on, restless, to another. Fickle Raggles!—But perhaps he had not met the civic corporation that could engage and hold his critical fancy.

Through the ancient poets we have learned that the cities are feminine. So they were to poet Raggles; and his mind carried a concrete and clear conception of the figure that symbolized and typified each one that he had wooed.

Chicago seemed to swoop down upon him with a breezy suggestion of Mrs. Partington, plumes and patchouli, and to disturb his rest with a soaring and beautiful song of future promise. But Raggles would awake to a sense of shivering cold and a haunting impression of ideals lost in a depressing aura of potato salad and fish.

Thus Chicago affected him. Perhaps there is a vagueness and inaccuracy in the description; but that is Raggles's fault. He should have recorded his sensations in magazine poems.

Pittsburg impressed him as the play of "Othello" performed in the Russian language in a railroad station by Dockstader's minstrels. A royal and generous lady this Pittsburg, though—homely, hearty, with flushed face, washing the dishes in a silk dress and white kid slippers, and bidding Raggles sit before the roaring fireplace and drink champagne with his pigs' feet and fried potatoes.

New Orleans had simply gazed down upon him from a balcony. He could see her pensive, starry eyes and catch the flutter of her fan, and that was all. Only once he came face to face with her. It was at dawn, when she was flushing the red bricks of the banquette with a pail of water. She laughed and hummed a chansonette and filled Raggles's shoes with ice-cold water. Allons!

Boston construed herself to the poetic Raggles in an erratic and singular way. It seemed to him that he had drunk cold tea and that the city was a white, cold cloth that had been bound tightly around his brow to spur him to some unknown but tremendous mental effort. And, after all, he came to shovel snow for a livelihood; and the cloth, becoming wet, tightened its knots and could not be removed.

Indefinite and unintelligible ideas, you will say; but your disapprobation should be tempered with gratitude, for these are poets' fancies—and suppose you had come upon them in verse!

One day Raggles came and laid siege to the heart of the great city of Manhattan. She was the greatest of all; and he wanted to learn her note in the scale; to taste and appraise and classify and solve and label her and arrange her with the other cities that had given him up the secret of their individuality. And here we cease to be Raggles's translator and become his chronicler.

Raggles landed from a ferry-boat one morning and walked into the core of the town with the blasée air of a cosmopolite. He was dressed with care to play the *rôle* of an "unidentified man." No country, race, class, clique, union, party clan or bowling association could have claimed him. His clothing, which had been donated to him piece-meal by citizens of different height, but same number of inches around the heart, was not yet as uncomfortable to his figure as those speciments of raiment, self-measured, that are railroaded to you by transcontinental tailors with a suit case, suspenders, silk handkerchief and pearl studs as a bonus. Without money—as a poet should be—but with the ardor of an astronomer discovering a new star in the chorus of the milky way, or a man who has seen ink suddenly flow from his fountain pen, Raggles wandered into the great city.

Late in the afternoon he drew out of the roar and commotion with a look of dumb terror on his countenance. He was defeated, puzzled, discomfited, frightened. Other cities had been to him as long primer to read; as country maidens quickly to fathom; as send-price-of-subscription-with-answer rebuses to solve; as oyster cocktails to swallow; but here was one as cold, glittering, serene, impossible as a four-carat diamond in a window to a lover outside fingering damply in his pocket his ribbon-counter salary.

The greetings of the other cities he had known—their homespun kindliness, their human gamut of rough charity, friendly curses, garrulous curiosity and easily estimated credulity or indifference. This city of Manhattan gave him no clue; it was walled against him. Like a river of adamant it flowed past him in the streets. Never an eye was turned upon him; no voice spoke to him. His heart yearned for the clap of Pittsburg's sooty hand on his shoulder; for Chicago's menacing but social yawp in his ear; for the pale and eleemosynary stare through the Bostonian eyeglass—even for the precipitate but unmalicious boot-toe of Louisville or St. Louis.

On Broadway Raggles, successful suitor of many cities, stood, bashful, like any country swain. For the first time he experienced the poignant humiliation of being ignored. And when he tried to reduce this brilliant, swiftly changing, ice-cold city to a formula he failed utterly. Poet though he was, it offered him no color similes, no points of comparison, no flaw in its polished facets, no handle by which he could hold it up and view its shape and structure, as he familiarly and often contemptuously had done with other towns. The houses were interminable ramparts loopholed for defense; the people were bright but bloodless specters passing in sinister and selfish array.

The thing that weighed heaviest on Raggles's soul and clogged his poet's fancy was the spirit of absolute egotism that seemed to saturate the people as toys are saturated with paint. Each one that he considered appeared a monster of abominable and insolent conceit. Humanity was gone from them; they were toddling idols of stone and varnish, worshiping themselves and greedy for though oblivious of worship from their fellow graven images. Frozen, cruel, implacable, impervious, cut to an identical pattern, they hurried on their ways like statues brought by some miracles to motion, while soul and feeling lay unaroused in the reluctant marble.

Gradually Raggles became conscious of certain types. One was an elderly gentleman with a snow-white, short beard, pink, unwrinkled face and stony, sharp blue eyes, attired in the fashion of a gilded youth, who seemed to personify the city's wealth, ripeness and frigid unconcern. Another type was a woman, tall, beautiful, clear as a steel engraving, goddess-like, calm, clothed like the princesses of old, with eyes as coldly blue as the reflection of sunlight on a glacier. And another was a by-product of this town of marionettes—a broad, swaggering, grim, threateningly sedate fellow, with a jowl as large as a harvested wheat field, the complexion of a baptized infant and the knuckles of a prize-fighter. This type leaned against cigar signs and viewed the world with frappéd contumely.

A poet is a sensitive creature, and Raggles soon shrivelled in the bleak embrace of the undecipherable. The chill, sphinx-like, ironical, illegible, unnatural, ruthless expression of the city left him downcast and bewildered. Had it no heart? Better the woodpile, the scolding of vinegar-faced housewives at back doors, the kindly spleen of bartenders behind provincial free-lunch counters, the amiable truculence of rural constables, the kicks, arrests and happy-go-lucky chances of the other vulgar, loud, crude cities than this freezing heartlessness.

Raggles summoned his courage and sought alms from the populace. Unheeding, regardless, they passed on without the wink of an eyelash to testify that they were conscious of his existence. And then he said to himself that this fair but pitiless city of Manhattan was without a soul; that its inhabitants were manikins moved by wires and springs, and that he was alone in a great wilderness.

Raggles started to cross the street. There was a blast, a roar, a hissing and a crash as something struck him and hurled him over and over six yards from where he had been. As he was coming down like the stick of a rocket the earth and all the cities thereof turned to a fractured dream.

Raggles opened his eyes. First an odor made itself known to him—an odor of the earliest spring flowers of Paradise. And then a hand soft as a falling petal touched his brow. Bending over him was the woman clothed like the princess of old, with blue eyes, now soft and humid with human sympathy. Under his head on the pavement were silks and furs. With Raggles's hat in his hand and with his face pinker than ever from a vehement burst of oratory against reckless driving, stood the elderly gentleman who personified the city's wealth and ripeness. From a nearby café hurried the by-product with the vast jowl and baby complexion, bearing a glass full of a crimson fluid that suggested delightful possibilities.

"Drink dis, sport," said the by-product, holding the glass to Raggles's lips.

Hundreds of people huddled around in a moment, their faces wearing the deepest concern. Two flattering and gorgeous policemen got into the circle and pressed back the overplus of Samaritans. An old lady in a black shawl spoke loudly of camphor; a newsboy slipped one of his papers beneath Raggles's elbow, where it lay on the muddy pavement. A brisk young man with a notebook was asking for names.

A bell clanged importantly, and the ambulance cleaned a lane through the crowd. A cool surgeon slipped into the midst of affairs.

"How do you feel, old man?" asked the surgeon, stooping easily to his task. The princess of silks and satins wiped a red drop or two from Raggles's brow with a fragrant cobweb.

"Me?" said Raggles, with a seraphic smile, "I feel fine."

He had found the heart of his new city.

In three days they let him leave his cot for the convalescent ward in the hospital. He had been in there an hour when the attendants heard sounds of conflict. Upon investigation they found that Raggles had assaulted and damaged a brother convalescent—a glowering transient whom a freight train collision had sent in to be patched up.

"What's all this about?" inquired the head nurse.

"He was runnin' down me town," said Raggles.

"What town?" asked the nurse.

"Noo York," said Raggles.

22

The Pendulum

"Eighty-first street—let 'em out, please," yelled the shepherd in blue.

A flock of citizen sheep scrambled out and another flock scrambled aboard. Ding-ding! The cattle cars of the Manhattan Elevated rattled away, and John Perkins drifted down the stairway of the station with the released flock.

John walked slowly toward his flat. Slowly, because in the lexicon of his daily life there was no such word as "perhaps." There are no surprises awaiting a man who has been married two years and lives in a flat. As he walked John Perkins prophesied to himself with gloomy and downtrodden cynicism the foregone conclusions of the monotonous day.

Katy would meet him at the door with a kiss flavored with cold cream and butter-scotch. He would remove his coat, sit upon a macadamized lounge and read, in the evening paper, of Russians and Japs slaughtered by the deadly linotype. For dinner there would be pot roast, a salad flavored with a dressing warranted not to crack or injure the leather, stewed rhubarb and the bottle of strawberry marmalade blushing at the certificate of chemical purity on its label. After dinner Katy would show him the new patch in her crazy quilt that the iceman had cut for her off the end of his four-in-hand. At half-past seven they would spread newspapers over the furniture to catch the pieces of plastering that fell when the fat man in the flat overhead began to take his physical culture exercises. Exactly at eight Hickey & Mooney, of the vaudeville team (unbooked) in the flat across the hall, would yield to the gentle influence of *delirium tremens* and begin to overturn chairs under the delusion that Hammerstein was pursuing them with a five-hundred-dollar-a-week contract. Then the gent at the window across the air-shaft would get out his flute; the nightly gas leak would steal forth to frolic in the highways; the dumbwaiter would slip off its trolley; the janitor would drive Mrs. Zanowitski's five children once more across the Yalu, the lady with the champagne shoes and the Skye terrier would trip downstairs and paste her Thursday name over her bell and letter-box—and the evening routine of the Frogmore flats would be under way.

John Perkins knew these things would happen. And he knew that at a quarter past eight he would summon his nerve and reach for his hat, and that his wife would deliver this speech in a querulous tone:

"Now, where are you going, I'd like to know, John Perkins?"

"Thought I'd drop up to McCloskey's," he would answer, "and play a game or two of pool with the fellows."

Of late such had been John Perkins's habit. At ten or eleven he would return. Sometimes Katy would be asleep; sometimes waiting up, ready to melt in the crucible of her ire a little more gold plating from the wrought steel chains of matrimony. For these things Cupid will have to answer when he stands at the bar of justice with his victims from the Frogmore flats.

Tonight John Perkins encountered a tremendous upheaval of the commonplace when he reached his door. No Katy was there with her affectionate, confectionate kiss. The three rooms seemed in portentous disorder. All about lay her things in confusion. Shoes in the middle of the floor, curling tongs, hair bows, kimonos, powder box, jumbled together on dresser and chairs—this was not Katy's way. With a sinking heart John saw the comb with a curling cloud of her brown hair among its teeth.

Some unusual hurry and perturbation must have possessed her, for she always carefully placed these combings in the little blue vase on the mantel to be some day formed into the coveted feminine "rat."

Hanging conspicuously to the gas jet by a string was a folded paper. John seized it. It was a note from his wife running thus:

Dear John: I just had a telegram saying mother is very sick. I am going to take the 4.30 train. Brother Sam is going to meet me at the depot there. There is cold mutton in the ice box. I hope it isn't her quinzy again. Pay the milkman 50 cents. She had it bad last spring. Don't forget to write to the company about the gas meter, and your good socks are in the top drawer. I will write tomorrow.
Hastily, KATY.

Never during their two years of matrimony had he and Katy been separated for a night. John read the note over and over in a dumbfounded way. Here was a break in a routine that had never varied, and it left him dazed.

There on the back of a chair hung, pathetically empty and formless, the red wrapper with black dots that she always wore while getting the meals. Her week-day clothes had been tossed here and there in her haste. A little paper bag of her favorite butter-scotch lay with its string yet unwound. A daily paper sprawled on the floor, gaping rectangularly where a railroad time-table had been clipped from it. Everything in the room spoke of a loss, of an essence gone, of its soul and life departed. John Perkins stood among the dead remains with a queer feeling of desolation in his heart.

He began to set the rooms tidy as well as he could. When he touched her clothes a thrill of something like terror went through him. He had never thought what existence would be without Katy. She had become so thoroughly annealed into his life that she was like the air he breathed—necessary but scarcely noticed. Now, without warning, she was gone, vanished, as completely absent as if she had never existed. Of course it would be only for a few days, or at most a week or two, but it seemed to him as if the very hand of death had pointed a finger at his secure and uneventful home.

John dragged the cold mutton from the ice-box, made coffee and sat down to a lonely meal face to face with the strawberry marmalade's shameless certificate of purity. Bright among withdrawn blessings now appeared to him the ghosts of pot roasts and the salad with tan polish dressing. His home was dismantled. A quinzied mother-in-law had knocked his *lares and penates* sky-high. After his solitary meal John sat at a front window.

He did not care to smoke. Outside the city roared to him to come join in its dance of folly and pleasure. The night was his. He might go forth unquestioned and thrum the strings of jollity as free as any gay bachelor there. He might carouse and wander and have his fling until dawn if he liked; and there would be no wrathful Katy waiting for him, bearing the chalice that held the dregs of his joy. He might play pool at McCloskey's with his roistering friends until Aurora dimmed the electric bulbs if he chose. The hymeneal strings that had curbed him always when the Frogmore flats had palled upon him were loosened. Katy was gone.

John Perkins was not accustomed to analyzing his emotions. But as he sat in his Katy-bereft 10×12 parlor he hit unerringly upon the keynote of his discomfort. He knew now that Katy was necessary to his happiness. His feeling for her, lulled into unconsciousness by the dull round of domesticity, had been sharply stirred by the loss of her presence. Has it not been dinned into us by proverb and sermon and fable that we never prize the music till the sweet-voiced bird has flown—or in other no less florid and true utterances?

"I'm a double-dyed dub," mused John Perkins, "the way I've been treating Katy. Off every night playing pool and bumming with the boys instead of staying home with her. The poor girl here all alone with nothing to amuse her, and me acting that way! John Perkins, you're the worst kind of a shine. I'm going to make it up for the little girl. I'll take her out and let her see some amusement. And I'll cut out the McCloskey gang right from this minute."

Yes, there was the city roaring outside for John Perkins to come dance in the train of Momus. And at McCloskey's the boys were knocking the balls idly into the pockets against the hour for the nightly game. But no primrose way nor clicking cue could woo the remorseful soul of Perkins the bereft. The thing that was his, lightly held and half scorned, had been taken away from him, and he wanted it. Backward to a certain man named Adam, whom the cherubim bounced from the orchard, could Perkins, the remorseful, trace his descent.

Near the right hand of John Perkins stood a chair. On the back of it stood Katy's blue shirtwaist. It still retained something of her contour. Midway of the sleeves were fine, individual wrinkles made by the movements of her arms in working for his comfort and pleasure. A delicate but impelling odor of bluebells came from it. John took it and looked long and soberly at the unresponsive grenadine. Katy had never been unresponsive. Tears:—yes, tears—came into John Perkins's eyes. When she came back things would be different. He would make up for all his neglect. What was life without her?

The door opened. Katy walked in carrying a little hand satchel. John stared at her stupidly.

"My! I'm glad to get back," said Katy. "Ma wasn't sick to amount to anything. Sam was at the depot, and said she just had a little spell, and got all right soon after they telegraphed. So I took the next train back. I'm just dying for a cup of coffee."

Nobody heard the click and rattle of the cog-wheels as the third-floor front of the Frogmore flats buzzed its machinery back into the Order of Things. A band slipped, a spring was touched, the gear was adjusted and the wheels revolve in their old orbit.

John Perkins looked at the clock. It was 8.15. He reached for his hat and walked to the door.

"Now, where are you going, I'd like to know, John Perkins?" asked Katy, in a querulous tone.

"Thought I'd drop up to McCloskey's," said John, "and play a game or two of pool with the fellows."

23

The Pimienta Pancakes

While we were rounding up a bunch of the Triangle-O cattle in the Frio bottoms a projecting branch of a dead mesquite caught my wooden stirrup and gave my ankle a wrench that laid me up in camp for a week.

On the third day of my compulsory idleness I crawled out near the grub wagon, and reclined helpless under the conversational fire of Judson Odom, the camp cook. Jud was a monologist by nature, whom Destiny, with customary blundering, had set in a profession wherein he was bereaved, for the greater portion of his time, of an audience.

Therefore, I was manna in the desert of Jud's obmutescence.

Betimes I was stirred by invalid longings for something to eat that did not come under the caption of "grub." I had visions of the maternal pantry "deep as first love, and wild with all regret," and then I asked:

"Jud, can you make pancakes?"

Jud laid down his six-shooter, with which he was preparing to pound an antelope steak, and stood over me in what I felt to be a menacing attitude. He further endorsed my impression that his pose was resentful by fixing upon me with his light blue eyes a look of cold suspicion.

"Say, you," he said, with candid, though not excessive, choler, "did you mean that straight, or was you trying to throw the gaff into me? Some of the boys been telling you about me and that pancake racket?"

"No, Jud," I said, sincerely, "I meant it. It seems to me I'd swap my pony and saddle for a stack of buttered brown pancakes with some first crop, open kettle, New Orleans sweetening. Was there a story about pancakes?"

Jud was mollified at once when he saw that I had not been dealing in allusions. He brought some mysterious bags and tin boxes from the grub wagon and set them in the shade of the hackberry where I lay reclined. I watched him as he began to arrange them leisurely and untie their many strings.

"No, not a story," said Jud, as he worked, "but just the logical disclosures in the case of me and that pink-eyed snoozer from Mired Mule Canada and Miss Willella Learight. I don't mind telling you.

"I was punching then for old Bill Toomey, on the San Miguel. One day I gets all ensnared up in aspirations for to eat some canned grub that hasn't ever mooed or baaed or grunted or been in peck measures. So, I gets on my bronc and pushes the wind for Uncle Emsley Telfair's store at the Pimienta Crossing on the Nueces.

"About three in the afternoon I throwed my bridle rein over a mesquite limb and walked the last twenty yards into Uncle Emsley's store. I got up on the counter and told Uncle Emsley that the signs pointed to the devastation of the fruit crop of the world. In a minute I had a bag of crackers and a long-handled spoon, with an open can each of apricots and pineapples and cherries and greengages beside of me with Uncle Emsley busy chopping away with the hatchet at the yellow clings. I was feeling like Adam before the apple stampede, and was digging my spurs into the side of the counter and working with my twenty-four-inch spoon when I happened to look out of the window into the yard of Uncle Emsley's house, which was next to the store.

"There was a girl standing there—an imported girl with fixings on— philandering with a croquet maul and amusing herself by watching my style of encouraging the fruit canning industry.

"I slid off the counter and delivered up my shovel to Uncle Emsley.

"'That's my niece,' says he; 'Miss Willella Learight, down from Palestine on a visit. Do you want that I should make you acquainted?'

"'The Holy Land,' I says to myself, my thoughts milling some as I tried to run 'em into the corral. 'Why not? There was sure angels in Pales—Why, yes, Uncle Emsley,' I says out loud, 'I'd be awful edified to meet Miss Learight.'

"So Uncle Emsley took me out in the yard and gave us each other's entitlements.

"I never was shy about women. I never could understand why some men who can break a mustang before breakfast and shave in the dark, get all left-handed and full of perspiration and excuses when they see a bold of calico draped around what belongs to it. Inside of eight minutes me and Miss Willella was aggravating the croquet balls around as amiable as second cousins. She gave me a dig about the quantity of canned fruit I had eaten, and I got back at her, flat-footed, about how a certain lady named Eve started the fruit trouble in the first free-grass pasture—'Over in Palestine, wasn't it?' says I, as easy and pat as roping a one-year-old.

"That was how I acquired cordiality for the proximities of Miss Willella Learight; and the disposition grew larger as time passed. She was stopping at Pimienta Crossing for her health, which was very good, and for the climate, which was forty per cent hotter than Palestine. I rode over to see her once every week for a while; and then I figured it out that if I doubled the number of trips I would see her twice as often.

"One week I slipped in a third trip; and that's where the pancakes and the pink-eyed snoozer busted into the game.

"That evening, while I set on the counter with a peach and two damsons in my mouth, I asked Uncle Emsley how Miss Willella was.

"'Why,' says Uncle Emsley, 'she's gone riding with Jackson Bird, the sheep man from over at Mired Mule Canada.'

"I swallowed the peach seed and the two damson seeds. I guess somebody held the counter by the bridle while I got off; and then I walked out straight ahead till I butted against the mesquite where my roan was tied.

"'She's gone riding,' I whisper in my bronc's ear, 'with Birdstone Jack, the hired mule from Sheep Man's Canada. Did you get that, old Leather-and-Gallops?'

"That bronc of mine wept, in his way. He'd been raised a cow pony and he didn't care for snoozers.

"I went back and said to Uncle Emsley: 'Did you say a sheep man?'

"'I said a sheep man,' says Uncle Emsley again. 'You must have heard tell of Jackson Bird. He's got eight sections of grazing and four thousand head of the finest Merinos south of the Arctic Circle.'

"I went out and sat on the ground in the shade of the store and leaned against a prickly pear. I sifted sand into my boots with unthinking hands while I soliloquized a quantity about this bird with the Jackson plumage to his name.

"I never had believed in harming sheep men. I see one, one day, reading a Latin grammar on hossback, and I never touched him! They never irritated me like they do most cowmen. You wouldn't go to work now, and impair and disfigure snoozers, would you, that eat on tables and wear little shoes and speak to you on subjects? I had always let 'em pass, just as you would a jack-rabbit; with a polite word and a guess about the weather, but no stopping to swap canteens. I never thought it was worth while to be hostile with a snoozer. And because I'd been lenient, and let 'em live, here was one going around riding with Miss Willella Learight!

"An hour by sun they come loping back, and stopped at Uncle Emsley's gate. The sheep person helped her off; and they stood throwing each other sentences all sprightful and sagacious for a while. And then this feathered Jackson flies up in his saddle and raises his little stew-pot of a hat, and trots off in the direction of his mutton ranch. By this time I had turned the sand out of my boots and unpinned myself from the prickly pear; and by the time he gets half a mile out of Pimienta, I singlefoots up beside him on my bronc.

"I said that snoozer was pink-eyed, but he wasn't. His seeing arrangement was grey enough, but his eye-lashes was pink and his hair was sandy, and that gave you the idea. Sheep man?—he wasn't more than a lamb man, anyhow—a little thing with his neck involved in a yellow silk handkerchief, and shoes tied up in bow-knots.

"'Afternoon!' says I to him. 'You now ride with a equestrian who is commonly called Dead-Moral-Certainty Judson, on account of the way I shoot. When I want a stranger to know me I always introduce myself before the draw, for I never did like to shake hands with ghosts.'

"'Ah,' says he, just like that—'Ah, I'm glad to know you, Mr. Judson. I'm Jackson Bird, from over at Mired Mule Ranch.'

"Just then one of my eyes saw a roadrunner skipping down the hill with a young tarantula in his bill, and the other eye noticed a rabbit-hawk sitting on a dead limb in a water-elm. I popped over one after the other with my forty-five, just to show him. 'Two out of three,' says I. 'Birds just naturally seem to draw my fire wherever I go.'

"'Nice shooting,' says the sheep man, without a flutter. 'But don't you sometimes ever miss the third shot? Elegant fine rain that was last week for the young grass, Mr. Judson?' says he.

"'Willie,' says I, riding over close to his palfrey, 'your infatuated parents may have denounced you by the name of Jackson, but you sure moulted into a twittering Willie—let us slough off this here analysis of rain and the elements, and get down to talk that is outside the vocabulary of parrots. That is a bad habit you have got of riding with young ladies over at Pimienta. I've known birds,' says I, 'to be served on toast for less than that. Miss Willella,' says I, 'don't ever want any nest made out of sheep's wool by a tomtit of the Jacksonian branch of ornithology. Now, are you going to quit, or do you wish for to gallop up against this Dead-Moral-Certainty attachment to my name, which is good for two hyphens and at least one set of funeral obsequies?'

"Jackson Bird flushed up some, and then he laughed.

"'Why, Mr. Judson,' says he, 'you've got the wrong idea. I've called on Miss Learight a few times; but not for the purpose you imagine. My object is purely a gastronomical one.'

"I reached for my gun.

"'Any coyote,' says I, 'that would boast of dishonorable—'

"'Wait a minute,' says this Bird, 'till I explain. What would I do with a wife? If you ever saw that ranch of mine! I do my own cooking and mending. Eating—that's all the pleasure I get out of sheep raising. Mr. Judson, did you ever taste the pancakes that Miss Learight makes?'

"'Me? No,' I told him. 'I never was advised that she was up to any culinary maneuvers.'

"'They're golden sunshine,' says he, 'honey-browned by the ambrosial fires of Epicurus. I'd give two years of my life to get the recipe for making them pancakes. That's what I went to see Miss Learight for,' says Jackson Bird, 'but I haven't been able to get it from her. It's an old recipe that's been in the family for seventy-five years. They hand it down from one generation to another, but they don't give it away to outsiders. If I could get that recipe, so I could make them pancakes for myself on my ranch, I'd be a happy man,' says Bird.

"'Are you sure,' I says to him, 'that it ain't the hand that mixes the pancakes that you're after?'

"'Sure,' says Jackson. 'Miss Learight is a mighty nice girl, but I can assure you my intentions go no further than the gastro—' but he seen my hand going down to my holster and he changed his similitude—'than the desire to procure a copy of the pancake recipe,' he finishes.

"'You ain't such a bad little man,' says I, trying to be fair.'I was thinking some of making orphans of your sheep, but I'll let you fly away this time. But you stick to pancakes,' says I, 'as close as the middle one of a stack; and don't go and mistake sentiments for syrup, or there'll be singing at your ranch, and you won't hear it.'

"'To convince you that I am sincere,' says the sheep man, 'I'll ask you to help me. Miss Learight and you being closer friends, maybe she would do for you what she wouldn't for me. If you will get me a copy of that pancake recipe, I give you my word that I'll never call upon her again.'

"'That's fair,' I says, and I shook hands with Jackson Bird. 'I'll get it for you if I can, and glad to oblige.' And he turned off down the big pear flat on the Piedra, in the direction of Mired Mule; and I steered northwest for old Bill Toomey's ranch.

"It was five days afterward when I got another chance to ride over to Pimienta. Miss Willella and me passed a gratifying evening at Uncle Emsley's. She sang some, and exasperated the piano quite a lot with quotations from the operas. I gave imitations of a rattlesnake, and told her about Snaky McFee's new way of skinning cows, and described the trip I made to Saint Louis once. We was getting along in one another's estimations fine. Thinks I, if Jackson Bird can now be persuaded to migrate, I win. I recollect his promise about the pancake receipt, and I thinks I will persuade it from Miss Willella and give it to him; and then if I catches Birdie off of Mired Mule again, I'll make him hop the twig.

"So, along about ten o'clock, I put on a wheedling smile and says to Miss Willella: 'Now, if there's anything I do like better than the sight of a red steer on green grass it's the taste of a nice hot pancake smothered in sugar-house molasses.'

"Miss Willella gives a little jump on the piano stool, and looked at me curious.

"'Yes,' says she, 'they're real nice. What did you say was the name of that street in Saint Louis, Mr. Odom, where you lost your hat?'

"'Pancake Avenue,' says I, with a wink, to show her that I was on about the family receipt, and couldn't be side-corralled off of the subject. 'Come, now, Miss Willella,' I says; 'let's hear how you make 'em. Pancakes is just whirling in my head like wagon wheels. Start her off, now—pound of flour, eight dozen eggs, and so on. How does the catalogue of constituents run?'

"'Excuse me for a moment, please,' says Miss Willella, and she gives me a quick kind of sideways look, and slides off the stool. She ambled out into the other room, and directly Uncle Emsley comes in in his shirt sleeves, with a pitcher of water. He turns around to get a glass on the table, and I see a forty-five in his hip pocket. 'Great post-holes!' thinks I, 'but here's a family thinks a heap of cooking receipts, protecting it with firearms. I've known outfits that wouldn't do that much by a family feud.'

"'Drink this here down,' says Uncle Emsley, handing me the glass of water. 'You've rid too far today, Jud, and got yourself over-excited. Try to think about something else now.'

"'Do you know how to make them pancakes, Uncle Emsley?' I asked.

"'Well, I'm not as apprised in the anatomy of them as some,' says Uncle Emsley, 'but I reckon you take a sifter of plaster of Paris and a little dough and saleratus and corn meal, and mix 'em with eggs and buttermilk as usual. Is old Bill going to ship beeves to Kansas City again this spring, Jud?'

"That was all the pancake specifications I could get that night. I didn't wonder that Jackson Bird found it uphill work. So I dropped the subject and talked with Uncle Emsley for a while about hollow-horn and cyclones. And then Miss Willella came and said 'Good-night,' and I hit the breeze for the ranch.

"About a week afterward I met Jackson Bird riding out of Pimienta as I rode in, and we stopped on the road for a few frivolous remarks.

"'Got the bill of particulars for them flapjacks yet?' I asked him.

"'Well, no,' says Jackson. 'I don't seem to have any success in getting hold of it. Did you try?'

"'I did,' says I, 'and 'twas like trying to dig a prairie dog out of his hole with a peanut hull. That pancake receipt must be a jookalorum, the way they hold on to it.'

"'I'm most ready to give it up,' says Jackson, so discouraged in his pronunciations that I felt sorry for him; 'but I did want to know how to make them pancakes to eat on my lonely ranch,' says he. 'I lie awake at nights thinking how good they are.'

"'You keep on trying for it,' I tells him, 'and I'll do the same. One of us is bound to get a rope over its horns before long. Well, so-long, Jacksy.'

"You see, by this time we were on the peacefullest of terms. When I saw that he wasn't after Miss Willella, I had more endurable contemplations of that sandy-haired snoozer. In order to help out the ambitions of his appetite I kept on trying to get that receipt from Miss Willella. But every time I would say 'pancakes' she would get sort of remote and fidgety about the eye, and try to change the subject. If I held her to it she would slide out and round up Uncle Emsley with his pitcher of water and hip-pocket howitzer.

"One day I galloped over to the store with a fine bunch of blue verbenas that I cut out of a herd of wild flowers over on Poisoned Dog Prairie. Uncle Emsley looked at 'em with one eye shut and says:

"'Haven't ye heard the news?'

"'Cattle up?' I asks.

"'Willella and Jackson Bird was married in Palestine yesterday,' says he. 'Just got a letter this morning.'

"I dropped them flowers in a cracker-barrel, and let the news trickle in my ears and down toward my upper left-hand shirt pocket until it got to my feet.

"'Would you mind saying that over again once more, Uncle Emsley?' says I. 'Maybe my hearing has got wrong, and you only said that prime heifers was 4.80 on the hoof, or something like that.'

"'Married yesterday,' says Uncle Emsley, 'and gone to Waco and Niagara Falls on a wedding tour. Why, didn't you see none of the signs all along? Jackson Bird has been courting Willella ever since that day he took her out riding.'

"'Then,' says I, in a kind of yell, 'what was all this zizzaparoola he gives me about pancakes? Tell me *that*.'

"When I said 'pancakes' Uncle Emsley sort of dodged and stepped back.

"'Somebody's been dealing me pancakes from the bottom of the deck,' I says, 'and I'll find out. I believe you know. Talk up,' says I, 'or we'll mix a panful of batter right here.'

"I slid over the counter after Uncle Emsley. He grabbed at his gun, but it was in a drawer, and he missed it two inches. I got him by the front of his shirt and shoved him in a corner.

"'Talk pancakes,' says I, 'or be made into one. Does Miss Willella make 'em?'

"'She never made one in her life and I never saw one,' says Uncle Emsley, soothing. 'Calm down now, Jud—calm down. You've got excited, and that wound in your head is contaminating your sense of intelligence. Try not to think about pancakes.'

"'Uncle Emsley,' says I, 'I'm not wounded in the head except so far as my natural cognitive instincts run to runts. Jackson Bird told me he was calling on Miss Willella for the purpose of finding out her system of producing pancakes, and he asked me to help him get the bill of lading of the ingredients. I done so, with the results as you see. Have I been sodded down with Johnson grass by a pink-eyed snoozer, or what?'

"'Slack up your grip in my dress shirt,' says Uncle Emsley, 'and I'll tell you. Yes, it looks like Jackson Bird has gone and humbugged you some. The day after he went riding with Willella he came back and told me and her to watch out for you whenever you got to talking about pancakes. He said you was in camp once where they was cooking flapjacks, and one of the fellows cut you over the head with a frying pan. Jackson said that whenever you got overhot or excited that wound hurt you and made you kind of crazy, and you went raving about pancakes. He told us to just get you worked off of the subject and soothed down, and you wouldn't be dangerous. So, me and Willella done the best by you we knew how. Well, well,' says Uncle Emsley, 'that Jackson Bird is sure a seldom kind of a snoozer.'"

During the progress of Jud's story he had been slowly but deftly combining certain portions of the contents of his sacks and cans. Toward the close of it he set before me the finished product—a pair of red-hot, rich-hued pancakes on a tin plate. From some secret hoarding he also brought a lump of excellent butter and a bottle of golden syrup.

"How long ago did these things happen?" I asked him.

"Three years," said Jud. "They're living on the Mired Mule Ranch now. But I haven't seen either of 'em since. They say Jackson Bird was fixing his ranch up fine with rocking chairs and window curtains all the time he was putting me up the pancake tree. Oh, I got over it after a while. But the boys kept the racket up."

"Did you make these cakes by the famous recipe?" I asked.

"Didn't I tell you there wasn't no receipt?" said Jud. "The boys hollered pancakes till they got pancake hungry, and I cut this recipe out of a newspaper. How does the truck taste?"

"They're delicious," I answered. "Why don't you have some, too, Jud?"

I was sure I heard a sigh.

"Me?" said Jud. "I don't ever eat 'em."

24

The Ransom of Mack

Me and old Mack Lonsbury, we got out of that Little Hide-and-Seek gold mine affair with about $40,000 apiece. I say "old" Mack; but he wasn't old. Forty-one, I should say; but he always seemed old.

"Andy," he says to me, "I'm tired of hustling. You and me have been working hard together for three years. Say we knock off for a while, and spend some of this idle money we've coaxed our way."

"The proposition hits me just right," says I. "Let's be nabobs for a while and see how it feels. What'll we do—take in the Niagara Falls, or buck at faro?"

"For a good many years," says Mack, "I've thought that if I ever had extravagant money I'd rent a two-room cabin somewhere, hire a Chinaman to cook, and sit in my stocking feet and read Buckle's *History of Civilization*."

"That sounds self-indulgent and gratifying without vulgar ostentation," says I; "and I don't see how money could be better invested. Give me a cuckoo clock and a Sep Winner's Self-Instructor for the Banjo, and I'll join you."

A week afterwards me and Mack hits this small town of Pina, about thirty miles out from Denver, and finds an elegant two-room house that just suits us. We deposited half-a-peck of money in the Pina bank and shook hands with every one of the 340 citizens in the town. We brought along the Chinaman and the cuckoo clock and Buckle and the Instructor with us from Denver; and they made the cabin seem like home at once.

Never believe it when they tell you riches don't bring happiness. If you could have seen old Mack sitting in his rocking-chair with his blue-yarn sock feet up in the window and absorbing in that Buckle stuff through his specs you'd have seen a picture of content that would have made Rockefeller jealous. And I was learning to pick out "Old Zip Coon" on the banjo, and the cuckoo was on time with his remarks, and Ah Sing was messing up the atmosphere with the handsomest smell of ham and eggs that ever laid the honeysuckle in the shade. When it got too dark to make out Buckle's nonsense and the notes in the Instructor, me and Mack would light our pipes and talk about science and pearl diving and sciatica and Egypt and spelling and fish and trade-winds and leather and gratitude and eagles, and a lot of subjects that we'd never had time to explain our sentiments about before.

One evening Mack spoke up and asked me if I was much apprised in the habits and policies of women folks.

"Why, yes," says I, in a tone of voice; "I know 'em from Alfred to Omaha. The feminine nature and similitude," says I, "is as plain to my sight as the Rocky Mountains is to a blue-eyed burro. I'm onto all their little side-steps and punctual discrepancies."

"I tell you, Andy," says Mack, with a kind of sigh, "I never had the least amount of intersection with their predispositions. Maybe I might have had a proneness in respect to their vicinity, but I never took the time. I made my own living since I was fourteen; and I never seemed to get my ratiocinations equipped with the sentiments usually depicted toward the sect. I sometimes wish I had," says old Mack.

"They're an adverse study," says I, "and adapted to points of view. Although they vary in rationale, I have found 'em quite often obviously differing from each other in divergences of contrast."

"It seems to me," goes on Mack, "that a man had better take 'em in and secure his inspirations of the sect when he's young and so preordained. I let my chance go by; and I guess I'm too old now to go hopping into the curriculum."

"Oh, I don't know," I tells him. "Maybe you better credit yourself with a barrel of money and a lot of emancipation from a quantity of uncontent. Still, I don't regret my knowledge of 'em," I says. "It takes a man who understands the symptoms and by-plays of women-folks to take care of himself in this world."

We stayed on in Pina because we liked the place. Some folks might enjoy their money with noise and rapture and locomotion; but me and Mack we had had plenty of turmoils and hotel towels. The people were friendly; Ah Sing got the swing of the grub we liked; Mack and Buckle were as thick as two body-snatchers, and I was hitting out a cordial resemblance to "Buffalo Gals, Can't You Come Out Tonight," on the banjo.

One day I got a telegram from Speight, the man that was working on a mine I had an interest in out in New Mexico. I had to go out there; and I was gone two months. I was anxious to get back to Pina and enjoy life once more.

When I struck the cabin I nearly fainted. Mack was standing in the door; and if angels ever wept, I saw no reason why they should be smiling then.

That man was a spectacle. Yes; he was worse; he was a spyglass; he was the great telescope in the Lick Observatory. He had on a coat and shiny shoes and a white vest and a high silk hat; and a geranium as big as an order of spinach was spiked onto his front. And he was smirking and warping his face like an infernal storekeeper or a kid with colic.

"Hello, Andy," says Mack, out of his face. "Glad to see you back. Things have happened since you went away."

"I know it," says I, "and a sacrilegious sight it is. God never made you that way, Mack Lonsbury. Why do you scarify His works with this presumptuous kind of ribaldry?"

"Why, Andy," says he, "they've elected me justice of the peace since you left."

I looked at Mack close. He was restless and inspired. A justice of the peace ought to be disconsolate and assuaged.

Just then a young woman passed on the sidewalk; and I saw Mack kind of half snicker and blush, and then he raised up his hat and smiled and bowed, and she smiled and bowed, and went on by.

"No hope for you," says I, "if you've got the Mary-Jane infirmity at your age. I thought it wasn't going to take on you. And patent leather shoes! All this in two little short months!"

"I'm going to marry the young lady who just passed tonight," says Mack, in a kind of flutter.

"I forgot something at the post-office," says I, and walked away quick.

I overtook that young woman a hundred yards away. I raised my hat and told her my name. She was about nineteen; and young for her age. She blushed, and then looked at me cool, like I was the snow scene from the "Two Orphans."

"I understand you are to be married tonight," I said.

"Correct," says she. "You got any objections?"

"Listen, sissy," I begins.

"My name is Miss Rebosa Redd," says she in a pained way.

"I know it," says I. "Now, Rebosa, I'm old enough to have owed money to your father. And that old, specious, dressed-up, garbled, sea-sick ptomaine prancing about avidiously like an irremediable turkey gobbler with patent leather shoes on is my best friend. Why did you go and get him invested in this marriage business?"

"Why, he was the only chance there was," answers Miss Rebosa.

"Nay," says I, giving a sickening look of admiration at her complexion and style of features; "with your beauty you might pick any kind of a man. Listen, Rebosa. Old Mack ain't the man you want. He was twenty- two when you was *née* Reed, as the papers say. This bursting into bloom won't last with him. He's all ventilated with oldness and rectitude and decay. Old Mack's down with a case of Indian summer. He overlooked his bet when he was young; and now he's suing Nature for the interest on the promissory note he took from Cupid instead of the cash. Rebosa, are you bent on having this marriage occur?"

"Why, sure I am," says she, oscillating the pansies on her hat, "and so is somebody else, I reckon."

"What time is it to take place?" I asks.

"At six o'clock," says she.

I made up my mind right away what to do. I'd save old Mack if I could. To have a good, seasoned, ineligible man like that turn chicken for a girl that hadn't quit eating slate pencils and buttoning in the back was more than I could look on with easiness.

"Rebosa," says I, earnest, drawing upon my display of knowledge concerning the feminine intuitions of reason—"ain't there a young man in Pina—a nice young man that you think a heap of?"

"Yep," says Rebosa, nodding her pansies—"Sure there is! What do you think! Gracious!"

"Does he like you?" I asks. "How does he stand in the matter?"

"Crazy," says Rebosa. "Ma has to wet down the front steps to keep him from sitting there all the time. But I guess that'll be all over after tonight," she winds up with a sigh.

"Rebosa," says I, "you don't really experience any of this adoration called love for old Mack, do you?"

"Lord! No," says the girl, shaking her head. "I think he's as dry as a lava bed. The idea!"

"Who is this young man that you like, Rebosa?" I inquires.

"It's Eddie Bayles," says she. "He clerks in Crosby's grocery. But he don't make but thirty-five a month. Ella Noakes was wild about him once."

"Old Mack tells me," I says, "that he's going to marry you at six o'clock this evening."

"That's the time," says she. "It's to be at our house."

"Rebosa," says I, "listen to me. If Eddie Bayles had a thousand dollars cash—a thousand dollars, mind you, would buy him a store of his own—if you and Eddie had that much to excuse matrimony on, would you consent to marry him this evening at five o'clock?"

The girl looks at me a minute; and I can see these inaudible cogitations going on inside of her, as women will.

"A thousand dollars?" says she. "Of course I would."

"Come on," says I. "We'll go and see Eddie."

We went up to Crosby's store and called Eddie outside. He looked to be estimable and freckled; and he had chills and fever when I made my proposition.

"At five o'clock?" says he, "for a thousand dollars? Please don't wake me up! Well, you *are* the rich uncle retired from the spice business in India! I'll buy out old Crosby and run the store myself."

We went inside and got old man Crosby apart and explained it. I wrote my check for a thousand dollars and handed it to him. If Eddie and Rebosa married each other at five he was to turn the money over to them.

And then I gave 'em my blessing, and went to wander in the wild-wood for a season. I sat on a log and made cogitations on life and old age and the zodiac and the ways of women and all the disorder that goes with a lifetime. I passed myself congratulations that I had probably saved my old friend Mack from his attack of Indian summer. I knew when he got well of it and shed his infatuation and his patent leather shoes, he would feel grateful. "To keep old Mack disinvolved," thinks I, "from relapses like this, is worth more than a thousand dollars." And most of all I was glad that I'd made a study of women, and wasn't to be deceived any by their means of conceit and evolution.

It must have been half-past five when I got back home. I stepped in; and there sat old Mack on the back of his neck in his old clothes with his blue socks on the window and the *History of Civilization* propped up on his knees.

"This don't look like getting ready for a wedding at six," I says, to seem innocent.

"Oh," says Mack, reaching for his tobacco, "that was postponed back to five o'clock. They sent me over a note saying the hour had been changed. It's all over now. What made you stay away so long, Andy?"

"You heard about the wedding?" I asks.

"I operated it," says he. "I told you I was justice of the peace. The preacher is off East to visit his folks, and I'm the only one in town that can perform the dispensations of marriage. I promised Eddie and Rebosa a month ago I'd marry 'em. He's a busy lad; and he'll have a grocery of his own some day."

"He will," says I.

"There was lots of women at the wedding," says Mack, smoking up. "But I didn't seem to get any ideas from 'em. I wish I was informed in the structure of their attainments like you said you was."

"That was two months ago," says I, reaching up for the banjo.

25

The Tale of a Tainted Tenner

Money talks. But you may think that the conversation of a little old ten-dollar bill in New York would be nothing more than a whisper. Oh, very well! Pass up this *sotto voce* autobiography of an X if you like. If you are one of the kind that prefers to listen to John D's checkbook roar at you through a megaphone as it passes by, all right. But don't forget that small change can say a word to the point now and then. The next time you tip your grocer's clerk a silver quarter to give you extra weight of his boss's goods read the four words above the lady's head. How are they for repartee?

I am a ten-dollar Treasury note, series of 1901. You may have seen one in a friend's hand. On my face, in the center, is a picture of the bison Americanus, miscalled a buffalo by fifty or sixty millions of Americans. The heads of Capt. Lewis and Capt. Clark adorn the ends. On my back is the graceful figure of Liberty or Ceres or Maxine Elliot standing in the center of the stage on a conservatory plant. My references is—or are—Section 3,588, Revised Statutes. Ten cold, hard dollars—I don't say whether silver, gold, lead or iron—Uncle Sam will hand you over his counter if you want to cash me in.

I beg you will excuse any conversational breaks that I make—thanks, I knew you would—got that sneaking little respect and agreeable feeling toward even an X, haven't you? You see, a tainted bill doesn't have much chance to acquire a correct form of expression. I never knew a really cultured and educated person that could afford to hold a ten-spot any longer than it would take to do an Arthur Duffy to the nearest That's All! sign or delicatessen store.

For a six-year-old, I've had a lively and gorgeous circulation. I guess I've paid as many debts as the man who dies. I've been owned by a good many kinds of people. But a little old ragged, damp, dingy five-dollar silver certificate gave me a jar one day. I was next to it in the fat and bad-smelling purse of a butcher.

"Hey, you Sitting Bull," says I, "don't scrouge so. Anyhow, don't you think it's about time you went in on a customs payment and got reissued? For a series of 1899 you're a sight."

"Oh, don't get crackly just because you're a Buffalo bill," says the fiver. "You'd be limp, too, if you'd been stuffed down in a thick cotton-and-lisle-thread under an elastic all day, and the thermometer not a degree under 85 in the store."

"I never heard of a pocketbook like that," says I. "Who carried you?"

"A shop-girl," says the five-spot.

"What's that?" I had to ask.

"You'll never know till their millennium comes," says the fiver.

Just then a two-dollar bill behind me with a George Washington head, spoke up to the fiver:

"Aw, cut out yer kicks. Ain't lisle thread good enough for yer? If you was under all cotton like I've been today, and choked up with factory dust till the lady with the cornucopia on me sneezed half a dozen times, you'd have some reason to complain."

That was the next day after I arrived in New York. I came in a $500 package of tens to a Brooklyn bank from one of its Pennsylvania correspondents—and I haven't made the acquaintance of any of the five and two spot's friends' pocketbooks yet. Silk for mine, every time.

I was lucky money. I kept on the move. Sometimes I changed hands twenty times a day. I saw the inside of every business;

I fought for my owner's every pleasure. It seemed that on Saturday nights I never missed being slapped down on a bar. Tens were always slapped down, while ones and twos were slid over to the bartenders folded. I got in the habit of looking for mine, and I managed to soak in a little straight or some spilled Martini or Manhattan whenever I could. Once I got tied up in a great greasy roll of bills in a pushcart peddler's jeans. I thought I never would get in circulation again, for the future department store owner lived on eight cents' worth of dog meat and onions a day. But this peddler got into trouble one day on account of having his cart too near a crossing, and I was rescued. I always will feel grateful to the cop that got me. He changed me at a cigar store near the Bowery that was running a crap game in the back room. So it was the Captain of the precinct, after all, that did me the best turn, when he got his. He blew me for wine the next evening in a Broadway restaurant; and I really felt as glad to get back again as an Astor does when he sees the lights of Charing Cross.

A tainted ten certainly does get action on Broadway. I was alimony once, and got folded in a little dog-skin purse among a lot of dimes. They were bragging about the busy times there were in Ossining whenever three girls got hold of one of them during the ice cream season. But it's Slow Moving Vehicles Keep to the Right for the little Bok tips when you think of the way we bison plasters refuse to stick to anything during the rush lobster hour.

The first I ever heard of tainted money was one night when a good thing with a Van to his name threw me over with some other bills to buy a stack of blues.

About midnight a big, easy-going man with a fat face like a monk's and the eye of a janitor with his wages raised took me and a lot of other notes and rolled us into what is termed a "wad" among the money tainters.

"Ticket me for five hundred," said he to the banker, "and look out for everything, Charlie. I'm going out for a stroll in the glen before the moonlight fades from the brow of the cliff. If anybody finds the roof in their way there's $60,000 wrapped in a comic supplement in the upper left-hand corner of the safe. Be bold; everywhere be bold, but be not bowled over. 'Night."

I found myself between two $20 gold certificates. One of 'em says to me:

"Well, old shorthorn, you're in luck tonight. You'll see something of life. Old Jack's going to make the Tenderloin look like a hamburg steak."

"Explain," says I. "I'm used to joints, but I don't care for filet mignon with the kind of sauce you serve."

"'Xcuse me," said the twenty. "Old Jack is the proprietor of this gambling house. He's going on a whiz tonight because he offered $50,000 to a church and it refused to accept it because they said his money was tainted."

"What is a church?" I asked.

"Oh, I forgot," says the twenty, "that I was talking to a tenner. Of course you don't know. You're too much to put into the contribution basket, and not enough to buy anything at a bazaar. A church is—a large building in which pen-wipers and tidies are sold at $20 each."

I don't care much about chinning with gold certificates. There's a streak of yellow in 'em. All is not gold that's quitters.

Old Jack certainly was a gild-edged sport. When it came his time to loosen up he never referred the waiter to an actuary.

By and by it got around that he was smiting the rock in the wilderness; and all along Broadway things with cold noses and hot gullets fell in on our trail. The third Jungle Book was there waiting for somebody to put covers on it. Old Jack's money may have had a taint to it, but all the same he had orders for his Camembert piling up on him every minute. First his friends rallied round him; and then the fellows that his friends knew by sight; and then a few of his enemies buried the hatchet; and finally he was buying souvenirs for so many Neapolitan fisher maidens and butterfly octettes that the head waiters were 'phoning all over town for Julian Mitchell to please come around and get them into some kind of order.

At last we floated into an uptown café that I knew by heart. When the hod-carriers' union in jackets and aprons saw us coming the chief goal kicker called out: "Six—eleven—forty-two—nineteen—twelve" to his men, and they put on nose guards till it was clear whether we meant Port Arthur or Portsmouth. But old Jack wasn't working for the furniture and glass factories that night. He sat down quiet and sang "Ramble" in a half-hearted way. His feelings had been hurt, so the twenty told me, because his offer to the church had been refused.

But the wassail went on; and Brady himself couldn't have hammered the thirst mob into a better imitation of the real penchant for the stuff that you screw out of a bottle with a napkin.

Old Jack paid the twenty above me for a round, leaving me on the outside of his roll. He laid the roll on the table and sent for the proprietor.

"Mike," says he, "here's money that the good people have refused. Will it buy of your wares in the name of the devil? They say it's tainted."

"I will," says Mike, "and I'll put it in the drawer next to the bills that was paid to the parson's daughter for kisses at the church fair to build a new parsonage for the parson's daughter to live in."

At 1 o'clock when the hod-carriers were making ready to close up the front and keep the inside open, a woman slips in the door of the restaurant and comes up to Old Jack's table. You've seen the kind—black shawl, creepy hair, ragged skirt, white face, eyes a cross between Gabriel's and a sick kitten's—the kind of woman that's always on the lookout for an automobile or the mendicancy squad—and she stands there without a word and looks at the money.

Old Jack gets up, peels me off the roll and hands me to her with a bow.

"Madam," says he, just like actors I've heard, "here is a tainted bill. I am a gambler. This bill came to me tonight from a gentleman's son. Where he got it I do not know. If you will do me the favor to accept it, it is yours."

The woman took me with a trembling hand.

"Sir," said she, "I counted thousands of this issue of bills into packages when they were virgin from the presses. I was a clerk in the Treasury Department. There was an official to whom I owed my position. You say they are tainted now. If you only knew—but I won't say any more. Thank you with all my heart, sir—thank you—thank you."

Where do you suppose that woman carried me almost at a run? To a bakery. Away from Old Jack and a sizzling good time to a bakery. And I get changed, and she does a Sheridan-twenty-miles-away with a dozen rolls and a section of jelly cake as big as a turbine water-wheel. Of course I lost sight of her then, for I was snowed up in the bakery, wondering whether I'd get changed at the drug store the next day in an alum deal or paid over to the cement works.

A week afterward I butted up against one of the one-dollar bills the baker had given the woman for change.

"Hallo, E35039669," says I, "weren't you in the change for me in a bakery last Saturday night?"

"Yep," says the solitaire in his free and easy style.

"How did the deal turn out?" I asked.

"She blew E17051431 for mills and round steak," says the one-spot. "She kept me till the rent man came. It was a bum room with a sick kid in it. But you ought to have seen him go for the bread and tincture of formaldehyde. Half-starved, I guess. Then she prayed some. Don't get stuck up, tenner. We one-spots hear ten prayers, where you hear one. She said something about 'who giveth to the poor.' Oh, let's cut out the slum talk. I'm certainly tired of the company that keeps me. I wish I was big enough to move in society with you tainted bills."

"Shut up," says I; "there's no such thing. I know the rest of it. There's a 'lendeth to the Lord' somewhere in it. Now look on my back and read what you see there."

"This note is a legal tender at its face value for all debts public and private."

"This talk about tainted money makes me tired," says I.

26

The Trimmed Lamp

Of course there are two sides to the question. Let us look at the other. We often hear "shop-girls" spoken of. No such persons exist. There are girls who work in shops. They make their living that way. But why turn their occupation into an adjective? Let us be fair. We do not refer to the girls who live on Fifth Avenue as "marriage-girls."

Lou and Nancy were chums. They came to the big city to find work because there was not enough to eat at their homes to go around. Nancy was nineteen; Lou was twenty. Both were pretty, active, country girls who had no ambition to go on the stage.

The little cherub that sits up aloft guided them to a cheap and respectable boarding-house. Both found positions and became wage-earners. They remained chums. It is at the end of six months that I would beg you to step forward and be introduced to them. Meddlesome Reader: My Lady friends, Miss Nancy and Miss Lou. While you are shaking hands please take notice—cautiously—of their attire. Yes, cautiously; for they are as quick to resent a stare as a lady in a box at the horse show is.

Lou is a piece-work ironer in a hand laundry. She is clothed in a badly-fitting purple dress, and her hat plume is four inches too long; but her ermine muff and scarf cost $25, and its fellow beasts will be ticketed in the windows at $7.98 before the season is over. Her cheeks are pink, and her light blue eyes bright. Contentment radiates from her.

Nancy you would call a shop-girl—because you have the habit. There is no type; but a perverse generation is always seeking a type; so this is what the type should be. She has the high-ratted pompadour, and the exaggerated straight-front. Her skirt is shoddy, but has the correct flare. No furs protect her against the bitter spring air, but she wears her short broadcloth jacket as jauntily as though it were Persian lamb! On her face and in her eyes, remorseless type-seeker, is the typical shop-girl expression. It is a look of silent but contemptuous revolt against cheated womanhood; of sad prophecy of the vengeance to come. When she laughs her loudest the look is still there. The same look can be seen in the eyes of Russian peasants; and those of us left will see it some day on Gabriel's face when he comes to blow us up. It is a look that should wither and abash man; but he has been known to smirk at it and offer flowers—with a string tied to them.

Now lift your hat and come away, while you receive Lou's cheery "See you again," and the sardonic, sweet smile of Nancy that seems, somehow, to miss you and go fluttering like a white moth up over the housetops to the stars.

The two waited on the corner for Dan. Dan was Lou's steady company. Faithful? Well, he was on hand when Mary would have had to hire a dozen subpoena servers to find her lamb.

"Ain't you cold, Nance?" said Lou. "Say, what a chump you are for working in that old store for $8. a week! I made $18.50 last week. Of course ironing ain't as swell work as selling lace behind a counter, but it pays. None of us ironers make less than $10. And I don't know that it's any less respectful work, either."

"You can have it," said Nancy, with uplifted nose. "I'll take my eight a week and hall bedroom. I like to be among nice things and swell people. And look what a chance I've got! Why, one of our glove girls married a Pittsburg—steel maker, or blacksmith or something—the other day worth a million dollars. I'll catch a swell myself some time. I ain't bragging on my looks or anything;

but I'll take my chances where there's big prizes offered. What show would a girl have in a laundry?"

"Why, that's where I met Dan," said Lou, triumphantly. "He came in for his Sunday shirt and collars and saw me at the first board, ironing. We all try to get to work at the first board. Ella Maginnis was sick that day, and I had her place. He said he noticed my arms first, how round and white they was. I had my sleeves rolled up. Some nice fellows come into laundries. You can tell 'em by their bringing their clothes in suit cases; and turning in the door sharp and sudden."

"How can you wear a waist like that, Lou?" said Nancy, gazing down at the offending article with sweet scorn in her heavy-lidded eyes. "It shows fierce taste."

"This waist?" cried Lou, with wide-eyed indignation. "Why, I paid $16 for this waist. It's worth twenty-five. A woman left it to be laundered, and never called for it. The boss sold it to me. It's got yards and yards of hand embroidery on it. Better talk about that ugly, plain thing you've got on."

"This ugly, plain thing," said Nancy, calmly, "was copied from one that Mrs. Van Alstyne Fisher was wearing. The girls say her bill in the store last year was $12,000. I made mine, myself. It cost me $1.50. Ten feet away you couldn't tell it from hers."

"Oh, well," said Lou, good-naturedly, "if you want to starve and put on airs, go ahead. But I'll take my job and good wages; and after hours give me something as fancy and attractive to wear as I am able to buy."

But just then Dan came—a serious young man with a ready-made necktie, who had escaped the city's brand of frivolity—an electrician earning 30 dollars per week who looked upon Lou with the sad eyes of Romeo, and thought her embroidered waist a web in which any fly should delight to be caught.

"My friend, Mr. Owens—shake hands with Miss Danforth," said Lou.

"I'm mighty glad to know you, Miss Danforth," said Dan, with outstretched hand. "I've heard Lou speak of you so often."

"Thanks," said Nancy, touching his fingers with the tips of her cool ones, "I've heard her mention you—a few times."

Lou giggled.

"Did you get that handshake from Mrs. Van Alstyne Fisher, Nance?" she asked.

"If I did, you can feel safe in copying it," said Nancy.

"Oh, I couldn't use it, at all. It's too stylish for me. It's intended to set off diamond rings, that high shake is. Wait till I get a few and then I'll try it."

"Learn it first," said Nancy wisely, "and you'll be more likely to get the rings."

"Now, to settle this argument," said Dan, with his ready, cheerful smile, "let me make a proposition. As I can't take both of you up to Tiffany's and do the right thing, what do you say to a little vaudeville? I've got the tickets. How about looking at stage diamonds since we can't shake hands with the real sparklers?"

The faithful squire took his place close to the curb; Lou next, a little peacocky in her bright and pretty clothes; Nancy on the inside, slender, and soberly clothed as the sparrow, but with the true Van Alstyne Fisher walk—thus they set out for their evening's moderate diversion.

I do not suppose that many look upon a great department store as an educational institution. But the one in which Nancy worked was something like that to her. She was surrounded by beautiful things that breathed of taste and refinement. If you live in an atmosphere of luxury, luxury is yours whether your money pays for it, or another's.

The people she served were mostly women whose dress, manners, and position in the social world were quoted as criterions. From them Nancy began to take toll—the best from each according to her view.

From one she would copy and practice a gesture, from another an eloquent lifting of an eyebrow, from others, a manner of walking, of carrying a purse, of smiling, of greeting a friend, of addressing "inferiors in station." From her best beloved model, Mrs. Van Alstyne Fisher, she made requisition for that excellent thing, a soft, low voice as clear as silver and as perfect in articulation as the notes of a thrush. Suffused in the aura of this high social refinement and good breeding, it was impossible for her to escape a deeper effect of it. As good habits are said to be better than good principles, so, perhaps, good manners are better than good habits. The teachings of your parents may not keep alive your New England conscience; but if you sit on a straight-back chair and repeat the words "prisms and pilgrims" forty times the devil will flee from you. And when Nancy spoke in the Van Alstyne Fisher tones she felt the thrill of *noblesse oblige* to her very bones.

There was another source of learning in the great departmental school. Whenever you see three or four shop-girls gather in a bunch and jingle their wire bracelets as an accompaniment to apparently frivolous conversation, do not think that they are there for the purpose of criticizing the way Ethel does her back hair. The meeting may lack the dignity of the deliberative bodies of man; but it has all the importance of the occasion on which Eve and her first daughter first put their heads together to make Adam understand his proper place in the household. It is Woman's Conference for Common Defense and Exchange of Strategical Theories of Attack and Repulse upon and against the World, which is a Stage, and Man, its Audience who Persists in Throwing Bouquets Thereupon. Woman, the most helpless of the young of any animal—with the fawn's grace but without its fleetness; with the bird's beauty but without its power of flight; with the honey-bee's burden of sweetness but without its—Oh, let's drop that simile—some of us may have been stung.

During this council of war they pass weapons one to another, and exchange stratagems that each has devised and formulated out of the tactics of life.

"I says to 'im," says Sadie, "ain't you the fresh thing! Who do you suppose I am, to be addressing such a remark to me? And what do you think he says back to me?"

The heads, brown, black, flaxen, red, and yellow bob together; the answer is given; and the parry to the thrust is decided upon, to be used by each thereafter in passages-at-arms with the common enemy, man.

Thus Nancy learned the art of defense; and to women successful defense means victory.

The curriculum of a department store is a wide one. Perhaps no other college could have fitted her as well for her life's ambition—the drawing of a matrimonial prize.

Her station in the store was a favored one. The music room was near enough for her to hear and become familiar with the works of the best composers—at least to acquire the familiarity that passed for appreciation in the social world in which she was vaguely trying to set a tentative and aspiring foot. She absorbed the educating influence of art wares, of costly and dainty fabrics, of adornments that are almost culture to women.

The other girls soon became aware of Nancy's ambition. "Here comes your millionaire, Nancy," they would call to her whenever any man who looked the *rôle* approached her counter. It got to be a habit of men, who were hanging about while their women folk were shopping, to stroll over to the handkerchief counter and dawdle over the cambric squares. Nancy's imitation high-bred air and genuine dainty beauty was what attracted. Many men thus came to display their graces before her. Some of them may have been millionaires; others were certainly no more than their sedulous apes. Nancy learned to discriminate. There was a window at the end of the handkerchief counter; and she could see the rows of vehicles waiting for the shoppers in the street below. She looked and perceived that automobiles differ as well as do their owners.

Once a fascinating gentleman bought four dozen handkerchiefs, and wooed her across the counter with a King Cophetua air. When he had gone one of the girls said:

"What's wrong, Nance, that you didn't warm up to that fellow. He looks the swell article, all right, to me."

"Him?" said Nancy, with her coolest, sweetest, most impersonal, Van Alstyne Fisher smile; "not for mine. I saw him drive up outside. A 12 H. P. machine and an Irish chauffeur! And you saw what kind of handkerchiefs he bought—silk! And he's got dactylis on him. Give me the real thing or nothing, if you please."

Two of the most "refined" women in the store—a forelady and a cashier—had a few "swell gentlemen friends" with whom they now and then dined. Once they included Nancy in an invitation. The dinner took place in a spectacular café whose tables are engaged for New Year's eve a year in advance. There were two "gentlemen friends"—one without any hair on his head—high living ungrew it; and we can prove it—the other a young man whose worth and sophistication he impressed upon you in two convincing ways—he swore that all the wine was corked; and he wore diamond cuff buttons. This young man perceived irresistible excellencies in Nancy. His taste ran to shop-girls; and here was one that added the voice and manners of his high social world to the franker charms of her own caste. So, on the following day, he appeared in the store and made her a serious proposal of marriage over a box of hem-stitched, grass-bleached Irish linens. Nancy declined. A brown pompadour ten feet away had been using her eyes and ears. When the rejected suitor had gone she heaped carboys of upbraidings and horror upon Nancy's head.

"What a terrible little fool you are! That fellow's a millionaire—he's a nephew of old Van Skittles himself. And he was talking on the level, too. Have you gone crazy, Nance?"

"Have I?" said Nancy. "I didn't take him, did I? He isn't a millionaire so hard that you could notice it, anyhow. His family only allows him $20,000 a year to spend. The bald-headed fellow was guying him about it the other night at supper."

The brown pompadour came nearer and narrowed her eyes.

"Say, what do you want?" she inquired, in a voice hoarse for lack of chewing-gum. "Ain't that enough for you? Do you want to be a Mormon, and marry Rockefeller and Gladstone Dowie and the King of Spain and the whole bunch? Ain't $20,000 a year good enough for you?"

Nancy flushed a little under the level gaze of the black, shallow eyes.

"It wasn't altogether the money, Carrie," she explained. "His friend caught him in a rank lie the other night at dinner. It was about some girl he said he hadn't been to the theater with. Well, I can't stand a liar. Put everything together—I don't like him; and that settles it. When I sell out it's not going to be on any bargain day. I've got to have something that sits up in a chair like a man, anyhow. Yes, I'm looking out for a catch; but it's got to be able to do something more than make a noise like a toy bank."

"The physiopathic ward for yours!" said the brown pompadour, walking away.

These high ideas, if not ideals—Nancy continued to cultivate on $8 per week. She bivouacked on the trail of the great unknown "catch," eating her dry bread and tightening her belt day by day. On her face was the faint, soldierly, sweet, grim smile of the preordained man-hunter. The store was her forest; and many times she raised her rifle at game that seemed broad-antlered and big; but always some deep unerring instinct—perhaps of the huntress, perhaps of the woman—made her hold her fire and take up the trail again.

Lou flourished in the laundry. Out of her $18.50 per week she paid $6. for her room and board. The rest went mainly for clothes. Her opportunities for bettering her taste and manners were few compared with Nancy's. In the steaming laundry there was nothing but work, work and her thoughts of the evening pleasures to come. Many costly and showy fabrics passed under her iron; and it may be that her growing fondness for dress was thus transmitted to her through the conducting metal.

When the day's work was over Dan awaited her outside, her faithful shadow in whatever light she stood.

Sometimes he cast an honest and troubled glance at Lou's clothes that increased in conspicuity rather than in style; but this was no disloyalty; he deprecated the attention they called to her in the streets.

And Lou was no less faithful to her chum. There was a law that Nancy should go with them on whatsoever outings they might take. Dan bore the extra burden heartily and in good cheer. It might be said that Lou furnished the color, Nancy the tone, and Dan the weight of the distraction-seeking trio. The escort, in his neat but obviously ready-made suit, his ready-made tie and unfailing, genial, ready-made wit never startled or clashed. He was of that good kind that you are likely to forget while they are present, but remember distinctly after they are gone.

To Nancy's superior taste the flavor of these ready-made pleasures was sometimes a little bitter: but she was young; and youth is a gourmand, when it cannot be a gourmet.

"Dan is always wanting me to marry him right away," Lou told her once. "But why should I? I'm independent. I can do as I please with the money I earn; and he never would agree for me to keep on working afterward. And say, Nance, what do you want to stick to that old store for, and half starve and half dress yourself? I could get you a place in the laundry right now if you'd come. It seems to me that you could afford to be a little less stuck-up if you could make a good deal more money."

"I don't think I'm stuck-up, Lou," said Nancy, "but I'd rather live on half rations and stay where I am. I suppose I've got the habit. It's the chance that I want. I don't expect to be always behind a counter. I'm learning something new every day. I'm right up against refined and rich people all the time—even if I do only wait on them; and I'm not missing any pointers that I see passing around."

"Caught your millionaire yet?" asked Lou with her teasing laugh.

"I haven't selected one yet," answered Nancy. "I've been looking them over."

"Goodness! The idea of picking over 'em! Don't you ever let one get by you Nance—even if he's a few dollars shy. But of course you're joking—millionaires don't think about working girls like us."

"It might be better for them if they did," said Nancy, with cool wisdom. "Some of us could teach them how to take care of their money."

"If one was to speak to me," laughed Lou, "I know I'd have a duck-fit."

"That's because you don't know any. The only difference between swells and other people is you have to watch 'em closer. Don't you think that red silk lining is just a little bit too bright for that coat, Lou?"

Lou looked at the plain, dull olive jacket of her friend.

"Well, no I don't—but it may seem so beside that faded-looking thing you've got on."

"This jacket," said Nancy, complacently, "has exactly the cut and fit of one that Mrs. Van Alstyne Fisher was wearing the other day. The material cost me $3.98. I suppose hers cost about $100 more."

"Oh, well," said Lou lightly, "it don't strike me as millionaire bait. Shouldn't wonder if I catch one before you do, anyway."

Truly it would have taken a philosopher to decide upon the values of the theories held by the two friends. Lou, lacking that certain pride and fastidiousness that keeps stores and desks filled with girls working for the barest living, thumped away gaily with her iron in the noisy and stifling laundry. Her wages supported her even beyond the point of comfort; so that her dress profited until sometimes she cast a sidelong glance of impatience at the neat but inelegant apparel of Dan—Dan the constant, the immutable, the undeviating.

As for Nancy, her case was one of tens of thousands. Silk and jewels and laces and ornaments and the perfume and music of the fine world of good-breeding and taste—these were made for woman; they are her equitable portion. Let her keep near them if they are a part of life to her, and if she will. She is no traitor to herself, as Esau was; for she keeps her birthright and the pottage she earns is often very scant.

In this atmosphere Nancy belonged; and she throve in it and ate her frugal meals and schemed over her cheap dresses with a determined and contented mind. She already knew woman; and she was studying man, the animal, both as to his habits and eligibility. Some day she would bring down the game that she wanted; but she promised herself it would be what seemed to her the biggest and the best, and nothing smaller.

Thus she kept her lamp trimmed and burning to receive the bridegroom when he should come.

But, another lesson she learned, perhaps unconsciously. Her standard of values began to shift and change. Sometimes the dollar-mark grew blurred in her mind's eye, and shaped itself into letters that spelled such words as "truth" and "honor" and now and then just "kindness." Let us make a likeness of one who hunts the moose or elk in some mighty wood. He sees a little dell, mossy and embowered, where a rill trickles, babbling to him of rest and comfort. At these times the spear of Nimrod himself grows blunt.

So, Nancy wondered sometimes if Persian lamb was always quoted at its market value by the hearts that it covered.

One Thursday evening Nancy left the store and turned across Sixth Avenue westward to the laundry. She was expected to go with Lou and Dan to a musical comedy.

Dan was just coming out of the laundry when she arrived. There was a queer, strained look on his face.

"I thought I would drop around to see if they had heard from her," he said.

"Heard from who?" asked Nancy. "Isn't Lou there?"

"I thought you knew," said Dan. "She hasn't been here or at the house where she lived since Monday. She moved all her things from there. She told one of the girls in the laundry she might be going to Europe."

"Hasn't anybody seen her anywhere?" asked Nancy.

Dan looked at her with his jaws set grimly, and a steely gleam in his steady gray eyes.

"They told me in the laundry," he said, harshly, "that they saw her pass yesterday—in an automobile. With one of the millionaires, I suppose, that you and Lou were forever busying your brains about."

For the first time Nancy quailed before a man. She laid her hand that trembled slightly on Dan's sleeve.

"You've no right to say such a thing to me, Dan—as if I had anything to do with it!"

"I didn't mean it that way," said Dan, softening. He fumbled in his vest pocket.

"I've got the tickets for the show tonight," he said, with a gallant show of lightness. "If you—"

Nancy admired pluck whenever she saw it.

"I'll go with you, Dan," she said.

Three months went by before Nancy saw Lou again.

At twilight one evening the shop-girl was hurrying home along the border of a little quiet park. She heard her name called, and wheeled about in time to catch Lou rushing into her arms.

After the first embrace they drew their heads back as serpents do, ready to attack or to charm, with a thousand questions trembling on their swift tongues. And then Nancy noticed that prosperity had descended upon Lou, manifesting itself in costly furs, flashing gems, and creations of the tailors' art.

"You little fool!" cried Lou, loudly and affectionately. "I see you are still working in that store, and as shabby as ever. And how about that big catch you were going to make—nothing doing yet, I suppose?"

And then Lou looked, and saw that something better than prosperity had descended upon Nancy—something that shone brighter than gems in her eyes and redder than a rose in her cheeks, and that danced like electricity anxious to be loosed from the tip of her tongue.

"Yes, I'm still in the store," said Nancy, "but I'm going to leave it next week. I've made my catch—the biggest catch in the world. You won't mind now Lou, will you?—I'm going to be married to Dan—to Dan!—he's my Dan now—why, Lou!"

Around the corner of the park strolled one of those new-crop, smooth-faced young policemen that are making the force more endurable—at least to the eye. He saw a woman with an expensive fur coat, and diamond-ringed hands crouching down against the iron fence of the park sobbing turbulently, while a slender, plainly-dressed working girl leaned close, trying to console her. But the Gibsonian cop, being of the new order, passed on, pretending not to notice, for he was wise enough to know that these matters are beyond help so far as the power he represents is concerned, though he rap the pavement with his nightstick till the sound goes up to the furthermost stars.

27

Two Thanksgiving Day Gentlemen

There is one day that is ours. There is one day when all we Americans who are not self-made go back to the old home to eat saleratus biscuits and marvel how much nearer to the porch the old pump looks than it used to. Bless the day. President Roosevelt gives it to us. We hear some talk of the Puritans, but don't just remember who they were. Bet we can lick 'em, anyhow, if they try to land again. Plymouth Rocks? Well, that sounds more familiar. Lots of us have had to come down to hens since the Turkey Trust got its work in. But somebody in Washington is leaking out advance information to 'em about these Thanksgiving proclamations.

The big city east of the cranberry bogs has made Thanksgiving Day an institution. The last Thursday in November is the only day in the year on which it recognizes the part of America lying across the ferries. It is the one day that is purely American. Yes, a day of celebration, exclusively American.

And now for the story which is to prove to you that we have traditions on this side of the ocean that are becoming older at a much rapider rate than those of England are—thanks to our git-up and enterprise.

Stuffy Pete took his seat on the third bench to the right as you enter Union Square from the east, at the walk opposite the fountain. Every Thanksgiving Day for nine years he had taken his seat there promptly at 1 o'clock. For every time he had done so things had happened to him—Charles Dickensy things that swelled his waistcoat above his heart, and equally on the other side.

But today Stuffy Pete's appearance at the annual trysting place seemed to have been rather the result of habit than of the yearly hunger which, as the philanthropists seem to think, afflicts the poor at such extended intervals.

Certainly Pete was not hungry. He had just come from a feast that had left him of his powers barely those of respiration and locomotion. His eyes were like two pale gooseberries firmly imbedded in a swollen and gravy-smeared mask of putty. His breath came in short wheezes; a senatorial roll of adipose tissue denied a fashionable set to his upturned coat collar. Buttons that had been sewed upon his clothes by kind Salvation fingers a week before flew like popcorn, strewing the earth around him. Ragged he was, with a split shirt front open to the wishbone; but the November breeze, carrying fine snowflakes, brought him only a grateful coolness. For Stuffy Pete was overcharged with the caloric produced by a super-bountiful dinner, beginning with oysters and ending with plum pudding, and including (it seemed to him) all the roast turkey and baked potatoes and chicken salad and squash pie and ice cream in the world. Wherefore he sat, gorged, and gazed upon the world with after-dinner contempt.

The meal had been an unexpected one. He was passing a red brick mansion near the beginning of Fifth avenue, in which lived two old ladies of ancient family and a reverence for traditions. They even denied the existence of New York, and believed that Thanksgiving Day was declared solely for Washington Square. One of their traditional habits was to station a servant at the postern gate with orders to admit the first hungry wayfarer that came along after the hour of noon had struck, and banquet him to a finish. Stuffy Pete happened to pass by on his way to the park, and the seneschals gathered him in and upheld the custom of the castle.

After Stuffy Pete had gazed straight before him for ten minutes he was conscious of a desire for a more varied field of vision. With a tremendous effort he moved his head slowly to the left. And then his eyes bulged out fearfully, and his breath ceased, and the rough-shod ends of his short legs wriggled and rustled on the gravel.

For the Old Gentleman was coming across Fourth avenue toward his bench.

Every Thanksgiving Day for nine years the Old Gentleman had come there and found Stuffy Pete on his bench. That was a thing that the Old Gentleman was trying to make a tradition of. Every Thanksgiving Day for nine years he had found Stuffy there, and had led him to a restaurant and watched him eat a big dinner. They do those things in England unconsciously. But this is a young country, and nine years is not so bad. The Old Gentleman was a staunch American patriot, and considered himself a pioneer in American tradition. In order to become picturesque we must keep on doing one thing for a long time without ever letting it get away from us. Something like collecting the weekly dimes in industrial insurance. Or cleaning the streets.

The Old Gentleman moved, straight and stately, toward the Institution that he was rearing. Truly, the annual feeding of Stuffy Pete was nothing national in its character, such as the Magna Charta or jam for breakfast was in England. But it was a step. It was almost feudal. It showed, at least, that a Custom was not impossible to New Y—ahem!—America.

The Old Gentleman was thin and tall and sixty. He was dressed all in black, and wore the old-fashioned kind of glasses that won't stay on your nose. His hair was whiter and thinner than it had been last year, and he seemed to make more use of his big, knobby cane with the crooked handle.

As his established benefactor came up Stuffy wheezed and shuddered like some woman's over-fat pug when a street dog bristles up at him. He would have flown, but all the skill of Santos-Dumont could not have separated him from his bench. Well had the myrmidons of the two old ladies done their work.

"Good morning," said the Old Gentleman. "I am glad to perceive that the vicissitudes of another year have spared you to move in health about the beautiful world. For that blessing alone this day of thanksgiving is well proclaimed to each of us. If you will come with me, my man, I will provide you with a dinner that should make your physical being accord with the mental."

That is what the old Gentleman said every time. Every Thanksgiving Day for nine years. The words themselves almost formed an Institution. Nothing could be compared with them except the Declaration of Independence. Always before they had been music in Stuffy's ears. But now he looked up at the Old Gentleman's face with tearful agony in his own. The fine snow almost sizzled when it fell upon his perspiring brow. But the Old Gentleman shivered a little and turned his back to the wind.

Stuffy had always wondered why the Old Gentleman spoke his speech rather sadly. He did not know that it was because he was wishing every time that he had a son to succeed him. A son who would come there after he was gone—a son who would stand proud and strong before some subsequent Stuffy, and say: "In memory of my father." Then it would be an Institution.

But the Old Gentleman had no relatives. He lived in rented rooms in one of the decayed old family brownstone mansions in one of the quiet streets east of the park. In the winter he raised fuchsias in a little conservatory the size of a steamer trunk. In the spring he walked in the Easter parade. In the summer he lived at a farmhouse in the New Jersey hills, and sat in a wicker armchair, speaking of a butterfly, the *ornithoptera amphrisius*, that he hoped to find some day. In the autumn he fed Stuffy a dinner. These were the Old Gentleman's occupations.

Stuffy Pete looked up at him for a half minute, stewing and helpless in his own self-pity. The Old Gentleman's eyes were bright with the giving-pleasure. His face was getting more lined each year, but his little black necktie was in as jaunty a bow as ever, and the linen was beautiful and white, and his gray mustache was curled carefully at the ends. And then Stuffy made a noise that sounded like peas bubbling in a pot. Speech was intended; and as the Old Gentleman had heard the sounds nine times before, he rightly construed them into Stuffy's old formula of acceptance.

"Thankee, sir. I'll go with ye, and much obliged. I'm very hungry, sir."

The coma of repletion had not prevented from entering Stuffy's mind the conviction that he was the basis of an Institution. His Thanksgiving appetite was not his own; it belonged by all the sacred rights of established custom, if not, by the actual Statute of Limitations, to this kind old gentleman who bad preempted it. True, America is free; but in order to establish tradition some one must be a repetend—a repeating decimal. The heroes are not all heroes of steel and gold. See one here that wielded only weapons of iron, badly silvered, and tin.

The Old Gentleman led his annual protégé southward to the restaurant, and to the table where the feast had always occurred. They were recognized.

"Here comes de old guy," said a waiter, "dat blows dat same bum to a meal every Thanksgiving."

The Old Gentleman sat across the table glowing like a smoked pearl at his corner-stone of future ancient Tradition. The waiters heaped the table with holiday food—and Stuffy, with a sigh that was mistaken for hunger's expression, raised knife and fork and carved for himself a crown of imperishable bay.

No more valiant hero ever fought his way through the ranks of an enemy. Turkey, chops, soups, vegetables, pies, disappeared before him as fast as they could be served. Gorged nearly to the uttermost when he entered the restaurant, the smell of food had almost caused him to lose his honor as a gentleman, but he rallied like a true knight. He saw the look of beneficent happiness on the Old Gentleman's face—a happier look than even the fuchsias and the *ornithoptera amphrisius* had ever brought to it—and he had not the heart to see it wane.

In an hour Stuffy leaned back with a battle won. "Thankee kindly, sir," he puffed like a leaky steam pipe; "thankee kindly for a hearty meal." Then he arose heavily with glazed eyes and started toward the kitchen. A waiter turned him about like a top, and pointed him toward the door. The Old Gentleman carefully counted out $1.30 in silver change, leaving three nickels for the waiter.

They parted as they did each year at the door, the Old Gentleman going south, Stuffy north.

Around the first corner Stuffy turned, and stood for one minute. Then he seemed to puff out his rags as an owl puffs out his feathers, and fell to the sidewalk like a sun-stricken horse.

When the ambulance came the young surgeon and the driver cursed softly at his weight. There was no smell of whiskey to justify a transfer to the patrol wagon, so Stuffy and his two dinners went to the hospital. There they stretched him on a bed and began to test him for strange diseases, with the hope of getting a chance at some problem with the bare steel.

And lo! An hour later another ambulance brought the Old Gentleman. And they laid him on another bed and spoke of appendicitis, for he looked good for the bill.

But pretty soon one of the young doctors met one of the young nurses whose eyes he liked, and stopped to chat with her about the cases.

"That nice old gentleman over there, now," he said, "you wouldn't think that was a case of almost starvation. Proud old family, I guess. He told me he hadn't eaten a thing for three days."

28

One Thousand Dollars

"One thousand dollars," repeated Lawyer Tolman, solemnly and severely, "and here is the money."

Young Gillian gave a decidedly amused laugh as he fingered the thin package of new fifty-dollar notes.

"It's such a confoundedly awkward amount," he explained, genially, to the lawyer. "If it had been ten thousand a fellow might wind up with a lot of fireworks and do himself credit. Even fifty dollars would have been less trouble."

"You heard the reading of your uncle's will," continued Lawyer Tolman, professionally dry in his tones. "I do not know if you paid much attention to its details. I must remind you of one. You are required to render to us an account of the manner of expenditure of this $1,000 as soon as you have disposed of it. The will stipulates that. I trust that you will so far comply with the late Mr. Gillian's wishes."

"You may depend upon it," said the young man politely, "in spite of the extra expense it will entail. I may have to engage a secretary. I was never good at accounts."

Gillian went to his club. There he hunted out one whom he called Old Bryson.

Old Bryson was calm and forty and sequestered. He was in a corner reading a book, and when he saw Gillian approaching he sighed, laid down his book and took off his glasses.

"Old Bryson, wake up," said Gillian. "I've a funny story to tell you."

"I wish you would tell it to some one in the billiard room," said Old Bryson. "You know how I hate your stories."

"This is a better one than usual," said Gillian, rolling a cigarette; "and I'm glad to tell it to you. It's too sad and funny to go with the rattling of billiard balls. I've just come from my late uncle's firm of legal corsairs. He leaves me an even thousand dollars. Now, what can a man possibly do with a thousand dollars?"

"I thought," said Old Bryson, showing as much interest as a bee shows in a vinegar cruet, "that the late Septimus Gillian was worth something like half a million."

"He was," assented Gillian, joyously, "and that's where the joke comes in. He's left his whole cargo of doubloons to a microbe. That is, part of it goes to the man who invents a new bacillus and the rest to establish a hospital for doing away with it again. There are one or two trifling bequests on the side. The butler and the housekeeper get a seal ring and $10 each. His nephew gets $1,000."

"You've always had plenty of money to spend," observed Old Bryson.

"Tons," said Gillian. "Uncle was the fairy godmother as far as an allowance was concerned."

"Any other heirs?" asked Old Bryson.

"None." Gillian frowned at his cigarette and kicked the upholstered leather of a divan uneasily. "There is a Miss Hayden, a ward of my uncle, who lived in his house. She's a quiet thing—musical—the daughter of somebody who was unlucky enough to be his friend. I forgot to say that she was in on the seal ring and $10 joke, too. I wish I had been. Then I could have had two bottles of brut, tipped the waiter with the ring and had the whole business off my hands. Don't be superior and insulting, Old Bryson—tell me what a fellow can do with a thousand dollars."

Old Bryson rubbed his glasses and smiled. And when Old Bryson smiled, Gillian knew that he intended to be more offensive than ever.

"A thousand dollars," he said, "means much or little. One man may buy a happy home with it and laugh at Rockefeller. Another could send his wife South with it and save her life. A thousand dollars would buy pure milk for one hundred babies during June, July, and August and save fifty of their lives. You could count upon a half hour's diversion with it at faro in one of the fortified art galleries. It would furnish an education to an ambitious boy. I am told that a genuine Corot was secured for that amount in an auction room yesterday. You could move to a New Hampshire town and live respectably two years on it. You could rent Madison Square Garden for one evening with it, and lecture your audience, if you should have one, on the precariousness of the profession of heir presumptive."

"People might like you, Old Bryson," said Gillian, always unruffled, "if you wouldn't moralize. I asked you to tell me what I could do with a thousand dollars."

"You?" said Bryson, with a gentle laugh. "Why, Bobby Gillian, there's only one logical thing you could do. You can go buy Miss Lotta Lauriere a diamond pendant with the money, and then take yourself off to Idaho and inflict your presence upon a ranch. I advise a sheep ranch, as I have a particular dislike for sheep."

"Thanks," said Gillian, rising, "I thought I could depend upon you, Old Bryson. You've hit on the very scheme. I wanted to chuck the money in a lump, for I've got to turn in an account for it, and I hate itemizing."

Gillian phoned for a cab and said to the driver:

"The stage entrance of the Columbine Theatre."

Miss Lotta Lauriere was assisting nature with a powder puff, almost ready for her call at a crowded matinée, when her dresser mentioned the name of Mr. Gillian.

"Let it in," said Miss Lauriere. "Now, what is it, Bobby? I'm going on in two minutes."

"Rabbit-foot your right ear a little," suggested Gillian, critically. "That's better. It won't take two minutes for me. What do you say to a little thing in the pendant line? I can stand three ciphers with a figure one in front of 'em."

"Oh, just as you say," carolled Miss Lauriere. "My right glove, Adams. Say, Bobby, did you see that necklace Della Stacey had on the other night? Twenty-two hundred dollars it cost at Tiffany's. But, of course—pull my sash a little to the left, Adams."

"Miss Lauriere for the opening chorus!" cried the call boy without.

Gillian strolled out to where his cab was waiting.

"What would you do with a thousand dollars if you had it?" he asked the driver.

"Open a s'loon," said the cabby, promptly and huskily. "I know a place I could take money in with both hands. It's a four-story brick on a corner. I've got it figured out. Second story—Chinks and chop suey; third floor—manicures and foreign missions; fourth floor—poolroom. If you was thinking of putting up the cap—"

"Oh, no," said Gillian, "I merely asked from curiosity. I take you by the hour. Drive 'til I tell you to stop."

Eight blocks down Broadway Gillian poked up the trap with his cane and got out. A blind man sat upon a stool on the sidewalk selling pencils. Gillian went out and stood before him.

"Excuse me," he said, "but would you mind telling me what you would do if you had a thousand dollars?"

"You got out of that cab that just drove up, didn't you?" asked the blind man.

"I did," said Gillian.

"I guess you are all right," said the pencil dealer, "to ride in a cab by daylight. Take a look at that, if you like."

He drew a small book from his coat pocket and held it out. Gillian opened it and saw that it was a bank deposit book. It showed a balance of $1,785 to the blind man's credit.

Gillian returned the book and got into the cab.

"I forgot something," he said. "You may drive to the law offices of Tolman & Sharp, at —— Broadway."

Lawyer Tolman looked at him hostilely and inquiringly through his gold-rimmed glasses.

"I beg your pardon," said Gillian, cheerfully, "but may I ask you a question? It is not an impertinent one, I hope. Was Miss Hayden left anything by my uncle's will besides the ring and the $10?"

"Nothing," said Mr. Tolman.

"I thank you very much, sir," said Gillian, and on he went to his cab. He gave the driver the address of his late uncle's home.

Miss Hayden was writing letters in the library. She was small and slender and clothed in black. But you would have noticed her eyes. Gillian drifted in with his air of regarding the world as inconsequent.

"I've just come from old Tolman's," he explained. "They've been going over the papers down there. They found a—Gillian searched his memory for a legal term—they found an amendment or a post-script or something to the will. It seemed that the old boy loosened up a little on second thoughts and willed you a thousand dollars. I was driving up this way and Tolman asked me to bring you the money. Here it is. You'd better count it to see if it's right." Gillian laid the money beside her hand on the desk.

Miss Hayden turned white. "Oh!" she said, and again "Oh!"

Gillian half turned and looked out the window.

"I suppose, of course," he said, in a low voice, "that you know I love you."

"I am sorry," said Miss Hayden, taking up her money.

"There is no use?" asked Gillian, almost light-heartedly.

"I am sorry," she said again.

"May I write a note?" asked Gillian, with a smile, He seated himself at the big library table. She supplied him with paper and pen, and then went back to her *secrétaire*.

Gillian made out his account of his expenditure of the thousand dollars in these words:

"Paid by the black sheep, Robert Gillian, $1,000 on account of the eternal happiness, owed by Heaven to the best and dearest woman on earth."

Gillian slipped his writing into an envelope, bowed and went his way.

His cab stopped again at the offices of Tolman & Sharp.

"I have expended the thousand dollars," he said cheerily, to Tolman of the gold glasses, "and I have come to render account of it, as I agreed. There is quite a feeling of summer in the air—do you not think so, Mr. Tolman?" He tossed a white envelope on the lawyer's table. "You will find there a memorandum, sir, of the *modus operandi* of the vanishing of the dollars."

Without touching the envelope, Mr. Tolman went to a door and called his partner, Sharp. Together they explored the caverns of an immense safe. Forth they dragged, as trophy of their search a big envelope sealed with wax. This they forcibly invaded, and wagged their venerable heads together over its contents. Then Tolman became spokesman.

"Mr. Gillian," he said, formally, "there was a codicil to your uncle's will. It was intrusted to us privately, with instructions that it be not opened until you had furnished us with a full account of your handling of the $1,000 bequest in the will. As you have fulfilled the conditions, my partner and I have read the codicil. I do not wish to encumber your understanding with its legal phraseology, but I will acquaint you with the spirit of its contents.

"In the event that your disposition of the $1,000 demonstrates that you possess any of the qualifications that deserve reward, much benefit will accrue to you. Mr. Sharp and I are named as the judges, and I assure you that we will do our duty strictly according to justice—with liberality. We are not at all unfavorably disposed toward you, Mr. Gillian. But let us return to the letter of the codicil. If your disposal of the money in question has been prudent, wise, or unselfish, it is in our power to hand you over bonds to the value of $50,000, which have been placed in our hands for that purpose. But if—as our client, the late Mr. Gillian, explicitly provides—you have used this money as you have money in the past, I quote the late Mr. Gillian—in reprehensible dissipation among disreputable associates—the $50,000 is to be paid to Miriam Hayden, ward of the late Mr. Gillian, without delay. Now, Mr. Gillian, Mr. Sharp and I will examine your account in regard to the $1,000. You submit it in writing, I believe. I hope you will repose confidence in our decision."

Mr. Tolman reached for the envelope. Gillian was a little the quicker in taking it up. He tore the account and its cover leisurely into strips and dropped them into his pocket.

"It's all right," he said, smilingly. "There isn't a bit of need to bother you with this. I don't suppose you'd understand these itemized bets, anyway. I lost the thousand dollars on the races. Good-day to you, gentlemen."

Tolman & Sharp shook their heads mournfully at each other when Gillian left, for they heard him whistling gaily in the hallway as he waited for the elevator.

29

The Clarion Call

Half of this story can be found in the records of the Police Department; the other half belongs behind the business counter of a newspaper office.

One afternoon two weeks after Millionaire Norcross was found in his apartment murdered by a burglar, the murderer, while strolling serenely down Broadway ran plump against Detective Barney Woods.

"Is that you, Johnny Kernan?" asked Woods, who had been near-sighted in public for five years.

"No less," cried Kernan, heartily. "If it isn't Barney Woods, late and early of old Saint Jo! You'll have to show me! What are you doing East? Do the green-goods circulars get out that far?"

"I've been in New York some years," said Woods. "I'm on the city detective force."

"Well, well!" said Kernan, breathing smiling joy and patting the detective's arm.

"Come into Muller's," said Woods, "and let's hunt a quiet table. I'd like to talk to you awhile."

It lacked a few minutes to the hour of four. The tides of trade were not yet loosed, and they found a quiet corner of the café. Kernan, well dressed, slightly swaggering, self-confident, seated himself opposite the little detective, with his pale, sandy mustache, squinting eyes and ready-made cheviot suit.

"What business are you in now?" asked Woods. "You know you left Saint Jo a year before I did."

"I'm selling shares in a copper mine," said Kernan. "I may establish an office here. Well, well! And so old Barney is a New York detective. You always had a turn that way. You were on the police in Saint Jo after I left there, weren't you?"

"Six months," said Woods. "And now there's one more question, Johnny. I've followed your record pretty close ever since you did that hotel job in Saratoga, and I never knew you to use your gun before. Why did you kill Norcross?"

Kernan stared for a few moments with concentrated attention at the slice of lemon in his high-ball; and then he looked at the detective with a sudden, crooked, brilliant smile.

"How did you guess it, Barney?" he asked, admiringly. "I swear I thought the job was as clean and as smooth as a peeled onion. Did I leave a string hanging out anywhere?"

Woods laid upon the table a small gold pencil intended for a watch-charm.

"It's the one I gave you the last Christmas we were in Saint Jo. I've got your shaving mug yet. I found this under a corner of the rug in Norcross's room. I warn you to be careful what you say. I've got it put on to you, Johnny. We were old friends once, but I must do my duty. You'll have to go to the chair for Norcross."

Kernan laughed.

"My luck stays with me," said he. "Who'd have thought old Barney was on my trail!" He slipped one hand inside his coat. In an instant Woods had a revolver against his side.

"Put it away," said Kernan, wrinkling his nose. "I'm only investigating. Aha! It takes nine tailors to make a man, but one can do a man up. There's a hole in that vest pocket. I took that pencil off my chain and slipped it in there in case of a scrap. Put up your gun, Barney, and I'll tell you why I had to shoot Norcross. The old fool started down the hall after me, popping at the buttons on the back of my coat with a peevish little .22 and I had to stop him. The old lady was a darling. She just lay in bed and saw her $12,000 diamond necklace go without a chirp, while she begged like a panhandler to have back a little thin gold ring with a garnet worth about $3. I guess she married old Norcross for his money, all right. Don't they hang on to the little trinkets from the Man Who Lost Out, though? There were six rings, two brooches and a châtelaine watch. Fifteen thousand would cover the lot."

"I warned you not to talk," said Woods.

"Oh, that's all right," said Kernan. "The stuff is in my suit case at the hotel. And now I'll tell you why I'm talking. Because it's safe. I'm talking to a man I know. You owe me a thousand dollars, Barney Woods, and even if you wanted to arrest me your hand wouldn't make the move."

"I haven't forgotten," said Woods. "You counted out twenty fifties without a word. I'll pay it back some day. That thousand saved me and—well, they were piling my furniture out on the sidewalk when I got back to the house."

"And so," continued Kernan, "you being Barney Woods, born as true as steel, and bound to play a white man's game, can't lift a finger to arrest the man you're indebted to. Oh, I have to study men as well as Yale locks and window fastenings in my business. Now, keep quiet while I ring for the waiter. I've had a thirst for a year or two that worries me a little. If I'm ever caught the lucky sleuth will have to divide honors with old boy Booze. But I never drink during business hours. After a job I can crook elbows with my old friend Barney with a clear conscience. What are you taking?"

The waiter came with the little decanters and the siphon and left them alone again.

"You've called the turn," said Woods, as he rolled the little gold pencil about with a thoughtful fore-finger. "I've got to pass you up. I can't lay a hand on you. If I'd a-paid that money back—but I didn't, and that settles it. It's a bad break I'm making, Johnny, but I can't dodge it. You helped me once, and it calls for the same."

"I knew it," said Kernan, raising his glass, with a flushed smile of self-appreciation. "I can judge men. Here's to Barney, for—'he's a jolly good fellow.'"

"I don't believe," went on Woods quietly, as if he were thinking aloud, "that if accounts had been square between you and me, all the money in all the banks in New York could have bought you out of my hands tonight."

"I know it couldn't," said Kernan. "That's why I knew I was safe with you."

"Most people," continued the detective, "look sideways at my business. They don't class it among the fine arts and the professions. But I've always taken a kind of fool pride in it. And here is where I go 'busted.' I guess I'm a man first and a detective afterward. I've got to let you go, and then I've got to resign from the force. I guess I can drive an express wagon. Your thousand dollars is further off than ever, Johnny."

"Oh, you're welcome to it," said Kernan, with a lordly air. "I'd be willing to call the debt off, but I know you wouldn't have it. It was a lucky day for me when you borrowed it. And now, let's drop the subject. I'm off to the West on a morning train. I know a place out there where I can negotiate the Norcross sparks. Drink up, Barney, and forget your troubles. We'll have a jolly time while the police are knocking their heads together over the case. I've got one of my Sahara thirsts on tonight. But I'm in the hands—the unofficial hands—of my old friend Barney, and I won't even dream of a cop."

And then, as Kernan's ready finger kept the button and the waiter working, his weak point—a tremendous vanity and arrogant egotism, began to show itself. He recounted story after story of his successful plunderings, ingenious plots and infamous transgressions until Woods, with all his familiarity with evildoers, felt growing within him a cold abhorrence toward the utterly vicious man who had once been his benefactor.

"I'm disposed of, of course," said Woods, at length. "But I advise you to keep under cover for a spell. The newspapers may take up this Norcross affair. There has been an epidemic of burglaries and manslaughter in town this summer."

The word sent Kernan into a high glow of sullen and vindictive rage.

"To h——l with the newspapers," he growled. "What do they spell but brag and blow and boodle in box-car letters? Suppose they do take up a case—what does it amount to? The police are easy enough to fool; but what do the newspapers do? They send a lot of pin-head reporters around to the scene; and they make for the nearest saloon and have beer while they take photos of the bartender's oldest daughter in evening dress, to print as the fiancée of the young man in the tenth story, who thought he heard a noise below on the night of the murder. That's about as near as the newspapers ever come to running down Mr. Burglar."

"Well, I don't know," said Woods, reflecting. "Some of the papers have done good work in that line. There's the *Morning Mars*, for instance. It warmed up two or three trails, and got the man after the police had let 'em get cold."

"I'll show you," said Kernan, rising, and expanding his chest. "I'll show you what I think of newspapers in general, and your *Morning Mars* in particular."

Three feet from their table was the telephone booth. Kernan went inside and sat at the instrument, leaving the door open. He found a number in the book, took down the receiver and made his demand upon Central. Woods sat still, looking at the sneering, cold, vigilant face waiting close to the transmitter, and listened to the words that came from the thin, truculent lips curved into a contemptuous smile.

"That the *Morning Mars*? ... I want to speak to the managing editor... Why, tell him it's some one who wants to talk to him about the Norcross murder.

"You the editor? ... All right... I am the man who killed old Norcross... Wait! Hold the wire; I'm not the usual crank... Oh, there isn't the slightest danger. I've just been discussing it with a detective friend of mine. I killed the old man at 2:30 a. m. two weeks ago tomorrow... Have a drink with you? Now, hadn't you better leave that kind of talk to your funny man? Can't you tell whether a man's guying you or whether you're being offered the biggest scoop your dull dishrag of a paper ever had? ... Well, that's so; it's a bobtail scoop—but you can hardly expect me to ‹phone in my name and address... Why? Oh, because I heard you make a specialty of solving mysterious crimes that stump the police... No, that's not all. I want to tell you that your rotten, lying, penny sheet is of no more use in tracking an intelligent murderer or highwayman than a blind poodle would be... What? ... Oh, no, this isn't a rival newspaper office; you're getting it straight. I did the Norcross job, and I've got the jewels in my suit case at—'the name of the hotel could not be learned'—you recognize that phrase, don't you? I thought so. You've used it often enough. Kind of rattles you, doesn't it, to have the mysterious villain call up your great, big, all-powerful organ of right and justice and good government and tell you what a helpless old gas-bag you are? ... Cut that out; you're not that big a fool—no, you don't think I'm a fraud. I can tell it by your voice... Now, listen, and I'll give you a pointer that will prove it to you. Of course you've had this murder case worked over by your staff of bright young blockheads. Half of the second button on old Mrs. Norcross's nightgown is broken off. I saw it when I took the garnet ring off her finger. I thought it was a ruby... Stop that! it won't work."

Kernan turned to Woods with a diabolic smile.

"I've got him going. He believes me now. He didn't quite cover the transmitter with his hand when he told somebody to call up Central on another 'phone and get our number. I'll give him just one more dig, and then we'll make a 'get-away.'

"Hello! ... Yes. I'm here yet. You didn't think I'd run from such a little subsidized, turncoat rag of a newspaper, did you? ... Have me inside of forty-eight hours? Say, will you quit being funny? Now, you let grown men alone and attend to your business of hunting up divorce cases and street-car accidents and printing the filth and scandal that you make your living by. Good-by, old boy—sorry I haven't time to call on you. I'd feel perfectly safe in your *sanctum asinorum*. Tra-la!"

"He's as mad as a cat that's lost a mouse," said Kernan, hanging up the receiver and coming out. "And now, Barney, my boy, we'll go to a show and enjoy ourselves until a reasonable bedtime. Four hours' sleep for me, and then the west-bound."

The two dined in a Broadway restaurant. Kernan was pleased with himself. He spent money like a prince of fiction. And then a weird and gorgeous musical comedy engaged their attention. Afterward there was a late supper in a grill-room, with champagne, and Kernan at the height of his complacency.

Half-past three in the morning found them in a corner of an all-night café, Kernan still boasting in a vapid and rambling way, Woods thinking moodily over the end that had come to his usefulness as an upholder of the law.

But, as he pondered, his eye brightened with a speculative light.

"I wonder if it's possible," he said to himself, "I won-der if it's pos-si-ble!"

And then outside the café the comparative stillness of the early morning was punctured by faint, uncertain cries that seemed mere fireflies of sound, some growing louder, some fainter, waxing and waning amid the rumble of milk wagons and infrequent cars. Shrill cries they were when near—well-known cries that conveyed many meanings to the ears of those of the slumbering millions of the great city who waked to hear them. Cries that bore upon their significant, small volume the weight of a world's woe and laughter and delight and stress. To some, cowering beneath the protection of a night's ephemeral cover, they brought news of the hideous, bright day; to others, wrapped in happy sleep, they announced a morning that would dawn blacker than sable night. To many of the rich they brought a besom to sweep away what had been theirs while the stars shone; to the poor they brought—another day.

All over the city the cries were starting up, keen and sonorous, heralding the chances that the slipping of one cogwheel in the machinery of time had made; apportioning to the sleepers while they lay at the mercy of fate, the vengeance, profit, grief, reward and doom that the new figure in the calendar had brought them. Shrill and yet plaintive were the cries, as if the young voices grieved that so much evil and so little good was in their irresponsible hands. Thus echoed in the streets of the helpless city the transmission of the latest decrees of the gods, the cries of the newsboys—the Clarion Call of the Press.

Woods flipped a dime to the waiter, and said: "Get me a *Morning Mars*."

When the paper came he glanced at its first page, and then tore a leaf out of his memorandum book and began to write on it with the little gold pencil.

"What's the news?" yawned Kernan.

Woods flipped over to him the piece of writing:

"The New York *Morning Mars*:

"Please pay to the order of John Kernan the one thousand dollars reward coming to me for his arrest and conviction.

"BARNARD WOODS."

"I kind of thought they would do that," said Woods, "when you were jollying them so hard. Now, Johnny, you'll come to the police station with me."

30

The Third Ingredient

The (so-called) Vallambrosa Apartment-House is not an apartment-house. It is composed of two old-fashioned, brownstone-front residences welded into one. The parlor floor of one side is gay with the wraps and head-gear of a modiste; the other is lugubrious with the sophistical promises and grisly display of a painless dentist. You may have a room there for two dollars a week or you may have one for twenty dollars. Among the Vallambrosa's roomers are stenographers, musicians, brokers, shop-girls, space-rate writers, art students, wire-tappers, and other people who lean far over the banister-rail when the door-bell rings.

This treatise shall have to do with but two of the Vallambrosians—though meaning no disrespect to the others.

At six o'clock one afternoon Hetty Pepper came back to her third-floor rear $3.50 room in the Vallambrosa with her nose and chin more sharply pointed than usual. To be discharged from the department store where you have been working four years, and with only fifteen cents in your purse, does have a tendency to make your features appear more finely chiseled.

And now for Hetty's thumb-nail biography while she climbs the two flights of stairs.

She walked into the Biggest Store one morning four years before with seventy-five other girls, applying for a job behind the waist department counter. The phalanx of wage-earners formed a bewildering scene of beauty, carrying a total mass of blond hair sufficient to have justified the horseback gallops of a hundred Lady Godivas.

The capable, cool-eyed, impersonal, young, bald-headed man whose task it was to engage six of the contestants, was aware of a feeling of suffocation as if he were drowning in a sea of frangipanni, while white clouds, hand-embroidered, floated about him. And then a sail hove in sight. Hetty Pepper, homely of countenance, with small, contemptuous, green eyes and chocolate-colored hair, dressed in a suit of plain burlap and a common-sense hat, stood before him with every one of her twenty-nine years of life unmistakably in sight.

"You're on!" shouted the bald-headed young man, and was saved. And that is how Hetty came to be employed in the Biggest Store. The story of her rise to an eight-dollar-a-week salary is the combined stories of Hercules, Joan of Arc, Una, Job, and Little-Red-Riding-Hood. You shall not learn from me the salary that was paid her as a beginner. There is a sentiment growing about such things, and I want no millionaire store-proprietors climbing the fire-escape of my tenement-house to throw dynamite bombs into my skylight boudoir.

The story of Hetty's discharge from the Biggest Store is so nearly a repetition of her engagement as to be monotonous.

In each department of the store there is an omniscient, omnipresent, and omnivorous person carrying always a mileage book and a red necktie, and referred to as a "buyer." The destinies of the girls in his department who live on (see Bureau of Victual Statistics)—so much per week are in his hands.

This particular buyer was a capable, cool-eyed, impersonal, young, bald-headed man. As he walked along the aisles of his department he seemed to be sailing on a sea of frangipanni, while white clouds, machine-embroidered, floated around him. Too many sweets bring surfeit. He looked upon Hetty Pepper's homely countenance, emerald eyes, and chocolate-colored hair as a welcome oasis of green in a desert of cloying beauty. In a quiet angle of a counter he pinched her arm kindly, three inches above the elbow. She slapped him three feet away with one good blow of her muscular and not especially lily-white right. So, now you know why Hetty Pepper came to leave the Biggest Store at thirty minutes' notice, with one dime and a nickel in her purse.

This morning's quotations list the price of rib beef at six cents per (butcher's) pound. But on the day that Hetty was "released" by the B. S. the price was seven and one-half cents. That fact is what makes this story possible. Otherwise, the extra four cents would have—

But the plot of nearly all the good stories in the world is concerned with shorts who were unable to cover; so you can find no fault with this one.

Hetty mounted with her rib beef to her $3.50 third-floor back. One hot, savory beef-stew for supper, a night's good sleep, and she would be fit in the morning to apply again for the tasks of Hercules, Joan of Arc, Una, Job, and Little-Red-Riding-Hood.

In her room she got the granite-ware stew-pan out of the 2×4-foot china—er—I mean earthenware closet, and began to dig down in a rat's-nest of paper bags for the potatoes and onions. She came out with her nose and chin just a little sharper pointed.

There was neither a potato nor an onion. Now, what kind of a beef-stew can you make out of simply beef? You can make oyster-soup without oysters, turtle-soup without turtles, coffee-cake without coffee, but you can't make beef-stew without potatoes and onions.

But rib beef alone, in an emergency, can make an ordinary pine door look like a wrought-iron gambling-house portal to the wolf. With salt and pepper and a tablespoonful of flour (first well stirred in a little cold water) 'twill serve—'tis not so deep as a lobster à la Newburg nor so wide as a church festival doughnut; but 'twill serve.

Hetty took her stew-pan to the rear of the third-floor hall. According to the advertisements of the Vallambrosa there was running water to be found there. Between you and me and the water-meter, it only ambled or walked through the faucets; but technicalities have no place here. There was also a sink where housekeeping roomers often met to dump their coffee grounds and glare at one another's kimonos.

At this sink Hetty found a girl with heavy, gold-brown, artistic hair and plaintive eyes, washing two large "Irish" potatoes. Hetty knew the Vallambrosa as well as any one not owning "double hextra-magnifying eyes" could compass its mysteries. The kimonos were her encyclopedia, her "Who's What?" her clearinghouse of news, of goers and comers. From a rose-pink kimono edged with Nile green she had learned that the girl with the potatoes was a miniature-painter living in a kind of attic—or "studio," as they prefer to call it—on the top floor. Hetty was not certain in her mind what a miniature was; but it certainly wasn't a house; because house-painters, although they wear splashy overalls and poke ladders in your face on the street, are known to indulge in a riotous profusion of food at home.

The potato girl was quite slim and small, and handled her potatoes as an old bachelor uncle handles a baby who is cutting teeth. She had a dull shoemaker's knife in her right hand, and she had begun to peel one of the potatoes with it.

Hetty addressed her in the punctiliously formal tone of one who intends to be cheerfully familiar with you in the second round.

"Beg pardon," she said, "for butting into what's not my business, but if you peel them potatoes you lose out. They're new Bermudas. You want to scrape 'em. Lemme show you."

She took a potato and the knife, and began to demonstrate.

"Oh, thank you," breathed the artist. "I didn't know. And I *did* hate to see the thick peeling go; it seemed such a waste. But I thought they always had to be peeled. When you've got only potatoes to eat, the peelings count, you know."

"Say, kid," said Hetty, staying her knife, "you ain't up against it, too, are you?"

The miniature artist smiled starvedly.

"I suppose I am. Art—or, at least, the way I interpret it—doesn't seem to be much in demand. I have only these potatoes for my dinner. But they aren't so bad boiled and hot, with a little butter and salt."

"Child," said Hetty, letting a brief smile soften her rigid features, "Fate has sent me and you together. I've had it handed to me in the neck, too; but I've got a chunk of meat in my, room as big as a lap-dog. And I've done everything to get potatoes except pray for 'em. Let's me and you bunch our commissary departments and make a stew of 'em. We'll cook it in my room. If we only had an onion to go in it! Say, kid, you haven't got a couple of pennies that've slipped down into the lining of your last winter's sealskin, have you? I could step down to the corner and get one at old Giuseppe's stand. A stew without an onion is worse'n a matinée without candy."

"You may call me Cecilia," said the artist. "No; I spent my last penny three days ago."

"Then we'll have to cut the onion out instead of slicing it in," said Hetty. "I'd ask the janitress for one, but I don't want 'em hep just yet to the fact that I'm pounding the asphalt for another job. But I wish we did have an onion."

In the shop-girl's room the two began to prepare their supper. Cecilia's part was to sit on the couch helplessly and beg to be allowed to do something, in the voice of a cooing ring-dove. Hetty prepared the rib beef, putting it in cold salted water in the stew-pan and setting it on the one-burner gas-stove.

"I wish we had an onion," said Hetty, as she scraped the two potatoes.

On the wall opposite the couch was pinned a flaming, gorgeous advertising picture of one of the new ferry-boats of the P. U. F. F. Railroad that had been built to cut down the time between Los Angeles and New York City one-eighth of a minute.

Hetty, turning her head during her continuous monologue, saw tears running from her guest's eyes as she gazed on the idealised presentment of the speeding, foam-girdled transport.

"Why, say, Cecilia, kid," said Hetty, poising her knife, "is it as bad art as that? I ain't a critic; but I thought it kind of brightened up the room. Of course, a manicure-painter could tell it was a bum picture in a minute. I'll take it down if you say so. I wish to the holy Saint Potluck we had an onion."

But the miniature miniature-painter had tumbled down, sobbing, with her nose indenting the hard-woven drapery of the couch. Something was here deeper than the artistic temperament offended at crude lithography.

Hetty knew. She had accepted her *rôle* long ago. How scant the words with which we try to describe a single quality of a human being! When we reach the abstract we are lost. The nearer to Nature that the babbling of our lips comes, the better do we understand. Figuratively (let us say), some people are Bosoms, some are Hands, some are Heads, some are Muscles, some are Feet, some are Backs for burdens.

Hetty was a Shoulder. Hers was a sharp, sinewy shoulder; but all her life people had laid their heads upon it, metaphorically or actually, and had left there all or half their troubles. Looking at Life anatomically, which is as good a way as any, she was preordained to be a Shoulder. There were few truer collar-bones anywhere than hers.

Hetty was only thirty-three, and she had not yet outlived the little pang that visited her whenever the head of youth and beauty leaned upon her for consolation. But one glance in her mirror always served as an instantaneous pain-killer. So she gave one pale look into the crinkly old looking-glass on the wall above the gas-stove, turned down the flame a little lower from the bubbling beef and potatoes, went over to the couch, and lifted Cecilia's head to its confessional.

"Go on and tell me, honey," she said. "I know now that it ain't art that's worrying you. You met him on a ferry-boat, didn't you? Go on, Cecilia, kid, and tell your—your Aunt Hetty about it."

But youth and melancholy must first spend the surplus of sighs and tears that waft and float the barque of romance to its harbor in the delectable isles. Presently, through the stringy tendons that formed the bars of the confessional, the penitent—or was it the glorified communicant of the sacred flame—told her story without art or illumination.

"It was only three days ago. I was coming back on the ferry from Jersey City. Old Mr. Schrum, an art dealer, told me of a rich man in Newark who wanted a miniature of his daughter painted. I went to see him and showed him some of my work. When I told him the price would be fifty dollars he laughed at me like a hyena. He said an enlarged crayon twenty times the size would cost him only eight dollars.

"I had just enough money to buy my ferry ticket back to New York. I felt as if I didn't want to live another day. I must have looked as I felt, for I saw *him* on the row of seats opposite me, looking at me as if he understood. He was nice-looking, but oh, above everything else, he looked kind. When one is tired or unhappy or hopeless, kindness counts more than anything else.

"When I got so miserable that I couldn't fight against it any longer, I got up and walked slowly out the rear door of the ferry-boat cabin. No one was there, and I slipped quickly over the rail and dropped into the water. Oh, friend Hetty, it was cold, cold!

"For just one moment I wished I was back in the old Vallambrosa, starving and hoping. And then I got numb, and didn't care. And then I felt that somebody else was in the water close by me, holding me up. *He* had followed me, and jumped in to save me.

"Somebody threw a thing like a big, white doughnut at us, and he made me put my arms through the hole. Then the ferry-boat backed, and they pulled us on board. Oh, Hetty, I was so ashamed of my wickedness in trying to drown myself; and, besides, my hair had all tumbled down and was sopping wet, and I was such a sight.

"And then some men in blue clothes came around; and he gave them his card, and I heard him tell them he had seen me drop my purse on the edge of the boat outside the rail, and in leaning over to get it I had fallen overboard. And then I remembered having read in the papers that people who try to kill themselves are locked up in cells with people who try to kill other people, and I was afraid.

"But some ladies on the boat took me downstairs to the furnace-room and got me nearly dry and did up my hair. When the boat landed, *he* came and put me in a cab. He was all dripping himself, but laughed as if he thought it was all a joke. He begged me, but I wouldn't tell him my name nor where I lived, I was so ashamed."

"You were a fool, child," said Hetty, kindly. "Wait till I turn the light up a bit. I wish to Heaven we had an onion."

"Then he raised his hat," went on Cecilia, "and said: 'Very well. But I'll find you, anyhow. I'm going to claim my rights of salvage.' Then he gave money to the cab-driver and told him to take me where I wanted to go, and walked away. What is 'salvage,' Hetty?"

"The edge of a piece of goods that ain't hemmed," said the shop-girl. "You must have looked pretty well frazzled out to the little hero boy."

"It's been three days," moaned the miniature-painter, "and he hasn't found me yet."

"Extend the time," said Hetty. "This is a big town. Think of how many girls he might have to see soaked in water with their hair down before he would recognize you. The stew's getting on fine—but oh, for an onion! I'd even use a piece of garlic if I had it."

The beef and potatoes bubbled merrily, exhaling a mouth-watering savor that yet lacked something, leaving a hunger on the palate, a haunting, wistful desire for some lost and needful ingredient.

"I came near drowning in that awful river," said Cecilia, shuddering.

"It ought to have more water in it," said Hetty; "the stew, I mean. I'll go get some at the sink."

"It smells good," said the artist.

"That nasty old North River?" objected Hetty. "It smells to me like soap factories and wet setter-dogs—oh, you mean the stew. Well, I wish we had an onion for it. Did he look like he had money?"

"First, he looked kind," said Cecilia. "I'm sure he was rich; but that matters so little. When he drew out his bill-folder to pay the cab-man you couldn't help seeing hundreds and thousands of dollars in it. And I looked over the cab doors and saw him leave the ferry station in a motor-car; and the chauffeur gave him his bearskin to put on, for he was sopping wet. And it was only three days ago."

"What a fool!" said Hetty, shortly.

"Oh, the chauffeur wasn't wet," breathed Cecilia. "And he drove the car away very nicely."

"I mean *you*," said Hetty. "For not giving him your address."

"I never give my address to chauffeurs," said Cecilia, haughtily.

"I wish we had one," said Hetty, disconsolately.

"What for?"

"For the stew, of course—oh, I mean an onion."

Hetty took a pitcher and started to the sink at the end of the hall.

A young man came down the stairs from above just as she was opposite the lower step. He was decently dressed, but pale and haggard. His eyes were dull with the stress of some burden of physical or mental woe. In his hand he bore an onion—a pink, smooth, solid, shining onion as large around as a ninety-eight-cent alarm-clock.

Hetty stopped. So did the young man. There was something Joan of Arc-ish, Herculean, and Una-ish in the look and pose of the shop-lady—she had cast off the *rôles* of Job and Little-Red-Riding-Hood. The young man stopped at the foot of the stairs and coughed distractedly. He felt marooned, held up, attacked, assailed, levied upon, sacked, assessed, panhandled, browbeaten, though he knew not why. It was the look in Hetty's eyes that did it. In them he saw the Jolly Roger fly to the masthead and an able seaman with a dirk between his teeth scurry up the ratlines and nail it there. But as yet he did not know that the cargo he carried was the thing that had caused him to be so nearly blown out of the water without even a parley.

"*Beg* your pardon," said Hetty, as sweetly as her dilute acetic acid tones permitted, "but did you find that onion on the stairs? There was a hole in the paper bag; and I've just come out to look for it."

The young man coughed for half a minute. The interval may have given him the courage to defend his own property. Also, he clutched his pungent prize greedily, and, with a show of spirit, faced his grim waylayer.

"No," he said huskily, "I didn't find it on the stairs. It was given to me by Jack Bevens, on the top floor. If you don't believe it, ask him. I'll wait until you do."

"I know about Bevens," said Hetty, sourly. "He writes books and things up there for the paper-and-rags man. We can hear the postman guy him all over the house when he brings them thick envelopes back. Say—do you live in the Vallambrosa?"

"I do not," said the young man. "I come to see Bevens sometimes. He's my friend. I live two blocks west."

"What are you going to do with the onion?—*Begging* your pardon," said Hetty.

"I'm going to eat it."

"Raw?"

"Yes: as soon as I get home."

"Haven't you got anything else to eat with it?"

The young man considered briefly.

"No," he confessed; "there's not another scrap of anything in my diggings to eat. I think old Jack is pretty hard up for grub in his shack, too. He hated to give up the onion, but I worried him into parting with it."

"Man," said Hetty, fixing him with her world-sapient eyes, and laying a bony but impressive finger on his sleeve, "you've known trouble, too, haven't you?"

"Lots," said the onion owner, promptly. "But this onion is my own property, honestly come by. If you will excuse me, I must be going."

"Listen," said Hetty, paling a little with anxiety. "Raw onion is a mighty poor diet. And so is a beef-stew without one. Now, if you're Jack Bevens' friend, I guess you're nearly right. There's a little lady—a friend of mine—in my room there at the end of the hall. Both of us are out of luck; and we had just potatoes and meat between us. They're stewing now. But it ain't got any soul. There's something lacking to it. There's certain things in life that are naturally intended to fit and belong together. One is pink cheese-cloth and green roses, and one is ham and eggs, and one is Irish and trouble. And the other one is beef and potatoes *with* onions. And still another one is people who are up against it and other people in the same fix."

The young man went into a protracted paroxysm of coughing. With one hand he hugged his onion to his bosom.

"No doubt; no doubt," said he, at length. "But, as I said, I must be going, because—"

Hetty clutched his sleeve firmly.

"Don't be a Dago, Little Brother. Don't eat raw onions. Chip it in toward the dinner and line yourself inside with the best stew you ever licked a spoon over. Must two ladies knock a young gentleman down and drag him inside for the honor of dining with 'em? No harm shall befall you, Little Brother. Loosen up and fall into line."

The young man's pale face relaxed into a grin.

"Believe I'll go you," he said, brightening. "If my onion is good as a credential, I'll accept the invitation gladly."

"It's good as that, but better as seasoning," said Hetty. "You come and stand outside the door till I ask my lady friend if she has any objections. And don't run away with that letter of recommendation before I come out."

Hetty went into her room and closed the door. The young man waited outside.

"Cecilia, kid," said the shop-girl, oiling the sharp saw of her voice as well as she could, "there's an onion outside. With a young man attached. I've asked him in to dinner. You ain't going to kick, are you?"

"Oh, dear!" said Cecilia, sitting up and patting her artistic hair. She cast a mournful glance at the ferry-boat poster on the wall.

"Nit," said Hetty. "It ain't him. You're up against real life now. I believe you said your hero friend had money and automobiles. This is a poor skeezicks that's got nothing to eat but an onion. But he's easy-spoken and not a freshy. I imagine he's been a gentleman, he's so low down now. And we need the onion. Shall I bring him in? I'll guarantee his behavior."

"Hetty, dear," sighed Cecilia, "I'm so hungry. What difference does it make whether he's a prince or a burglar? I don't care. Bring him in if he's got anything to eat with him."

Hetty went back into the hall. The onion man was gone. Her heart missed a beat, and a gray look settled over her face except on her nose and cheek-bones. And then the tides of life flowed in again, for she saw him leaning out of the front window at the other end of the hall. She hurried there. He was shouting to some one below. The noise of the street overpowered the sound of her footsteps. She looked down over his shoulder, saw whom he was speaking to, and heard his words. He pulled himself in from the window-sill and saw her standing over him.

Hetty's eyes bored into him like two steel gimlets.

"Don't lie to me," she said, calmly. "What were you going to do with that onion?"

The young man suppressed a cough and faced her resolutely. His manner was that of one who had been bearded sufficiently.

"I was going to eat it," said he, with emphatic slowness; "just as I told you before."

"And you have nothing else to eat at home?"

"Not a thing."

"What kind of work do you do?"

"I am not working at anything just now."

"Then why," said Hetty, with her voice set on its sharpest edge, "do you lean out of windows and give orders to chauffeurs in green automobiles in the street below?"

The young man flushed, and his dull eyes began to sparkle.

"Because, madam," said he, in *accelerando* tones, "I pay the chauffeur's wages and I own the automobile—and also this onion—this onion, madam."

He flourished the onion within an inch of Hetty's nose. The shop-lady did not retreat a hair's-breadth.

"Then why do you eat onions," she said, with biting contempt, "and nothing else?"

"I never said I did," retorted the young man, heatedly. "I said I had nothing else to eat where I live. I am not a delicatessen store-keeper."

"Then why," pursued Hetty, inflexibly, "were you going to eat a raw onion?"

"My mother," said the young man, "always made me eat one for a cold. Pardon my referring to a physical infirmity; but you may have noticed that I have a very, very severe cold. I was going to eat the onion and go to bed. I wonder why I am standing here and apologizing to you for it."

"How did you catch this cold?" went on Hetty, suspiciously.

The young man seemed to have arrived at some extreme height of feeling. There were two modes of descent open to him—a burst of rage or a surrender to the ridiculous. He chose wisely; and the empty hall echoed his hoarse laughter.

"You're a dandy," said he. "And I don't blame you for being careful. I don't mind telling you. I got wet. I was on a North River ferry a few days ago when a girl jumped overboard. Of course, I—"

Hetty extended her hand, interrupting his story.

"Give me the onion," she said.

The young man set his jaw a trifle harder.

"Give me the onion," she repeated.

He grinned, and laid it in her hand.

Then Hetty's infrequent, grim, melancholy smile showed itself. She took the young man's arm and pointed with her other hand to the door of her room.

"Little Brother," she said, "go in there. The little fool you fished out of the river is there waiting for you. Go on in. I'll give you three minutes before I come. Potatoes is in there, waiting. Go on in, Onions."

After he had tapped at the door and entered, Hetty began to peel and wash the onion at the sink. She gave a gray look at the gray roofs outside, and the smile on her face vanished by little jerks and twitches.

"But it's us," she said, grimly, to herself, "it's *us* that furnished the beef."

31

The Voice of the City

Twenty-five years ago the school children used to chant their lessons. The manner of their delivery was a singsong recitative between the utterance of an Episcopal minister and the drone of a tired sawmill. I mean no disrespect. We must have lumber and sawdust.

I remember one beautiful and instructive little lyric that emanated from the physiology class. The most striking line of it was this:

"The shin-bone is the long-est bone in the hu-man bod-y."

What an inestimable boon it would have been if all the corporeal and spiritual facts pertaining to man had thus been tunefully and logically inculcated in our youthful minds! But what we gained in anatomy, music and philosophy was meagre.

The other day I became confused. I needed a ray of light. I turned back to those school days for aid. But in all the nasal harmonies we whined forth from those hard benches I could not recall one that treated of the voice of agglomerated mankind.

In other words, of the composite vocal message of massed humanity.

In other words, of the Voice of a Big City.

Now, the individual voice is not lacking. We can understand the song of the poet, the ripple of the brook, the meaning of the man who wants $5 until next Monday, the inscriptions on the tombs of the Pharaohs, the language of flowers, the "step lively" of the conductor, and the prelude of the milk cans at 4 a.m. Certain large-eared ones even assert that they are wise to the vibrations of the tympanum produced by concussion of the air emanating from Mr. H. James. But who can comprehend the meaning of the voice of the city?

I went out for to see.

First, I asked Aurelia. She wore white Swiss and a hat with flowers on it, and ribbons and ends of things fluttered here and there.

"Tell me," I said, stammeringly, for I have no voice of my own, "what does this big—er—enormous—er—whopping city say? It must have a voice of some kind. Does it ever speak to you? How do you interpret its meaning? It is a tremendous mass, but it must have a key."

"Like a Saratoga trunk?" asked Aurelia.

"No," said I. "Please do not refer to the lid. I have a fancy that every city has a voice. Each one has something to say to the one who can hear it. What does the big one say to you?"

"All cities," said Aurelia, judicially, "say the same thing. When they get through saying it there is an echo from Philadelphia. So, they are unanimous."

"Here are 4,000,000 people," said I, scholastically, "compressed upon an island, which is mostly lamb surrounded by Wall Street water. The conjunction of so many units into so small a space must result in an identity—or, or rather a homogeneity that finds its oral expression through a common channel. It is, as you might say, a consensus of translation, concentrating in a crystallized, general idea which reveals itself in what may be termed the Voice of the City. Can you tell me what it is?"

Aurelia smiled wonderfully. She sat on the high stoop. A spray of insolent ivy bobbed against her right ear. A ray of impudent moonlight flickered upon her nose. But I was adamant, nickel-plated.

"I must go and find out," I said, "what is the Voice of this City. Other cities have voices. It is an assignment. I must have it. New York," I continued, in a rising tone, "had better not hand me a cigar and say: 'Old man, I can't talk for publication.' No other city acts in that way. Chicago says, unhesitatingly, 'I will;' I Philadelphia says, 'I should;' New Orleans says, 'I used to;' Louisville says, 'Don't care if I do;' St. Louis says, 'Excuse me;' Pittsburg says, 'Smoke up.' Now, New York—"

Aurelia smiled.

"Very well," said I, "I must go elsewhere and find out."

I went into a palace, tile-floored, cherub-ceilinged and square with the cop. I put my foot on the brass rail and said to Billy Magnus, the best bartender in the diocese:

"Billy, you've lived in New York a long time—what kind of a song-and-dance does this old town give you? What I mean is, doesn't the gab of it seem to kind of bunch up and slide over the bar to you in a sort of amalgamated tip that hits off the burg in a kind of an epigram with a dash of bitters and a slice of—"

"Excuse me a minute," said Billy, "somebody's punching the button at the side door."

He went away; came back with an empty tin bucket; again vanished with it full; returned and said to me:

"That was Mame. She rings twice. She likes a glass of beer for supper. Her and the kid. If you ever saw that little skeesicks of mine brace up in his high chair and take his beer and— But, say, what was yours? I get kind of excited when I hear them two rings—was it the baseball score or gin fizz you asked for?"

"Ginger ale," I answered.

I walked up to Broadway. I saw a cop on the corner. The cops take kids up, women across, and men in. I went up to him.

"If I'm not exceeding the spiel limit," I said, "let me ask you. You see New York during its vocative hours. It is the function of you and your brother cops to preserve the acoustics of the city. There must be a civic voice that is intelligible to you. At night during your lonely rounds you must have heard it. What is the epitome of its turmoil and shouting? What does the city say to you?"

"Friend," said the policeman, spinning his club, "it don't say nothing. I get my orders from the man higher up. Say, I guess you're all right. Stand here for a few minutes and keep an eye open for the roundsman."

The cop melted into the darkness of the side street. In ten minutes he had returned.

"Married last Tuesday," he said, half gruffly. "You know how they are. She comes to that corner at nine every night for a—comes to say 'hello!' I generally manage to be there. Say, what was it you asked me a bit ago—what's doing in the city? Oh, there's a roof-garden or two just opened, twelve blocks up."

I crossed a crow's-foot of street-car tracks, and skirted the edge of an umbrageous park. An artificial Diana, gilded, heroic, poised, wind-ruled, on the tower, shimmered in the clear light of her namesake in the sky. Along came my poet, hurrying, hatted, haired, emitting dactyls, spondees and dactylis. I seized him.

"Bill," said I (in the magazine he is Cleon), "give me a lift. I am on an assignment to find out the Voice of the city. You see, it's a special order. Ordinarily a symposium comprising the views of Henry Clews, John L. Sullivan, Edwin Markham, May Irwin and Charles Schwab would be about all. But this is a different matter. We want a broad, poetic, mystic vocalization of the city's soul and meaning. You are the very chap to give me a hint. Some years ago a man got at the Niagara Falls and gave us its pitch. The note was about two feet below the lowest G on the piano. Now, you can't put New York into a note unless it's better indorsed than that. But give me an idea of what it would say if it should speak. It is bound to be a mighty and far-reaching utterance. To arrive at it we must take the tremendous crash of the chords of the day's traffic, the laughter and music of the night, the solemn tones of Dr. Parkhurst, the rag-time, the weeping, the stealthy hum of cab-wheels, the shout of the press agent, the tinkle of fountains on the roof gardens, the hullabaloo of the strawberry vender and the covers of *Everybody's Magazine*, the whispers of the lovers in the parks—all these sounds must go into your Voice—not combined, but mixed, and of the mixture an essence made; and of the essence an extract—an audible extract, of which one drop shall form the thing we seek."

"Do you remember," asked the poet, with a chuckle, "that California girl we met at Stiver's studio last week? Well, I'm on my way to see her. She repeated that poem of mine, 'The Tribute of Spring,' word for word. She's the smartest proposition in this town just at present. Say, how does this confounded tie look? I spoiled four before I got one to set right."

"And the Voice that I asked you about?" I inquired.

"Oh, she doesn't sing," said Cleon. "But you ought to hear her recite my 'Angel of the Inshore Wind.'"

I passed on. I cornered a newsboy and he flashed at me prophetic pink papers that outstripped the news by two revolutions of the clock's longest hand.

"Son," I said, while I pretended to chase coins in my penny pocket, "doesn't it sometimes seem to you as if the city ought to be able to talk? All these ups and downs and funny business and queer things happening every day—what would it say, do you think, if it could speak?"

"Quit yer kiddin'," said the boy. "Wot paper yer want? I got no time to waste. It's Mag's birthday, and I want thirty cents to git her a present."

Here was no interpreter of the city's mouthpiece. I bought a paper, and consigned its undeclared treaties, its premeditated murders and unfought battles to an ash can.

Again I repaired to the park and sat in the moon shade. I thought and thought, and wondered why none could tell me what I asked for.

And then, as swift as light from a fixed star, the answer came to me. I arose and hurried—hurried as so many reasoners must, back around my circle. I knew the answer and I hugged it in my breast as I flew, fearing lest some one would stop me and demand my secret.

Aurelia was still on the stoop. The moon was higher and the ivy shadows were deeper. I sat at her side and we watched a little cloud tilt at the drifting moon and go asunder quite pale and discomfited.

And then, wonder of wonders and delight of delights! our hands somehow touched, and our fingers closed together and did not part.

After half an hour Aurelia said, with that smile of hers:

"Do you know, you haven't spoken a word since you came back!"

"That," said I, nodding wisely, "is the Voice of the City."

32

While the Auto Waits

Promptly at the beginning of twilight, came again to that quiet corner of that quiet, small park the girl in gray. She sat upon a bench and read a book, for there was yet to come a half hour in which print could be accomplished.

To repeat: Her dress was gray, and plain enough to mask its impeccancy of style and fit. A large-meshed veil imprisoned her turban hat and a face that shone through it with a calm and unconscious beauty. She had come there at the same hour on the day previous, and on the day before that; and there was one who knew it.

The young man who knew it hovered near, relying upon burnt sacrifices to the great joss, Luck. His piety was rewarded, for, in turning a page, her book slipped from her fingers and bounded from the bench a full yard away.

The young man pounced upon it with instant avidity, returning it to its owner with that air that seems to flourish in parks and public places—a compound of gallantry and hope, tempered with respect for the policeman on the beat. In a pleasant voice, he risked an inconsequent remark upon the weather—that introductory topic responsible for so much of the world's unhappiness—and stood poised for a moment, awaiting his fate.

The girl looked him over leisurely; at his ordinary, neat dress and his features distinguished by nothing particular in the way of expression.

"You may sit down, if you like," she said, in a full, deliberate contralto. "Really, I would like to have you do so. The light is too bad for reading. I would prefer to talk."

The vassal of Luck slid upon the seat by her side with complaisance.

"Do you know," he said, speaking the formula with which park chairmen open their meetings, "that you are quite the stunningest girl I have seen in a long time? I had my eye on you yesterday. Didn't know somebody was bowled over by those pretty lamps of yours, did you, honeysuckle?"

"Whoever you are," said the girl, in icy tones, "you must remember that I am a lady. I will excuse the remark you have just made because the mistake was, doubtless, not an unnatural one—in your circle. I asked you to sit down; if the invitation must constitute me your honeysuckle, consider it withdrawn."

"I earnestly beg your pardon," pleaded the young ran. His expression of satisfaction had changed to one of penitence and humility. "It was my fault, you know—I mean, there are girls in parks, you know—that is, of course, you don't know, but—"

"Abandon the subject, if you please. Of course I know. Now, tell me about these people passing and crowding, each way, along these paths. Where are they going? Why do they hurry so? Are they happy?"

The young man had promptly abandoned his air of coquetry. His cue was now for a waiting part; he could not guess the *rôle* he would be expected to play.

"It *is* interesting to watch them," he replied, postulating her mood. "It is the wonderful drama of life. Some are going to supper and some to—er—other places. One wonders what their histories are."

"I do not," said the girl; "I am not so inquisitive. I come here to sit because here, only, can I be near the great, common, throbbing heart of humanity. My part in life is cast where its beats are never felt. Can you surmise why I spoke to you, Mr.—?"

"Parkenstacker," supplied the young man. Then he looked eager and hopeful.

"No," said the girl, holding up a slender finger, and smiling slightly. "You would recognize it immediately. It is impossible to keep one's name out of print. Or even one's portrait. This veil and this hat of my maid furnish me with an *incog*. You should have seen the chauffeur stare at it when he thought I did not see. Candidly, there are five or six names that belong in the holy of holies, and mine, by the accident of birth, is one of them. I spoke to you, Mr. Stackenpot—"

"Parkenstacker," corrected the young man, modestly.

"—Mr. Parkenstacker, because I wanted to talk, for once, with a natural man—one unspoiled by the despicable gloss of wealth and supposed social superiority. Oh! You do not know how weary I am of it—money, money, money! And of the men who surround me, dancing like little marionettes all cut by the same pattern. I am sick of pleasure, of jewels, of travel, of society, of luxuries of all kinds."

"I always had an idea," ventured the young man, hesitatingly, "that money must be a pretty good thing."

"A competence is to be desired. But when you have so many millions that—!" She concluded the sentence with a gesture of despair. "It is the monotony of it," she continued, "that palls. Drives, dinners, theaters, balls, suppers, with the gilding of superfluous wealth over it all. Sometimes the very tinkle of the ice in my champagne glass nearly drives me mad."

Mr. Parkenstacker looked ingenuously interested.

"I have always liked," he said, "to read and hear about the ways of wealthy and fashionable folks. I suppose I am a bit of a snob. But I like to have my information accurate. Now, I had formed the opinion that champagne is cooled in the bottle and not by placing ice in the glass."

The girl gave a musical laugh of genuine amusement.

"You should know," she explained, in an indulgent tone, "that we of the non-useful class depend for our amusement upon departure from precedent. Just now it is a fad to put ice in champagne. The idea was originated by a visiting Prince of Tartary while dining at the Waldorf. It will soon give way to some other whim. Just as at a dinner party this week on Madison Avenue a green kid glove was laid by the plate of each guest to be put on and used while eating olives."

"I see," admitted the young man, humbly.

"These special diversions of the inner circle do not become familiar to the common public."

"Sometimes," continued the girl, acknowledging his confession of error by a slight bow, "I have thought that if I ever should love a man it would be one of lowly station. One who is a worker and not a drone. But, doubtless, the claims of caste and wealth will prove stronger than my inclination. Just now I am besieged by two. One is a Grand Duke of a German principality. I think he has, or has had, a wife, somewhere, driven mad by his intemperance and cruelty. The other is an English Marquis, so cold and mercenary that I even prefer the diabolism of the Duke. What is it that impels me to tell you these things, Mr. Packenstacker?

"Parkenstacker," breathed the young man. "Indeed, you cannot know how much I appreciate your confidences."

The girl contemplated him with the calm, impersonal regard that befitted the difference in their stations.

"What is your line of business, Mr. Parkenstacker?" she asked.

"A very humble one. But I hope to rise in the world. Were you really in earnest when you said that you could love a man of lowly position?"

"Indeed I was. But I said 'might.' There is the Grand Duke and the Marquis, you know. Yes; no calling could be too humble were the man what I would wish him to be."

"I work," declared Mr. Parkenstacker, "in a restaurant."

The girl shrank slightly.

"Not as a waiter?" she said, a little imploringly. "Labor is noble, but personal attendance, you know—valets and—"

"I am not a waiter. I am cashier in"—on the street they faced that bounded the opposite side of the park was the brilliant electric sign "RESTAURANT"—"I am cashier in that restaurant you see there."

The girl consulted a tiny watch set in a bracelet of rich design upon her left wrist, and rose, hurriedly. She thrust her book into a glittering reticule suspended from her waist, for which, however, the book was too large.

"Why are you not at work?" she asked.

"I am on the night turn," said the young man; "it is yet an hour before my period begins. May I not hope to see you again?"

"I do not know. Perhaps—but the whim may not seize me again. I must go quickly now. There is a dinner, and a box at the play—and, oh! The same old round. Perhaps you noticed an automobile at the upper corner of the park as you came. One with a white body."

"And red running gear?" asked the young man, knitting his brows reflectively.

"Yes. I always come in that. Pierre waits for me there. He supposes me to be shopping in the department store across the square. Conceive of the bondage of the life wherein we must deceive even our chauffeurs. Good-night."

"But it is dark now," said Mr. Parkenstacker, "and the park is full of rude men. May I not walk—"

"If you have the slightest regard for my wishes," said the girl, firmly, "you will remain at this bench for ten minutes after I have left. I do not mean to accuse you, but you are probably aware that autos generally bear the monogram of their owner. Again, good-night."

Swift and stately she moved away through the dusk. The young man watched her graceful form as she reached the pavement at the park's edge, and turned up along it toward the corner where stood the automobile. Then he treacherously and unhesitatingly began to dodge and skim among the park trees and shrubbery in a course parallel to her route, keeping her well in sight.

When she reached the corner she turned her head to glance at the motor car, and then passed it, continuing on across the street. Sheltered behind a convenient standing cab, the young man followed her movements closely with his eyes. Passing down the sidewalk of the street opposite the park, she entered the restaurant with the blazing sign. The place was one of those frankly glaring establishments, all white paint and glass, where one may dine cheaply and conspicuously. The girl penetrated the restaurant to some retreat at its rear, whence she quickly emerged without her hat and veil.

The cashier's desk was well to the front. A red-haired girl an the stool climbed down, glancing pointedly at the clock as she did so. The girl in gray mounted in her place.

The young man thrust his hands into his pockets and walked slowly back along the sidewalk. At the corner his foot struck a small, paper-covered volume lying there, sending it sliding to the edge of the turf. By its picturesque cover he recognized it as the book the girl had been reading. He picked it up carelessly, and saw that its title was "New Arabian Nights," the author being of the name of Stevenson. He dropped it again upon the grass, and lounged, irresolute, for a minute. Then he stepped into the automobile, reclined upon the cushions, and said two words to the chauffeur:

"Club, Henri."

33

Buried Treasure

There are many kinds of fools. Now, will everybody please sit still until they are called upon specifically to rise?

I had been every kind of fool except one. I had expended my patrimony, pretended my matrimony, played poker, lawn-tennis, and bucket-shops—parted soon with my money in many ways. But there remained one rule of the wearer of cap and bells that I had not played. That was the Seeker after Buried Treasure. To few does the delectable furor come. But of all the would-be followers in the hoof-prints of King Midas none has found a pursuit so rich in pleasurable promise.

But, going back from my theme a while—as lame pens must do—I was a fool of the sentimental sort. I saw May Martha Mangum, and was hers. She was eighteen, the color of the white ivory keys of a new piano, beautiful, and possessed by the exquisite solemnity and pathetic witchery of an unsophisticated angel doomed to live in a small, dull, Texas prairie-town. She had a spirit and charm that could have enabled her to pluck rubies like raspberries from the crown of Belgium or any other sporty kingdom, but she did not know it, and I did not paint the picture for her.

You see, I wanted May Martha Mangum for to have and to hold. I wanted her to abide with me, and put my slippers and pipe away every day in places where they cannot be found of evenings.

May Martha's father was a man hidden behind whiskers and spectacles. He lived for bugs and butterflies and all insects that fly or crawl or buzz or get down your back or in the butter. He was an etymologist, or words to that effect. He spent his life seining the air for flying fish of the June-bug order, and then sticking pins through 'em and calling 'em names.

He and May Martha were the whole family. He prized her highly as a fine specimen of the *racibus humanus* because she saw that he had food at times, and put his clothes on right side before, and kept his alcohol-bottles filled. Scientists, they say, are apt to be absent-minded.

There was another besides myself who thought May Martha Mangum one to be desired. That was Goodloe Banks, a young man just home from college. He had all the attainments to be found in books—Latin, Greek, philosophy, and especially the higher branches of mathematics and logic.

If it hadn't been for his habit of pouring out this information and learning on every one that he addressed, I'd have liked him pretty well. But, even as it was, he and I were, you would have thought, great pals.

We got together every time we could because each of us wanted to pump the other for whatever straws we could to find which way the wind blew from the heart of May Martha Mangum—rather a mixed metaphor; Goodloe Banks would never have been guilty of that. That is the way of rivals.

You might say that Goodloe ran to books, manners, culture, rowing, intellect, and clothes. I would have put you in mind more of baseball and Friday-night debating societies—by way of culture—and maybe of a good horseback rider.

But in our talks together, and in our visits and conversation with May Martha, neither Goodloe Banks nor I could find out which one of us she preferred. May Martha was a natural-born non-committal, and knew in her cradle how to keep people guessing.

As I said, old man Mangum was absent-minded. After a long time he found out one day—a little butterfly must have told him—that two young men were trying to throw a net over the head of the young person, a daughter, or some such technical appendage, who looked after his comforts.

I never knew scientists could rise to such occasions. Old Mangum orally labeled and classified Goodloe and myself easily among the lowest orders of the vertebrates; and in English, too, without going any further into Latin than the simple references to *Orgetorix, Rex Helvetii*—which is as far as I ever went, myself. And he told us that if he ever caught us around his house again he would add us to his collection.

Goodloe Banks and I remained away five days, expecting the storm to subside. When we dared to call at the house again May Martha Mangum and her father were gone. Gone! The house they had rented was closed. Their little store of goods and chattels was gone also.

And not a word of farewell to either of us from May Martha—not a white, fluttering note pinned to the hawthorn-bush; not a chalk-mark on the gate-post nor a post-card in the post-office to give us a clew.

For two months Goodloe Banks and I—separately—tried every scheme we could think of to track the runaways. We used our friendship and influence with the ticket-agent, with livery-stable men, railroad conductors, and our one lone, lorn constable, but without results.

Then we became better friends and worse enemies than ever. We forgathered in the back room of Snyder's saloon every afternoon after work, and played dominoes, and laid conversational traps to find out from each other if anything had been discovered. That is the way of rivals.

Now, Goodloe Banks had a sarcastic way of displaying his own learning and putting me in the class that was reading "Poor Jane Ray, her bird is dead, she cannot play." Well, I rather liked Goodloe, and I had a contempt for his college learning, and I was always regarded as good-natured, so I kept my temper. And I was trying to find out if he knew anything about May Martha, so I endured his society.

In talking things over one afternoon he said to me:

"Suppose you do find her, Ed, whereby would you profit? Miss Mangum has a mind. Perhaps it is yet uncultured, but she is destined for higher things than you could give her. I have talked with no one who seemed to appreciate more the enchantment of the ancient poets and writers and the modern cults that have assimilated and expended their philosophy of life. Don't you think you are wasting your time looking for her?"

"My idea," said I, "of a happy home is an eight-room house in a grove of live-oaks by the side of a *charco* on a Texas prairie. A piano," I went on, "with an automatic player in the sitting-room, three thousand head of cattle under fence for a starter, a buckboard and ponies always hitched at a post for ‹the missus'—and May Martha Mangum to spend the profits of the ranch as she pleases, and to abide with me, and put my slippers and pipe away every day in places where they cannot be found of evenings. That," said I, "is what is to be; and a fig—a dried, Smyrna, dago-stand fig—for your curriculums, cults, and philosophy."

"She is meant for higher things," repeated Goodloe Banks.

"Whatever she is meant for," I answered, just now she is out of pocket. And I shall find her as soon as I can without aid of the colleges."

"The game is blocked," said Goodloe, putting down a domino; and we had the beer.

Shortly after that a young farmer whom I knew came into town and brought me a folded blue paper. He said his grandfather had just died. I concealed a tear, and he went on to say that the old man had jealously guarded this paper for twenty years. He left it to his family as part of his estate, the rest of which consisted of two mules and a hypotenuse of non-arable land.

The sheet of paper was of the old, blue kind used during the rebellion of the abolitionists against the secessionists. It was dated June 14, 1863, and it described the hiding-place of ten burro-loads of gold and silver coin valued at three hundred thousand dollars. Old Rundle—grandfather of his grandson, Sam—was given the information by a Spanish priest who was in on the treasure-burying, and who died many years before—no, afterward—in old Rundle's house. Old Rundle wrote it down from dictation.

"Why didn't your father look this up?" I asked young Rundle.

"He went blind before he could do so," he replied.

"Why didn't you hunt for it yourself?" I asked.

"Well," said he, "I've only known about the paper for ten years. First there was the spring ploughin' to do, and then choppin' the weeds out of the corn; and then come takin' fodder; and mighty soon winter was on us. It seemed to run along that way year after year."

That sounded perfectly reasonable to me, so I took it up with young Lee Rundle at once.

The directions on the paper were simple. The whole burro cavalcade laden with the treasure started from an old Spanish mission in Dolores County. They travelled due south by the compass until they reached the Alamito River. They forded this, and buried the treasure on the top of a little mountain shaped like a pack-saddle standing in a row between two higher ones. A heap of stones marked the place of the buried treasure. All the party except the Spanish priest were killed by Indians a few days later. The secret was a monopoly. It looked good to me.

Lee Rundle suggested that we rig out a camping outfit, hire a surveyor to run out the line from the Spanish mission, and then spend the three hundred thousand dollars seeing the sights in Fort Worth. But, without being highly educated, I knew a way to save time and expense.

We went to the State land-office and had a practical, what they call a "working," sketch made of all the surveys of land from the old mission to the Alamito River. On this map I drew a line due southward to the river. The length of lines of each survey and section of land was accurately given on the sketch. By these we found the point on the river and had a "connection" made with it and an important, well-identified corner of the Los Animos five-league survey—a grant made by King Philip of Spain.

By doing this we did not need to have the line run out by a surveyor. It was a great saving of expense and time.

So, Lee Rundle and I fitted out a two-horse wagon team with all the accessories, and drove a hundred and forty-nine miles to

Chico, the nearest town to the point we wished to reach. There we picked up a deputy county surveyor. He found the corner of the Los Animos survey for us, ran out the five thousand seven hundred and twenty varas west that our sketch called for, laid a stone on the spot, had coffee and bacon, and caught the mail-stage back to Chico.

I was pretty sure we would get that three hundred thousand dollars. Lee Rundle's was to be only one-third, because I was paying all the expenses. With that two hundred thousand dollars I knew I could find May Martha Mangum if she was on earth. And with it I could flutter the butterflies in old man Mangum's dovecot, too. If I could find that treasure!

But Lee and I established camp. Across the river were a dozen little mountains densely covered by cedar-brakes, but not one shaped like a pack-saddle. That did not deter us. Appearances are deceptive. A pack-saddle, like beauty, may exist only in the eye of the beholder.

I and the grandson of the treasure examined those cedar-covered hills with the care of a lady hunting for the wicked flea. We explored every side, top, circumference, mean elevation, angle, slope, and concavity of every one for two miles up and down the river. We spent four days doing so. Then we hitched up the roan and the dun, and hauled the remains of the coffee and bacon the one hundred and forty-nine miles back to Concho City.

Lee Rundle chewed much tobacco on the return trip. I was busy driving, because I was in a hurry.

As shortly as could be after our empty return Goodloe Banks and I forgathered in the back room of Snyder's saloon to play dominoes and fish for information. I told Goodloe about my expedition after the buried treasure.

"If I could have found that three hundred thousand dollars," I said to him, "I could have scoured and sifted the surface of the earth to find May Martha Mangum."

"She is meant for higher things," said Goodloe. "I shall find her myself. But, tell me how you went about discovering the spot where this unearthed increment was imprudently buried."

I told him in the smallest detail. I showed him the draughtsman's sketch with the distances marked plainly upon it.

After glancing over it in a masterly way, he leaned back in his chair and bestowed upon me an explosion of sardonic, superior, collegiate laughter.

"Well, you *are* a fool, Jim," he said, when he could speak.

"It's your play," said I, patiently, fingering my double-six.

"Twenty," said Goodloe, making two crosses on the table with his chalk.

"Why am I a fool?" I asked. "Buried treasure has been found before in many places."

"Because," said he, "in calculating the point on the river where your line would strike you neglected to allow for the variation. The variation there would be nine degrees west. Let me have your pencil."

Goodloe Banks figured rapidly on the back of an envelope.

"The distance, from north to south, of the line run from the Spanish mission," said he, "is exactly twenty-two miles. It was run by a pocket-compass, according to your story. Allowing for the variation, the point on the Alamito River where you should have searched for your treasure is exactly six miles and nine hundred and forty-five varas farther west than the place you hit upon. Oh, what a fool you are, Jim!"

"What is this variation that you speak of?" I asked. "I thought figures never lied."

"The variation of the magnetic compass," said Goodloe, "from the true meridian."

He smiled in his superior way; and then I saw come out in his face the singular, eager, consuming cupidity of the seeker after buried treasure.

"Sometimes," he said with the air of the oracle, "these old traditions of hidden money are not without foundation. Suppose you let me look over that paper describing the location. Perhaps together we might—"

The result was that Goodloe Banks and I, rivals in love, became companions in adventure. We went to Chico by stage from Huntersburg, the nearest railroad town. In Chico we hired a team drawing a covered spring-wagon and camping paraphernalia. We had the same surveyor run out our distance, as revised by Goodloe and his variations, and then dismissed him and sent him on his homeward road.

It was night when we arrived. I fed the horses and made a fire near the bank of the river and cooked supper. Goodloe would have helped, but his education had not fitted him for practical things.

But while I worked he cheered me with the expression of great thoughts handed down from the dead ones of old. He quoted some translations from the Greek at much length.

"Anacreon," he explained. "That was a favorite passage with Miss Mangum—as I recited it."

"She is meant for higher things," said I, repeating his phrase.

"Can there be anything higher," asked Goodloe, "than to dwell in the society of the classics, to live in the atmosphere of learning and culture? You have often decried education. What of your wasted efforts through your ignorance of simple mathematics? How soon would you have found your treasure if my knowledge had not shown you your error?"

"We'll take a look at those hills across the river first," said I, "and see what we find. I am still doubtful about variations. I have been brought up to believe that the needle is true to the pole."

The next morning was a bright June one. We were up early and had breakfast. Goodloe was charmed. He recited—Keats, I think it was, and Kelly or Shelley—while I broiled the bacon. We were getting ready to cross the river, which was little more than a shallow creek there, and explore the many sharp-peaked cedar-covered hills on the other side.

"My good Ulysses," said Goodloe, slapping me on the shoulder while I was washing the tin breakfast-plates, "let me see the enchanted document once more. I believe it gives directions for climbing the hill shaped like a pack-saddle. I never saw a pack-saddle. What is it like, Jim?"

"Score one against culture," said I. "I'll know it when I see it."

Goodloe was looking at old Rundle's document when he ripped out a most uncollegiate swear-word.

"Come here," he said, holding the paper up against the sunlight. "Look at that," he said, laying his finger against it.

On the blue paper—a thing I had never noticed before—I saw stand out in white letters the word and figures: "Malvern, 1898."

"What about it?" I asked.

"It's the water-mark," said Goodloe. "The paper was manufactured in 1898. The writing on the paper is dated 1863. This is a palpable fraud."

"Oh, I don't know," said I. "The Rundles are pretty reliable, plain, uneducated country people. Maybe the paper manufacturers tried to perpetrate a swindle."

And then Goodloe Banks went as wild as his education permitted. He dropped the glasses off his nose and glared at me.

"I've often told you you were a fool," he said. "You have let yourself be imposed upon by a clodhopper. And you have imposed upon me."

"How," I asked, "have I imposed upon you?"

"By your ignorance," said he. "Twice I have discovered serious flaws in your plans that a common-school education should have enabled you to avoid. And," he continued, "I have been put to expense that I could ill afford in pursuing this swindling quest. I am done with it."

I rose and pointed a large pewter spoon at him, fresh from the dish-water.

"Goodloe Banks," I said, "I care not one parboiled navy bean for your education. I always barely tolerated it in any one, and I despised it in you. What has your learning done for you? It is a curse to yourself and a bore to your friends. Away," I said—"away with your water-marks and variations! They are nothing to me. They shall not deflect me from the quest."

I pointed with my spoon across the river to a small mountain shaped like a pack-saddle.

"I am going to search that mountain," I went on, "for the treasure. Decide now whether you are in it or not. If you wish to let a water-mark or a variation shake your soul, you are no true adventurer. Decide."

A white cloud of dust began to rise far down the river road. It was the mail-wagon from Hesperus to Chico. Goodloe flagged it.

"I am done with the swindle," said he, sourly. "No one but a fool would pay any attention to that paper now. Well, you always were a fool, Jim. I leave you to your fate."

He gathered his personal traps, climbed into the mail-wagon, adjusted his glasses nervously, and flew away in a cloud of dust.

After I had washed the dishes and staked the horses on new grass, I crossed the shallow river and made my way slowly through the cedar-brakes up to the top of the hill shaped like a pack-saddle.

It was a wonderful June day. Never in my life had I seen so many birds, so many butter-flies, dragon-flies, grasshoppers, and such winged and stinged beasts of the air and fields.

I investigated the hill shaped like a pack-saddle from base to summit. I found an absolute absence of signs relating to buried treasure. There was no pile of stones, no ancient blazes on the trees, none of the evidences of the three hundred thousand dollars, as set forth in the document of old man Rundle.

I came down the hill in the cool of the afternoon. Suddenly, out of the cedar-brake I stepped into a beautiful green valley where a tributary small stream ran into the Alamito River.

And there I was startled to see what I took to be a wild man, with unkempt beard and ragged hair, pursuing a giant butterfly with brilliant wings.

"Perhaps he is an escaped madman," I thought; and wondered how he had strayed so far from seats of education and learning.

And then I took a few more steps and saw a vine-covered cottage near the small stream. And in a little grassy glade I saw May Martha Mangum plucking wild flowers.

She straightened up and looked at me. For the first time since I knew her I saw her face—which was the color of the white keys of a new piano—turn pink. I walked toward her without a word. She let the gathered flowers trickle slowly from her hand to the grass.

"I knew you would come, Jim," she said clearly. "Father wouldn't let me write, but I knew you would come."

What followed you may guess—there was my wagon and team just across the river.

I've often wondered what good too much education is to a man if he can't use it for himself. If all the benefits of it are to go to others, where does it come in?

For May Martha Mangum abides with me. There is an eight-room house in a live-oak grove, and a piano with an automatic player, and a good start toward the three thousand head of cattle is under fence.

And when I ride home at night my pipe and slippers are put away in places where they cannot be found.

But who cares for that? Who cares—who cares?

34

Friends in San Rosario

The west-bound train stopped at San Rosario on time at 8.20 a.m. A man with a thick black-leather wallet under his arm left the train and walked rapidly up the main street of the town. There were other passengers who also got off at San Rosario, but they either slouched limberly over to the railroad eating-house or the Silver Dollar saloon, or joined the groups of idlers about the station.

Indecision had no part in the movements of the man with the wallet. He was short in stature, but strongly built, with very light, closely-trimmed hair, smooth, determined face, and aggressive, gold-rimmed nose glasses. He was well dressed in the prevailing Eastern style. His air denoted a quiet but conscious reserve force, if not actual authority.

After walking a distance of three squares he came to the centre of the town's business area. Here another street of importance crossed the main one, forming the hub of San Rosario's life and commerce. Upon one corner stood the post-office. Upon another Rubensky's Clothing Emporium. The other two diagonally opposing corners were occupied by the town's two banks, the First National and the Stockmen's National. Into the First

National Bank of San Rosario the newcomer walked, never slowing his brisk step until he stood at the cashier's window. The bank opened for business at nine, and the working force was already assembled, each member preparing his department for the day's business. The cashier was examining the mail when he noticed the stranger standing at his window.

"Bank doesn't open 'til nine," he remarked curtly, but without feeling. He had had to make that statement so often to early birds since San Rosario adopted city banking hours.

"I am well aware of that," said the other man, in cool, brittle tones. "Will you kindly receive my card?"

The cashier drew the small, spotless parallelogram inside the bars of his wicket, and read:

J. F. C. Nettlewick

National Bank Examiner

"Oh—er—will you walk around inside, Mr.—er—Nettlewick. Your first visit—didn't know your business, of course. Walk right around, please."

The examiner was quickly inside the sacred precincts of the bank, where he was ponderously introduced to each employee in turn by Mr. Edlinger, the cashier—a middle-aged gentleman of deliberation, discretion, and method.

"I was kind of expecting Sam Turner round again, pretty soon," said Mr. Edlinger. "Sam's been examining us now, for about four years. I guess you'll find us all right, though, considering the tightness in business. Not overly much money on hand, but able to stand the storms, sir, stand the storms."

"Mr. Turner and I have been ordered by the Comptroller to exchange districts," said the examiner, in his decisive, formal tones. "He is covering my old territory in Southern Illinois and Indiana. I will take the cash first, please."

Perry Dorsey, the teller, was already arranging his cash on the counter for the examiner's inspection. He knew it was right to a cent, and he had nothing to fear, but he was nervous and flustered. So was every man in the bank. There was something so icy and swift, so impersonal and uncompromising about this man that his very presence seemed an accusation. He looked to be a man who would never make nor overlook an error.

Mr. Nettlewick first seized the currency, and with a rapid, almost juggling motion, counted it by packages. Then he spun the sponge cup toward him and verified the count by bills. His thin, white fingers flew like some expert musician's upon the keys of a piano. He dumped the gold upon the counter with a crash, and the coins whined and sang as they skimmed across the marble slab from the tips of his nimble digits. The air was full of fractional currency when he came to the halves and quarters. He counted the last nickle and dime. He had the scales brought, and he weighed every sack of silver in the vault. He questioned Dorsey concerning each of the cash memoranda—certain checks, charge slips, etc., carried over from the previous day's work—with unimpeachable courtesy, yet with something so mysteriously momentous in his frigid manner, that the teller was reduced to pink cheeks and a stammering tongue.

This newly-imported examiner was so different from Sam Turner. It had been Sam's way to enter the bank with a shout, pass the cigars, and tell the latest stories he had picked up on his rounds. His customary greeting to Dorsey had been, "Hello, Perry! Haven't skipped out with the boodle yet, I see." Turner's way of counting the cash had been different, too. He would finger the packages of bills in a tired kind of way, and then go into the vault and kick over a few sacks of silver, and the thing was done. Halves and quarters and dimes? Not for Sam Turner. "No chicken feed for me," he would say when they were set before him. "I'm not in the agricultural department." But, then, Turner was a Texan, an old friend of the bank's president, and had known Dorsey since he was a baby.

While the examiner was counting the cash, Major Thomas B. Kingman—known to every one as "Major Tom"—the president of the First National, drove up to the side door with his old dun horse and buggy, and came inside. He saw the examiner busy with the money, and, going into the little "pony corral," as he called it, in which his desk was railed off, he began to look over his letters.

Earlier, a little incident had occurred that even the sharp eyes of the examiner had failed to notice. When he had begun his work at the cash counter, Mr. Edlinger had winked significantly at Roy Wilson, the youthful bank messenger, and nodded his head slightly toward the front door. Roy understood, got his hat, and walked leisurely out, with his collector's book under his arm. Once outside, he made a bee-line for the Stockmen's National. That bank was also getting ready to open. No customers had, as yet, presented themselves.

"Say, you people!" cried Roy, with the familiarity of youth and long acquaintance, "you want to get a move on you. There's a new bank examiner over at the First, and he's a stem-winder. He's counting nickels on Perry, and he's got the whole outfit bluffed. Mr. Edlinger gave me the tip to let you know."

Mr. Buckley, president of the Stockmen's National—a stout, elderly man, looking like a farmer dressed for Sunday—heard Roy from his private office at the rear and called him.

"Has Major Kingman come down to the bank yet?" he asked of the boy.

"Yes, sir, he was just driving up as I left," said Roy.

"I want you to take him a note. Put it into his own hands as soon as you get back."

Mr. Buckley sat down and began to write.

Roy returned and handed to Major Kingman the envelope containing the note. The major read it, folded it, and slipped it into his vest pocket. He leaned back in his chair for a few moments as if he were meditating deeply, and then rose and went into the vault. He came out with the bulky, old-fashioned leather note case stamped on the back in gilt letters, "Bills Discounted." In this were the notes due the bank with their attached securities, and the major, in his rough way, dumped the lot upon his desk and began to sort them over.

By this time Nettlewick had finished his count of the cash. His pencil fluttered like a swallow over the sheet of paper on which he had set his figures. He opened his black wallet, which seemed to be also a kind of secret memorandum book, made a few rapid figures in it, wheeled and transfixed Dorsey with the glare of his spectacles. That look seemed to say: "You're safe this time, but—"

"Cash all correct," snapped the examiner. He made a dash for the individual bookkeeper, and, for a few minutes there was a fluttering of ledger leaves and a sailing of balance sheets through the air.

"How often do you balance your pass-books?" he demanded, suddenly.

"Er—once a month," faltered the individual bookkeeper, wondering how many years they would give him.

"All right," said the examiner, turning and charging upon the general bookkeeper, who had the statements of his foreign banks and their reconcilement memoranda ready. Everything there was found to be all right. Then the stub book of the certificates of deposit. Flutter—flutter—zip—zip—check! All right. List of over-drafts, please. Thanks. H'm-m. Unsigned bills of the bank, next. All right.

Then came the cashier's turn, and easy-going Mr. Edlinger rubbed his nose and polished his glasses nervously under the quick fire of questions concerning the circulation, undivided profits, bank real estate, and stock ownership.

Presently Nettlewick was aware of a big man towering above him at his elbow—a man sixty years of age, rugged and hale, with a rough, grizzled beard, a mass of gray hair, and a pair of penetrating blue eyes that confronted the formidable glasses of the examiner without a flicker.

"Er—Major Kingman, our president—er—Mr. Nettlewick," said the cashier.

Two men of very different types shook hands. One was a finished product of the world of straight lines, conventional methods, and formal affairs. The other was something freer, wider, and nearer to nature. Tom Kingman had not been cut to any pattern. He had been mule-driver, cowboy, ranger, soldier, sheriff, prospector, and cattleman. Now, when he was bank president, his old comrades from the prairies, of the saddle, tent, and trail found no change in him. He had made his fortune when Texas cattle were at the high tide of value, and had organized the First National Bank of San Rosario. In spite of his largeness of heart and sometimes unwise generosity toward his old friends, the bank had prospered, for Major Tom Kingman knew men as well as he knew cattle. Of late years the cattle business had known a depression, and the major's bank was one of the few whose losses had not been great.

"And now," said the examiner, briskly, pulling out his watch, "the last thing is the loans. We will take them up now, if you please."

He had gone through the First National at almost record-breaking speed—but thoroughly, as he did everything. The running order of the bank was smooth and clean, and that had facilitated his work. There was but one other bank in the town. He received from the Government a fee of twenty-five dollars for each bank that he examined. He should be able to go over those loans and discounts in half an hour. If so, he could examine the other bank immediately afterward, and catch the 11.45, the only other train that day in the direction he was working. Otherwise, he would have to spend the night and Sunday in this uninteresting Western town. That was why Mr. Nettlewick was rushing matters.

"Come with me, sir," said Major Kingman, in his deep voice, that united the Southern drawl with the rhythmic twang of the West; "We will go over them together. Nobody in the bank knows those notes as I do. Some of 'em are a little wobbly on their legs, and some are mavericks without extra many brands on their backs, but they'll most all pay out at the round-up."

The two sat down at the president's desk. First, the examiner went through the notes at lightning speed, and added up their total, finding it to agree with the amount of loans carried on the book of daily balances. Next, he took up the larger loans, inquiring scrupulously into the condition of their endorsers or securities. The new examiner's mind seemed to course and turn and make unexpected dashes hither and thither like a bloodhound seeking a trail. Finally he pushed aside all the notes except a few, which he arranged in a neat pile before him, and began a dry, formal little speech.

"I find, sir, the condition of your bank to be very good, considering the poor crops and the depression in the cattle interests of your state. The clerical work seems to be done accurately and punctually. Your past-due paper is moderate in amount, and promises only a small loss. I would recommend the calling in of your large loans, and the making of only sixty and ninety day or call loans until general business revives. And now, there is one thing more, and I will have finished with the bank. Here are six notes aggregating something like $40,000. They are secured, according to their faces, by various stocks, bonds, shares, etc. to the value of $70,000. Those securities are missing from the notes to which they should be attached. I suppose you have them in the safe or vault. You will permit me to examine them."

Major Tom's light-blue eyes turned unflinchingly toward the examiner.

"No, sir," he said, in a low but steady tone; "those securities are neither in the safe nor in the vault. I have taken them. You may hold me personally responsible for their absence."

Nettlewick felt a slight thrill. He had not expected this. He had struck a momentous trail when the hunt was drawing to a close.

"Ah!" said the examiner. He waited a moment, and then continued: "May I ask you to explain more definitely?"

"The securities were taken by me," repeated the major. "It was not for my own use, but to save an old friend in trouble. Come in here, sir, and we'll talk it over."

He led the examiner into the bank's private office at the rear, and closed the door. There was a desk, and a table, and half-a-dozen leather-covered chairs. On the wall was the mounted head of a Texas steer with horns five feet from tip to tip. Opposite hung the major's old cavalry saber that he had carried at Shiloh and Fort Pillow.

Placing a chair for Nettlewick, the major seated himself by the window, from which he could see the post-office and the carved limestone front of the Stockmen's National. He did not speak at once, and Nettlewick felt, perhaps, that the ice could be broken by something so near its own temperature as the voice of official warning.

"Your statement," he began, "since you have failed to modify it, amounts, as you must know, to a very serious thing. You are aware, also, of what my duty must compel me to do. I shall have to go before the United States Commissioner and make—"

"I know, I know," said Major Tom, with a wave of his hand. "You don't suppose I'd run a bank without being posted on national banking laws and the revised statutes! Do your duty. I'm not asking any favors. But, I spoke of my friend. I did want you to hear me tell you about Bob."

Nettlewick settled himself in his chair. There would be no leaving San Rosario for him that day. He would have to telegraph to the Comptroller of the Currency; he would have to swear out a warrant before the United States Commissioner for the arrest of Major Kingman; perhaps he would be ordered to close the bank on account of the loss of the securities. It was not the first crime the examiner had unearthed. Once or twice the terrible upheaval of human emotions that his investigations had loosed had almost caused a ripple in his official calm. He had seen bank men kneel and plead and cry like women for a chance—an hour's time—the overlooking of a single error. One cashier had shot himself at his desk before him. None of them had taken it with the dignity and coolness of this stern old Westerner. Nettlewick felt that he owed it to him at least to listen if he wished to talk. With his elbow on the arm of his chair, and his square chin resting upon the fingers of his right hand, the bank examiner waited to hear the confession of the president of the First National Bank of San Rosario.

"When a man's your friend," began Major Tom, somewhat didactically, "for forty years, and tried by water, fire, earth, and cyclones, when you can do him a little favor you feel like doing it."

("Embezzle for him $70,000 worth of securities," thought the examiner.)

"We were cowboys together, Bob and I," continued the major, speaking slowly, and deliberately, and musingly, as if his thoughts were rather with the past than the critical present, "and we prospected together for gold and silver over Arizona, New Mexico, and a good part of California. We were both in the war of 'sixty-one, but in different commands. We've fought Indians and horse thieves side by side; we've starved for weeks in a cabin in the Arizona mountains, buried twenty feet deep in snow; we've ridden herd together when the wind blew so hard the lightning couldn't strike—well, Bob and I have been through some rough spells since the first time we met in the branding camp of the old Anchor-Bar ranch. And during that time we've found it necessary more than once to help each other out of tight places. In those days it was expected of a man to stick to his friend, and he didn't ask any credit for it. Probably next day you'd need him to get at your back and help stand off a band of Apaches, or put a tourniquet on your leg above a rattlesnake bite and ride for whisky. So, after all, it was give and take, and if you didn't stand square with your pardner, why, you might be shy one when you needed him. But Bob was a man who was willing to go further than that. He never played a limit.

"Twenty years ago I was sheriff of this county, and I made Bob my chief deputy. That was before the boom in cattle when we both made our stake. I was sheriff and collector, and it was a big thing for me then. I was married, and we had a boy and a girl—a four and a six year old. There was a comfortable house next to the courthouse, furnished by the county, rent free, and I was saving some money. Bob did most of the office work. Both of us had seen rough times and plenty of rustling and danger, and I tell you it was great to hear the rain and the sleet dashing against the windows of nights, and be warm and safe and comfortable, and know you could get up in the morning and be shaved and have folks call you 'mister.' And then, I had the finest wife and kids that ever struck the range, and my old friend with me enjoying the first fruits of prosperity and white shirts, and I guess I was happy. Yes, I was happy about that time."

The major sighed and glanced casually out of the window. The bank examiner changed his position, and leaned his chin upon his other hand.

"One winter," continued the major, "the money for the county taxes came pouring in so fast that I didn't have time to take the stuff to the bank for a week. I just shoved the checks into a cigar box and the money into a sack, and locked them in the big safe that belonged to the sheriff's office.

"I had been overworked that week, and was about sick, anyway. My nerves were out of order, and my sleep at night didn't seem to rest me. The doctor had some scientific name for it, and I was taking medicine. And so, added to the rest, I went to bed at night with that money on my mind. Not that there was much need of being worried, for the safe was a good one, and nobody but Bob and I knew the combination. On Friday night there was about $6,500 in cash in the bag. On Saturday morning I went to the office as usual. The safe was locked, and Bob was writing at his desk. I opened the safe, and the money was gone. I called Bob, and roused everybody in the court-house to announce the robbery. It struck me that Bob took it pretty quiet, considering how much it reflected upon both him and me.

"Two days went by and we never got a clew. It couldn't have been burglars, for the safe had been opened by the combination in the proper way. People must have begun to talk, for one afternoon in comes Alice—that's my wife—and the boy and girl, and Alice stamps her foot, and her eyes flash, and she cries out, 'The lying wretches—Tom, Tom!' and I catch her in a faint, and bring her 'round little by little, and she lays her head down and cries and cries for the first time since she took Tom Kingman's name and fortunes. And Jack and Zilla—the youngsters—they were always wild as tiger cubs to rush at Bob and climb all over him whenever they were allowed to come to the court-house—they stood and kicked their little shoes, and herded together like scared partridges. They were having their first trip down into the shadows of life. Bob was working at his desk, and he got up and went out without a word. The grand jury was in session then, and the next morning Bob went before them and confessed that he stole the money. He said he lost it in a poker game. In fifteen minutes they had found a true bill and sent me the warrant to arrest the man with whom I'd been closer than a thousand brothers for many a year.

"I did it, and then I said to Bob, pointing: 'There's my house, and here's my office, and up there's Maine, and out that way is California, and over there is Florida—and that's your range 'til court meets. You're in my charge, and I take the responsibility. You be here when you're wanted.'

"'Thanks, Tom,' he said, kind of carelessly; 'I was sort of hoping you wouldn't lock me up. Court meets next Monday, so, if you don't object, I'll just loaf around the office until then. I've got one favour to ask, if it isn't too much. If you'd let the kids come out in the yard once in a while and have a romp I'd like it.'

"'Why not?' I answered him. 'They're welcome, and so are you. And come to my house, the same as ever.' You see, Mr. Nettlewick, you can't make a friend of a thief, but neither can you make a thief of a friend, all at once."

The examiner made no answer. At that moment was heard the shrill whistle of a locomotive pulling into the depot. That was the train on the little, narrow-gauge road that struck into San Rosario from the south. The major cocked his ear and listened for a moment, and looked at his watch. The narrow-gauge was in on time—10.35. The major continued:

"So Bob hung around the office, reading the papers and smoking. I put another deputy to work in his place, and after a while, the first excitement of the case wore off.

"One day when we were alone in the office Bob came over to where I was sitting. He was looking sort of grim and blue—the same look he used to get when he'd been up watching for Indians all night or herd-riding.

"'Tom,' says he, 'it's harder than standing off redskins; it's harder than lying in the lava desert forty miles from water; but I'm going to stick it out to the end. You know that's been my style. But if you'd tip me the smallest kind of a sign—if you'd just say, "Bob I understand," why, it would make it lots easier.'

"I was surprised. 'I don't know what you mean, Bob,' I said. 'Of course, you know that I'd do anything under the sun to help you that I could. But you've got me guessing.'

"'All right, Tom,' was all he said, and he went back to his newspaper and lit another cigar.

"It was the night before court met when I found out what he meant. I went to bed that night with that same old, light-headed, nervous feeling come back upon me. I dropped off to sleep about midnight. When I awoke I was standing half dressed in one of the court-house corridors. Bob was holding one of my arms, our family doctor the other, and Alice was shaking me and half crying. She had sent for the doctor without my knowing it, and when he came they had found me out of bed and missing, and had begun a search.

"'Sleep-walking,' said the doctor.

"All of us went back to the house, and the doctor told us some remarkable stories about the strange things people had done while in that condition. I was feeling rather chilly after my trip out, and, as my wife was out of the room at the time, I pulled open the door of an old wardrobe that stood in the room and dragged out a big quilt I had seen in there. With it tumbled out the bag of money for stealing which Bob was to be tried—and convicted—in the morning.

"'How the jumping rattlesnakes did that get there?' I yelled, and all hands must have seen how surprised I was. Bob knew in a flash.

"'You darned old snoozer,' he said, with the old-time look on his face, 'I saw you put it there. I watched you open the safe and take it out, and I followed you. I looked through the window and saw you hide it in that wardrobe.'

"'Then, you blankety-blank, flop-eared, sheep-headed coyote, what did you say you took it, for?'

"'Because,' said Bob, simply, 'I didn't know you were asleep.'

"I saw him glance toward the door of the room where Jack and Zilla were, and I knew then what it meant to be a man's friend from Bob's point of view."

Major Tom paused, and again directed his glance out of the window. He saw some one in the Stockmen's National Bank reach and draw a yellow shade down the whole length of its plate-glass, big front window, although the position of the sun did not seem to warrant such a defensive movement against its rays.

Nettlewick sat up straight in his chair. He had listened patiently, but without consuming interest, to the major's story. It had impressed him as irrelevant to the situation, and it could certainly have no effect upon the consequences. Those Western people, he thought, had an exaggerated sentimentality. They were not business-like. They needed to be protected from their friends. Evidently the major had concluded. And what he had said amounted to nothing.

"May I ask," said the examiner, "if you have anything further to say that bears directly upon the question of those abstracted securities?"

"Abstracted securities, sir!" Major Tom turned suddenly in his chair, his blue eyes flashing upon the examiner. "What do you mean, sir?"

He drew from his coat pocket a batch of folded papers held together by a rubber band, tossed them into Nettlewick's hands, and rose to his feet.

"You'll find those securities there, sir, every stock, bond, and share of 'em. I took them from the notes while you were counting the cash. Examine and compare them for yourself."

The major led the way back into the banking room. The examiner, astounded, perplexed, nettled, at sea, followed. He felt that he had been made the victim of something that was not exactly a hoax, but that left him in the shoes of one who had been played upon, used, and then discarded, without even an inkling of the game. Perhaps, also, his official position had been irreverently juggled with. But there was nothing he could take hold of. An official report of the matter would be an absurdity. And, somehow, he felt that he would never know anything more about the matter than he did then.

Frigidly, mechanically, Nettlewick examined the securities, found them to tally with the notes, gathered his black wallet, and rose to depart.

"I will say," he protested, turning the indignant glare of his glasses upon Major Kingman, "that your statements—your misleading statements, which you have not condescended to explain—do not appear to be quite the thing, regarded either as business or humour. I do not understand such motives or actions."

Major Tom looked down at him serenely and not unkindly.

"Son," he said, "there are plenty of things in the chaparral, and on the prairies, and up the canyons that you don't understand. But I want to thank you for listening to a garrulous old man's prosy story. We old Texans love to talk about our adventures and our old comrades, and the home folks have long ago learned to run when we begin with 'Once upon a time,' so we have to spin our yarns to the stranger within our gates."

The major smiled, but the examiner only bowed coldly, and abruptly quitted the bank. They saw him travel diagonally across the street in a straight line and enter the Stockmen's National Bank.

Major Tom sat down at his desk, and drew from his vest pocket the note Roy had given him. He had read it once, but hurriedly, and now, with something like a twinkle in his eyes, he read it again. These were the words he read:

DEAR TOM:
I hear there's one of Uncle Sam's grayhounds going through you, and that means that we'll catch him inside of a couple of hours, maybe. Now, I want you to do something for me. We've got just $2,200 in the bank, and the law requires that we have $20,000. I let Ross and Fisher have $18,000 late yesterday afternoon to buy up that Gibson bunch of cattle. They'll realise $40,000 in less than thirty days on the transaction, but that won't make my cash on hand look any prettier to that bank examiner. Now, I can't show him those notes, for they're just plain notes of hand without any security in sight, but you know very well that Pink Ross and Jim Fisher are two of the finest white men God ever made, and they'll do the square thing. You remember Jim Fisher—he was the one who shot that faro dealer in El Paso. I wired Sam Bradshaw's bank to send me $20,000, and it will get in on the narrow-gauge at 10.35. You can't let a bank examiner in to count $2,200 and close your doors. Tom, you hold that examiner. Hold him. Hold him if you have to rope him and sit on his head. Watch our front window after the narrow-gauge gets in, and when we've got the cash inside we'll pull down the shade for a signal. Don't turn him loose till then. I'm counting on you, Tom.
Your Old Pard,
BOB BUCKLY,
Prest. Stockmen's National.

The major began to tear the note into small pieces and throw them into his waste basket. He gave a satisfied little chuckle as he did so.

"Confounded old reckless cowpuncher!" he growled, contentedly, "that pays him some on account for what he tried to do for me in the sheriff's office twenty years ago."

35

THE PASSING OF BLACK EAGLE

For some months of a certain year a grim bandit infested the Texas border along the Rio Grande. Peculiarly striking to the optic nerve was this notorious marauder. His personality secured him the title of "Black Eagle, the Terror of the Border." Many fearsome tales are on record concerning the doings of him and his followers. Suddenly, in the space of a single minute, Black Eagle vanished from earth. He was never heard of again. His own band never even guessed the mystery of his disappearance. The border ranches and settlements feared he would come again to ride and ravage the mesquite flats. He never will. It is to disclose the fate of Black Eagle that this narrative is written.

The initial movement of the story is furnished by the foot of a bartender in St. Louis. His discerning eye fell upon the form of Chicken Ruggles as he pecked with avidity at the free lunch. Chicken was a "hobo." He had a long nose like the bill of a fowl, an inordinate appetite for poultry, and a habit of gratifying it without expense, which accounts for the name given him by his fellow vagrants.

Physicians agree that the partaking of liquids at meal times is not a healthy practice. The hygiene of the saloon promulgates the opposite. Chicken had neglected to purchase a drink to accompany his meal. The bartender rounded the counter, caught the injudicious diner by the ear with a lemon squeezer, led him to the door and kicked him into the street.

Thus the mind of Chicken was brought to realize the signs of coming winter. The night was cold; the stars shone with unkindly brilliancy; people were hurrying along the streets in two egotistic, jostling streams. Men had donned their overcoats, and Chicken knew to an exact percentage the increased difficulty of coaxing dimes from those buttoned-in vest pockets. The time had come for his annual exodus to the south.

A little boy, five or six years old, stood looking with covetous eyes in a confectioner's window. In one small hand he held an empty two-ounce vial; in the other he grasped tightly something flat and round, with a shining milled edge. The scene presented a field of operations commensurate to Chicken's talents and daring. After sweeping the horizon to make sure that no official tug was cruising near, he insidiously accosted his prey. The boy, having been early taught by his household to regard altruistic advances with extreme suspicion, received the overtures coldly.

Then Chicken knew that he must make one of those desperate, nerve-shattering plunges into speculation that fortune sometimes requires of those who would win her favor. Five cents was his capital, and this he must risk against the chance of winning what lay within the close grasp of the youngster's chubby hand. It was a fearful lottery, Chicken knew. But he must accomplish his end by strategy, since he had a wholesome terror of plundering infants by force. Once, in a park, driven by hunger, he had committed an onslaught upon a bottle of peptonized infant's food in the possession of an occupant of a baby carriage. The outraged infant had so promptly opened its mouth and pressed the button that communicated with the welkin that help arrived, and Chicken did his thirty days in a snug coop. Wherefore he was, as he said, "leary of kids."

Beginning artfully to question the boy concerning his choice of sweets, he gradually drew out the information he wanted. Mamma said he was to ask the drug store man for ten cents' worth of paregoric in the bottle; he was to keep his hand shut tight over the dollar; he must not stop to talk to anyone in the street; he must ask the drug-store man to wrap up the change and put it in the pocket of his trousers. Indeed, they had pockets—two of them! And he liked chocolate creams best.

Chicken went into the store and turned plunger. He invested his entire capital in C.A.N.D.Y. stocks, simply to pave the way to the greater risk following.

He gave the sweets to the youngster, and had the satisfaction of perceiving that confidence was established. After that it was easy to obtain leadership of the expedition; to take the investment by the hand and lead it to a nice drug store he knew of in the same block. There Chicken, with a parental air, passed over the dollar and called for the medicine, while the boy crunched his candy, glad to be relieved of the responsibility of the purchase. And then the successful investor, searching his pockets, found an overcoat button— the extent of his winter trousseau—and, wrapping it carefully, placed the ostensible change in the pocket of confiding juvenility. Setting the youngster's face homeward, and patting him benevolently on the back—for Chicken's heart was as soft as those of his feathered namesakes—the speculator quit the market with a profit of 1,700 per cent. on his invested capital.

Two hours later an Iron Mountain freight engine pulled out of the railroad yards, Texas bound, with a string of empties. In one of the cattle cars, half buried in excelsior, Chicken lay at ease. Beside him in his nest was a quart bottle of very poor whiskey and a paper bag of bread and cheese. Mr. Ruggles, in his private car, was on his trip south for the winter season.

For a week that car was trundled southward, shifted, laid over, and manipulated after the manner of rolling stock, but Chicken stuck to it, leaving it only at necessary times to satisfy his hunger and thirst. He knew it must go down to the cattle country, and San Antonio, in the heart of it, was his goal. There the air was salubrious and mild; the people indulgent and long-suffering. The bartenders there would not kick him. If he should eat too long or too often at one place they would swear at him as if by rote and without heat. They swore so drawlingly, and they rarely paused short of their full vocabulary, which was copious, so that Chicken had often gulped a good meal during the process of the vituperative prohibition. The season there was always spring-like; the plazas were pleasant at night, with music and gaiety; except during the slight and infrequent cold snaps one could sleep comfortably out of doors in case the interiors should develop inhospitability.

At Texarkana his car was switched to the I. and G.N. Then still southward it trailed until, at length, it crawled across the Colorado bridge at Austin, and lined out, straight as an arrow, for the run to San Antonio.

When the freight halted at that town Chicken was fast asleep. In ten minutes the train was off again for Laredo, the end of the road. Those empty cattle cars were for distribution along the line at points from which the ranches shipped their stock.

When Chicken awoke his car was stationary. Looking out between the slats he saw it was a bright, moonlit night. Scrambling out, he saw his car with three others abandoned on a little siding in a wild and lonesome country. A cattle pen and chute stood on one side of the track. The railroad bisected a vast, dim ocean of prairie, in the midst of which Chicken, with his futile rolling stock, was as completely stranded as was Robinson with his land-locked boat.

A white post stood near the rails. Going up to it, Chicken read the letters at the top, S. A. 90. Laredo was nearly as far to the south. He was almost a hundred miles from any town. Coyotes began to yelp in the mysterious sea around him. Chicken felt lonesome. He had lived in Boston without an education, in Chicago without nerve, in Philadelphia without a sleeping place, in New York without a pull, and in Pittsburg sober, and yet he had never felt so lonely as now.

Suddenly through the intense silence, he heard the whicker of a horse. The sound came from the side of the track toward the east, and Chicken began to explore timorously in that direction. He stepped high along the mat of curly mesquit grass, for he was afraid of everything there might be in this wilderness—snakes, rats, brigands, centipedes, mirages, cowboys, fandangoes, tarantulas, tamales—he had read of them in the story papers. Rounding a clump of prickly pear that reared high its fantastic and menacing array of rounded heads, he was struck to shivering terror by a snort and a thunderous plunge, as the horse, himself startled, bounded away some fifty yards, and then resumed his grazing. But here was the one thing in the desert that Chicken did not fear. He had been reared on a farm; he had handled horses, understood them, and could ride.

Approaching slowly and speaking soothingly, he followed the animal, which, after its first flight, seemed gentle enough, and secured the end of the twenty-foot lariat that dragged after him in the grass. It required him but a few moments to contrive the rope into an ingenious nose-bridle, after the style of the Mexican *borsal*. In another he was upon the horse's back and off at a splendid lope, giving the animal free choice of direction. "He will take me somewhere," said Chicken to himself.

It would have been a thing of joy, that untrammelled gallop over the moonlit prairie, even to Chicken, who loathed exertion, but that his mood was not for it. His head ached; a growing thirst was upon him; the "somewhere" whither his lucky mount might convey him was full of dismal peradventure.

And now he noted that the horse moved to a definite goal. Where the prairie lay smooth he kept his course straight as an arrow's toward the east. Deflected by hill or arroyo or impractical spinous brakes, he quickly flowed again into the current, charted by his unerring instinct. At last, upon the side of a gentle rise, he suddenly subsided to a complacent walk. A stone's cast away stood a little mott of coma trees; beneath it a *jacal* such as the Mexicans erect—a one- room house of upright poles daubed with clay and roofed with grass or tule reeds. An experienced eye would have estimated the spot as the headquarters of a small sheep ranch. In the moonlight the ground in the nearby corral showed pulverized to a level smoothness by the hoofs of the sheep. Everywhere was carelessly distributed the paraphernalia of the place—ropes, bridles, saddles, sheep pelts, wool sacks, feed troughs, and camp litter. The barrel of drinking water stood in the end of the two-horse wagon near the door. The harness was piled, promiscuous, upon the wagon tongue, soaking up the dew.

Chicken slipped to earth, and tied the horse to a tree. He halloed again and again, but the house remained quiet. The door stood open, and he entered cautiously. The light was sufficient for him to see that no one was at home. The room was that of a bachelor ranch-man who was content with the necessaries of life. Chicken rummaged intelligently until he found what he had hardly dared hope for—a small, brown jug that still contained something near a quart of his desire.

Half an hour later, Chicken—now a gamecock of hostile aspect—emerged from the house with unsteady steps. He had drawn upon the absent ranch-man's equipment to replace his own ragged attire. He wore a suit of coarse brown ducking, the coat being a sort of rakish bolero, jaunty to a degree. Boots he had donned, and spurs that whirred with every lurching step. Buckled around him was a belt full of cartridges with a big six-shooter in each of its two holsters.

Prowling about, he found blankets, a saddle and bridle with which he caparisoned his steed. Again mounting, he rode swiftly away, singing a loud and tuneless song.

~

Bud King's band of desperadoes, outlaws and horse and cattle thieves were in camp at a secluded spot on the bank of the Frio. Their depredations in the Rio Grande country, while no bolder than usual, had been advertised more extensively, and Captain Kinney's company of rangers had been ordered down to look after them. Consequently, Bud King, who was a wise general, instead of cutting out a hot trail for the upholders of the law, as his men wished to do, retired for the time to the prickly fastnesses of the Frio valley.

Though the move was a prudent one, and not incompatible with Bud's well-known courage, it raised dissension among the members of the band. In fact, while they thus lay ingloriously *perdu* in the brush, the question of Bud King's fitness for the leadership was argued, with closed doors, as it were, by his followers. Never before had Bud's skill or efficiency been brought to criticism; but his glory was wandering (and such is glory's fate) in the light of a newer star. The sentiment of the band was crystallizing into the opinion that Black Eagle could lead them with more lustre, profit, and distinction.

This Black Eagle—sub-titled the "Terror of the Border"—had been a member of the gang about three months.

One night while they were in camp on the San Miguel water-hole a solitary horseman on the regulation fiery steed dashed in among them. The newcomer was of a portentous and devastating aspect. A beak-like nose with a predatory curve projected above a mass of bristling, blue- black whiskers. His eye was cavernous and fierce. He was spurred, sombreroed, booted, garnished with revolvers, abundantly drunk, and very much unafraid. Few people in the country drained by the Rio Bravo would have cared thus to invade alone the camp of Bud King. But this fell bird swooped fearlessly upon them and demanded to be fed.

Hospitality in the prairie country is not limited. Even if your enemy pass your way you must feed him before you shoot him. You must empty your larder into him before you empty your lead. So the stranger of undeclared intentions was set down to a mighty feast.

A talkative bird he was, full of most marvellous loud tales and exploits, and speaking a language at times obscure but never colourless. He was a new sensation to Bud King's men, who rarely encountered new types. They hung, delighted, upon his vainglorious boasting, the spicy strangeness of his lingo, his contemptuous familiarity with life, the world, and remote places, and the extravagant frankness with which he conveyed his sentiments.

To their guest the band of outlaws seemed to be nothing more than a congregation of country bumpkins whom he was "stringing for grub" just as he would have told his stories at the back door of a farmhouse to wheedle a meal. And, indeed, his ignorance was not without excuse, for the "bad man" of the Southwest does not run to extremes. Those brigands might justly have been taken for a little party of peaceable rustics assembled for a fish-fry or pecan gathering. Gentle of manner, slouching of gait, soft-voiced, unpicturesquely clothed; not one of them presented to the eye any witness of the desperate records they had earned.

For two days the glittering stranger within the camp was feasted. Then, by common consent, he was invited to become a member of the band. He consented, presenting for enrollment the prodigious name of "Captain Montressor." This name was immediately overruled by the band, and "Piggy" substituted as a compliment to the awful and insatiate appetite of its owner.

Thus did the Texas border receive the most spectacular brigand that ever rode its chaparral.

For the next three months Bud King conducted business as usual, escaping encounters with law officers and being content with reasonable profits. The band ran off some very good companies of horses from the ranges, and a few bunches of fine cattle which they got safely across the Rio Grande and disposed of to fair advantage. Often the band would ride into the little villages and Mexican settlements, terrorizing the inhabitants and plundering for the provisions and ammunition they needed. It was during these bloodless raids that Piggy's ferocious aspect and frightful voice gained him a renown more widespread and glorious than those other gentle-voiced and sad-faced desperadoes could have acquired in a lifetime.

The Mexicans, most apt in nomenclature, first called him The Black Eagle, and used to frighten the babes by threatening them with tales of the dreadful robber who carried off little children in his great beak. Soon the name extended, and Black Eagle, the Terror of the Border, became a recognized factor in exaggerated newspaper reports and ranch gossip.

The country from the Nueces to the Rio Grande was a wild but fertile stretch, given over to the sheep and cattle ranches. Range was free; the inhabitants were few; the law was mainly a letter, and the pirates met with little opposition until the flaunting and garish Piggy gave the band undue advertisement. Then McKinney's ranger company headed for those precincts, and Bud King knew that it meant grim and sudden war or else temporary retirement. Regarding the risk to be unnecessary, he drew off his band to an almost inaccessible spot on the bank of the Frio. Wherefore, as has been said, dissatisfaction arose among the members, and impeachment proceedings against Bud were premeditated, with Black Eagle in high favor for the succession. Bud King was not unaware of the sentiment, and he called aside Cactus Taylor, his trusted lieutenant, to discuss it.

"If the boys," said Bud, "ain't satisfied with me, I'm willing to step out. They're buckin' against my way of handlin' 'em. And 'specially because I concludes to hit the brush while Sam Kinney is ridin' the line. I saves 'em from bein' shot or sent up on a state contract, and they up and says I'm no good."

"It ain't so much that," explained Cactus, "as it is they're plum locoed about Piggy. They want them whiskers and that nose of his to split the wind at the head of the column."

"There's somethin' mighty seldom about Piggy," declared Bud, musingly. "I never yet see anything on the hoof that he exactly grades up with. He can shore holler a plenty and he straddles a hoss from where you laid the chunk. But he ain't never been smoked yet. You know, Cactus, we ain't had a row since he's been with us. Piggy's all right for skearin' the greaser kids and layin' waste a cross-roads store. I reckon he's the finest canned oyster buccaneer and cheese pirate that ever was, but how's his appetite for fightin'? I've knowed some citizens you'd think was starvin' for trouble get a bad case of dyspepsy the first dose of lead they had to take."

"He talks all spraddled out," said Cactus, "'bout the rookuses he's been in. He claims to have saw the elephant and hearn the owl."

"I know," replied Bud, using the cowpuncher's expressive phrase of skepticism, "but it sounds to me!"

This conversation was held one night in camp while the other members of the band—eight in number—were sprawling around the fire, lingering over their supper. When Bud and Cactus ceased talking they heard Piggy's formidable voice holding forth to the others as usual while he was engaged in checking, though never satisfying, his ravening appetite.

"Wat's de use," he was saying, "of chasin' little red cowses and hosses 'round for t'ousands of miles? Dere ain't nuttin' in it. Gallopin' t'rough dese bushes and briers, and gettin' a t'irst dat a brewery couldn't put out, and missin' meals! Say! You know what I'd do if I was main finger of dis bunch? I'd stick up a train. I'd blow de express car and make hard dollars where you guys get wind. Youse makes me tired. Dis sook-cow kind of cheap sport gives me a pain."

Later on, a deputation waited on Bud. They stood on one leg, chewed mesquit twigs and circumlocuted, for they hated to hurt his feelings. Bud foresaw their business, and made it easy for them. Bigger risks and larger profits was what they wanted.

The suggestion of Piggy's about holding up a train had fired their imagination and increased their admiration for the dash and boldness of the instigator. They were such simple, artless, and custom-bound bush-rangers that they had never before thought of extending their habits beyond the running off of live-stock and the shooting of such of their acquaintances as ventured to interfere.

Bud acted "on the level," agreeing to take a subordinate place in the gang until Black Eagle should have been given a trial as leader.

After a great deal of consultation, studying of time-tables, and discussion of the country's topography, the time and place for carrying out their new enterprise was decided upon. At that time there was a feedstuff famine in Mexico and a cattle famine in certain parts of the United States, and there was a brisk international trade. Much money was being shipped along the railroads that connected the two republics. It was agreed that the most promising place for the contemplated robbery was at Espina, a little station on the I. and G.N., about forty miles north of Laredo. The train stopped there one minute; the country around was wild and unsettled; the station consisted of but one house in which the agent lived.

Black Eagle's band set out, riding by night. Arriving in the vicinity of Espina they rested their horses all day in a thicket a few miles distant.

The train was due at Espina at 10.30 P.M. They could rob the train and be well over the Mexican border with their booty by daylight the next morning.

To do Black Eagle justice, he exhibited no signs of flinching from the responsible honors that had been conferred upon him.

He assigned his men to their respective posts with discretion, and coached them carefully as to their duties. On each side of the track four of the band were to lie concealed in the chaparral. Gotch-Ear Rodgers was to stick up the station agent. Bronco

Charlie was to remain with the horses, holding them in readiness. At a spot where it was calculated the engine would be when the train stopped, Bud King was to lie hidden on one side, and Black Eagle himself on the other. The two would get the drop on the engineer and fireman, force them to descend and proceed to the rear. Then the express car would be looted, and the escape made. No one was to move until Black Eagle gave the signal by firing his revolver. The plan was perfect.

At ten minutes to train time every man was at his post, effectually concealed by the thick chaparral that grew almost to the rails. The night was dark and lowering, with a fine drizzle falling from the flying gulf clouds. Black Eagle crouched behind a bush within five yards of the track. Two six-shooters were belted around him. Occasionally he drew a large black bottle from his pocket and raised it to his mouth.

A star appeared far down the track which soon waxed into the headlight of the approaching train. It came on with an increasing roar; the engine bore down upon the ambushing desperadoes with a glare and a shriek like some avenging monster come to deliver them to justice. Black Eagle flattened himself upon the ground. The engine, contrary to their calculations, instead of stopping between him and Bud King's place of concealment, passed fully forty years farther before it came to a stand.

The bandit leader rose to his feet and peered through the bush. His men all lay quiet, awaiting the signal. Immediately opposite Black Eagle was a thing that drew his attention. Instead of being a regular passenger train it was a mixed one. Before him stood a box car, the door of which, by some means, had been left slightly open. Black Eagle went up to it and pushed the door farther open. An odor came forth—a damp, rancid, familiar, musty, intoxicating, beloved odor stirring strongly at old memories of happy days and travels. Black Eagle sniffed at the witching smell as the returned wanderer smells of the rose that twines his boyhood's cottage home. Nostalgia seized him. He put his hand inside. Excelsior—dry, springy, curly, soft, enticing, covered the floor. Outside the drizzle had turned to a chilling rain.

The train bell clanged. The bandit chief unbuckled his belt and cast it, with its revolvers, upon the ground. His spurs followed quickly, and his broad sombrero. Black Eagle was moulting. The train started with a rattling jerk. The ex-Terror of the Border scrambled into the box car and closed the door. Stretched luxuriously upon the excelsior, with the black bottle clasped closely to his breast, his eyes closed, and a foolish, happy smile upon his terrible features Chicken Ruggles started upon his return trip.

Undisturbed, with the band of desperate bandits lying motionless, awaiting the signal to attack, the train pulled out from Espina. As its speed increased, and the black masses of chaparral went whizzing past on either side, the express messenger, lighting his pipe, looked through his window and remarked, feelingly:

"What a jim-dandy place for a hold-up!"

36

Two Renegades

In the Gate City of the South the Confederate Veterans were reuniting; and I stood to see them march, beneath the tangled flags of the great conflict, to the hall of their oratory and commemoration.

While the irregular and halting line was passing I made onslaught upon it and dragged from the ranks my friend Barnard O'Keefe, who had no right to be there. For he was a Northerner born and bred; and what should he be doing halloing for the Stars and Bars among those gray and moribund veterans? And why should he be trudging, with his shining, martial, humorous, broad face, among those warriors of a previous and alien generation?

I say I dragged him forth, and held him till the last hickory leg and waving goatee had stumbled past. And then I hustled him out of the crowd into a cool interior; for the Gate City was stirred that day, and the hand-organs wisely eliminated "Marching Through Georgia" from their repertories.

"Now, what deviltry are you up to?" I asked of O'Keefe when there were a table and things in glasses between us.

O'Keefe wiped his heated face and instigated a commotion among the floating ice in his glass before he chose to answer.

"I am assisting at the wake," said he, "of the only nation on earth that ever did me a good turn. As one gentleman to another, I am ratifying and celebrating the foreign policy of the late Jefferson Davis, as fine a statesman as ever settled the financial question of a country. Equal ratio—that was his platform—a barrel of money for a barrel of flour—a pair of $20 bills for a pair of boots—a hatful of currency for a new hat—say, ain't that simple compared with W. J. B's little old oxidized plank?"

"What talk is this?" I asked. "Your financial digression is merely a subterfuge. Why were you marching in the ranks of the Confederate Veterans?"

"Because, my lad," answered O'Keefe, "the Confederate Government in its might and power interposed to protect and defend Barnard O'Keefe against immediate and dangerous assassination at the hands of a blood- thirsty foreign country after the Unites States of America had overruled his appeal for protection, and had instructed Private Secretary Cortelyou to reduce his estimate of the Republican majority for 1905 by one vote."

"Come, Barney," said I, "the Confederate States of America has been out of existence nearly forty years. You do not look older yourself. When was it that the deceased government exerted its foreign policy in your behalf?"

"Four months ago," said O'Keefe, promptly. "The infamous foreign power I alluded to is still staggering from the official blow dealt it by Mr. Davis's contraband aggregation of states. That's why you see me cake-walking with the ex-rebs to the illegitimate tune about 'simmon-seeds and cotton. I vote for the Great Father in Washington, but I am not going back on Mars' Jeff. You say the Confederacy has been dead forty years? Well, if it hadn't been for it, I'd have been breathing today with soul so dead I couldn't have whispered a single cuss-word about my native land. The O'Keefes are not overburdened with ingratitude."

I must have looked bewildered. "The war was over," I said vacantly, "in—"

O'Keefe laughed loudly, scattering my thoughts.

"Ask old Doc Millikin if the war is over!" he shouted, hugely diverted. "Oh, no! Doc hasn't surrendered yet. And the Confederate States! Well, I just told you they bucked officially and solidly and nationally against a foreign government four months ago and kept me from being shot. Old Jeff's country stepped in and brought me off under its wing while Roosevelt was having a gunboat repainted and waiting for the National Campaign Committee to look up whether I had ever scratched the ticket."

"Isn't there a story in this, Barney?" I asked.

"No," said O'Keefe; "but I'll give you the facts. You know I went down to Panama when this irritation about a canal began. I thought I'd get in on the ground floor. I did, and had to sleep on it, and drink water with little zoos in it; so, of course, I got the Chagres fever. That was in a little town called San Juan on the coast.

"After I got the fever hard enough to kill a Port-au-Prince nigger, I had a relapse in the shape of Doc Millikin.

"There was a doctor to attend a sick man! If Doc Millikin had your case, he made the terrors of death seem like an invitation to a donkey-party. He had the bedside manners of a Piute medicine-man and the soothing presence of a dray loaded with iron bridge-girders. When he laid his hand on your fevered brow you felt like Cap John Smith just before Pocahontas went his bail.

"Well, this old medical outrage floated down to my shack when I sent for him. He was build like a shad, and his eyebrows was black, and his white whiskers trickled down from his chin like milk coming out of a sprinkling-pot. He had a nigger boy along carrying an old tomato-can full of calomel, and a saw.

"Doc felt my pulse, and then he began to mess up some calomel with an agricultural implement that belonged to the trowel class.

"'I don't want any death-mask made yet, Doc,' I says, 'nor my liver put in a plaster-of-Paris cast. I'm sick; and it's medicine I need, not frescoing.'

"'You're a blame Yankee, ain't you?' asked Doc, going on mixing up his Portland cement.

"'I'm from the North,' says I, 'but I'm a plain man, and don't care for mural decorations. When you get the Isthmus all asphalted over with that boll-weevil prescription, would you mind giving me a dose of pain-killer, or a little strychnine on toast to ease up this feeling of unhealthiness that I have got?"

"'They was all sassy, just like you,' says old Doc, 'but we lowered their temperature considerable. Yes, sir, I reckon we sent a good many of ye over to old *mortuis nisi bonum*. Look at Antietam and Bull Run and Seven Pines and around Nashville! There never was a battle where we didn't lick ye unless you was ten to our one. I knew you were a blame Yankee the minute I laid eyes on you.'

"'Don't reopen the chasm, Doc,' I begs him. 'Any Yankeeness I may have is geographical; and, as far as I am concerned, a Southerner is as good as a Filipino any day. I'm feeling to bad too argue. Let's have secession without misrepresentation, if you say so; but what I need is more laudanum and less Lundy's Lane. If you're mixing that compound gefloxide of gefloxicum for me, please fill my ears with it before you get around to the battle of Gettysburg, for there is a subject full of talk.'

"By this time Doc Millikin had thrown up a line of fortifications on square pieces of paper; and he says to me: 'Yank, take one of these powders every two hours. They won't kill you. I'll be around again about sundown to see if you're alive.'

"Old Doc's powders knocked the chagres. I stayed in San Juan, and got to knowing him better. He was from Mississippi, and the red-hottest Southerner that ever smelled mint. He made Stonewall Jackson and R. E. Lee look like Abolitionists. He had a family somewhere down near Yazoo City; but he stayed away from the States on account of an uncontrollable liking he had for the absence of a Yankee government. Him and me got as thick personally as the Emperor of Russia and the dove of peace, but sectionally we didn't amalgamate.

"'Twas a beautiful system of medical practice introduced by old Doc into that isthmus of land. He'd take that bracket-saw and the mild chloride and his hypodermic, and treat anything from yellow fever to a personal friend.

"Besides his other liabilities Doc could play a flute for a minute or two. He was guilty of two tunes—'Dixie' and another one that was mighty close to the 'Suwanee River'—you might say one of its tributaries. He used to come down and sit with me while

I was getting well, and aggrieve his flute and say unreconstructed things about the North. You'd have thought that the smoke from the first gun at Fort Sumter was still floating around in the air.

"You know that was about the time they staged them property revolutions down there, that wound up in the fifth act with the thrilling canal scene where Uncle Sam has nine curtain-calls holding Miss Panama by the hand, while the bloodhounds keep Senator Morgan treed up in a cocoanut-palm.

"That's the way it wound up; but at first it seemed as if Colombia was going to make Panama look like one of the $3.98 kind, with dents made in it in the factory, like they wear at North Beach fish fries. For mine, I played the straw-hat crowd to win; and they gave me a colonel's commission over a brigade of twenty-seven men in the left wing and second joint of the insurgent army.

"The Colombian troops were awfully rude to us. One day when I had my brigade in a sandy spot, with its shoes off doing a battalion drill by squads, the Government army rushed from behind a bush at us, acting as noisy and disagreeable as they could.

"My troops enfiladed, left-faced, and left the spot. After enticing the enemy for three miles or so we struck a brier-patch and had to sit down. When we were ordered to throw up our toes and surrender we obeyed. Five of my best staff-officers fell, suffering extremely with stone-bruised heels.

"Then and there those Colombians took your friend Barney, sir, stripped him of the insignia of his rank, consisting of a pair of brass knuckles and a canteen of rum, and dragged him before a military court. The presiding general went through the usual legal formalities that sometimes cause a case to hang on the calendar of a South American military court as long as ten minutes. He asked me my age, and then sentenced me to be shot.

"They woke up the court interpreter, an American named Jenks, who was in the rum business and vice versa, and told him to translate the verdict.

"Jenks stretched himself and took a morphine tablet.

"'You've got to back up against th' 'dobe, old man,' says he to me. 'Three weeks, I believe, you get. Haven't got a chew of fine-cut on you, have you?'

"'Translate that again, with foot-notes and a glossary,' says I. 'I don't know whether I'm discharged, condemned, or handed over to the Gerry Society.'

"'Oh,' says Jenks, 'don't you understand? You're to be stood up against a 'dobe wall and shot in two or three weeks—three, I think, they said.'

"'Would you mind asking 'em which?' says I. 'A week don't amount to much after you're dead, but it seems a real nice long spell while you are alive.'

"'It's two weeks,' says the interpreter, after inquiring in Spanish of the court. 'Shall I ask 'em again?'

"'Let be,' says I. 'Let's have a stationary verdict. If I keep on appealing this way they'll have me shot about ten days before I was captured. No, I haven't got any fine-cut.'

"They sends me over to the *calaboza* with a detachment of colored postal-telegraph boys carrying Enfield rifles, and I am locked up in a kind of brick bakery. The temperature in there was just about the kind mentioned in the cooking recipes that call for a quick oven.

"Then I gives a silver dollar to one of the guards to send for the United States consul. He comes around in pajamas, with a pair of glasses on his nose and a dozen or two inside of him.

"'I'm to be shot in two weeks,' says I. 'And although I've made a memorandum of it, I don't seem to get it off my mind. You want to call up Uncle Sam on the cable as quick as you can and get him all worked up about it. Have 'em send the *Kentucky* and the *Kearsage* and the *Oregon* down right away. That'll be about enough battleships; but it wouldn't hurt to have a couple of cruisers and a torpedo-boat destroyer, too. And—say, if Dewey isn't busy, better have him come along on the fastest one of the fleet.'

"'Now, see here, O'Keefe,' says the consul, getting the best of a hiccup, 'what do you want to bother the State Department about this matter for?'

"'Didn't you hear me?' says I; 'I'm to be shot in two weeks. Did you think I said I was going to a lawn-party? And it wouldn't hurt of Roosevelt could get the Japs to send down the *Yellowyamtiskookum* or the *Ogotosingsing* or some other first-class cruisers to help. It would make me feel safer.'

"'Now, what you want,' says the consul, 'is not to get excited. I'll send you over some chewing tobacco and some banana fritters when I go back. The United States can't interfere in this. You know you were caught insurging against the government, and you're subject to the laws of this country. To tell the truth, I've had an intimation from the State Department—unofficially, of course—that whenever a soldier of fortune demands a fleet of gunboats in a case of revolutionary *katzenjammer*, I should cut the cable, give him all the tobacco he wants, and after he's shot take his clothes, if they fit me, for part payment of my salary.'

"'Consul,' says I to him, 'this is a serious question. You are representing Uncle Sam. This ain't any little international tomfoolery, like a universal peace congress or the christening of the *Shamrock IV*. I'm an American citizen and I demand protection. I demand the Mosquito fleet, and Schley, and the Atlantic squadron, and Bob Evans, and General E. Byrd Grubb, and two or three protocols. What are you going to do about it?'

"'Nothing doing,' says the consul.

"'Be off with you, then,' says I, out of patience with him, 'and send me Doc Millikin. Ask Doc to come and see me.'

"Doc comes and looks through the bars at me, surrounded by dirty soldiers, with even my shoes and canteen confiscated, and he looks mightily pleased.

"'Hello, Yank,' says he, 'getting a little taste of Johnson's Island, now, ain't ye?'

"'Doc,' says I, 'I've just had an interview with the U.S. consul. I gather from his remarks that I might just as well have been caught selling suspenders in Kishineff under the name of Rosenstein as to be in my present condition. It seems that the only maritime aid I am to receive from the United States is some navy-plug to chew. Doc,' says I, 'can't you suspend hostility on the slavery question long enough to do something for me?'

"'It ain't been my habit,' Doc Millikin answers, 'to do any painless dentistry when I find a Yank cutting an eye-tooth. So the Stars and Stripes ain't lending any marines to shell the huts of the Colombian cannibals, hey? Oh, say, can you see by the dawn's early light the star-spangled banner has fluked in the fight? What's the matter with the War Department, hey? It's a great thing to be a citizen of a gold- standard nation, ain't it?'

"'Rub it in, Doc, all you want,' says I. 'I guess we're weak on foreign policy.'

"'For a Yank,' says Doc, putting on his specs and talking more mild, 'you ain't so bad. If you had come from below the line I reckon I would have liked you right smart. Now since your country has gone back on you, you have to come to the old doctor whose cotton you burned and whose mules who stole and whose niggers you freed to help you. Ain't that so, Yank?'

"'It is,' says I heartily, 'and let's have a diagnosis of the case right away, for in two weeks' time all you can do is to hold an autopsy and I don't want to be amputated if I can help it.'

"'Now,' says Doc, business-like, 'it's easy enough for you to get out of this scrape. Money'll do it. You've got to pay a long string of 'em from General Pomposo down to this anthropoid ape guarding your door. About $10,000 will do the trick. Have you got the money?'

"'Me?' says I. 'I've got one Chili dollar, two *real* pieces, and a *medio*.'

"'Then if you've any last words, utter 'em,' says that old reb. 'The roster of your financial budget sounds quite much to be like the noise of a requiem.'

"'Change the treatment,' says I. 'I admit that I'm short. Call a consultation or use radium or smuggle me in some saws or something.'

"'Yank,' says Doc Millikin, 'I've a good notion to help you. There's only one government in the world that can get you out of this difficulty; and that's the Confederate States of America, the grandest nation that ever existed.'

"Just as you said to me I says to Doc; 'Why, the Confederacy ain't a nation. It's been absolved forty years ago.'

"'That's a campaign lie,' says Doc. 'She's running along as solid as the Roman Empire. She's the only hope you've got. Now, you, being a Yank, have got to go through with some preliminary obsequies before you can get official aid. You've got to take the oath of allegiance to the Confederate Government. Then I'll guarantee she does all she can for you. What do you say, Yank?—it's your last chance.'

"'If you're fooling with me, Doc,' I answers, 'you're no better than the United States. But as you say it's the last chance, hurry up and swear me. I always did like the corn whiskey and 'possum anyhow. I believe I'm half Southerner by nature. I'm willing to try the Klu-klux in place of the khaki. Get brisk.'

"Doc Millikin thinks awhile, and then he offers me this oath of allegiance to take without any kind of a chaser:

"'I, Barnard O'Keefe, Yank, being of sound body but a Republican mind, hereby swear to transfer my fealty, respect, and allegiance to the Confederate States of America, and the government thereof in consideration of said government, through its official acts and powers, obtaining my freedom and release from confinement and sentence of death brought about by the exuberance of my Irish proclivities and my general pizenness as a Yank.'

"I repeated these words after Doc, but they seemed to me a kind of hocus-pocus; and I don't believe any life-insurance company in the world would have issued me a policy on the strength of 'em.

"Doc went away saying he would communicate with his government immediately.

"Say—you can imagine how I felt—me to be shot in two weeks and my only hope for help being in a government that's been dead so long that it isn't even remembered except on Decoration Day and when Joe Wheeler signs the voucher for his pay-check. But it was all there was in sight; and somehow I thought Doc Millikin had something up his old alpaca sleeve that wasn't all foolishness.

"Around to the jail comes old Doc again in about a week. I was flea- bitten, a mite sarcastic, and fundamentally hungry.

"'Any Confederate ironclads in the offing?' I asks. 'Do you notice any sounds resembling the approach of Jeb Stewart's cavalry overland or Stonewall Jackson sneaking up in the rear? If you do, I wish you'd say so.'

"'It's too soon yet for help to come,' says Doc.

"'The sooner the better,' says I. 'I don't care if it gets in fully fifteen minutes before I am shot; and if you happen to lay eyes on

Beauregard or Albert Sidney Johnston or any of the relief corps, wig- wag 'em to hike along.'

"'There's been no answer received yet,' says Doc.

"'Don't forget,' says I, 'that there's only four days more. I don't know how you propose to work this thing, Doc,' I says to him; 'but it seems to me I'd sleep better if you had got a government that was alive and on the map—like Afghanistan or Great Britain, or old man Kruger's kingdom, to take this matter up. I don't mean any disrespect to your Confederate States, but I can't help feeling that my chances of being pulled out of this scrape was decidedly weakened when General Lee surrendered.'

"'It's your only chance,' said Doc; 'don't quarrel with it. What did your own country do for you?'

"It was only two days before the morning I was to be shot, when Doc Millikin came around again.

"'All right, Yank,' says he. 'Help's come. The Confederate States of America is going to apply for your release. The representatives of the government arrived on a fruit-steamer last night.'

"'Bully!' says I—'bully for you, Doc! I suppose it's marines with a Gatling. I'm going to love your country all I can for this.'

"'Negotiations,' says old Doc, 'will be opened between the two governments at once. You will know later today if they are successful.'

"About four in the afternoon a soldier in red trousers brings a paper round to the jail, and they unlocks the door and I walks out. The guard at the door bows and I bows, and I steps into the grass and wades around to Doc Millikin's shack.

"Doc was sitting in his hammock playing 'Dixie,' soft and low and out of tune, on his flute. I interrupted him at 'Look away! Look away!' and shook his hand for five minutes.

"'I never thought,' says Doc, taking a chew fretfully, 'that I'd ever try to save any blame Yank's life. But, Mr. O'Keefe, I don't see but what you are entitled to be considered part human, anyhow. I never thought Yanks had any of the rudiments of decorum and laudability about them. I reckon I might have been too aggregative in my tabulation. But it ain't me you want to thank—it's the Confederate States of America.'

"'And I'm much obliged to 'em,' says I. 'It's a poor man that wouldn't be patriotic with a country that's saved his life. I'll drink to the Stars and Bars whenever there's a flagstaff and a glass convenient. But where,' says I, 'are the rescuing troops? If there was a gun fired or a shell burst, I didn't hear it.'

"Doc Millikin raises up and points out the window with his flute at the banana-steamer loading with fruit.

"'Yank,' says he, 'there's a steamer that's going to sail in the morning. If I was you, I'd sail on it. The Confederate Government's done all it can for you. There wasn't a gun fired. The negotiations were carried on secretly between the two nations by the purser of that steamer. I got him to do it because I didn't want to appear in it. Twelve thousand dollars was paid to the officials in bribes to let you go.'

"'Man!' says I, sitting down hard—'twelve thousand—how will I ever—who could have—where did the money come from?'

"'Yazoo City,' says Doc Millikin: 'I've got a little saved up there. Two barrels full. It looks good to these Colombians. 'Twas Confederate money, every dollar of it. Now do you see why you'd better leave before they try to pass some of it on an expert?'

"'I do,' says I.

"'Now let's hear you give the password,' says Doc Millikin.

"'Hurrah for Jeff Davis!' says I.

"'Correct,' says Doc. 'And let me tell you something: The next tune I learn on my flute is going to be "Yankee Doodle." I reckon there's some Yanks that are not so pizen. Or, if you was me, would you try "The Red, White, and Blue"?'"

37

Roads of Destiny

I go to seek on many roads
What is to be.
True heart and strong, with love to light—
Will they not bear me in the fight
To order, shun or wield or mould
My Destiny?
Unpublished Poems of David Mignot.

The song was over. The words were David's; the air, one of the countryside. The company about the inn table applauded heartily, for the young poet paid for the wine. Only the notary, M. Papineau, shook his head a little at the lines, for he was a man of books, and he had not drunk with the rest.

David went out into the village street, where the night air drove the wine vapor from his head. And then he remembered that he and Yvonne had quarreled that day, and that he had resolved to leave his home that night to seek fame and honor in the great world outside.

"When my poems are on every man's tongue," he told himself, in a fine exhilaration, "she will, perhaps, think of the hard words she spoke this day."

Except the roisterers in the tavern, the village folk were abed. David crept softly into his room in the shed of his father's cottage and made a bundle of his small store of clothing. With this upon a staff, he set his face outward upon the road that ran from Vernoy.

He passed his father's herd of sheep, huddled in their nightly pen—the sheep he herded daily, leaving them to scatter while he wrote verses on scraps of paper. He saw a light yet shining in Yvonne's window, and a weakness shook his purpose of a sudden. Perhaps that light meant that she rued, sleepless, her anger, and that morning might—But, no! His decision was made. Vernoy was no place for him. Not one soul there could share his thoughts. Out along that road lay his fate and his future.

Three leagues across the dim, moonlit champaign ran the road, straight as a ploughman's furrow. It was believed in the village that the road ran to Paris, at least; and this name the poet whispered often to himself as he walked. Never so far from Vernoy had David traveled before.

The Left Branch

Three leagues, then, the road ran, and turned into a puzzle. It joined with another and a larger road at right angles. David stood, uncertain, for a while, and then took the road to the left.

Upon this more important highway were, imprinted in the dust, wheel tracks left by the recent passage of some vehicle. Some half an hour later these traces were verified by the sight of a ponderous carriage mired in a little brook at the bottom of a steep hill. The driver and postilions were shouting and tugging at the horses' bridles. On the road at one side stood a huge, black-clothed man and a slender lady wrapped in a long, light cloak.

David saw the lack of skill in the efforts of the servants. He quietly assumed control of the work. He directed the outriders to cease their clamor at the horses and to exercise their strength upon the wheels. The driver alone urged the animals with his familiar voice; David himself heaved a powerful shoulder at the rear of the carriage, and with one harmonious tug the great vehicle rolled up on solid ground. The outriders climbed to their places.

David stood for a moment upon one foot. The huge gentleman waved a hand. "You will enter the carriage," he said, in a voice large, like himself, but smoothed by art and habit. Obedience belonged in the path of such a voice. Brief as was the young poet's hesitation, it was cut shorter still by a renewal of the command. David's foot went to the step. In the darkness he perceived dimly the form of the lady upon the rear seat. He was about to seat himself opposite, when the voice again swayed him to its will. "You will sit at the lady's side."

The gentleman swung his great weight to the forward seat. The carriage proceeded up the hill. The lady was shrunk, silent, into her corner. David could not estimate whether she was old or young, but a delicate, mild perfume from her clothes stirred his poet's fancy to the belief that there was loveliness beneath the mystery. Here was an adventure such as he had often imagined. But as yet he held no key to it, for no word was spoken while he sat with his impenetrable companions.

In an hour's time David perceived through the window that the vehicle traversed the street of some town. Then it stopped in front of a closed and darkened house, and a postilion alighted to hammer impatiently upon the door. A latticed window above flew wide and a night-capped head popped out.

"Who are ye that disturb honest folk at this time of night? My house is closed. 'Tis too late for profitable travelers to be abroad. Cease knocking at my door, and be off."

"Open!" spluttered the postilion, loudly; "open for Monsiegneur the Marquis de Beaupertuys."

"Ah!" cried the voice above. "Ten thousand pardons, my lord. I did not know—the hour is so late—at once shall the door be opened, and the house placed at my lord's disposal."

Inside was heard the clink of chain and bar, and the door was flung open. Shivering with chill and apprehension, the landlord of the Silver Flagon stood, half clad, candle in hand, upon the threshold.

David followed the Marquis out of the carriage. "Assist the lady," he was ordered. The poet obeyed. He felt her small hand tremble as he guided her descent. "Into the house," was the next command.

The room was the long dining-hall of the tavern. A great oak table ran down its length. The huge gentleman seated himself in a chair at the nearer end. The lady sank into another against the wall, with an air of great weariness. David stood, considering how best he might now take his leave and continue upon his way.

"My lord," said the landlord, bowing to the floor, "h-had I ex-expected this honor, entertainment would have been ready. T-t-there is wine and cold fowl and m-m-maybe—"

"Candles," said the marquis, spreading the fingers of one plump white hand in a gesture he had.

"Y-yes, my lord." He fetched half a dozen candles, lighted them, and set them upon the table.

"If monsieur would, perhaps, deign to taste a certain Burgundy—there is a cask—"

"Candles," said monsieur, spreading his fingers.

"Assuredly—quickly—I fly, my lord."

A dozen more lighted candles shone in the hall. The great bulk of the marquis overflowed his chair. He was dressed in fine black from head to foot save for the snowy ruffles at his wrist and throat. Even the hilt and scabbard of his sword were black. His expression was one of sneering pride. The ends of an upturned mustache reached nearly to his mocking eyes.

The lady sat motionless, and now David perceived that she was young, and possessed of pathetic and appealing beauty. He was startled from the contemplation of her forlorn loveliness by the booming voice of the marquis.

"What is your name and pursuit?"

"David Mignot. I am a poet."

The mustache of the marquis curled nearer to his eyes.

"How do you live?"

"I am also a shepherd; I guarded my father's flock," David answered, with his head high, but a flush upon his cheek.

"Then listen, master shepherd and poet, to the fortune you have blundered upon tonight. This lady is my niece, Mademoiselle Lucie de Varennes. She is of noble descent and is possessed of ten thousand francs a year in her own right. As to her charms, you have but to observe for yourself. If the inventory pleases your shepherd's heart, she becomes your wife at a word. Do not interrupt me. Tonight I conveyed her to the *château* of the Comte de Villemaur, to whom her hand had been promised. Guests were present; the priest was waiting; her marriage to one eligible in rank and fortune was ready to be accomplished. At the alter this demoiselle, so meek and dutiful, turned upon me like a leopardess, charged me with cruelty and crimes, and broke, before the gaping priest, the troth I had plighted for her. I swore there and then, by ten thousand devils, that she should marry the first man we met after leaving the *château,* be he prince, charcoal-burner, or thief. You, shepherd, are the first. Mademoiselle must be wed this night. If not you, then another. You have ten minutes in which to make your decision. Do not vex me with words or questions. Ten minutes, shepherd; and they are speeding."

The marquis drummed loudly with his white fingers upon the table. He sank into a veiled attitude of waiting. It was as if some great house had shut its doors and windows against approach. David would have spoken, but the huge man's bearing stopped his tongue. Instead, he stood by the lady's chair and bowed.

"Mademoiselle," he said, and he marveled to find his words flowing easily before so much elegance and beauty. "You have heard me say I was a shepherd. I have also had the fancy, at times, that I am a poet. If it be the test of a poet to adore and cherish the beautiful, that fancy is now strengthened. Can I serve you in any way, mademoiselle?"

The young woman looked up at him with eyes dry and mournful. His frank, glowing face, made serious by the gravity of the adventure, his strong, straight figure and the liquid sympathy in his blue eyes, perhaps, also, her imminent need of long-denied help and kindness, thawed her to sudden tears.

"Monsieur," she said, in low tones, "you look to be true and kind. He is my uncle, the brother of my father, and my only relative. He loved my mother, and he hates me because I am like her. He has made my life one long terror. I am afraid of his very looks, and never before dared to disobey him. But tonight he would have married me to a man three times my age. You will forgive me for bringing this vexation upon you, monsieur. You will, of course, decline this mad act he tries to force upon you. But let me thank you for your generous words, at least. I have had none spoken to me in so long."

There was now something more than generosity in the poet's eyes. Poet he must have been, for Yvonne was forgotten; this fine, new loveliness held him with its freshness and grace. The subtle perfume from her filled him with strange emotions. His tender look fell warmly upon her. She leaned to it, thirstily.

"Ten minutes," said David, "is given me in which to do what I would devote years to achieve. I will not say I pity you, mademoiselle; it would not be true—I love you. I cannot ask love from you yet, but let me rescue you from this cruel man, and, in time, love may come. I think I have a future; I will not always be a shepherd. For the present I will cherish you with all my heart and make your life less sad. Will you trust your fate to me, mademoiselle?"

"Ah, you would sacrifice yourself from pity!"

"From love. The time is almost up, mademoiselle."

"You will regret it, and despise me."

"I will live only to make you happy, and myself worthy of you."

Her fine small hand crept into his from beneath her cloak.

"I will trust you," she breathed, "with my life. And—and love—may not be so far off as you think. Tell him. Once away from the power of his eyes I may forget."

David went and stood before the marquis. The black figure stirred, and the mocking eyes glanced at the great hall clock.

"Two minutes to spare. A shepherd requires eight minutes to decide whether he will accept a bride of beauty and income! Speak up, shepherd, do you consent to become mademoiselle's husband?"

"Mademoiselle," said David, standing proudly, "has done me the honour to yield to my request that she become my wife."

"Well said!" said the marquis. "You have yet the making of a courtier in you, master shepherd. Mademoiselle could have drawn a worse prize, after all. And now to be done with the affair as quick as the Church and the devil will allow!"

He struck the table soundly with his sword hilt. The landlord came, knee-shaking, bringing more candles in the hope of anticipating the great lord's whims. "Fetch a priest," said the marquis, "a priest; do you understand? In ten minutes have a priest here, or—"

The landlord dropped his candles and flew.

The priest came, heavy-eyed and ruffled. He made David Mignot and Lucie de Verennes man and wife, pocketed a gold piece that the marquis tossed him, and shuffled out again into the night.

"Wine," ordered the marquis, spreading his ominous fingers at the host.

"Fill glasses," he said, when it was brought. He stood up at the head of the table in the candlelight, a black mountain of venom and conceit, with something like the memory of an old love turned to poison in his eyes, as it fell upon his niece.

"Monsieur Mignot," he said, raising his wineglass, "drink after I say this to you: You have taken to be your wife one who will make your life a foul and wretched thing. The blood in her is an inheritance running black lies and red ruin. She will bring you shame and anxiety. The devil that descended to her is there in her eyes and skin and mouth that stoop even to beguile a peasant. There is your promise, monsieur poet, for a happy life. Drink your wine. At last, mademoiselle, I am rid of you."

The marquis drank. A little grievous cry, as if from a sudden wound, came from the girl's lips. David, with his glass in his hand, stepped forward three paces and faced the marquis. There was little of a shepherd in his bearing.

"Just now," he said, calmly, "you did me the honor to call me 'monsieur.' May I hope, therefore that my marriage to mademoiselle has placed me somewhat nearer to you in—let us say, reflected rank—has given me the right to stand more as an equal to monseigneur in a certain little piece of business I have in my mind?"

"You may hope, shepherd," sneered the marquis.

"Then," said David, dashing his glass of wine into the contemptuous eyes that mocked him, "perhaps you will condescend to fight me."

The fury of the great lord outbroke in one sudden curse like a blast from a horn. He tore his sword from its black sheath; he called to the hovering landlord: "A sword there, for this lout!" He turned to the lady, with a laugh that chilled her heart, and said: "You put much labour upon me, madame. It seems I must find you a husband and make you a widow in the same night."

"I know not sword-play," said David. He flushed to make the confession before his lady.

"'I know not sword-play,'" mimicked the marquis. "Shall we fight like peasants with oaken cudgels? *Hola!* François, my pistols!"

A postilion brought two shining great pistols ornamented with carven silver, from the carriage holsters. The marquis tossed one upon the table near David's hand. "To the other end of the table," he cried; "even a shepherd may pull a trigger. Few of them attain the honor to die by the weapon of a De Beaupertuys."

The shepherd and the marquis faced each other from the ends of the long table. The landlord, in an ague of terror, clutched the air and stammered: "M-M-Monseigneur, for the love of Christ! Not in my house!—Do not spill blood—it will ruin my custom—" The look of the marquis, threatening him, paralyzed his tongue.

"Coward," cried the lord of Beaupertuys, "cease chattering your teeth long enough to give the word for us, if you can."

Mine host's knees smote the floor. He was without a vocabulary. Even sounds were beyond him. Still, by gestures he seemed to beseech peace in the name of his house and custom.

"I will give the word," said the lady, in a clear voice. She went up to David and kissed him sweetly. Her eyes were sparkling bright, and color had come to her cheek. She stood against the wall, and the two men leveled their pistols for her count.

"*Un—deux—trois!*"

The two reports came so nearly together that the candles flickered but once. The marquis stood, smiling, the fingers of his left hand resting, outspread, upon the end of the table. David remained erect, and turned his head very slowly, searching for his wife with his eyes. Then, as a garment falls from where it is hung, he sank, crumpled, upon the floor.

With a little cry of terror and despair, the widowed maid ran and stooped above him. She found his wound, and then looked up with her old look of pale melancholy. "Through his heart," she whispered. "Oh, his heart!"

"Come," boomed the great voice of the marquis, "out with you to the carriage! Daybreak shall not find you on my hands. Wed you shall be again, and to a living husband, this night. The next we come upon, my lady, highwayman or peasant. If the road yields no other, then the churl that opens my gates. Out with you into the carriage!"

The marquis, implacable and huge, the lady wrapped again in the mystery of her cloak, the postilion bearing the weapons—all moved out to the waiting carriage. The sound of its ponderous wheels rolling away echoed through the slumbering village. In the hall of the Silver Flagon the distracted landlord wrung his hands above the slain poet's body, while the flames of the four and twenty candles danced and flickered on the table.

The Right Branch

Three leagues, then, the road ran, and turned into a puzzle. It joined with another and a larger road at right angles. David stood, uncertain, for a while, and then took the road to the right.

Whither it led he knew not, but he was resolved to leave Vernoy far behind that night. He traveled a league and then passed a large *château* which showed testimony of recent entertainment. Lights shone from every window; from the great stone gateway ran a tracery of wheel tracks drawn in the dust by the vehicles of the guests.

Three leagues farther and David was weary. He rested and slept for a while on a bed of pine boughs at the roadside. Then up and on again along the unknown way.

Thus for five days he traveled the great road, sleeping upon Nature's balsamic beds or in peasants' ricks, eating of their black, hospitable bread, drinking from streams or the willing cup of the goatherd.

At length he crossed a great bridge and set his foot within the smiling city that has crushed or crowned more poets than all the rest of the world. His breath came quickly as Paris sang to him in a little undertone her vital chant of greeting—the hum of voice and foot and wheel.

High up under the eaves of an old house in the Rue Conti, David paid for lodging, and set himself, in a wooden chair, to his poems. The street, once sheltering citizens of import and consequence, was now given over to those who ever follow in the wake of decline.

The houses were tall and still possessed of a ruined dignity, but many of them were empty save for dust and the spider. By night there was the clash of steel and the cries of brawlers straying restlessly from inn to inn. Where once gentility abode was now but a rancid and rude incontinence. But here David found housing commensurate to his scant purse. Daylight and candlelight found him at pen and paper.

One afternoon he was returning from a foraging trip to the lower world, with bread and curds and a bottle of thin wine. Halfway up his dark stairway he met—or rather came upon, for she rested on the stair—a young woman of a beauty that should balk even the justice of a poet's imagination. A loose, dark cloak, flung open, showed a rich gown beneath. Her eyes changed swiftly with every little shade of thought. Within one moment they would be round and artless like a child's, and long and cozening like a gypsy's. One hand raised her gown, undraping a little shoe, high-heeled, with its ribbons dangling, untied. So heavenly she was, so unfitted to stoop, so qualified to charm and command! Perhaps she had seen David coming, and had waited for his help there.

Ah, would monsieur pardon that she occupied the stairway, but the shoe!—the naughty shoe! Alas! it would not remain tied. Ah! If monsieur *would* be so gracious!

The poet's fingers trembled as he tied the contrary ribbons. Then he would have fled from the danger of her presence, but the eyes grew long and cozening, like a gypsy's, and held him. He leaned against the balustrade, clutching his bottle of sour wine.

"You have been so good," she said, smiling. "Does monsieur, perhaps, live in the house?"

"Yes, madame. I—I think so, madame."

"Perhaps in the third story, then?"

"No, Madame; higher up."

The lady fluttered her fingers with the least possible gesture of impatience.

"Pardon. Certainly I am not discreet in asking. Monsieur will forgive me? It is surely not becoming that I should inquire where he lodges."

"Madame, do not say so. I live in the—"

"No, no, no; do not tell me. Now I see that I erred. But I cannot lose the interest I feel in this house and all that is in it. Once it was my home. Often I come here but to dream of those happy days again. Will you let that be my excuse?"

"Let me tell you, then, for you need no excuse," stammered the poet. "I live in the top floor—the small room where the stairs turn."

"In the front room?" asked the lady, turning her head side-wise.

"The rear, madame."

The lady sighed, as if with relief.

"I will detain you no longer then, monsieur," she said, employing the round and artless eye. "Take good care of my house. Alas! Only the memories of it are mine now. Adieu, and accept my thanks for your courtesy."

She was gone, leaving but a smile and a trace of sweet perfume. David climbed the stairs as one in slumber. But he awoke from it, and the smile and the perfume lingered with him and never afterward did either seem quite to leave him. This lady of whom he knew nothing drove him to lyrics of eyes, chansons of swiftly conceived love, odes to curling hair, and sonnets to slippers on slender feet.

Poet he must have been, for Yvonne was forgotten; this fine, new loveliness held him with its freshness and grace. The subtle perfume about her filled him with strange emotions.

On a certain night three persons were gathered about a table in a room on the third floor of the same house. Three chairs and the table and a lighted candle upon it was all the furniture. One of the persons was a huge man, dressed in black. His expression was one of sneering pride. The ends of his upturned mustache reached nearly to his mocking eyes. Another was a lady, young and beautiful, with eyes that could be round and artless, as a child's, or long and cozening, like a gypsy's, but were now keen and ambitious, like any other conspirator's. The third was a man of action, a combatant, a bold and impatient executive, breathing fire and steel. He was addressed by the others as Captain Desrolles.

This man struck the table with his fist, and said, with controlled violence:

"Tonight. Tonight as he goes to midnight mass. I am tired of the plotting that gets nowhere. I am sick of signals and ciphers and secret meetings and such *baragouin*. Let us be honest traitors. If France is to be rid of him, let us kill in the open, and not hunt with snares and traps. Tonight, I say. I back my words. My hand will do the deed. Tonight, as he goes to mass."

The lady turned upon him a cordial look. Woman, however wedded to plots, must ever thus bow to rash courage. The big man stroked his upturned mustache.

"Dear captain," he said, in a great voice, softened by habit, "this time I agree with you. Nothing is to be gained by waiting. Enough of the palace guards belong to us to make the endeavor a safe one."

"Tonight," repeated Captain Desrolles, again striking the table. "You have heard me, marquis; my hand will do the deed."

"But now," said the huge man, softly, "comes a question. Word must be sent to our partisans in the palace, and a signal agreed upon. Our stanchest men must accompany the royal carriage. At this hour what messenger can penetrate so far as the south doorway? Ribouet is stationed there; once a message is placed in his hands, all will go well."

"I will send the message," said the lady.

"You, countess?" said the marquis, raising his eyebrows. "Your devotion is great, we know, but—"

"Listen!" exclaimed the lady, rising and resting her hands upon the table; "in a garret of this house lives a youth from the provinces as guileless and tender as the lambs he tended there. I have met him twice or thrice upon the stairs. I questioned him, fearing that he might dwell too near the room in which we are accustomed to meet. He is mine, if I will. He writes poems in his garret, and I think he dreams of me. He will do what I say. He shall take the message to the palace."

The marquis rose from his chair and bowed. "You did not permit me to finish my sentence, countess," he said. "I would have said: 'Your devotion is great, but your wit and charm are infinitely greater.'"

While the conspirators were thus engaged, David was polishing some lines addressed to his *amorette d'escalier*. He heard a timorous knock at his door, and opened it, with a great throb, to behold her there, panting as one in straits, with eyes wide open and artless, like a child's.

"Monsieur," she breathed, "I come to you in distress. I believe you to be good and true, and I know of no other help. How I flew through the streets among the swaggering men! Monsieur, my mother is dying. My uncle is a captain of guards in the palace of the king. Some one must fly to bring him. May I hope—"

"Mademoiselle," interrupted David, his eyes shining with the desire to do her service, "your hopes shall be my wings. Tell me how I may reach him."

The lady thrust a sealed paper into his hand.

"Go to the south gate—the south gate, mind—and say to the guards there, 'The falcon has left his nest.' They will pass you, and you will go to the south entrance to the palace. Repeat the words, and give this letter to the man who will reply 'Let him strike when he will.' This is the password, monsieur, entrusted to me by my uncle, for now when the country is disturbed and men plot against the king's life, no one without it can gain entrance to the palace grounds after nightfall. If you will, monsieur, take him this letter so that my mother may see him before she closes her eyes."

"Give it me," said David, eagerly. "But shall I let you return home through the streets alone so late? I—"

"No, no—fly. Each moment is like a precious jewel. Some time," said the lady, with eyes long and cozening, like a gypsy's, "I will try to thank you for your goodness."

The poet thrust the letter into his breast, and bounded down the stairway. The lady, when he was gone, returned to the room below.

The eloquent eyebrows of the marquis interrogated her.

"He is gone," she said, "as fleet and stupid as one of his own sheep, to deliver it."

The table shook again from the batter of Captain Desrolles's fist.

"Sacred name!" he cried; "I have left my pistols behind! I can trust no others."

"Take this," said the marquis, drawing from beneath his cloak a shining, great weapon, ornamented with carven silver. "There are none truer. But guard it closely, for it bears my arms and crest, and already I am suspected. Me, I must put many leagues between myself and Paris this night. Tomorrow must find me in my *château*. After you, dear countess."

The marquis puffed out the candle. The lady, well cloaked, and the two gentlemen softly descended the stairway and flowed into the crowd that roamed along the narrow pavements of the Rue Conti.

David sped. At the south gate of the king's residence a halberd was laid to his breast, but he turned its point with the words; "The falcon has left his nest."

"Pass, brother," said the guard, "and go quickly."

On the south steps of the palace they moved to seize him, but again the *mot de passe* charmed the watchers. One among them stepped forward and began: "Let him strike—" but a flurry among the guards told of a surprise. A man of keen look and soldierly stride suddenly pressed through them and seized the letter which David held in his hand. "Come with me," he said, and led him inside the great hall. Then he tore open the letter and read it. He beckoned to a man uniformed as an officer of musketeers, who was passing. "Captain Tetreau, you will have the guards at the south entrance and the south gate arrested and confined. Place men known to be loyal in their places." To David he said: "Come with me."

He conducted him through a corridor and an anteroom into a spacious chamber, where a melancholy man, somberly dressed, sat brooding in a great, leather-covered chair. To that man he said:

"Sire, I have told you that the palace is as full of traitors and spies as a sewer is of rats. You have thought, sire, that it was my fancy. This man penetrated to your very door by their connivance. He bore a letter which I have intercepted. I have brought him here that your majesty may no longer think my zeal excessive."

"I will question him," said the king, stirring in his chair. He looked at David with heavy eyes dulled by an opaque film. The poet bent his knee.

"From where do you come?" asked the king.

"From the village of Vernoy, in the province of Eure-et-Loir, sire."

"What do you follow in Paris?"

"I—I would be a poet, sire."

"What did you in Vernoy?"

"I minded my father's flock of sheep."

The king stirred again, and the film lifted from his eyes.

"Ah! in the fields!"

"Yes, sire."

"You lived in the fields; you went out in the cool of the morning and lay among the hedges in the grass. The flock distributed itself upon the hillside; you drank of the living stream; you ate your sweet, brown bread in the shade, and you listened, doubtless, to blackbirds piping in the grove. Is not that so, shepherd?"

"It is, sire," answered David, with a sigh; "and to the bees at the flowers, and, maybe, to the grape gatherers singing on the hill."

"Yes, yes," said the king, impatiently; "maybe to them; but surely to the blackbirds. They whistled often, in the grove, did they not?"

"Nowhere, sire, so sweetly as in Eure-et-Loir. I have endeavored to express their song in some verses that I have written."

"Can you repeat those verses?" asked the king, eagerly. "A long time ago I listened to the blackbirds. It would be something better than a kingdom if one could rightly construe their song.

And at night you drove the sheep to the fold and then sat, in peace and tranquility, to your pleasant bread. Can you repeat those verses, shepherd?"

"They run this way, sire," said David, with respectful ardor:

"'Lazy shepherd, see your lambkins
Skip, ecstatic, on the mead;
See the firs dance in the breezes,
Hear Pan blowing at his reed.

"Hear us calling from the tree-tops,
See us swoop upon your flock;
Yield us wool to make our nests warm
In the branches of the—'"

"If it please your majesty," interrupted a harsh voice, "I will ask a question or two of this rhymester. There is little time to spare. I crave pardon, sire, if my anxiety for your safety offends."

"The loyalty," said the king, "of the Duke d'Aumale is too well proven to give offence." He sank into his chair, and the film came again over his eyes.

"First," said the duke, "I will read you the letter he brought:

"'Tonight is the anniversary of the dauphin's death. If he goes, as is his custom, to midnight mass to pray for the soul of his son, the falcon will strike, at the corner of the Rue Esplanade. If this be his intention, set a red light in the upper room at the southwest corner of the palace, that the falcon may take heed.'

"Peasant," said the duke, sternly, "you have heard these words. Who gave you this message to bring?"

"My lord duke," said David, sincerely, "I will tell you. A lady gave it me. She said her mother was ill, and that this writing would fetch her uncle to her bedside. I do not know the meaning of the letter, but I will swear that she is beautiful and good."

"Describe the woman," commanded the duke, "and how you came to be her dupe."

"Describe her!" said David with a tender smile. "You would command words to perform miracles. Well, she is made of sunshine and deep shade. She is slender, like the alders, and moves with their grace. Her eyes change while you gaze into them; now round, and then half shut as the sun peeps between two clouds. When she comes, heaven is all about her; when she leaves, there is chaos and a scent of hawthorn blossoms. She came to see me in the Rue Conti, number twenty-nine."

"It is the house," said the duke, turning to the king, "that we have been watching. Thanks to the poet's tongue, we have a picture of the infamous Countess Quebedaux."

"Sire and my lord duke," said David, earnestly, "I hope my poor words have done no injustice. I have looked into that lady's eyes. I will stake my life that she is an angel, letter or no letter."

The duke looked at him steadily. "I will put you to the proof," he said, slowly. "Dressed as the king, you shall, yourself, attend mass in his carriage at midnight. Do you accept the test?"

David smiled. "I have looked into her eyes," he said. "I had my proof there. Take yours how you will."

Half an hour before twelve the Duke d'Aumale, with his own hands, set a red lamp in a southwest window of the palace. At ten minutes to the hour, David, leaning on his arm, dressed as the king, from top to toe, with his head bowed in his cloak, walked slowly from the royal apartments to the waiting carriage. The duke assisted him inside and closed the door. The carriage whirled away along its route to the cathedral.

On the *qui vive* in a house at the corner of the Rue Esplanade was Captain Tetreau with twenty men, ready to pounce upon the conspirators when they should appear.

But it seemed that, for some reason, the plotters had slightly altered their plans. When the royal carriage had reached the Rue Christopher, one square nearer than the Rue Esplanade, forth from it burst Captain Desrolles, with his band of would-be regicides, and assailed the equipage. The guards upon the carriage, though surprised at the premature attack, descended and fought valiantly. The noise of conflict attracted the force of Captain Tetreau, and they came pelting down the street to the rescue. But, in the meantime, the desperate Desrolles had torn open the door of the king's carriage, thrust his weapon against the body of the dark figure inside, and fired.

Now, with loyal reinforcements at hand, the street rang with cries and the rasp of steel, but the frightened horses had dashed away. Upon the cushions lay the dead body of the poor mock king and poet, slain by a ball from the pistol of Monseigneur, the Marquis de Beaupertuys.

THE MAIN ROAD

Three leagues, then, the road ran, and turned into a puzzle. It joined with another and a larger road at right angles. David stood, uncertain, for a while, and then sat himself to rest upon its side.

Whither these roads led he knew not. Either way there seemed to lie a great world full of chance and peril. And then, sitting there, his eye fell upon a bright star, one that he and Yvonne had named for theirs. That set him thinking of Yvonne, and he wondered if he had not been too hasty. Why should he leave her and his home because a few hot words had come between them? Was love so brittle a thing that jealousy, the very proof of it, could break it? Mornings always brought a cure for the little heartaches of evening. There was yet time for him to return home without any one in the sweetly sleeping village of Vernoy being the wiser. His heart was Yvonne's; there where he had lived always he could write his poems and find his happiness.

David rose, and shook off his unrest and the wild mood that had tempted him. He set his face steadfastly back along the road he had come. By the time he had retraveled the road to Vernoy, his desire to rove was gone. He passed the sheepfold, and the sheep scurried, with a drumming flutter, at his late footsteps, warming his heart by the homely sound. He crept without noise into his little room and lay there, thankful that his feet had escaped the distress of new roads that night.

How well he knew woman's heart! The next evening Yvonne was at the well in the road where the young congregated in order that the *curé* might have business. The corner of her eye was engaged in a search for David, albeit her set mouth seemed unrelenting. He saw the look; braved the mouth, drew from it a recantation and, later, a kiss as they walked homeward together.

Three months afterwards they were married. David's father was shrewd and prosperous. He gave them a wedding that was heard of three leagues away. Both the young people were favorites in the village. There was a procession in the streets, a dance on the green; they had the marionettes and a tumbler out from Dreux to delight the guests.

Then a year, and David's father died. The sheep and the cottage descended to him. He already had the seemliest wife in the village. Yvonne's milk pails and her brass kettles were bright—*ouf!* They blinded you in the sun when you passed that way. But you must keep your eyes upon her yard, for her flower beds were so neat and gay they restored to you your sight. And you might hear her sing, aye, as far as the double chestnut tree above Père Gruneau's blacksmith forge.

But a day came when David drew out paper from a long-shut drawer, and began to bite the end of a pencil. Spring had come again and touched his heart. Poet he must have been, for now Yvonne was well-nigh forgotten. This fine new loveliness of earth held him with its witchery and grace. The perfume from her woods and meadows stirred him strangely. Daily had he gone forth with his flock, and brought it safe at night. But now he stretched himself under the hedge and pieced words together on his bits of paper. The sheep strayed, and the wolves, perceiving that difficult poems make easy mutton, ventured from the woods and stole his lambs.

David's stock of poems grew larger and his flock smaller. Yvonne's nose and temper waxed sharp and her talk blunt. Her pans and kettles grew dull, but her eyes had caught their flash. She pointed out to the poet that his neglect was reducing the flock and bringing woe upon the household. David hired a boy to guard the sheep, locked himself in the little room at the top of the cottage, and wrote more poems. The boy, being a poet by nature, but not furnished with an outlet in the way of writing, spent his time in slumber. The wolves lost no time in discovering that poetry and sleep are practically the same; so the flock steadily grew smaller. Yvonne's ill temper increased at an equal rate. Sometimes she would stand in the yard and rail at David through his high window. Then you could hear her as far as the double chestnut tree above Père Gruneau's blacksmith forge.

M. Papineau, the kind, wise, meddling old notary, saw this, as he saw everything at which his nose pointed. He went to David, fortified himself with a great pinch of snuff, and said:

"Friend Mignot, I affixed the seal upon the marriage certificate of your father. It would distress me to be obliged to attest a paper signifying the bankruptcy of his son. But that is what you are coming to. I speak as an old friend. Now, listen to what I have to say. You have your heart set, I perceive, upon poetry. At Dreux, I have a friend, one Monsieur Bril—Georges Bril. He lives in a little cleared space in a houseful of books. He is a learned man; he visits Paris each year; he himself has written books. He will tell you when the catacombs were made, how they found out the names of the stars, and why the plover has a long bill. The meaning and the form of poetry is to him as intelligent as the baa of a sheep is to you. I will give you a letter to him, and you shall take him your poems and let him read them. Then you will know if you shall write more, or give your attention to your wife and business."

"Write the letter," said David, "I am sorry you did not speak of this sooner."

At sunrise the next morning he was on the road to Dreux with the precious roll of poems under his arm. At noon he wiped the dust from his feet at the door of Monsieur Bril. That learned man broke the seal of M. Papineau's letter, and sucked up its contents through his gleaming spectacles as the sun draws water. He took David inside to his study and sat him down upon a little island beat upon by a sea of books.

Monsieur Bril had a conscience. He flinched not even at a mass of manuscript the thickness of a finger length and rolled to an incorrigible curve. He broke the back of the roll against his knee and began to read. He slighted nothing; he bored into the lump as a worm into a nut, seeking for a kernel.

Meanwhile, David sat, marooned, trembling in the spray of so much literature. It roared in his ears. He held no chart or compass for voyaging in that sea. Half the world, he thought, must be writing books.

Monsieur Bril bored to the last page of the poems. Then he took off his spectacles, and wiped them with his handkerchief.

"My old friend, Papineau, is well?" he asked.

"In the best of health," said David.

"How many sheep have you, Monsieur Mignot?"

"Three hundred and nine, when I counted them yesterday. The flock has had ill fortune. To that number it has decreased from eight hundred and fifty."

"You have a wife and home, and lived in comfort. The sheep brought you plenty. You went into the fields with them and lived in the keen air and ate the sweet bread of contentment. You had but to be vigilant and recline there upon nature's breast, listening to the whistle of the blackbirds in the grove. Am I right thus far?"

"It was so," said David.

"I have read all your verses," continued Monsieur Bril, his eyes wandering about his sea of books as if he conned the horizon for a sail. "Look yonder, through that window, Monsieur Mignot; tell me what you see in that tree."

"I see a crow," said David, looking.

"There is a bird," said Monsieur Bril, "that shall assist me where I am disposed to shirk a duty. You know that bird, Monsieur Mignot; he is the philosopher of the air. He is happy through submission to his lot. None so merry or full-crawed as he with his whimsical eye and rollicking step. The fields yield him what he desires. He never grieves that his plumage is not gay, like the oriole's. And you have heard, Monsieur Mignot, the notes that nature has given him? Is the nightingale any happier, do you think?"

David rose to his feet. The crow cawed harshly from his tree.

"I thank you, Monsieur Bril," he said, slowly. "There was not, then, one nightingale among all those croaks?"

"I could not have missed it," said Monsieur Bril, with a sigh. "I read every word. Live your poetry, man; do not try to write it any more."

"I thank you," said David, again. "And now I will be going back to my sheep."

"If you would dine with me," said the man of books, "and overlook the smart of it, I will give you reasons at length."

"No," said the poet, "I must be back in the fields cawing at my sheep."

Back along the road to Vernoy he trudged with his poems under his arm. When he reached his village he turned into the shop of one Zeigler, a Jew out of Armenia, who sold anything that came to his hand.

"Friend," said David, "wolves from the forest harass my sheep on the hills. I must purchase firearms to protect them. What have you?"

"A bad day, this, for me, friend Mignot," said Zeigler, spreading his hands, "for I perceive that I must sell you a weapon that will not fetch a tenth of its value. Only last I week I bought from a peddlar a wagon full of goods that he procured at a sale by a *commissionaire* of the crown. The sale was of the *château* and belongings of a great lord—I know not his title—who has been banished for conspiracy against the king. There are some choice firearms in the lot. This pistol—oh, a weapon fit for a prince!—it shall be only forty francs to you, friend Mignot—if I lose ten by the sale. But perhaps an arquebuse—"

"This will do," said David, throwing the money on the counter. "Is it charged?"

"I will charge it," said Zeigler. "And, for ten francs more, add a store of powder and ball."

David laid his pistol under his coat and walked to his cottage. Yvonne was not there. Of late she had taken to gadding much among the neighbors. But a fire was glowing in the kitchen stove. David opened the door of it and thrust his poems in upon the coals. As they blazed up they made a singing, harsh sound in the flue.

"The song of the crow!" said the poet.

He went up to his attic room and closed the door. So quiet was the village that a score of people heard the roar of the great pistol. They flocked thither, and up the stairs where the smoke, issuing, drew their notice.

The men laid the body of the poet upon his bed, awkwardly arranging it to conceal the torn plumage of the poor black crow. The women chattered in a luxury of zealous pity. Some of them ran to tell Yvonne.

M. Papineau, whose nose had brought him there among the first, picked up the weapon and ran his eye over its silver mountings with a mingled air of connoisseurship and grief.

"The arms," he explained, aside, to the *curé*, "and crest of Monseigneur, the Marquis de Beaupertuys."

38

A Municipal Report

The cities are full of pride, Challenging each to each—This from her mountainside, That from her burthened beach. R. KIPLING.

Fancy a novel about Chicago or Buffalo, let us say, or Nashville, Tennessee! There are just three big cities in the United States that are "story cities"—New York, of course, New Orleans, and, best of the lot, San Francisco.—FRANK NORRIS.

East is East, and West is San Francisco, according to Californians. Californians are a race of people; they are not merely inhabitants of a State. They are the Southerners of the West. Now, Chicagoans are no less loyal to their city; but when you ask them why, they stammer and speak of lake fish and the new Odd Fellows Building. But Californians go into detail.

Of course they have, in the climate, an argument that is good for half an hour while you are thinking of your coal bills and heavy underwear. But as soon as they come to mistake your silence for conviction, madness comes upon them, and they picture the city of the Golden Gate as the Bagdad of the New World. So far, as a matter of opinion, no refutation is necessary. But, dear cousins all (from Adam and Eve descended), it is a rash one who will lay his finger on the map and say: "In this town there can be no romance—what could happen here?" Yes, it is a bold and a rash deed to challenge in one sentence history, romance, and Rand and McNally.

NASHVILLE—A city, port of delivery, and the capital of the State of Tennessee, is on the Cumberland River and on the N. C. & St. L. and the L. & N. railroads. This city is regarded as the most important educational centre in the South.

I stepped off the train at 8 P.M. Having searched the thesaurus in vain for adjectives, I must, as a substitution, hie me to comparison in the form of a recipe.

Take a London fog 30 parts; malaria 10 parts; gas leaks 20 parts; dewdrops gathered in a brick yard at sunrise, 25 parts; odor of honeysuckle 15 parts. Mix.

The mixture will give you an approximate conception of a Nashville drizzle. It is not so fragrant as a moth-ball nor as thick as pea-soup; but 'tis enough—'twill serve.

I went to a hotel in a tumbril. It required strong self-suppression for me to keep from climbing to the top of it and giving an imitation of Sidney Carton. The vehicle was drawn by beasts of a bygone era and driven by something dark and emancipated.

I was sleepy and tired, so when I got to the hotel I hurriedly paid it the fifty cents it demanded (with approximate lagniappe, I assure you). I knew its habits; and I did not want to hear it prate about its old "marster" or anything that happened "befo' de wah."

The hotel was one of the kind described as "renovated." That means $20,000 worth of new marble pillars, tiling, electric lights and brass cuspidors in the lobby, and a new L. & N. time table and a lithograph of Lookout Mountain in each one of the great rooms above. The management was without reproach, the attention full of exquisite Southern courtesy, the service as slow as the progress of a snail and as good-humored as Rip Van Winkle. The food was worth traveling a thousand miles for. There is no other hotel in the world where you can get such chicken livers *en brochette*.

At dinner I asked a Negro waiter if there was anything doing in town. He pondered gravely for a minute, and then replied: "Well, boss, I don't really reckon there's anything at all doin' after sundown."

Sundown had been accomplished; it had been drowned in the drizzle long before. So that spectacle was denied me. But I went forth upon the streets in the drizzle to see what might be there.

It is built on undulating grounds; and the streets are lighted by electricity at a cost of $32,470 per annum.

As I left the hotel there was a race riot. Down upon me charged a company of freedmen, or Arabs, or Zulus, armed with—no, I saw with relief that they were not rifles, but whips. And I saw dimly a caravan of black, clumsy vehicles; and at the reassuring shouts, "Kyar you anywhere in the town, boss, fuh fifty cents," I reasoned that I was merely a "fare" instead of a victim.

I walked through long streets, all leading uphill. I wondered how those streets ever came down again. Perhaps they didn't until they were "graded." On a few of the "main streets" I saw lights in stores here and there; saw street cars go by conveying worthy burghers hither and yon; saw people pass engaged in the art of conversation, and heard a burst of semi-lively laughter issuing from a soda-water and ice-cream parlor. The streets other than "main" seemed to have enticed upon their borders houses consecrated to peace and domesticity. In many of them lights shone behind discreetly drawn window shades; in a few pianos tinkled orderly and irreproachable music. There was, indeed, little "doing." I wished I had come before sundown. So I returned to my hotel.

In November, 1864, the Confederate General Hood advanced against Nashville, where he shut up a National force under General Thomas. The latter then sallied forth and defeated the Confederates in a terrible conflict.

All my life I have heard of, admired, and witnessed the fine marksmanship of the South in its peaceful conflicts in the tobacco-chewing regions. But in my hotel a surprise awaited me. There were twelve bright, new, imposing, capacious brass cuspidors in the great lobby, tall enough to be called urns and so wide-mouthed that the crack pitcher of a lady baseball team should have been able to throw a ball into one of them at five paces distant. But, although a terrible battle had raged and was still raging, the enemy had not suffered. Bright, new, imposing, capacious, untouched, they stood. But, shades of Jefferson Brick! the tile floor—the beautiful tile floor! I could not avoid thinking of the battle of Nashville, and trying to draw, as is my foolish habit, some deductions about hereditary marksmanship.

Here I first saw Major (by misplaced courtesy) Wentworth Caswell. I knew him for a type the moment my eyes suffered from the sight of him. A rat has no geographical habitat. My old friend, A. Tennyson, said, as he so well said almost everything:

Prophet, curse me the blabbing lip, And curse me the British vermin, the rat.

Let us regard the word "British" as interchangeable *ad lib*. A rat is a rat.

This man was hunting about the hotel lobby like a starved dog that had forgotten where he had buried a bone. He had a face of great acreage, red, pulpy, and with a kind of sleepy massiveness like that of Buddha. He possessed one single virtue—he was very smoothly shaven. The mark of the beast is not indelible upon a man until he goes about with a stubble. I think that if he had not used his razor that day I would have repulsed his advances, and the criminal calendar of the world would have been spared the addition of one murder.

I happened to be standing within five feet of a cuspidor when Major Caswell opened fire upon it. I had been observant enough to perceive that the attacking force was using Gatlings instead of squirrel rifles; so I side-stepped so promptly that the major seized the opportunity to apologize to a noncombatant. He had the blabbing lip. In four minutes he had become my friend and had dragged me to the bar.

I desire to interpolate here that I am a Southerner. But I am not one by profession or trade. I eschew the string tie, the slouch hat, the Prince Albert, the number of bales of cotton destroyed by Sherman, and plug chewing. When the orchestra plays Dixie I do not cheer. I slide a little lower on the leather-cornered seat and, well, order another Würzburger and wish that Longstreet had—but what's the use?

Major Caswell banged the bar with his fist, and the first gun at Fort Sumter re-echoed. When he fired the last one at Appomattox I began to hope. But then he began on family trees, and demonstrated that Adam was only a third cousin of a collateral branch of the Caswell family. Genealogy disposed of, he took up, to my distaste, his private family matters. He spoke of his wife, traced her descent back to Eve, and profanely denied any possible rumor that she may have had relations in the land of Nod.

By this time I was beginning to suspect that he was trying to obscure by noise the fact that he had ordered the drinks, on the chance that I would be bewildered into paying for them. But when they were down he crashed a silver dollar loudly upon the bar. Then, of course, another serving was obligatory. And when I had paid for that I took leave of him brusquely; for I wanted no more of him. But before I had obtained my release he had prated loudly of an income that his wife received, and showed a handful of silver money.

When I got my key at the desk the clerk said to me courteously: "If that man Caswell has annoyed you, and if you would like to make a complaint, we will have him ejected. He is a nuisance, a loafer, and without any known means of support, although he seems to have some money most the time. But we don't seem to be able to hit upon any means of throwing him out legally."

"Why, no," said I, after some reflection; "I don't see my way clear to making a complaint. But I would like to place myself on record as asserting that I do not care for his company. Your town," I continued, "seems to be a quiet one. What manner of entertainment, adventure, or excitement have you to offer to the stranger within your gates?"

"Well, sir," said the clerk, "there will be a show here next Thursday. It is—I'll look it up and have the announcement sent up to your room with the ice water. Good night."

After I went up to my room I looked out the window. It was only about ten o'clock, but I looked upon a silent town. The drizzle continued, spangled with dim lights, as far apart as currants in a cake sold at the Ladies' Exchange.

"A quiet place," I said to myself, as my first shoe struck the ceiling of the occupant of the room beneath mine. "Nothing of the life here that gives color and variety to the cities in the East and West. Just a good, ordinary, humdrum, business town."

Nashville occupies a foremost place among the manufacturing centers of the country. It is the fifth boot and shoe market in the United States, the largest candy and cracker manufacturing city in the South, and does an enormous wholesale dry-goods, grocery, and drug business.

I must tell you how I came to be in Nashville, and I assure you the digression brings as much tedium to me as it does to you. I was traveling elsewhere on my own business, but I had a commission from a Northern literary magazine to stop over there and establish a personal connection between the publication and one of its contributors, Azalea Adair.

Adair (there was no clue to the personality except the handwriting) had sent in some essays (lost art!) and poems that had made the editors swear approvingly over their one o'clock luncheon. So they had commissioned me to round up said Adair and corner by contract his or her output at two cents a word before some other publisher offered her ten or twenty.

At nine o'clock the next morning, after my chicken livers *en brochette* (try them if you can find that hotel), I strayed out into the drizzle, which was still on for an unlimited run. At the first corner I came upon Uncle Cæsar. He was a stalwart Negro, older than the pyramids, with gray wool and a face that reminded me of Brutus, and a second afterwards of the late King Cettiwayo. He wore the most remarkable coat that I ever had seen or expect to see. It reached to his ankles and had once been a Confederate gray in colors. But rain and sun and age had so variegated it that Joseph's coat, beside it, would have faded to a pale monochrome. I must linger with that coat, for it has to do with the story—the story that is so long in coming, because you can hardly expect anything to happen in Nashville.

Once it must have been the military coat of an officer. The cape of it had vanished, but all adown its front it had been frogged and tasseled magnificently. But now the frogs and tassles were gone. In their stead had been patiently stitched (I surmised by some surviving "black mammy") new frogs made of cunningly twisted common hempen twine. This twine was frayed and disheveled. It must have been added to the coat as a substitute for vanished splendors, with tasteless but painstaking devotion, for it followed faithfully the curves of the long-missing frogs. And, to complete the comedy and pathos of the garment, all its buttons were gone save one. The second button from the top alone remained. The coat was fastened by other twine strings tied through the buttonholes and other holes rudely pierced in the opposite side. There was never such a weird garment so fantastically bedecked and of so many mottled hues. The lone button was the size of a half-dollar, made of yellow horn and sewed on with coarse twine.

This Negro stood by a carriage so old that Ham himself might have started a hack line with it after he left the ark with the two animals hitched to it. As I approached he threw open the door, drew out a feather duster, waved it without using it, and said in deep, rumbling tones:

"Step right in, suh; ain't a speck of dust in it—jus' got back from a funeral, suh."

I inferred that on such gala occasions carriages were given an extra cleaning. I looked up and down the street and perceived that there was little choice among the vehicles for hire that lined the curb. I looked in my memorandum book for the address of Azalea Adair.

"I want to go to 861 Jessamine Street," I said, and was about to step into the hack. But for an instant the thick, long, gorilla-like arm of the old Negro barred me. On his massive and saturnine face a look of sudden suspicion and enmity flashed for a moment. Then, with quickly returning conviction, he asked blandishingly: "What are you gwine there for, boss?"

"What is it to you?" I asked, a little sharply.

"Nothin', suh, jus' nothin'. Only it's a lonesome kind of part of town and few folks ever has business out there. Step right in. The seats is clean—jes' got back from a funeral, suh."

A mile and a half it must have been to our journey's end. I could hear nothing but the fearful rattle of the ancient hack over the uneven brick paving; I could smell nothing but the drizzle, now further flavored with coal smoke and something like a mixture of tar and oleander blossoms. All I could see through the streaming windows were two rows of dim houses.

The city has an area of 10 square miles; 181 miles of streets, of which 137 miles are paved; a system of water-works that cost $2,000,000, with 77 miles of mains.

Eight-sixty-one Jessamine Street was a decayed mansion. Thirty yards back from the street it stood, outmerged in a splendid grove of trees and untrimmed shrubbery. A row of box bushes overflowed and almost hid the paling fence from sight; the gate was kept closed by a rope noose that encircled the gate post and the first paling of the gate. But when you got inside you saw that 861 was a shell, a shadow, a ghost of former grandeur and excellence. But in the story, I have not yet got inside.

When the hack had ceased from rattling and the weary quadrupeds came to a rest I handed my jehu his fifty cents with an additional quarter, feeling a glow of conscious generosity, as I did so. He refused it.

"It's two dollars, suh," he said.

"How's that?" I asked. "I plainly heard you call out at the hotel: 'Fifty cents to any part of the town.'"

"It's two dollars, suh," he repeated obstinately. "It's a long ways from the hotel."

"It is within the city limits and well within them." I argued. "Don't think that you have picked up a greenhorn Yankee. Do you see those hills over there?" I went on, pointing toward the east (I could not see them, myself, for the drizzle); "well, I was born and raised on their other side. You old fool nigger, can't you tell people from other people when you see 'em?"

The grim face of King Cettiwayo softened. "Is you from the South, suh? I reckon it was them shoes of yourn fooled me. They is somethin' sharp in the toes for a Southern gen'l'man to wear."

"Then the charge is fifty cents, I suppose?" said I inexorably.

His former expression, a mingling of cupidity and hostility, returned, remained ten seconds, and vanished.

"Boss," he said, "fifty cents is right; but I *needs* two dollars, suh; I'm *obleeged* to have two dollars. I ain't *demandin'* it now, suh; after I know whar you's from; I'm jus' sayin' that I *has* to have two dollars tonight, and business is mighty po'."

Peace and confidence settled upon his heavy features. He had been luckier than he had hoped. Instead of having picked up a greenhorn, ignorant of rates, he had come upon an inheritance.

"You confounded old rascal," I said, reaching down to my pocket, "you ought to be turned over to the police."

For the first time I saw him smile. He knew; *he knew*. HE KNEW.

I gave him two one-dollar bills. As I handed them over I noticed that one of them had seen parlous times. Its upper right-hand corner was missing, and it had been torn through the middle, but joined again. A strip of blue tissue paper, pasted over the split, preserved its negotiability.

Enough of the African bandit for the present: I left him happy, lifted the rope and opened a creaky gate.

The house, as I said, was a shell. A paint brush had not touched it in twenty years. I could not see why a strong wind should not have bowled it over like a house of cards until I looked again at the trees that hugged it close—the trees that saw the battle of Nashville and still drew their protecting branches around it against storm and enemy and cold.

Azalea Adair, fifty years old, white-haired, a descendant of the cavaliers, as thin and frail as the house she lived in, robed in the cheapest and cleanest dress I ever saw, with an air as simple as a queen's, received me.

The reception room seemed a mile square, because there was nothing in it except some rows of books, on unpainted white-pine bookshelves, a cracked marble-top table, a rag rug, a hairless horsehair sofa and two or three chairs. Yes, there was a picture on the wall, a colored crayon drawing of a cluster of pansies. I looked around for the portrait of Andrew Jackson and the pine-cone hanging basket but they were not there.

Azalea Adair and I had conversation, a little of which will be repeated to you. She was a product of the old South, gently nurtured in the sheltered life. Her learning was not broad, but was deep and of splendid originality in its somewhat narrow scope. She had been educated at home, and her knowledge of the world was derived from inference and by inspiration. Of such is the precious, small group of essayists made. While she talked to me I kept brushing my fingers, trying, unconsciously, to rid them guiltily of the absent dust from the half-calf backs of Lamb, Chaucer, Hazlitt, Marcus Aurelius, Montaigne and Hood. She was exquisite, she was a valuable discovery. Nearly everybody nowadays knows too much—oh, so much too much—of real life.

I could perceive clearly that Azalea Adair was very poor. A house and a dress she had, not much else, I fancied. So, divided between my duty to the magazine and my loyalty to the poets and essayists who fought Thomas in the valley of the Cumberland, I listened to her voice, which was like a harpsichord's, and found that I could not speak of contracts. In the presence of the nine Muses and the three Graces one hesitated to lower the topic to two cents. There would have to be another colloquy after I had regained my commercialism. But I spoke of my mission, and three o'clock of the next afternoon was set for the discussion of the business proposition.

"Your town," I said, as I began to make ready to depart (which is the time for smooth generalities), "seems to be a quiet, sedate place. A home town, I should say, where few things out of the ordinary ever happen."

It carries on an extensive trade in stoves and hollow ware with the West and South, and its flouring mills have a daily capacity of more than 2,000 barrels.

Azalea Adair seemed to reflect.

"I have never thought of it that way," she said, with a kind of sincere intensity that seemed to belong to her. "Isn't it in the still, quiet places that things do happen? I fancy that when God began to create the earth on the first Monday morning one could have leaned out one's window and heard the drops of mud splashing from His trowel as He built up the everlasting hills. What did the noisiest project in the world—I mean the building of the Tower of Babel—result in finally? A page and a half of Esperanto in the *North American Review*."

"Of course," said I platitudinously, "human nature is the same everywhere; but there is more color—er—more drama and movement and—er—romance in some cities than in others."

"On the surface," said Azalea Adair. "I have traveled many times around the world in a golden airship wafted on two wings—print and dreams. I have seen (on one of my imaginary tours) the Sultan of Turkey bowstring with his own hands one of his wives who had uncovered her face in public. I have seen a man in Nashville tear up his theatre tickets because his wife was going out with her face covered—with rice powder. In San Francisco's Chinatown I saw the slave girl Sing Yee dipped slowly, inch by inch, in boiling almond oil to make her swear she would never see her American lover again. She gave in when the boiling oil had reached three inches above her knee. At a euchre party in East Nashville the other night I saw Kitty Morgan cut dead by seven of her schoolmates and lifelong friends because she had married a house painter. The boiling oil was sizzling as high as her heart; but I wish you could have seen the fine little smile that she carried from table to table. Oh, yes, it is a humdrum town. Just a few miles of red brick houses and mud and lumber yards."

Some one knocked hollowly at the back of the house. Azalea Adair breathed a soft apology and went to investigate the sound. She came back in three minutes with brightened eyes, a faint flush on her cheeks, and ten years lifted from her shoulders.

"You must have a cup of tea before you go," she said, "and a sugar cake."

She reached and shook a little iron bell. In shuffled a small Negro girl about twelve, barefoot, not very tidy, glowering at me with thumb in mouth and bulging eyes.

Azalea Adair opened a tiny, worn purse and drew out a dollar bill, a dollar bill with the upper right-hand corner missing, torn in two pieces, and pasted together again with a strip of blue tissue paper. It was one of the bills I had given the piratical Negro—there was no doubt about it.

"Go up to Mr. Baker's store on the corner, Impy," she said, handing the girl the dollar bill, "and get a quarter of a pound of tea—the kind he always sends me—and ten cents worth of sugar cakes. Now, hurry. The supply of tea in the house happens to be exhausted," she explained to me.

Impy left by the back way. Before the scrape of her hard, bare feet had died away on the back porch, a wild shriek—I was sure it was hers—filled the hollow house. Then the deep, gruff tones of an angry man's voice mingled with the girl's further squeals and unintelligible words.

Azalea Adair rose without surprise or emotion and disappeared. For two minutes I heard the hoarse rumble of the man's voice; then something like an oath and a slight scuffle, and she returned calmly to her chair.

"This is a roomy house," she said, "and I have a tenant for part of it. I am sorry to have to rescind my invitation to tea. It was impossible to get the kind I always use at the store. Perhaps tomorrow, Mr. Baker will be able to supply me."

I was sure that Impy had not had time to leave the house. I inquired concerning street-car lines and took my leave. After I was well on my way I remembered that I had not learned Azalea Adair's name. But tomorrow would do.

That same day I started in on the course of iniquity that this uneventful city forced upon me. I was in the town only two days, but in that time I managed to lie shamelessly by telegraph, and to be an accomplice—after the fact, if that is the correct legal term—to a murder.

As I rounded the corner nearest my hotel the Afrite coachman of the polychromatic, nonpareil coat seized me, swung open the dungeony door of his peripatetic sarcophagus, flirted his feather duster and began his ritual: "Step right in, boss. Carriage is clean—jus' got back from a funeral. Fifty cents to any—"

And then he knew me and grinned broadly. "'Scuse me, boss; you is de gen'l'man what rid out with me dis mawnin'. Thank you kindly, suh."

"I am going out to 861 again tomorrow afternoon at three," said I, "and if you will be here, I'll let you drive me. So you know Miss Adair?" I concluded, thinking of my dollar bill.

"I belonged to her father, Judge Adair, suh," he replied.

"I judge that she is pretty poor," I said. "She hasn't much money to speak of, has she?"

For an instant I looked again at the fierce countenance of King Cettiwayo, and then he changed back to an extortionate old Negro hack driver.

"She ain't gwine to starve, suh," he said slowly. "She has reso'ces, suh; she has reso'ces."

"I shall pay you fifty cents for the trip," said I.

"Dat is puffeckly correct, suh," he answered humbly. "I jus' *had* to have dat two dollars dis mawnin', boss."

I went to the hotel and lied by electricity. I wired the magazine: "A. Adair holds out for eight cents a word."

The answer that came back was: "Give it to her quick you duffer."

Just before dinner "Major" Wentworth Caswell bore down upon me with the greetings of a long-lost friend. I have seen few men whom I have so instantaneously hated, and of whom it was so difficult to be rid. I was standing at the bar when he invaded me; therefore I could not wave the white ribbon in his face. I would have paid gladly for the drinks, hoping, thereby, to escape another; but he was one of those despicable, roaring, advertising bibbers who must have brass bands and fireworks attend upon every cent that they waste in their follies.

With an air of producing millions he drew two one-dollar bills from a pocket and dashed one of them upon the bar. I looked once more at the dollar bill with the upper right-hand corner missing, torn through the middle, and patched with a strip of blue tissue paper. It was my dollar bill again. It could have been no other.

I went up to my room. The drizzle and the monotony of a dreary, eventless Southern town had made me tired and listless. I remember that just before I went to bed I mentally disposed of the mysterious dollar bill (which might have formed the clew to a tremendously fine detective story of San Francisco) by saying to myself sleepily: "Seems as if a lot of people here own stock in the Hack-Driver's Trust. Pays dividends promptly, too. Wonder if—" Then I fell asleep.

King Cettiwayo was at his post the next day, and rattled my bones over the stones out to 861. He was to wait and rattle me back again when I was ready.

Azalea Adair looked paler and cleaner and frailer than she had looked on the day before. After she had signed the contract at eight cents per word she grew still paler and began to slip out of her chair. Without much trouble I managed to get her up on the antediluvian horsehair sofa and then I ran out to the sidewalk and yelled to the coffee-colored Pirate to bring a doctor. With a wisdom that I had not expected in him, he abandoned his team and struck off up the street afoot, realizing the value of speed. In ten minutes he returned with a grave, gray-haired and capable man of medicine. In a few words (worth much less than eight cents each) I explained to him my presence in the hollow house of mystery. He bowed with stately understanding, and turned to the old Negro.

"Uncle Cæsar," he said calmly, "Run up to my house and ask Miss Lucy to give you a cream pitcher full of fresh milk and half a tumbler of port wine. And hurry back. Don't drive—run. I want you to get back sometime this week."

It occurred to me that Dr. Merriman also felt a distrust as to the speeding powers of the land-pirate's steeds. After Uncle Cæsar was gone, lumberingly, but swiftly, up the street, the doctor looked me over with great politeness and as much careful calculation until he had decided that I might do.

"It is only a case of insufficient nutrition," he said. "In other words, the result of poverty, pride, and starvation. Mrs. Caswell has many devoted friends who would be glad to aid her, but she will accept nothing except from that old Negro, Uncle Cæsar, who was once owned by her family."

"Mrs. Caswell!" said I, in surprise. And then I looked at the contract and saw that she had signed it "Azalea Adair Caswell."

"I thought she was Miss Adair," I said.

"Married to a drunken, worthless loafer, sir," said the doctor. "It is said that he robs her even of the small sums that her old servant contributes toward her support."

When the milk and wine had been brought the doctor soon revived Azalea Adair. She sat up and talked of the beauty of the autumn leaves that were then in season, and their height of color. She referred lightly to her fainting seizure as the outcome of an old palpitation of the heart. Impy fanned her as she lay on the sofa. The doctor was due elsewhere, and I followed him to the door. I told him that it was within my power and intentions to make a reasonable advance of money to Azalea Adair on future contributions to the magazine, and he seemed pleased.

"By the way," he said, "perhaps you would like to know that you have had royalty for a coachman. Old Cæsar's grandfather was a king in Congo. Cæsar himself has royal ways, as you may have observed."

As the doctor was moving off I heard Uncle Cæsar's voice inside: "Did he get bofe of dem two dollars from you, Mis' Zalea?"

"Yes, Cæsar," I heard Azalea Adair answer weakly. And then I went in and concluded business negotiations with our contributor. I assumed the responsibility of advancing fifty dollars, putting it as a necessary formality in binding our bargain. And then Uncle Cæsar drove me back to the hotel.

Here ends all of the story as far as I can testify as a witness. The rest must be only bare statements of facts.

At about six o'clock I went out for a stroll. Uncle Cæsar was at his corner. He threw open the door of his carriage, flourished his duster and began his depressing formula: "Step right in, suh. Fifty cents to anywhere in the city—hack's puffickly clean, suh—jus' got back from a funeral—"

And then he recognized me. I think his eyesight was getting bad. His coat had taken on a few more faded shades of color, the twine strings were more frayed and ragged, the last remaining button—the button of yellow horn—was gone. A motley descendant of kings was Uncle Cæsar!

About two hours later I saw an excited crowd besieging the front of a drug store. In a desert where nothing happens this was manna; so I wedged my way inside. On an extemporized couch of empty boxes and chairs was stretched the mortal corporeality of Major Wentworth Caswell. A doctor was testing him for the immortal ingredient. His decision was that it was conspicuous by its absence.

The erstwhile Major had been found dead on a dark street and brought by curious and ennuied citizens to the drug store. The late human being had been engaged in terrific battle—the details showed that. Loafer and reprobate though he had been, he had been also a warrior. But he had lost. His hands were yet clinched so tightly that his fingers would not be opened. The gentle citizens who had know him stood about and searched their vocabularies to find some good words, if it were possible, to speak of him. One kind-looking man said, after much thought: "When 'Cas' was about fo'teen he was one of the best spellers in school."

While I stood there the fingers of the right hand of "the man that was" which hung down the side of a white pine box, relaxed, and dropped something at my feet. I covered it with one foot quietly, and a little later on I picked it up and pocketed it. I reasoned that in his last struggle his hand must have seized that object unwittingly and held it in a death grip.

At the hotel that night the main topic of conversation, with the possible exceptions of politics and prohibition, was the demise of Major Caswell. I heard one man say to a group of listeners:

"In my opinion, gentlemen, Caswell was murdered by some of these no-account niggers for his money. He had fifty dollars this afternoon which he showed to several gentlemen in the hotel. When he was found the money was not on his person."

I left the city the next morning at nine, and as the train was crossing the bridge over the Cumberland River I took out of my pocket a yellow horn overcoat button the size of a fifty-cent piece, with frayed ends of coarse twine hanging from it, and cast it out of the window into the slow, muddy waters below.

I wonder what's doing in Buffalo!

39

Girl

In gilt letters on the ground glass of the door of room No. 962 were the words: "Robbins & Hartley, Brokers." The clerks had gone. It was past five, and with the solid tramp of a drove of prize Percherons, scrub-women were invading the cloud-capped twenty-story office building. A puff of red-hot air flavored with lemon peelings, soft-coal smoke and train oil came in through the half-open windows.

Robbins, fifty, something of an overweight beau, and addicted to first nights and hotel palm-rooms, pretended to be envious of his partner's commuter's joys.

"Going to be something doing in the humidity line tonight," he said. "You out-of-town chaps will be the people, with your katydids and moonlight and long drinks and things out on the front porch."

Hartley, twenty-nine, serious, thin, good-looking, nervous, sighed and frowned a little.

"Yes," said he, "we always have cool nights in Floralhurst, especially in the winter."

A man with an air of mystery came in the door and went up to Hartley.

"I've found where she lives," he announced in the portentous half-whisper that makes the detective at work a marked being to his fellow men.

Hartley scowled him into a state of dramatic silence and quietude. But by that time Robbins had got his cane and set his tie pin to his liking, and with a debonair nod went out to his metropolitan amusements.

"Here is the address," said the detective in a natural tone, being deprived of an audience to foil.

Hartley took the leaf torn out of the sleuth's dingy memorandum book. On it were penciled the words "Vivienne Arlington, No. 341 East—th Street, care of Mrs. McComus."

"Moved there a week ago," said the detective. "Now, if you want any shadowing done, Mr. Hartley, I can do you as fine a job in that line as anybody in the city. It will be only $7 a day and expenses. Can send in a daily typewritten report, covering—"

"You needn't go on," interrupted the broker. "It isn't a case of that kind. I merely wanted the address. How much shall I pay you?"

"One day's work," said the sleuth. "A tenner will cover it."

Hartley paid the man and dismissed him. Then he left the office and boarded a Broadway car. At the first large crosstown artery of travel he took an eastbound car that deposited him in a decaying avenue, whose ancient structures once sheltered the pride and glory of the town.

Walking a few squares, he came to the building that he sought. It was a new flat-house, bearing carved upon its cheap stone portal its sonorous name, "The Vallambrosa." Fire-escapes zigzagged down its front—these laden with household goods, drying clothes, and squalling children evicted by the midsummer heat. Here and there a pale rubber plant peeped from the miscellaneous mass, as if wondering to what kingdom it belonged—vegetable, animal or artificial.

Hartley pressed the "McComus" button. The door latch clicked spasmodically— now hospitably, now doubtfully, as though in anxiety whether it might be admitting friends or duns. Hartley entered and began to climb the stairs after the manner of those who seek their friends in city flat-houses—which is the manner of a boy who climbs an apple-tree, stopping when he comes upon what he wants.

On the fourth floor he saw Vivienne standing in an open door. She invited him inside, with a nod and a bright, genuine smile. She placed a chair for him near a window, and poised herself gracefully upon the edge of one of those Jekyll-and-Hyde pieces of furniture that are masked and mysteriously hooded, unguessable bulks by day and inquisitorial racks of torture by night.

Hartley cast a quick, critical, appreciative glance at her before speaking, and told himself that his taste in choosing had been flawless.

Vivienne was about twenty-one. She was of the purest Saxon type. Her hair was a ruddy golden, each filament of the neatly gathered mass shining with its own luster and delicate graduation of color. In perfect harmony were her ivory-clear complexion and deep sea-blue eyes that looked upon the world with the ingenuous calmness of a mermaid or the pixie of an undiscovered mountain stream. Her frame was strong and yet possessed the grace of absolute naturalness. And yet with all her Northern clearness and frankness of line and coloring, there seemed to be something of the tropics in her—something of languor in the droop of her pose, of love of ease in her ingenious complacency of satisfaction and comfort in the mere act of breathing—something that seemed to claim for her a right as a perfect work of nature to exist and be admired equally with a rare flower or some beautiful, milk-white dove among its sober-hued companions.

She was dressed in a white waist and dark skirt—that discreet masquerade of goose-girl and duchess.

"Vivienne," said Hartley, looking at her pleadingly, "you did not answer my last letter. It was only by nearly a week's search that I found where you had moved to. Why have you kept me in suspense when you knew how anxiously I was waiting to see you and hear from you?"

The girl looked out the window dreamily.

"Mr. Hartley," she said hesitatingly, "I hardly know what to say to you. I realize all the advantages of your offer, and sometimes I feel sure that I could be contented with you. But, again, I am doubtful. I was born a city girl, and I am afraid to bind myself to a quiet suburban life."

"My dear girl," said Hartley, ardently, "have I not told you that you shall have everything that your heart can desire that is in my power to give you? You shall come to the city for the theaters, for shopping and to visit your friends as often as you care to. You can trust me, can you not?"

"To the fullest," she said, turning her frank eyes upon him with a smile. "I know you are the kindest of men, and that the girl you get will be a lucky one. I learned all about you when I was at the Montgomerys'."

"Ah!" exclaimed Hartley, with a tender, reminiscent light in his eye; "I remember well the evening I first saw you at the Montgomerys'. Mrs. Montgomery was sounding your praises to me all the evening. And she hardly did you justice. I shall never forget that supper. Come, Vivienne, promise me. I want you. You'll never regret coming with me. No one else will ever give you as pleasant a home."

The girl sighed and looked down at her folded hands.

A sudden jealous suspicion seized Hartley.

"Tell me, Vivienne," he asked, regarding her keenly, "is there another—is there some one else?"

A rosy flush crept slowly over her fair cheeks and neck.

"You shouldn't ask that, Mr. Hartley," she said, in some confusion. "But I will tell you. There is one other—but he has no right—I have promised him nothing."

"His name?" demanded Hartley, sternly.

"Townsend."

"Rafford Townsend!" exclaimed Hartley, with a grim tightening of his jaw. "How did that man come to know you? After all I've done for him—"

"His auto has just stopped below," said Vivienne, bending over the window-sill. "He's coming for his answer. Oh I don't know what to do!"

The bell in the flat kitchen whirred. Vivienne hurried to press the latch button.

"Stay here," said Hartley. "I will meet him in the hall."

Townsend, looking like a Spanish grandee in his light tweeds, Panama hat and curling black mustache, came up the stairs three at a time. He stopped at sight of Hartley and looked foolish.

"Go back," said Hartley, firmly, pointing downstairs with his forefinger.

"Hullo!" said Townsend, feigning surprise. "What's up? What are you doing here, old man?"

"Go back," repeated Hartley, inflexibly. "The Law of the Jungle. Do you want the Pack to tear you in pieces? The kill is mine."

"I came here to see a plumber about the bathroom connections," said Townsend, bravely.

"All right," said Hartley. "You shall have that lying plaster to stick upon your traitorous soul. But, go back." Townsend went downstairs, leaving a bitter word to be wafted up the draught of the staircase. Hartley went back to his wooing.

"Vivienne," said he, masterfully. "I have got to have you. I will take no more refusals or dilly-dallying."

"When do you want me?" she asked.

"Now. As soon as you can get ready."

She stood calmly before him and looked him in the eye.

"Do you think for one moment," she said, "that I would enter your home while Héloise is there?"

Hartley cringed as if from an unexpected blow. He folded his arms and paced the carpet once or twice.

"She shall go," he declared grimly. Drops stood upon his brow. "Why should I let that woman make my life miserable? Never have I seen one day of freedom from trouble since I have known her. You are right, Vivienne. Héloise must be sent away before I can take you home. But she shall go. I have decided. I will turn her from my doors."

"When will you do this?" asked the girl.

Hartley clinched his teeth and bent his brows together.

"Tonight," he said, resolutely. "I will send her away tonight."

"Then," said Vivienne, "my answer is 'yes.' Come for me when you will."

She looked into his eyes with a sweet, sincere light in her own. Hartley could scarcely believe that her surrender was true, it was so swift and complete.

"Promise me," he said feelingly, "on your word and honor."

"On my word and honor," repeated Vivienne, softly.

At the door he turned and gazed at her happily, but yet as one who scarcely trusts the foundations of his joy.

"Tomorrow," he said, with a forefinger of reminder uplifted.

"Tomorrow," she repeated with a smile of truth and candor.

In an hour and forty minutes Hartley stepped off the train at Floralhurst. A brisk walk of ten minutes brought him to the gate of a handsome two-story cottage set upon a wide and well-tended lawn. Halfway to the house he was met by a woman with jet-black braided hair and flowing white summer gown, who half strangled him without apparent cause.

When they stepped into the hall she said:

"Mamma's here. The auto is coming for her in half an hour. She came to dinner, but there's no dinner."

"I've something to tell you," said Hartley. "I thought to break it to you gently, but since your mother is here we may as well out with it."

He stooped and whispered something at her ear.

His wife screamed. Her mother came running into the hall. The dark-haired woman screamed again — the joyful scream of a well-beloved and petted woman.

"Oh, Mamma!" she cried ecstatically, "what do you think? Vivienne is coming to cook for us! She is the one that stayed with the Montgomerys a whole year. And now, Billy, dear," she concluded, "you must go right down into the kitchen and discharge Héloise. She has been drunk again the whole day long."

Robbins, fifty, something of an overweight beau, and addicted to first nights and hotel palm-rooms, pretended to be envious of his partner's commuter's joys.

"Going to be something doing in the humidity line tonight," he said. "You out-of-town chaps will be the people, with your katydids and moonlight and long drinks and things out on the front porch."

Hartley, twenty-nine, serious, thin, good-looking, nervous, sighed and frowned a little.

"Yes," said he, "we always have cool nights in Floralhurst, especially in the winter."

A man with an air of mystery came in the door and went up to Hartley.

"I've found where she lives," he announced in the portentous half-whisper that makes the detective at work a marked being to his fellow men.

Hartley scowled him into a state of dramatic silence and quietude. But by that time Robbins had got his cane and set his tie pin to his liking, and with a debonair nod went out to his metropolitan amusements.

"Here is the address," said the detective in a natural tone, being deprived of an audience to foil.

Hartley took the leaf torn out of the sleuth's dingy memorandum book. On it were penciled the words "Vivienne Arlington, No. 341 East—th Street, care of Mrs. McComus."

"Moved there a week ago," said the detective. "Now, if you want any shadowing done, Mr. Hartley, I can do you as fine a job in that line as anybody in the city. It will be only $7 a day and expenses. Can send in a daily typewritten report, covering—"

"You needn't go on," interrupted the broker. "It isn't a case of that kind. I merely wanted the address. How much shall I pay you?"

"One day's work," said the sleuth. "A tenner will cover it."

Hartley paid the man and dismissed him. Then he left the office and boarded a Broadway car. At the first large crosstown artery of travel he took an eastbound car that deposited him in a decaying avenue, whose ancient structures once sheltered the pride and glory of the town.

Walking a few squares, he came to the building that he sought. It was a new flat-house, bearing carved upon its cheap stone portal its sonorous name, "The Vallambrosa." Fire-escapes zigzagged down its front—these laden with household goods, drying clothes, and squalling children evicted by the midsummer heat. Here and there a pale rubber plant peeped from the miscellaneous mass, as if wondering to what kingdom it belonged—vegetable, animal or artificial.

Hartley pressed the "McComus" button. The door latch clicked spasmodically— now hospitably, now doubt- fully, as though in anxiety whether it might be admitting friends or duns.

Hartley entered and began to climb the stairs after the manner of those who seek their friends in city flat-houses—which is the manner of a boy who climbs an apple-tree, stopping when he comes upon what he wants.

On the fourth floor he saw Vivienne standing in an open door. She invited him inside, with a nod and a bright, genuine smile. She placed a chair for him near a window, and poised herself gracefully upon the edge of one of those Jekyll-and-Hyde pieces of furniture that are masked and mysteriously hooded, unguessable bulks by day and inquisitorial racks of torture by night.

Hartley cast a quick, critical, appreciative glance at her before speaking, and told himself that his taste in choosing had been flawless.

Vivienne was about twenty-one. She was of the purest Saxon type. Her hair was a ruddy golden, each filament of the neatly gathered mass shining with its own luster and delicate graduation of color. In perfect harmony were her ivory-clear complexion and deep sea-blue eyes that looked upon the world with the ingenuous calmness of a mermaid or the pixie of an undiscovered mountain stream. Her frame was strong and yet possessed the grace of absolute naturalness. And yet with all her Northern clearness and frankness of line and coloring, there seemed to be something of the tropics in her—something of languor in the droop of her pose, of love of ease in her ingenious complacency of satisfaction and comfort in the mere act of breathing—something that seemed to claim for her a right as a perfect work of nature to exist and be admired equally with a rare flower or some beautiful, milk-white dove among its sober-hued companions.

She was dressed in a white waist and dark skirt - that discreet masquerade of goose-girl and duchess.

"Vivienne," said Hartley, looking at her pleadingly, "you did not answer my last letter. It was only by nearly a week's search that I found where you had moved to. Why have you kept me in suspense when you knew how anxiously I was waiting to see you and hear from you?"

The girl looked out the window dreamily.

"Mr. Hartley," she said hesitatingly, "I hardly know what to say to you. I realize all the advantages of your offer, and sometimes I feel sure that I could be contented with you. But, again, I am doubtful. I was born a city girl, and I am afraid to bind myself to a quiet sub- urban life."

"My dear girl," said Hartley, ardently, "have I not told you that you shall have everything that your heart can desire that is in my power to give you? You shall come to the city for the theaters, for shopping and to visit your friends as often as you care to. You can trust me, can you not?"

"To the fullest," she said, turning her frank eyes upon him with a smile. "I know you are the kindest of men, and that the girl you get will be a lucky one. I learned all about you when I was at the Montgomerys'."

"Ah!" exclaimed Hartley, with a tender, reminiscent light in his eye; "I remember well the evening I first saw you at the Montgomerys'. Mrs. Montgomery was sound- ing your praises to me all the evening. And she hardly did you justice. I shall never forget that supper. Come, Vivienne, promise me. I want you. You'll never regret coming with me. No one else will ever give you as pleasant a home."

The girl sighed and looked down at her folded hands.

A sudden jealous suspicion seized Hartley.

"Tell me, Vivienne," he asked, regarding her keenly, "is there another—is there some one else?"

A rosy flush crept slowly over her fair cheeks and neck.

"You shouldn't ask that, Mr. Hartley," she said, in some confusion. "But I will tell you. There is one other—but he has no right—I have promised him nothing."

"His name?" demanded Hartley, sternly.

"Townsend."

"Rafford Townsend!" exclaimed Hartley, with a grim tightening of his jaw. "How did that man come to know you? After all I've done for him—"

"His auto has just stopped below," said Vivienne, bending over the window-sill. "He's coming for his answer. Oh I don't know what to do!"

The bell in the flat kitchen whirred. Vivienne hurried to press the latch button.

"Stay here," said Hartley. "I will meet him in the hall."

Townsend, looking like a Spanish grandee in his light tweeds, Panama hat and curling black mustache, came up the stairs three at a time. He stopped at sight of Hartley and looked foolish.

"Go back," said Hartley, firmly, pointing downstairs with his forefinger.

"Hullo!" said Townsend, feigning surprise. "What's up? What are you doing here, old man?"

"Go back," repeated Hartley, inflexibly. "The Law of the Jungle. Do you want the Pack to tear you in pieces? The kill is mine."

"I came here to see a plumber about the bathroom connections," said Townsend, bravely.

"All right," said Hartley. "You shall have that lying plaster to stick upon your traitorous soul. But, go back." Townsend went downstairs, leaving a bitter word to be wafted up the draught of the staircase. Hartley went back to his wooing.

"Vivienne," said he, masterfully. "I have got to have you. I will take no more refusals or dilly-dallying."

"When do you want me?" she asked.

"Now. As soon as you can get ready."

She stood calmly before him and looked him in the eye.

"Do you think for one moment," she said, "that I would enter your home while Héloise is there?"

Hartley cringed as if from an unexpected blow. He folded his arms and paced the carpet once or twice.

"She shall go," he declared grimly. Drops stood upon his brow. "Why should I let that woman make my life miserable? Never have I seen one day of freedom from trouble since I have known her. You are right, Vivienne. Héloise must be sent away before I can take you home. But she shall go. I have decided. I will turn her from my doors."

"When will you do this?" asked the girl.

Hartley clinched his teeth and bent his brows together.

"Tonight," he said, resolutely. "I will send her away tonight."

"Then," said Vivienne, "my answer is 'yes.' Come for me when you will."

She looked into his eyes with a sweet, sincere light in her own. Hartley could scarcely believe that her surrender was true, it was so swift and complete.

"Promise me," he said feelingly, "on your word and honor."

"On my word and honor," repeated Vivienne, softly.

At the door he turned and gazed at her happily, but yet as one who scarcely trusts the foundations of his joy.

"Tomorrow," he said, with a forefinger of reminder uplifted.

"Tomorrow," she repeated with a smile of truth and candor.

In an hour and forty minutes Hartley stepped off the train at Floralhurst. A brisk walk of ten minutes brought him to the gate of a handsome two-story cottage set upon a wide and well-tended lawn. Halfway to the house he was met by a woman with jet-black braided hair and flowing white summer gown, who half strangled him without apparent cause.

When they stepped into the hall she said:

"Mamma's here. The auto is coming for her in half an hour. She came to dinner, but there's no dinner."

"I've something to tell you," said Hartley. "I thought to break it to you gently, but since your mother is here we may as well out with it."

He stooped and whispered something at her ear.

His wife screamed. Her mother came running into the hall. The dark-haired woman screamed again- the joyful scream of a well-beloved and petted woman.

"Oh, Mamma!" she cried ecstatically, "what do you think? Vivienne is coming to cook for us! She is the one that stayed with the Montgomerys a whole year. And now, Billy, dear," she concluded, "you must go right down into the kitchen and discharge Héloise. She has been drunk again the whole day long."

40

The Gold That Glittered

A story with a moral appended is like the bill of a mosquito. It bores you, and then injects a stinging drop to irritate your conscience. Therefore let us have the moral first and be done with it. All is not gold that glitters, but it is a wise child that keeps the stopper in his bottle of testing acid.

Where Broadway skirts the corner of the square presided over by George the Veracious is the Little Rialto. Here stand the actors of that quarter, and this is their shibboleth: "'Nit,' says I to Frohman, 'you can't touch me for a kopeck less than two-fifty per,' and out I walks."

Westward and southward from the Thespian glare are one or two streets where a Spanish-American colony has huddled for a little tropical warmth in the nipping North. The center of life in this precinct is "El Refugio," a café and restaurant that caters to the volatile exiles from the South. Up from Chili, Bolivia, Colombia, the rolling republics of Central America and the ireful islands of the Western Indies flit the cloaked and sombreroed señores, who are scattered like burning lava by the political eruptions of their several countries. Hither they come to lay counterplots, to bide their time, to solicit funds, to enlist filibusterers, to smuggle out arms and ammunitions, to play the game at long taw. In El Refugio, they find the atmosphere in which they thrive.

In the restaurant of El Refugio are served compounds delightful to the palate of the man from Capricorn or Cancer. Altruism must halt the story thus long. On, diner, weary of the culinary subterfuges of the Gallic chef, hie thee to El Refugio! There only will you find a fish—bluefish, shad or pompano from the Gulf—baked after the Spanish method. Tomatoes give it color, individuality and soul; chili colorado bestows upon it zest, originality and fervor; unknown herbs furnish piquancy and mystery, and—but its crowning glory deserves a new sentence. Around it, above it, beneath it, in its vicinity—but never in it—hovers an ethereal aura, an effluvium so rarefied and delicate that only the Society for Psychical Research could note its origin. Do not say that garlic is in the fish at El Refugio. It is not otherwise than as if the spirit of Garlic, flitting past, has wafted one kiss that lingers in the parsley-crowned dish as haunting as those kisses in life, "by hopeless fancy feigned on lips that are for others." And then, when Conchito, the waiter, brings you a plate of brown frijoles and a carafe of wine that has never stood still between Oporto and El Refugio—ah, Dios!

One day a Hamburg-American liner deposited upon Pier No. 55 Gen. Perrico Ximenes Villablanca Falcon, a passenger from Cartagena. The General was between a claybank and a bay in complexion, had a 42-inch waist and stood 5 feet 4 with his Du Barry heels. He had the mustache of a shooting-gallery proprietor, he wore the full dress of a Texas congressman and had the important aspect of an uninstructed delegate.

Gen. Falcon had enough English under his hat to enable him to inquire his way to the street in which El Refugio stood. When he reached that neighborhood he saw a sign before a respectable red-brick house that read, "Hotel Español." In the window was a card in Spanish, "Aqui se habla Español." The General entered, sure of a congenial port.

In the cozy office was Mrs. O'Brien, the proprietress. She had blond—oh, unimpeachably blond hair. For the rest she was amiability, and ran largely to inches around. Gen. Falcon brushed the floor with his broad-brimmed hat, and emitted a quantity of

Spanish, the syllables sounding like firecrackers gently popping their way down the string of a bunch.

"Spanish or Dago?" asked Mrs. O'Brien, pleasantly.

"I am a Colombian, madam," said the General, proudly. "I speak the Spanish. The advisement in your window say the Spanish he is spoken here. How is that?"

"Well, you've been speaking it, ain't you?" said the madam. "I'm sure I can't."

At the Hotel Español General Falcon engaged rooms and established himself. At dusk he sauntered out upon the streets to view the wonders of this roaring city of the North. As he walked he thought of the wonderful golden hair of Mme. O'Brien. "It is here," said the General to himself, no doubt in his own language, "that one shall find the most beautiful señoras in the world. I have not in my Colombia viewed among our beauties one so fair. But no! It is not for the General Falcon to think of beauty. It is my country that claims my devotion."

At the corner of Broadway and the Little Rialto the General became involved. The street cars bewildered him, and the fender of one upset him against a pushcart laden with oranges. A cab driver missed him an inch with a hub, and poured barbarous execrations upon his head. He scrambled to the sidewalk and skipped again in terror when the whistle of a peanut-roaster puffed a hot scream in his ear. "*Válgame Dios*! What devil's city is this?"

As the General fluttered out of the streamers of passers like a wounded snipe he was marked simultaneously as game by two hunters. One was "Bully" McGuire, whose system of sport required the use of a strong arm and the misuse of an eight-inch piece of lead pipe. The other Nimrod of the asphalt was "Spider" Kelley, a sportsman with more refined methods.

In pouncing upon their self-evident prey, Mr. Kelley was a shade the quicker. His elbow fended accurately the onslaught of Mr. McGuire.

"G'wan!" he commanded harshly. "I saw it first." McGuire slunk away, awed by superior intelligence.

"Pardon me," said Mr. Kelley, to the General, "but you got balled up in the shuffle, didn't you? Let me assist you." He picked up the General's hat and brushed the dust from it.

The ways of Mr. Kelley could not but succeed. The General, bewildered and dismayed by the resounding streets, welcomed his deliverer as a caballero with a most disinterested heart.

"I have a desire," said the General, "to return to the hotel of O'Brien, in which I am stop. Caramba! señor, there is a loudness and rapidness of going and coming in the city of this Nueva York."

Mr. Kelley's politeness would not suffer the distinguished Colombian to brave the dangers of the return unaccompanied. At the door of the Hotel Español they paused. A little lower down on the opposite side of the street shone the modest illuminated sign of El Refugio. Mr. Kelley, to whom few streets were unfamiliar, knew the place exteriorly as a "Dago joint." All foreigners Mr. Kelley classed under the two heads of "Dagoes" and Frenchmen. He proposed to the General that they repair thither and substantiate their acquaintance with a liquid foundation.

An hour later found General Falcon and Mr. Kelley seated at a table in the conspirator's corner of El Refugio. Bottles and glasses were between them. For the tenth time the General confided the secret of his mission to the Estados Unidos. He was here, he declared, to purchase arms—2,000 stands of Winchester rifles—for the Colombian revolutionists. He had drafts in his pocket drawn by the Cartagena Bank on its New York correspondent for $25,000. At other tables other revolutionists were shouting their political secrets to their fellow-plotters; but none was as loud as the General. He pounded the table; he hallooed for some wine; he roared to his friend that his errand was a secret one, and not to be hinted at to a living soul. Mr. Kelley himself was stirred to sympathetic enthusiasm. He grasped the General's hand across the table.

"Monseer," he said, earnestly, "I don't know where this country of yours is, but I'm for it. I guess it must be a branch of the United States, though, for the poetry guys and the schoolmarms call us Columbia, too, sometimes. It's a lucky thing for you that you butted into me to-night. I'm the only man in New York that can get this gun deal through for you. The Secretary of War of the United States is me best friend. He's in the city now, and I'll see him for you to-morrow. In the meantime, monseer, you keep them drafts tight in your inside pocket. I'll call for you to-morrow, and take you to see him. Say! that ain't the District of Columbia you're talking about, is it?" concluded Mr. Kelley, with a sudden qualm. "You can't capture that with no 2,000 guns—it's been tried with more."

"No, no, no!" exclaimed the General. "It is the Republic of Colombia—it is a g-r-reat republic on the top side of America of the South. Yes. Yes."

"All right," said Mr. Kelley, reassured. "Now suppose we trek along home and go by-by. I'll write to the Secretary to-night and make a date with him. It's a ticklish job to get guns out of New York. McClusky himself can't do it."

They parted at the door of the Hotel Español. The General rolled his eyes at the moon and sighed.

"It is a great country, your Nueva York," he said. "Truly the cars in the streets devastate one, and the engine that cooks the nuts terribly makes a squeak in the ear. But, ah, Señor Kelley—the señoras with hair of much goldness, and admirable fatness—they are magnificas! Muy magnificas!"

Kelley went to the nearest telephone booth and called up McCrary's café, far up on Broadway. He asked for Jimmy Dunn.

"Is that Jimmy Dunn?" asked Kelley.

"Yes," came the answer.

"You're a liar," sang back Kelley, joyfully. "You're the Secretary of War. Wait there till I come up. I've got the finest thing down here in the way of a fish you ever baited for. It's a Colorado-maduro, with a gold band around it and free coupons enough to buy a red hall lamp and a statuette of Psyche rubbering in the brook. I'll be up on the next car."

Jimmy Dunn was an A. M. of Crookdom. He was an artist in the confidence line. He never saw a bludgeon in his life; and he scorned knockout drops. In fact, he would have set nothing before an intended victim but the purest of drinks, if it had been possible to procure such a thing in New York. It was the ambition of "Spider" Kelley to elevate himself into Jimmy's class.

These two gentlemen held a conference that night at McCrary's. Kelley explained.

"He's as easy as a gumshoe. He's from the Island of Colombia, where there's a strike, or a feud, or something going on, and they've sent him up here to buy 2,000 Winchesters to arbitrate the thing with. He showed me two drafts for $10,000 each, and one for $5,000 on a bank here. 'S truth, Jimmy, I felt real mad with him because he didn't have it in thousand-dollar bills, and hand it to me on a silver waiter. Now, we've got to wait till he goes to the bank and gets the money for us."

They talked it over for two hours, and then Dunn said; "Bring him to No. —— Broadway, at four o'clock to-morrow afternoon."

In due time Kelley called at the Hotel Español for the General. He found the wily warrior engaged in delectable conversation with Mrs. O'Brien.

"The Secretary of War is waitin' for us," said Kelley.

The General tore himself away with an effort.

"Ay, señor," he said, with a sigh, "duty makes a call. But, señor, the señoras of your Estados Unidos—how beauties! For exemplification, take you la Madame O'Brien—*que magnifica*! She is one goddess—one Juno—what you call one ox-eyed Juno."

Now Mr. Kelley was a wit; and better men have been shriveled by the fire of their own imagination.

"Sure!" he said with a grin; "but you mean a peroxide Juno, don't you?"

Mrs. O'Brien heard, and lifted an auriferous head. Her businesslike eye rested for an instant upon the disappearing form of Mr. Kelley. Except in street cars one should never be unnecessarily rude to a lady.

When the gallant Colombian and his escort arrived at the Broadway address, they were held in an anteroom for half an hour, and then admitted into a well-equipped office where a distinguished looking man, with a smooth face, wrote at a desk. General Falcon was presented to the Secretary of War of the United States, and his mission made known by his old friend, Mr. Kelley.

"Ah—Colombia!" said the Secretary, significantly, when he was made to understand; "I'm afraid there will be a little difficulty in that case. The President and I differ in our sympathies there. He prefers the established government, while I—" the secretary gave the General a mysterious but encouraging smile. "You, of course, know, General Falcon, that since the Tammany war, an act of Congress has been passed requiring all manufactured arms and ammunition exported from this country to pass through the War Department. Now, if I can do anything for you I will be glad to do so to oblige my old friend, Mr. Kelley. But it must be in absolute secrecy, as the President, as I have said, does not regard favorably the efforts of your revolutionary party in Colombia. I will have my orderly bring a list of the available arms now in the warehouse."

The Secretary struck a bell, and an orderly with the letters A. D. T. on his cap stepped promptly into the room.

"Bring me Schedule B of the small arms inventory," said the Secretary.

The orderly quickly returned with a printed paper. The Secretary studied it closely.

"I find," he said, "that in Warehouse 9, of Government stores, there is shipment of 2,000 stands of Winchester rifles that were ordered by the Sultan of Morocco, who forgot to send the cash with his order. Our rule is that legal-tender money must be paid down at the time of purchase. My dear Kelley, your friend, General Falcon, shall have this lot of arms, if he desires it, at the manufacturer's price. And you will forgive me, I am sure, if I curtail our interview. I am expecting the Japanese Minister and Charles Murphy every moment!"

As one result of this interview, the General was deeply grateful to his esteemed friend, Mr. Kelley. As another, the nimble Secretary of War was extremely busy during the next two days buying empty rifle cases and filling them with bricks, which were then stored in a warehouse rented for that purpose. As still another, when the General returned to the Hotel Español, Mrs. O'Brien went up to him, plucked a thread from his lapel, and said:

"Say, señor, I don't want to 'butt in,' but what does that monkey-faced, cat-eyed, rubber-necked tin horn tough want with you?"

"*Sangre de mi vida!*" exclaimed the General. "Impossible it is that you speak of my good friend, Señor Kelley."

"Come into the summer garden," said Mrs. O'Brien. "I want to have a talk with you."

Let us suppose that an hour has elapsed.

"And you say," said the General, "that for the sum of $18,000 can be purchased the furnishment of the house and the lease of one year with this garden so lovely—so resembling unto the patios of my cara Colombia?"

"And dirt cheap at that," sighed the lady.

"*Ah, Dios!*" breathed General Falcon. "What to me is war and politics? This spot is one paradise. My country it have other brave heroes to continue the fighting. What to me should be glory and the shooting of mans? Ah! no. It is here I have found one angel. Let us buy the Hotel Español and you shall be mine, and the money shall not be waste on guns."

Mrs. O'Brien rested her blond pompadour against the shoulder of the Colombian patriot.

"Oh, señor," she sighed, happily, "ain't you terrible!"

Two days later was the time appointed for the delivery of the arms to the General. The boxes of supposed rifles were stacked in the rented warehouse, and the Secretary of War sat upon them, waiting for his friend Kelley to fetch the victim.

Mr. Kelley hurried, at the hour, to the Hotel Español. He found the General behind the desk adding up accounts.

"I have decide," said the General, "to buy not guns. I have today buy the insides of this hotel, and there shall be marrying of the General Perrico Ximenes Villablanca Falcon with la Madame O'Brien."

Mr. Kelley almost strangled.

"Say, you old bald-headed bottle of shoe polish," he spluttered, "you're a swindler—that's what you are! You've bought a boarding house with money belonging to your infernal country, wherever it is."

"Ah," said the General, footing up a column, "that is what you call politics. War and revolution they are not nice. Yes. It is not best that one shall always follow Minerva. No. It is of quite desirable to keep hotels and be with that Juno—that ox-eyed Juno. Ah! What hair of the gold it is that she have!"

Mr. Kelley choked again.

"Ah, Senor Kelley!" said the General, feelingly and finally, "is it that you have never eaten of the corned beef hash that Madame O'Brien she make?"

41

The Ransom of Red Chief

It looked like a good thing: but wait till I tell you. We were down South, in Alabama—Bill Driscoll and myself—when this kidnapping idea struck us. It was, as Bill afterward expressed it, "during a moment of temporary mental apparition"; but we didn't find that out till later.

There was a town down there, as flat as a flannel-cake, and called Summit, of course. It contained inhabitants of as undeleterious and self-satisfied a class of peasantry as ever clustered around a Maypole.

Bill and me had a joint capital of about six hundred dollars, and we needed just two thousand dollars more to pull off a fraudulent town-lot scheme in Western Illinois with. We talked it over on the front steps of the hotel. Philoprogenitiveness, says we, is strong in semi-rural communities; therefore and for other reasons, a kidnapping project ought to do better there than in the radius of newspapers that send reporters out in plain clothes to stir up talk about such things. We knew that Summit couldn't get after us with anything stronger than constables and maybe some lackadaisical bloodhounds and a diatribe or two in the *Weekly Farmers' Budget*. So, it looked good.

We selected for our victim the only child of a prominent citizen named Ebenezer Dorset. The father was respectable and tight, a mortgage fancier and a stern, upright collection-plate passer and forecloser. The kid was a boy of ten, with bas-relief freckles, and hair the color of the cover of the magazine you buy at the news-stand when you want to catch a train. Bill and me figured that Ebenezer would melt down for a ransom of two thousand dollars to a cent. But wait till I tell you.

About two miles from Summit was a little mountain, covered with a dense cedar brake. On the rear elevation of this mountain was a cave. There we stored provisions. One evening after sundown, we drove in a buggy past old Dorset's house. The kid was in the street, throwing rocks at a kitten on the opposite fence.

"Hey, little boy!" says Bill, "would you like to have a bag of candy and a nice ride?"

The boy catches Bill neatly in the eye with a piece of brick.

"That will cost the old man an extra five hundred dollars," says Bill, climbing over the wheel.

That boy put up a fight like a welter-weight cinnamon bear; but, at last, we got him down in the bottom of the buggy and drove away. We took him up to the cave and I hitched the horse in the cedar brake. After dark I drove the buggy to the little village, three miles away, where we had hired it, and walked back to the mountain.

Bill was pasting court-plaster over the scratches and bruises on his features. There was a fire burning behind the big rock at the entrance of the cave, and the boy was watching a pot of boiling coffee, with two buzzard tail-feathers stuck in his red hair. He points a stick at me when I come up, and says:

"Ha! cursed paleface, do you dare to enter the camp of Red Chief, the terror of the plains?

"He's all right now," says Bill, rolling up his trousers and examining some bruises on his shins. "We're playing Indian. We're making Buffalo Bill's show look like magic-lantern views of Palestine in the town hall. I'm Old Hank, the Trapper, Red Chief's captive, and I'm to be scalped at daybreak. By Geronimo! that kid can kick hard."

Yes, sir, that boy seemed to be having the time of his life. The fun of camping out in a cave had made him forget that he was a captive himself. He immediately christened me Snake-eye, the Spy, and announced that, when his braves returned from the warpath, I was to be broiled at the stake at the rising of the sun.

Then we had supper; and he filled his mouth full of bacon and bread and gravy, and began to talk. He made a during-dinner speech something like this:

"I like this fine. I never camped out before; but I had a pet 'possum once, and I was nine last birthday. I hate to go to school. Rats ate up sixteen of Jimmy Talbot's aunt's speckled hen's eggs. Are there any real Indians in these woods? I want some more gravy. Does the trees moving make the wind blow? We had five puppies. What makes your nose so red, Hank? My father has lots of money. Are the stars hot? I whipped Ed Walker twice, Saturday. I don't like girls. You dassent catch toads unless with a string. Do oxen make any noise? Why are oranges round? Have you got beds to sleep on in this cave? Amos Murray has got six toes. A parrot can talk, but a monkey or a fish can't. How many does it take to make twelve?"

Every few minutes he would remember that he was a pesky redskin, and pick up his stick rifle and tiptoe to the mouth of the cave to rubber for the scouts of the hated paleface. Now and then he would let out a war-whoop that made Old Hank the Trapper shiver. That boy had Bill terrorized from the start.

"Red Chief," says I to the kid, "would you like to go home?"

"Aw, what for?" says he. "I don't have any fun at home. I hate to go to school. I like to camp out. You won't take me back home again, Snake-eye, will you?"

"Not right away," says I. "We'll stay here in the cave a while."

"All right!" says he. "That'll be fine. I never had such fun in all my life."

We went to bed about eleven o'clock. We spread down some wide blankets and quilts and put Red Chief between us. We weren't afraid he'd run away. He kept us awake for three hours, jumping up and reaching for his rifle and screeching: "Hist! pard," in mine and Bill's ears, as the fancied crackle of a twig or the rustle of a leaf revealed to his young imagination the stealthy approach of the outlaw band. At last, I fell into a troubled sleep, and dreamed that I had been kidnapped and chained to a tree by a ferocious pirate with red hair.

Just at daybreak, I was awakened by a series of awful screams from Bill. They weren't yells, or howls, or shouts, or whoops, or yawps, such as you'd expect from a manly set of vocal organs—they were simply indecent, terrifying, humiliating screams, such as women emit when they see ghosts or caterpillars. It's an awful thing to hear a strong, desperate, fat man scream incontinently in a cave at daybreak.

I jumped up to see what the matter was. Red Chief was sitting on Bill's chest, with one hand twined in Bill's hair. In the other he had the sharp case-knife we used for slicing bacon; and he was industriously and realistically trying to take Bill's scalp, according to the sentence that had been pronounced upon him the evening before.

I got the knife away from the kid and made him lie down again. But, from that moment, Bill's spirit was broken. He laid down on his side of the bed, but he never closed an eye again in sleep as long as that boy was with us. I dozed off for a while, but along toward sun-up I remembered that Red Chief had said I was to be burned at the stake at the rising of the sun. I wasn't nervous or afraid; but I sat up and lit my pipe and leaned against a rock.

"What you getting up so soon for, Sam?" asked Bill.

"Me?" says I. "Oh, I got a kind of a pain in my shoulder. I thought sitting up would rest it."

"You're a liar!" says Bill. "You're afraid. You was to be burned at sunrise, and you was afraid he'd do it. And he would, too, if he could find a match. Ain't it awful, Sam? Do you think anybody will pay out money to get a little imp like that back home?"

"Sure," said I. "A rowdy kid like that is just the kind that parents dote on. Now, you and the Chief get up and cook breakfast, while I go up on the top of this mountain and reconnoiter."

I went up on the peak of the little mountain and ran my eye over the contiguous vicinity. Over toward Summit I expected to see the sturdy yeomanry of the village armed with scythes and pitchforks beating the countryside for the dastardly kidnappers. But what I saw was a peaceful landscape dotted with one man ploughing with a dun mule. Nobody was dragging the creek; no couriers dashed hither and yon, bringing tidings of no news to the distracted parents. There was a sylvan attitude of somnolent sleepiness pervading that section of the external outward surface of Alabama that lay exposed to my view. "Perhaps," says I to myself, "it has not yet been discovered that the wolves have borne away the tender lambkin from the fold. Heaven help the wolves!" says I, and I went down the mountain to breakfast.

When I got to the cave I found Bill backed up against the side of it, breathing hard, and the boy threatening to smash him with a rock half as big as a cocoanut.

"He put a red-hot boiled potato down my back," explained Bill, "and then mashed it with his foot; and I boxed his ears. Have you got a gun about you, Sam?"

I took the rock away from the boy and kind of patched up the argument. "I'll fix you," says the kid to Bill. "No man ever yet struck the Red Chief but what he got paid for it. You better beware!"

After breakfast the kid takes a piece of leather with strings wrapped around it out of his pocket and goes outside the cave unwinding it.

"What's he up to now?" says Bill, anxiously. "You don't think he'll run away, do you, Sam?"

"No fear of it," says I. "He don't seem to be much of a home body. But we've got to fix up some plan about the ransom. There don't seem to be much excitement around Summit on account of his disappearance; but maybe they haven't realized yet that he's gone. His folks may think he's spending the night with Aunt Jane or one of the neighbors. Anyhow, he'll be missed today. Tonight we must get a message to his father demanding the two thousand dollars for his return."

Just then we heard a kind Of war-whoop, such as David might have emitted when he knocked out the champion Goliath. It was a sling that Red Chief had pulled out of his pocket, and he was whirling it around his head.

I dodged, and heard a heavy thud and a kind of a sigh from Bill, like a horse gives out when you take his saddle off. A niggerhead rock the size of an egg had caught Bill just behind his left ear.

He loosened himself all over and fell in the fire across the frying pan of hot water for washing the dishes. I dragged him out and poured cold water on his head for half an hour.

By and by, Bill sits up and feels behind his ear and says: "Sam, do you know who my favorite Biblical character is?"

"Take it easy," says I. "You'll come to your senses presently."

"King Herod," says he. "You won't go away and leave me here alone, will you, Sam?"

I went out and caught that boy and shook him until his freckles rattled.

"If you don't behave," says I, "I'll take you straight home. Now, are you going to be good, or not?"

"I was only funning," says he sullenly. "I didn't mean to hurt Old Hank. But what did he hit me for? I'll behave, Snake-eye, if you won't send me home, and if you'll let me play the Black Scout today."

"I don't know the game," says I. "That's for you and Mr. Bill to decide. He's your playmate for the day. I'm going away for a while, on business. Now, you come in and make friends with him and say you are sorry for hurting him, or home you go, at once."

I made him and Bill shake hands, and then I took Bill aside and told him I was going to Poplar Cove, a little village three miles from the cave, and find out what I could about how the kidnapping had been regarded in Summit. Also, I thought it best to send a peremptory letter to old man Dorset that day, demanding the ransom and dictating how it should be paid.

"You know, Sam," says Bill, "I've stood by you without batting an eye in earthquakes, fire and flood—in poker games, dynamite outrages, police raids, train robberies and cyclones. I never lost my nerve yet till we kidnapped that two-legged skyrocket of a kid. He's got me going. You won't leave me long with him, will you, Sam?"

"I'll be back some time this afternoon," says I. "You must keep the boy amused and quiet till I return. And now we'll write the letter to old Dorset."

Bill and I got paper and pencil and worked on the letter while Red Chief, with a blanket wrapped around him, strutted up and down, guarding the mouth of the cave. Bill begged me tearfully to make the ransom fifteen hundred dollars instead of two thousand. "I ain't attempting," says he, "to decry the celebrated moral aspect of parental affection, but we're dealing with humans, and it ain't human for anybody to give up two thousand dollars for that forty-pound chunk of freckled wildcat. I'm willing to take a chance at fifteen hundred dollars. You can charge the difference up to me."

So, to relieve Bill, I acceded, and we collaborated a letter that ran this way:

> *Ebenezer Dorset, Esq.:*
>
> We have your boy concealed in a place far from Summit. It is useless for you or the most skillful detectives to attempt to find him. Absolutely, the only terms on which you can have him restored to you are these: We demand fifteen hundred dollars in large bills for his return; the money to be left at midnight tonight at the same spot and in the same box as your reply—as hereinafter described. If you agree to these terms, send your answer in writing by a solitary messenger tonight at half-past eight o'clock. After crossing Owl Creek, on the road to Poplar Cove, there are three large trees about a hundred yards apart, close to the fence of the wheat field on the right-hand side. At the bottom of the fence-post, opposite the third tree, will be found a small pasteboard box.
>
> The messenger will place the answer in this box and return immediately to Summit.
>
> If you attempt any treachery or fail to comply with our demand as stated, you will never see your boy again.
>
> If you pay the money as demanded, he will be returned to you safe and well within three hours. These terms are final, and if you do not accede to them no further communication will be attempted.
>
> TWO DESPERATE MEN.

I addressed this letter to Dorset, and put it in my pocket. As I was about to start, the kid comes up to me and says:

"Aw, Snake-eye, you said I could play the Black Scout while you was gone."

"Play it, of course," says I. "Mr. Bill will play with you. What kind of a game is it?"

"I'm the Black Scout," says Red Chief, "and I have to ride to the stockade to warn the settlers that the Indians are coming. I'm tired of playing Indian myself. I want to be the Black Scout."

"All right," says I. "It sounds harmless to me. I guess Mr. Bill will help you foil the pesky savages."

"What am I to do?" asks Bill, looking at the kid suspiciously.

"You are the hoss," says Black Scout. "Get down on your hands and knees. How can I ride to the stockade without a hoss?"

"You'd better keep him interested," said I, "till we get the scheme going. Loosen up."

Bill gets down on his all fours, and a look comes in his eye like a rabbit's when you catch it in a trap.

"How far is it to the stockade, kid?" he asks, in a husky manner of voice.

"Ninety miles," says the Black Scout. "And you have to hump yourself to get there on time. Whoa, now!"

The Black Scout jumps on Bill's back and digs his heels in his side.

"For Heaven's sake," says Bill, "hurry back, Sam, as soon as you can. I wish we hadn't made the ransom more than a thousand. Say, you quit kicking me or I'll get up and warm you good."

I walked over to Poplar Cove and sat around the post-office and store, talking with the chawbacons that came in to trade. One whiskerando says that he hears Summit is all upset on account of Elder Ebenezer Dorset's boy having been lost or stolen. That was all I wanted to know. I bought some smoking tobacco, referred casually to the price of black-eyed peas, posted my letter surreptitiously and came away. The postmaster said the mail-carrier would come by in an hour to take the mail on to Summit.

When I got back to the cave Bill and the boy were not to be found. I explored the vicinity of the cave, and risked a yodel or two, but there was no response.

So I lighted my pipe and sat down on a mossy bank to await developments.

In about half an hour I heard the bushes rustle, and Bill wabbled out into the little glade in front of the cave. Behind him was the kid, stepping softly like a scout, with a broad grin on his face. Bill stopped, took off his hat and wiped his face with a red handkerchief. The kid stopped about eight feet behind him.

"Sam," says Bill, "I suppose you'll think I'm a renegade, but I couldn't help it. I'm a grown person with masculine proclivities and habits of self-defense, but there is a time when all systems of egotism and predominance fail. The boy is gone. I have sent him home. All is off. There was martyrs in old times," goes on Bill, "that suffered death rather than give up the particular graft they enjoyed. None of 'em ever was subjugated to such supernatural tortures as I have been. I tried to be faithful to our articles of depredation; but there came a limit."

"What's the trouble, Bill?" I asks him.

"I was rode," says Bill, "the ninety miles to the stockade, not barring an inch. Then, when the settlers was rescued, I was given oats. Sand ain't a palatable substitute. And then, for an hour I had to try to explain to him why there was nothin' in holes, how a road can run both ways and what makes the grass green. I tell you, Sam, a human can only stand so much. I takes him by the neck of his clothes and drags him down the mountain. On the way he kicks my legs black-and-blue from the knees down; and I've got to have two or three bites on my thumb and hand cauterized.

"But he's gone"—continues Bill—"gone home. I showed him the road to Summit and kicked him about eight feet nearer there at one kick. I'm sorry we lose the ransom; but it was either that or Bill Driscoll to the madhouse."

Bill is puffing and blowing, but there is a look of ineffable peace and growing content on his rose-pink features.

"Bill," says I, "there isn't any heart disease in your family, is there?

"No," says Bill, "nothing chronic except malaria and accidents. Why?"

"Then you might turn around," says I, "and have a took behind you."

Bill turns and sees the boy, and loses his complexion and sits down plump on the round and begins to pluck aimlessly at grass and little sticks. For an hour I was afraid for his mind. And then

I told him that my scheme was to put the whole job through immediately and that we would get the ransom and be off with it by midnight if old Dorset fell in with our proposition. So Bill braced up enough to give the kid a weak sort of a smile and a promise to play the Russian in a Japanese war with him is soon as he felt a little better.

I had a scheme for collecting that ransom without danger of being caught by counter-plots that ought to commend itself to professional kidnappers. The tree under which the answer was to be left—and the money later on—was close to the road fence with big, bare fields on all sides. If a gang of constables should be watching for any one to come for the note they could see him a long way off crossing the fields or in the road. But no, sirree! At half-past eight I was up in that tree as well hidden as a tree toad, waiting for the messenger to arrive.

Exactly on time, a half-grown boy rides up the road on a bicycle, locates the pasteboard box at the foot of the fence-post, slips a folded piece of paper into it and pedals away again back toward Summit.

I waited an hour and then concluded the thing was square. I slid down the tree, got the note, slipped along the fence till I struck the woods, and was back at the cave in another half an hour. I opened the note, got near the lantern and read it to Bill. It was written with a pen in a crabbed hand, and the sum and substance of it was this:

> *Two Desperate Men.*
>
> *Gentlemen:* I received your letter today by post, in regard to the ransom you ask for the return of my son. I think you are a little high in your demands, and I hereby make you a counter-proposition, which I am inclined to believe you will accept. You bring Johnny home and pay me two hundred and fifty dollars in cash, and I agree to take him off your hands. You had better come at night, for the neighbors believe he is lost, and I couldn't be responsible for what they would do to anybody they saw bringing him back. Very respectfully,
>
> EBENEZER DORSET.

"Great pirates of Penzance!" says I; "of all the impudent—"

But I glanced at Bill, and hesitated. He had the most appealing look in his eyes I ever saw on the face of a dumb or a talking brute.

"Sam," says he, "what's two hundred and fifty dollars, after all? We've got the money. One more night of this kid will send me to a bed in Bedlam. Besides being a thorough gentleman, I think Mr. Dorset is a spendthrift for making us such a liberal offer. You ain't going to let the chance go, are you?"

"Tell you the truth, Bill," says I, "this little he ewe lamb has somewhat got on my nerves too. We'll take him home, pay the ransom and make our get-away."

We took him home that night. We got him to go by telling him that his father had bought a silver-mounted rifle and a pair of moccasins for him, and we were going to hunt bears the next day.

It was just twelve o'clock when we knocked at Ebenezer's front door. Just at the moment when I should have been abstracting the fifteen hundred dollars from the box under the tree, according to the original proposition, Bill was counting out two hundred and fifty dollars into Dorset's hand.

When the kid found out we were going to leave him at home he started up a howl like a calliope and fastened himself as tight as a leech to Bill's leg. His father peeled him away gradually, like a porous plaster.

"How long can you hold him?" asks Bill.

"I'm not as strong as I used to be," says old Dorset, "but I think I can promise you ten minutes."

"Enough," says Bill. "In ten minutes I shall cross the Central, Southern and Middle Western States, and be legging it trippingly for the Canadian border."

And, as dark as it was, and as fat as Bill was, and as good a runner as I am, he was a good mile and a half out of Summit before I could catch up with him.

42

The Poet and the Peasant

The other day a poet friend of mine, who has lived in close communion with nature all his life, wrote a poem and took it to an editor.

It was a living pastoral, full of the genuine breath of the fields, the song of birds, and the pleasant chatter of trickling streams.

When the poet called again to see about it, with hopes of a beefsteak dinner in his heart, it was handed back to him with the comment:

"Too artificial."

Several of us met over spaghetti and Dutchess County chianti, and swallowed indignation with slippery forkfuls.

And there we dug a pit for the editor. With us was Conant, a well-arrived writer of fiction—a man who had trod on asphalt all his life, and who had never looked upon bucolic scenes except with sensations of disgust from the windows of express trains.

Conant wrote a poem and called it "The Doe and the Brook." It was a fine specimen of the kind of work you would expect from a poet who had strayed with Amaryllis only as far as the florist's windows, and whose sole ornithological discussion had been carried on with a waiter. Conant signed this poem, and we sent it to the same editor.

But this has very little to do with the story.

Just as the editor was reading the first line of the poem, on the next morning, a being stumbled off the West Shore ferryboat, and loped slowly up Forty-second Street.

The invader was a young man with light blue eyes, a hanging lip and hair the exact color of the little orphan's (afterward discovered to be the earl's daughter) in one of Mr. Blaney's plays. His trousers were corduroy, his coat short-sleeved, with buttons in the middle of his back. One bootleg was outside the corduroys. You looked expectantly, though in vain, at his straw hat for ear holes, its shape inaugurating the suspicion that it had been ravaged from a former equine possessor. In his hand was a valise—description of it is an impossible task; a Boston man would not have carried his lunch and law books to his office in it. And above one ear, in his hair, was a wisp of hay—the rustic's letter of credit, his badge of innocence, the last clinging touch of the Garden of Eden lingering to shame the gold-brick men.

Knowingly, smilingly, the city crowds passed him by. They saw the raw stranger stand in the gutter and stretch his neck at the tall buildings. At this they ceased to smile, and even to look at him. It had been done so often. A few glanced at the antique valise to see what Coney "attraction" or brand of chewing gum he might be thus dinning into his memory. But for the most part he was ignored. Even the newsboys looked bored when he scampered like a circus clown out of the way of cabs and street cars.

At Eighth Avenue stood "Bunco Harry," with his dyed mustache and shiny, good-natured eyes. Harry was too good an artist not to be pained at the sight of an actor overdoing his part. He edged up to the countryman, who had stopped to open his mouth at a jewelry store window, and shook his head.

"Too thick, pal," he said, critically—"too thick by a couple of inches. I don't know what your lay is; but you've got the properties too thick. That hay, now—why, they don't even allow that on Proctor's circuit any more."

"I don't understand you, mister," said the green one. "I'm not lookin' for any circus. I've just run down from Ulster County to look at the town, bein' that the hayin's over with. Gosh! But it's a whopper. I thought Poughkeepsie was some punkins; but this here town is five times as big."

"Oh, well," said "Bunco Harry," raising his eyebrows, "I didn't mean to butt in. You don't have to tell. I thought you ought to tone down a little, so I tried to put you wise. Wish you success at your graft, whatever it is. Come and have a drink, anyhow."

"I wouldn't mind having a glass of lager beer," acknowledged the other.

They went to a café frequented by men with smooth faces and shifty eyes, and sat at their drinks.

"I'm glad I come across you, mister," said Haylocks. "How'd you like to play a game or two of seven-up? I've got the keerds."

He fished them out of Noah's valise—a rare, inimitable deck, greasy with bacon suppers and grimy with the soil of cornfields.

"Bunco Harry" laughed loud and briefly.

"Not for me, sport," he said, firmly. "I don't go against that make-up of yours for a cent. But I still say you've overdone it. The Reubs haven't dressed like that since '79. I doubt if you could work Brooklyn for a key-winding watch with that layout."

"Oh, you needn't think I ain't got the money," boasted Haylocks. He drew forth a tightly rolled mass of bills as large as a teacup, and laid it on the table.

"Got that for my share of grandmother's farm," he announced. "There's $950 in that roll. Thought I'd come to the city and look around for a likely business to go into."

"Bunco Harry" took up the roll of money and looked at it with almost respect in his smiling eyes.

"I've seen worse," he said, critically. "But you'll never do it in them clothes. You want to get light tan shoes and a black suit and a straw hat with a colored band, and talk a good deal about Pittsburg and freight differentials, and drink sherry for breakfast in order to work off phony stuff like that."

"What's his line?" asked two or three shifty-eyed men of "Bunco Harry" after Haylocks had gathered up his impugned money and departed.

"The queer, I guess," said Harry. "Or else he's one of Jerome's men. Or some guy with a new graft. He's too much hayseed.

Maybe that his—I wonder now—oh, no, it couldn't have been real money."

Haylocks wandered on. Thirst probably assailed him again, for he dived into a dark groggery on a side street and bought beer. At first sight of him their eyes brightened; but when his insistent and exaggerated rusticity became apparent their expressions changed to wary suspicion.

Haylocks swung his valise across the bar.

"Keep that a while for me, mister," he said, chewing at the end of a virulent claybank cigar. "I'll be back after I knock around a spell. And keep your eye on it, for there's $950 inside of it, though maybe you wouldn't think so to look at me."

Somewhere outside a phonograph struck up a band piece, and Haylocks was off for it, his coat-tail buttons flopping in the middle of his back.

"Divvy, Mike," said the men hanging upon the bar, winking openly at one another.

"Honest, now," said the bartender, kicking the valise to one side. "You don't think I'd fall to that, do you? Anybody can see he ain't no jay. One of McAdoo's come-on squad, I guess. He's a shine if he made himself up. There ain't no parts of the country now where they dress like that since they run rural free delivery to Providence, Rhode Island. If he's got nine-fifty in that valise it's a ninety-eight cent Waterbury that's stopped at ten minutes to ten."

When Haylocks had exhausted the resources of Mr. Edison to amuse he returned for his valise. And then down Broadway he gallivanted, culling the sights with his eager blue eyes. But still and evermore Broadway rejected him with curt glances and sardonic smiles. He was the oldest of the "gags" that the city must endure. He was so flagrantly impossible, so ultra rustic, so exaggerated beyond the most freakish products of the barnyard, the hayfield and the vaudeville stage, that he excited only weariness and suspicion. And the wisp of hay in his hair was so genuine, so fresh and redolent of the meadows, so clamorously rural that even a shell-game man would have put up his peas and folded his table at the sight of it.

Haylocks seated himself upon a flight of stone steps and once more exhumed his roll of yellow-backs from the valise. The outer one, a twenty, he shucked off and beckoned to a newsboy.

"Son," said he, "run somewhere and get this changed for me. I'm mighty nigh out of chicken feed. I guess you'll get a nickel if you'll hurry up."

A hurt look appeared through the dirt on the newsy's face.

"Aw, watchert'ink! G'wan and get yer funny bill changed yerself. Dey ain't no farm clothes yer got on. G'wan wit yer stage money."

On a corner lounged a keen-eyed steerer for a gambling-house. He saw Haylocks, and his expression suddenly grew cold and virtuous.

"Mister," said the rural one. "I've heard of places in this here town where a fellow could have a good game of old sledge or peg a card at keno. I got $950 in this valise, and I come down from old Ulster to see the sights. Know where a fellow could get action on about $9 or $10? I'm goin' to have some sport, and then maybe I'll buy out a business of some kind."

The steerer looked pained, and investigated a white speck on his left forefinger nail.

"Cheese it, old man," he murmured, reproachfully. "The Central Office must be bughouse to send you out looking like such a gillie. You couldn't get within two blocks of a sidewalk crap game in them Tony Pastor props. The recent Mr. Scotty from Death Valley has got you beat a crosstown block in the way of Elizabethan scenery and mechanical accessories. Let it be skiddoo for yours. Nay, I know of no gilded halls where one may bet a patrol wagon on the ace."

Rebuffed once again by the great city that is so swift to detect artificialities, Haylocks sat upon the curb and presented his thoughts to hold a conference.

"It's my clothes," said he; "durned if it ain't. They think I'm a hayseed and won't have nothin' to do with me. Nobody never made fun of this hat in Ulster County. I guess if you want folks to notice you in New York you must dress up like they do."

So Haylocks went shopping in the bazaars where men spake through their noses and rubbed their hands and ran the tape line ecstatically over the bulge in his inside pocket where reposed a red nubbin of corn with an even number of rows. And messengers bearing parcels and boxes streamed to his hotel on Broadway within the lights of Long Acre.

At 9 o'clock in the evening one descended to the sidewalk whom Ulster County would have foresworn. Bright tan were his shoes; his hat the latest block. His light gray trousers were deeply creased; a gay blue silk handkerchief flapped from the breast pocket of his elegant English walking coat. His collar might have graced a laundry window; his blond hair was trimmed close; the wisp of hay was gone.

For an instant he stood, resplendent, with the leisurely air of a boulevardier concocting in his mind the route for his evening pleasures. And then he turned down the gay, bright street with the easy and graceful tread of a millionaire.

But in the instant that he had paused the wisest and keenest eyes in the city had enveloped him in their field of vision. A stout man with gray eyes picked two of his friends with a lift of his eyebrows from the row of loungers in front of the hotel.

"The juiciest jay I've seen in six months," said the man with gray eyes. "Come along."

It was half-past eleven when a man galloped into the West Forty-seventh Street Police Station with the story of his wrongs.

"Nine hundred and fifty dollars," he gasped, "all my share of grandmother's farm."

The desk sergeant wrung from him the name Jabez Bulltongue, of Locust Valley farm, Ulster County, and then began to take descriptions of the strong-arm gentlemen.

When Conant went to see the editor about the fate of his poem, he was received over the head of the office boy into the inner office that is decorated with the statuettes by Rodin and J. G. Brown.

"When I read the first line of 'The Doe and the Brook,'" said the editor, "I knew it to be the work of one whose life has been heart to heart with Nature. The finished art of the line did not blind me to that fact. To use a somewhat homely comparison, it was as if a wild, free child of the woods and fields were to don the garb of fashion and walk down Broadway. Beneath the apparel the man would show."

"Thanks," said Conant. "I suppose the check will be round on Thursday, as usual."

The morals of this story have somehow gotten mixed. You can take your choice of "Stay on the Farm" or "Don't Write Poetry."

43

The Greater Coney

"Next Sunday," said Dennis Carnahan, "I'll be after going down to see the new Coney Island that's risen like a phoenix bird from the ashes of the old resort. I'm going with Norah Flynn, and we'll fall victims to all the dry goods deceptions, from the red-flannel eruption of Mount Vesuvius to the pink silk ribbons on the race-suicide problems in the incubator kiosk.

"Was I there before? I was. I was there last Tuesday. Did I see the sights? I did not.

"Last Monday I amalgamated myself with the Bricklayers' Union, and in accordance with the rules I was ordered to quit work the same day on account of a sympathy strike with the Lady Salmon Canners' Lodge No.2, of Tacoma, Washington.

"'Twas disturbed I was in mind and proclivities by losing me job, bein' already harassed in me soul on account of havin' quarreled with Norah Flynn a week before by reason of hard words spoken at the Dairymen and Street-Sprinkler Drivers' semi-annual ball, caused by jealousy and prickly heat and that divil, Andy Coghlin.

"So, I says, it will be Coney for Tuesday; and if the chutes and the short change and the green-corn silk between the teeth don't create diversions and get me feeling better, then I don't know at all.

"Ye will have heard that Coney has received moral reconstruction. The old Bowery, where they used to take your tintype by force and give ye knockout drops before having your palm read, is now called the Wall Street of the island. The wienerwurst stands are required by law to keep a news ticker in 'em; and the doughnuts are examined every four years by a retired steamboat inspector. The nigger man's head that was used by the old patrons to throw baseballs at is now illegal; and, by order of the Police Commissioner the image of a man drivin' an automobile has been substituted. I hear that the old immoral amusements have been suppressed. People who used to go down from New York to sit in the sand and dabble in the surf now give up their quarters to squeeze through turnstiles and see imitations of city fires and floods painted on canvas. The reprehensible and degradin' resorts that disgraced old Coney are said to be wiped out. The wipin'-out process consists of raisin' the price from 10 cents to 25 cents, and hirin' a blonde named Maudie to sell tickets instead of Micky, the Bowery Bite. That's what they say—I don't know.

"But to Coney I goes a-Tuesday. I gets off the 'L' and starts for the glitterin' show. 'Twas a fine sight. The Babylonian towers and the Hindoo roof gardens was blazin' with thousands of electric lights, and the streets was thick with people. 'Tis a true thing they say that Coney levels all rank. I see millionaires eatin' popcorn and trampin' along with the crowd; and I see eight-dollar-a-week clothin'-store clerks in red automobiles fightin' one another for who'd squeeze the horn when they come to a corner.

"'I made a mistake,' I says to myself. 'Twas not Coney I needed. When a man's sad 'tis not scenes of hilarity he wants. 'Twould be far better for him to meditate in a graveyard or to attend services at the Paradise Roof Gardens. 'Tis no consolation when a man's lost his sweetheart to order hot corn and have the waiter bring him the powdered sugar cruet instead of salt and then conceal himself, or to have Zozookum, the gipsy palmist, tell him that he has three children and to look out for another serious calamity; price twenty-five cents.

"I walked far away down on the beach, to the ruins of an old pavilion near one corner of this new private park, Dreamland. A year ago that old pavilion was standin' up straight and the old-style waiters was slammin' a week's supply of clam chowder down in front of you for a nickel and callin' you 'cully' friendly, and vice was rampant, and you got back to New York with enough change to take a car at the bridge. Now they tell me that they serve Welsh rabbits on Surf Avenue, and you get the right change back in the movin'-picture joints.

"I sat down at one side of the old pavilion and looked at the surf spreadin' itself on the beach, and thought about the time me and Norah Flynn sat on that spot last summer. 'Twas before reform struck the island; and we was happy. We had tintypes and chowder in the ribald dives, and the Egyptian Sorceress of the Nile told Norah out of her hand, while I was waitin' in the door, that 'twould be the luck of her to marry a red-headed gossoon with two crooked legs, and I was overrunnin' with joy on account of the allusion. And 'twas there that Norah Flynn put her two hands in mine a year before and we talked of flats and the things she could cook and the love business that goes with such episodes. And that was Coney as we loved it, and as the hand of Satan was upon it, friendly and noisy and your money's worth, with no fence around the ocean and not too many electric lights to show the sleeve of a black serge coat against a white shirtwaist.

"I sat with my back to the parks where they had the moon and the dreams and the steeples corralled, and longed for the old Coney. There wasn't many people on the beach. Lots of them was feedin' pennies into the slot machines to see the 'Interrupted Courtship' in the movin' pictures; and a good many was takin' the sea air in the Canals of Venice and some was breathin' the smoke of the sea battle by actual warships in a tank filled with real water. A few was down on the sands enjoyin' the moonlight and the water. And the heart of me was heavy for the new morals of the old island, while the bands behind me played and the sea pounded on the bass drum in front.

"And directly I got up and walked along the old pavilion, and there on the other side of, half in the dark, was a slip of a girl sittin' on the tumble-down timbers, and unless I'm a liar she was cryin' by herself there, all alone.

"'Is it trouble you are in, now, Miss,' says I; 'and what's to be done about it?'

"''Tis none of your business at all, Denny Carnahan,' says she, sittin' up straight. And it was the voice of no other than Norah Flynn.

"'Then it's not,' says I, 'and we're after having a pleasant evening, Miss Flynn. Have ye seen the sights of this new Coney Island, then? I presume ye have come here for that purpose,' says I.

"'I have,' says she. 'Me mother and Uncle Tim they are waiting beyond. 'Tis an elegant evening I've had. I've seen all the attractions that be.'

"'Right ye are,' says I to Norah; and I don't know when I've been that amused. After disportin' me-self among the most laughable moral improvements of the revised shell games I took meself to the shore for the benefit of the cool air. 'And did ye observe the Durbar, Miss Flynn?'

"'I did,' says she, reflectin'; 'but 'tis not safe, I'm thinkin', to ride down them slantin' things into the water.'

"'How did ye fancy the shoot the chutes?' I asks.

"'True, then, I'm afraid of guns,' says Norah. 'They make such noise in my ears. But Uncle Tim, he shot them, he did, and won cigars. 'Tis a fine time we had this day, Mr. Carnahan.'

"'I'm glad you've enjoyed yerself,' I says. 'I suppose you've had a roarin' fine time seein' the sights. And how did the incubators and the helter-skelter and the midgets suit the taste of ye?'

"'I—I wasn't hungry,' says Norah, faint. 'But mother ate a quantity of all of 'em. I'm that pleased with the fine things in the new Coney Island,' says she, 'that it's the happiest day I've seen in a long time, at all.'

"'Did you see Venice?' says I.

"'We did,' says she. 'She was a beauty. She was all dressed in red, she was, with—'

"I listened no more to Norah Flynn. I stepped up and I gathered her in my arms.

"'Tis a story-teller ye are, Norah Flynn', says I. 'Ye've seen no more of the greater Coney Island than I have meself. Come, now, tell the truth—ye came to sit by the old pavilion by the waves where you sat last summer and made Dennis Carnahan a happy man. Speak up, and tell the truth.'

"Norah stuck her nose against me vest.

"'I despise it, Denny,' she says, half cryin'. 'Mother and Uncle Tim went to see the shows, but I came down here to think of you. I couldn't bear the lights and the crowd. Are you forgivin' me, Denny, for the words we had?'

"'Twas me fault,' says I. 'I came here for the same reason meself. Look at the lights, Norah,' I says, turning my back to the sea—'ain't they pretty?'

"'They are,' says Norah, with her eyes shinin'; 'and do ye hear the bands playin'? Oh, Denny, I think I'd like to see it all.'

"'The old Coney is gone, darlin',' I says to her. 'Everything moves. When a man's glad it's not scenes of sadness he wants. 'Tis a greater Coney we have here, but we couldn't see it till we got in the humor for it. Next Sunday, Norah darlin', we'll see the new place from end to end."

44

Law and Order

I found myself in Texas recently, revisiting old places and vistas. At a sheep ranch where I had sojourned many years ago, I stopped for a week. And, as all visitors do, I heartily plunged into the business at hand, which happened to be that of dipping the sheep.

Now, this process is so different from ordinary human baptism that it deserves a word of itself. A vast iron cauldron with half the fires of Avernus beneath it is partly filled with water that soon boils furiously. Into that is cast concentrated lye, lime, and sulphur, which is allowed to stew and fume until the witches' broth is strong enough to scorch the third arm of Palladino herself.

Then this concentrated brew is mixed in a long, deep vat with cubic gallons of hot water, and the sheep are caught by their hind legs and flung into the compound. After being thoroughly ducked by means of a forked pole in the hands of a gentleman detailed for that purpose, they are allowed to clamber up an incline into a corral and dry or die, as the state of their constitutions may decree. If you ever caught an able-bodied, two-year-old mutton by the hind legs and felt the 750 volts of kicking that he can send though your arm seventeen times before you can hurl him into the vat, you will, of course, hope that he may die instead of dry.

But this is merely to explain why Bud Oakley and I gladly stretched ourselves on the bank of the nearby *charco* after the dipping, glad for the welcome inanition and pure contact with the earth after our muscle-racking labours. The flock was a small one, and we finished at three in the afternoon; so Bud brought from the *morral* on his saddle horn, coffee and a coffeepot and a big hunk of bread and some side bacon. Mr. Mills, the ranch owner and my old friend, rode away to the ranch with his force of Mexican *trabajadores*.

While the bacon was frizzling nicely, there was the sound of horses' hoofs behind us. Bud's six-shooter lay in its scabbard ten feet away from his hand. He paid not the slightest heed to the approaching horseman. This attitude of a Texas ranch-man was so different from the old-time custom that I marveled. Instinctively I turned to inspect the possible foe that menaced us in the rear. I saw a horseman dressed in black, who might have been a lawyer or a parson or an undertaker, trotting peaceably along the road by the *arroyo*.

Bud noticed my precautionary movement and smiled sarcastically and sorrowfully.

"You've been away too long," said he. "You don't need to look around any more when anybody gallops up behind you in this state, unless something hits you in the back; and even then it's liable to be only a bunch of tracts or a petition to sign against the trusts. I never looked at that *hombre* that rode by; but I'll bet a quart of sheep dip that he's some double-dyed son of a popgun out rounding up prohibition votes."

"Times have changed, Bud," said I, oracularly. "Law and order is the rule now in the South and the Southwest."

I caught a cold gleam from Bud's pale blue eyes.

"Not that I—" I began, hastily.

"Of course you don't," said Bud warmly. "You know better. You've lived here before. Law and order, you say? Twenty years ago we had 'em here. We only had two or three laws, such as against murder before witnesses, and being caught stealing horses, and voting the Republican ticket. But how is it now? All we get is orders; and the laws go out of the state. Them legislators set up there at Austin and don't do nothing but make laws against kerosene oil and schoolbooks being brought into the state. I reckon they was afraid some man would go home some evening after work and light up and get an education and go to work and make laws to repeal aforesaid laws. Me, I'm for the old days when law and order meant what they said. A law was a law, and a order was a order."

"But—" I began.

"I was going on," continued Bud, "while this coffee is boiling, to describe to you a case of genuine law and order that I knew of once in the times when cases was decided in the chambers of a six-shooter instead of a supreme court.

"You've heard of old Ben Kirkman, the cattle king? His ranch run from the Nueces to the Rio Grande. In them days, as you know, there was cattle barons and cattle kings. The difference was this: when a cattleman went to San Antone and bought beer for the newspaper reporters and only give them the number of cattle he actually owned, they wrote him up for a baron. When he bought 'em champagne wine and added in the amount of cattle he had stole, they called him a king.

"Luke Summers was one of his range bosses. And down to the king's ranch comes one day a bunch of these Oriental people from New York or Kansas City or thereabouts. Luke was detailed with a squad to ride about with 'em, and see that the rattlesnakes got fair warning when they was coming, and drive the deer out of their way. Among the bunch was a black-eyed girl that wore a number two shoe. That's all I noticed about her. But Luke must have seen more, for he married her one day before the *caballard* started back, and went over on Canada Verde and set up a ranch of his own. I'm skipping over the sentimental stuff on purpose, because I never saw or wanted to see any of it. And Luke takes me along with him because we was old friends and I handled cattle to suit him.

"I'm skipping over much what followed, because I never saw or wanted to see any of it—but three years afterward there was a boy kid stumbling and blubbering around the galleries and floors of Luke's ranch. I never had no use for kids; but it seems they did. And I'm skipping over much what followed until one day out to the ranch drives in hacks and buckboards a lot of Mrs. Summers's friends from the East—a sister or so and two or three men. One looked like an uncle to somebody; and one looked like nothing; and the other one had on corkscrew pants and spoke in a tone of voice. I never liked a man who spoke in a tone of voice.

"I'm skipping over much what followed; but one afternoon when I rides up to the ranch house to get some orders about a drove of beeves that was to be shipped, I hears something like a popgun go off. I waits at the hitching rack, not wishing to intrude on private affairs. In a little while Luke comes out and gives some orders to some of his Mexican hands, and they go and hitch up sundry and divers vehicles; and mighty soon out comes one of the sisters or so and some of the two or three men. But two of the two or three men carries between 'em the corkscrew man who spoke in a tone of voice, and lays him flat down in one of the wagons. And they all might have been seen wending their way away.

"'Bud,' says Luke to me, 'I want you to fix up a little and go up to San Antone with me.'

"'Let me get on my Mexican spurs,' says I, 'and I'm your company.'

"One of the sisters or so seems to have stayed at the ranch with Mrs. Summers and the kid. We rides to Encinal and catches the International, and hits San Antone in the morning. After breakfast Luke steers me straight to the office of a lawyer. They go in a room and talk and then come out.

"'Oh, there won't be any trouble, Mr. Summers,' says the lawyer. 'I'll acquaint Judge Simmons with the facts today; and the matter will be put through as promptly as possible. Law and order reigns in this state as swift and sure as any in the country.'

"'I'll wait for the decree if it won't take over half an hour,' says Luke.

"'Tut, tut,' says the lawyer man. 'Law must take its course. Come back day after tomorrow at half-past nine.'

"At that time me and Luke shows up, and the lawyer hands him a folded document. And Luke writes him out a check.

"On the sidewalk Luke holds up the paper to me and puts a finger the size of a kitchen door latch on it and says:

"'Decree of ab-so-lute divorce with cus-to-dy of the child.'

"'Skipping over much what has happened of which I know nothing,' says I, 'it looks to me like a split. Couldn't the lawyer man have made it a strike for you?'

"'Bud,' says he, in a pained style, 'that child is the one thing I have to live for. *She* may go; but the boy is mine!—think of it—I have cus-to-dy of the child.'

"'All right,' says I. 'If it's the law, let's abide by it. But I think,' says I, 'that Judge Simmons might have used exemplary clemency, or whatever is the legal term, in our case.'

"You see, I wasn't inveigled much into the desirableness of having infants around a ranch, except the kind that feed themselves and sell for so much on the hoof when they grow up. But Luke was struck with that sort of parental foolishness that I never could understand. All the way riding from the station back to the ranch, he kept pulling that decree out of his pocket and laying his finger on the back of it and reading off to me the sum and substance of it. 'Cus-to-dy of the child, Bud,' says he. 'Don't forget it—cus-to-dy of the child.'

"But when we hits the ranch we finds our decree of court obviated, *nolle prossed*, and remanded for trial. Mrs. Summers and the kid was gone. They tell us that an hour after me and Luke had started for San Antone she had a team hitched and lit out for the nearest station with her trunks and the youngster.

"Luke takes out his decree once more and reads off its emoluments.

"'It ain't possible, Bud,' says he, 'for this to be. It's contrary to law and order. It's wrote as plain as day here—"Cus-to-dy of the child."'

"'There is what you might call a human leaning,' says I, 'toward smashing 'em both—not to mention the child.'

"'Judge Simmons,' goes on Luke, 'is a incorporated officer of the law. She can't take the boy away. He belongs to me by statutes passed and approved by the state of Texas.'

"'And he's removed from the jurisdiction of mundane mandamuses,' says I, 'by the unearthly statutes of female partiality. Let us praise the Lord and be thankful for whatever small mercies—' I begins; but I see Luke don't listen to me.

Tired as he was, he calls for a fresh horse and starts back again for the station.

"He come back two weeks afterward, not saying much.

"'We can't get the trail,' says he; 'but we've done all the telegraphing that the wires'll stand, and we've got these city rangers they call detectives on the lookout. In the meantime, Bud,' says he, 'we'll round up them cows on Brush Creek, and wait for the law to take its course.'"

"And after that we never alluded to allusions, as you might say.

"Skipping over much what happened in the next twelve years, Luke was made sheriff of Mojada County. He made me his office deputy. Now, don't get in your mind no wrong apparitions of a office deputy doing sums in a book or mashing letters in a cider press. In them days his job was to watch the back windows so nobody didn't plug the sheriff in the rear while he was adding up mileage at his desk in front. And in them days I had qualifications for the job. And there was law and order in Mojada County, and schoolbooks, and all the whiskey you wanted, and the Government built its own battleships instead of collecting nickels from the school children to do it with. And, as I say, there was law and order instead of enactments and restrictions such as disfigure our umpire state today. We had our office at Bildad, the county seat, from which we emerged forth on necessary occasions to soothe whatever fracases and unrest that might occur in our jurisdiction.

"Skipping over much what happened while me and Luke was sheriff, I want to give you an idea of how the law was respected in them days. Luke was what you would call one of the most conscious men in the world. He never knew much book law, but he had the inner emoluments of justice and mercy inculcated into his system. If a respectable citizen shot a Mexican or held up a train and cleaned out the safe in the express car, and Luke ever got hold of him, he'd give the guilty party such a reprimand and a cussin' out that he'd probable never do it again. But once let somebody steal a horse (unless it was a Spanish pony), or cut a wire fence, or otherwise impair the peace and indignity of Mojada County, Luke and me would be on 'em with habeas corpuses and smokeless powder and all the modern inventions of equity and etiquette.

"We certainly had our county on a basis of lawfulness. I've known persons of Eastern classification with little spotted caps and buttoned-up shoes to get off the train at Bildad and eat sandwiches at the railroad station without being shot at or even roped and drug about by the citizens of the town.

"Luke had his own ideas of legality and justice. He was kind of training me to succeed him when he went out of office. He was always looking ahead to the time when he'd quit sheriffing. What he wanted to do was to build a yellow house with lattice-work under the porch and have hens scratching in the yard. The one main thing in his mind seemed to be the yard.

"'Bud,' he says to me, 'by instinct and sentiment I'm a contractor. I want to be a contractor. That's what I'll be when I get out of office.'

"'What kind of a contractor?' says I. 'It sounds like a kind of a business to me. You ain't going to haul cement or establish branches or work on a railroad, are you?'

"'You don't understand,' says Luke. 'I'm tired of space and horizons and territory and distances and things like that. What I want is reasonable contraction. I want a yard with a fence around it that you can go out and set on after supper and listen to whip-poor-wills,' says Luke.

"That's the kind of a man he was. He was home-like, although he'd had bad luck in such investments. But he never talked about them times on the ranch. It seemed like he'd forgotten about it. I wondered how, with his ideas of yards and chickens and notions of lattice-work, he'd seemed to have got out of his mind that kid of his that had been taken away from him, unlawful, in spite of his decree of court. But he wasn't a man you could ask about such things as he didn't refer to in his own conversation.

"I reckon he'd put all his emotions and ideas into being sheriff. I've read in books about men that was disappointed in these poetic and fine-haired and high-collared affairs with ladies renouncing truck of that kind and wrapping themselves up into some occupation like painting pictures, or herding sheep, or science, or teaching school—something to make 'em forget. Well, I guess that was the way with Luke. But, as he couldn't paint pictures, he took it out in rounding up horse thieves and in making Mojada County a safe place to sleep in if you was well armed and not afraid of requisitions or tarantulas.

"One day there passes through Bildad a bunch of these money investors from the East, and they stopped off there, Bildad being the dinner station on the I. & G. N. They was just coming back from Mexico looking after mines and such. There was five of 'em—four solid parties, with gold watch chains, that would grade up over two hundred pounds on the hoof, and one kid about seventeen or eighteen.

"This youngster had on one of them cowboy suits such as tenderfoots bring West with 'em; and you could see he was aching to wing a couple of Indians or bag a grizzly or two with the little pearl-handled gun he had buckled around his waist.

"I walked down to the depot to keep an eye on the outfit and see that they didn't locate any land or scare the cow ponies hitched in front of Murchison's store or act otherwise unseemly. Luke was away after a gang of cattle thieves down on the Frio, and I always looked after the law and order when he wasn't there.

"After dinner this boy comes out of the dining-room while the train was waiting, and prances up and down the platform ready to shoot all antelope, lions, or private citizens that might endeavor to molest or come too near him. He was a good-looking kid; only he was like all them tenderfoots—he didn't know a law-and-order town when he saw it.

"By and by along comes Pedro Johnson, the proprietor of the Crystal Palace *chili-con-carne* stand in Bildad. Pedro was a man who liked to amuse himself; so he kind of herd rides this youngster, laughing at him, tickled to death. I was too far away to hear, but the kid seems to mention some remarks to Pedro, and Pedro goes up and slaps him about nine feet away, and laughs harder than ever. And then the boy gets up quicker than he fell and jerks out his little pearl-handle, and—bing! bing! bing! Pedro gets it three times in special and treasured portions of his carcass. I saw the dust fly off his clothes every time the bullets hit. Sometimes them little thirty-twos cause worry at close range.

"The engine bell was ringing, and the train starting off slow. I goes up to the kid and places him under arrest, and takes away his gun. But the first thing I knew that *caballard* of capitalists makes a break for the train. One of ‹em hesitates in front of me for a second, and kind of smiles and shoves his hand up against my chin, and I sort of laid down on the platform and took a nap. I never was afraid of guns; but I don't want any person except a barber to take liberties like that with my face again. When I woke up, the whole outfit—train, boy, and all—was gone. I asked about Pedro, and they told me the doctor said he would recover provided his wounds didn't turn out to be fatal.

"When Luke got back three days later, and I told him about it, he was mad all over.

"'Why'n't you telegraph to San Antone,' he asks, 'and have the bunch arrested there?'

"'Oh, well,' says I, 'I always did admire telegraphy; but astronomy was what I had took up just then.' That capitalist sure knew how to gesticulate with his hands.

"Luke got madder and madder. He investigates and finds in the depot a card one of the men had dropped that gives the address of some *hombre* called Scudder in New York City.

"'Bud,' says Luke, 'I'm going after that bunch. I'm going there and get the man or boy, as you say he was, and bring him back. I'm sheriff of Mojada County, and I shall keep law and order in its precincts while I'm able to draw a gun. And I want you to go with me. No Eastern Yankee can shoot up a respectable and well-known citizen of Bildad, 'specially with a thirty-two calibre, and escape the law. Pedro Johnson,' says Luke, 'is one of our most prominent citizens and business men. I'll appoint Sam Bell acting sheriff with penitentiary powers while I'm away, and you and me will take the six forty-five northbound tomorrow evening and follow up this trail.'

"'I'm your company,' says I. 'I never see this New York, but I'd like to. But, Luke,' says I, 'don't you have to have a dispensation or a habeas corpus or something from the state, when you reach out that far for rich men and malefactors?'

"'Did I have a requisition,' says Luke, 'when I went over into the Brazos bottoms and brought back Bill Grimes and two more for holding up the International? Did me and you have a search warrant or a posse comitatus when we rounded up them six Mexican cow thieves down in Hidalgo? It's my business to keep order in Mojada County.'

"'And it's my business as office deputy,' says I, 'to see that business is carried on according to law. Between us both we ought to keep things pretty well cleaned up.'

"So, the next day, Luke packs a blanket and some collars and his mileage book in a haversack, and him and me hits the breeze for New York. It was a powerful long ride. The seats in the cars was too short for six-footers like us to sleep comfortable on; and the conductor had to keep us from getting off at every town that had five-story houses in it. But we got there finally; and we seemed to see right away that he was right about it.

"'Luke,' says I, 'as office deputy and from a law standpoint, it don't look to me like this place is properly and legally in the jurisdiction of Mojada County, Texas.'

"'From the standpoint of order,' says he, 'it's amenable to answer for its sins to the properly appointed authorities from Bildad to Jerusalem.'

"'Amen,' says I. 'But let's turn our trick sudden, and ride. I don't like the looks of this place.'

"'Think of Pedro Johnson,' says Luke, 'a friend of mine and yours shot down by one of these gilded abolitionists at his very door!'

"'It was at the door of the freight depot,' says I. 'But the law will not be balked at a quibble like that.'

"We put up at one of them big hotels on Broadway. The next morning I goes down about two miles of stairsteps to the bottom and hunts for Luke. It ain't no use. It looks like San Jacinto day in San Antone. There's a thousand folks milling around in a kind of a roofed-over plaza with marble pavements and trees growing right out of 'em, and I see no more chance of finding Luke than if we was hunting each other in the big pear flat down below Old Fort Ewell. But soon Luke and me runs together in one of the turns of them marble alleys.

"'It ain't no use, Bud,' says he. 'I can't find no place to eat at. I've been looking for restaurant signs and smelling for ham all over the camp. But I'm used to going hungry when I have to. Now,' says he, 'I'm going out and get a hack and ride down to the address on this Scudder card. You stay here and try to hustle some grub. But I doubt if you'll find it. I wish we'd brought along some cornmeal and bacon and beans. I'll be back when I see this Scudder, if the trail ain't wiped out.'

"So I starts foraging for breakfast. For the honour of old Mojada County I didn't want to seem green to them abolitionists, so every time I turned a corner in them marble halls I went up to the first desk or counter I see and looks around for grub. If I didn't see what I wanted I asked for something else. In about half an hour I had a dozen cigars, five story magazines, and seven or eight railroad time-tables in my pockets, and never a smell of coffee or bacon to point out the trail.

"Once a lady sitting at a table and playing a game kind of like pushpin told me to go into a closet that she called Number 3. I went in and shut the door, and the blamed thing lit itself up. I set down on a stool before a shelf and waited. Thinks I, 'This is a private dining-room.' But no waiter never came. When I got to sweating good and hard, I goes out again.

"'Did you get what you wanted?' says she.

"'No, ma'am,' says I. 'Not a bite.'

"'Then there's no charge,' says she.

"'Thanky, ma'am,' says I, and I takes up the trail again.

"By and by I thinks I'll shed etiquette; and I picks up one of them boys with blue clothes and yellow buttons in front, and he leads me to what he calls the caffay breakfast room. And the first thing I lays my eyes on when I go in is that boy that had shot Pedro Johnson. He was setting all alone at a little table, hitting a egg with a spoon like he was afraid he'd break it.

"I takes the chair across the table from him; and he looks insulted and makes a move like he was going to get up.

"'Keep still, son,' says I. 'You're apprehended, arrested, and in charge of the Texas authorities. Go on and hammer that egg some more if it's the inside of it you want. Now, what did you shoot Mr. Johnson, of Bildad, for?'

"And may I ask who you are?' says he.

"'You may,' says I. 'Go ahead.'

"'I suppose you're on,' says this kid, without batting his eyes. 'But what are you eating? Here, waiter!' he calls out, raising his finger. 'Take this gentleman's order.

"'A beefsteak,' says I, 'and some fried eggs and a can of peaches and a quart of coffee will about suffice.'

"We talk awhile about the sundries of life and then he says:

"'What are you going to do about that shooting? I had a right to shoot that man,' says he. 'He called me names that I couldn't overlook, and then he struck me. He carried a gun, too. What else could I do?'

"'We'll have to take you back to Texas,' says I.

"'I'd like to go back,' says the boy, with a kind of a grin—'if it wasn't on an occasion of this kind. It's the life I like. I've always wanted to ride and shoot and live in the open air ever since I can remember.'

"'Who was this gang of stout parties you took this trip with?' I asks.

"'My stepfather,' says he, 'and some business partners of his in some Mexican mining and land schemes.'

"'I saw you shoot Pedro Johnson,' says I, 'and I took that little popgun away from you that you did it with. And when I did so I noticed three or four little scars in a row over your right eyebrow. You've been in rookus before, haven't you?'

"'I've had these scars ever since I can remember,' says he. 'I don't know how they came there.'

"'Was you ever in Texas before?' says I.

"'Not that I remember of,' says he. 'But I thought I had when we struck the prairie country. But I guess I hadn't.'

"'Have you got a mother?' I asks.

"'She died five years ago,' says he.

"Skipping over the most of what followed—when Luke came back I turned the kid over to him. He had seen Scudder and told him what he wanted; and it seems that Scudder got active with one of these telephones as soon as he left. For in about an hour afterward there comes to our hotel some of these city rangers in everyday clothes that they call detectives, and marches the whole outfit of us to what they call a magistrate's court. They accuse Luke of attempted kidnapping, and ask him what he has to say.

"'This snipe,' says Luke to the judge, 'shot and willfully punctured with malice and forethought one of the most respected and prominent citizens of the town of Bildad, Texas, Your Honor. And in so doing laid himself liable to the penitence of law and order. And I hereby make claim and demand restitution of the State of New York City for the said alleged criminal; and I know he done it.'

"'Have you the usual and necessary requisition papers from the governor of your state?' asks the judge.

"'My usual papers,' says Luke, 'was taken away from me at the hotel by these gentlemen who represent law and order in your city. They was two Colt's .45's that I've packed for nine years; and if I don't get 'em back, there'll be more trouble. You can ask anybody in Mojada County about Luke Summers. I don't usually need any other kind of papers for what I do.'

"I see the judge looks mad, so I steps up and says:

"'Your Honor, the aforesaid defendant, Mr. Luke Summers, sheriff of Mojada County, Texas, is as fine a man as ever threw a rope or upheld the statutes and codicils of the greatest state in the Union. But he—'

"The judge hits his table with a wooden hammer and asks who I am.

"Bud Oakley,' says I. 'Office deputy of the sheriff's office of Mojada County, Texas. Representing,' says I, 'the Law. Luke Summers,' I goes on, 'represents Order. And if Your Honor will give me about ten minutes in private talk, I'll explain the whole thing to you, and show you the equitable and legal requisition papers which I carry in my pocket.'

"The judge kind of half smiles and says he will talk with me in his private room. In there I put the whole thing up to him in such language as I had, and when we goes outside, he announces the verdict that the young man is delivered into the hands of the Texas authorities; and calls the next case.

"Skipping over much of what happened on the way back, I'll tell you how the thing wound up in Bildad.

"When we got the prisoner in the sheriff's office, I says to Luke:

"'You, remember that kid of yours—that two-year old that they stole away from you when the bust-up come?'

"Luke looks black and angry. He'd never let anybody talk to him about that business, and he never mentioned it himself.

"'Toe the mark,' says I. 'Do you remember when he was toddling around on the porch and fell down on a pair of Mexican spurs and cut four little holes over his right eye? Look at the prisoner,' says I, 'look at his nose and the shape of his head and—why, you old fool, don't you know your own son?—I knew him,' says I, 'when he perforated Mr. Johnson at the depot.'

"Luke comes over to me shaking all over. I never saw him lose his nerve before.

"'Bud,' says he. 'I've never had that boy out of my mind one day or one night since he was took away. But I never let on. But can we hold him?— Can we make him stay?— I'll make the best man of him that ever put his foot in a stirrup. Wait a minute,' says he, all excited and out of his mind—'I've got some-thing here in my desk—I reckon it'll hold legal yet—I've looked at it a thousand times—"Cus-to-dy of the child,"' says Luke—'"Cus-to-dy of the child." We can hold him on that, can't we? Le'me see if I can find that decree.'

"Luke begins to tear his desk to pieces.

"'Hold on,' says I. 'You are Order and I'm Law. You needn't look for that paper, Luke. It ain't a decree any more. It's requisition papers. It's on file in that Magistrate's office in New York. I took it along when we went, because I was office deputy and knew the law.'

"'I've got him back,' says Luke. 'He's mine again. I never thought—'

"'Wait a minute,' says I. 'We've got to have law and order. You and me have got to preserve 'em both in Mojada County according to our oath and conscience. The kid shot Pedro Johnson, one of Bildad's most prominent and—'

"'Oh, hell!' says Luke. 'That don't amount to anything. That fellow was half Mexican, anyhow.'"

45

Let Me Feel Your Pulse

So I went to a doctor.

"How long has it been since you took any alcohol into your system?" he asked.

Turning my head side-wise, I answered, "Oh, quite awhile."

He was a young doctor, somewhere between twenty and forty. He wore heliotrope socks, but he looked like Napoleon. I liked him immensely.

"Now," said he, "I am going to show you the effect of alcohol upon your circulation." I think it was "circulation" he said; though it may have been "advertising."

He bared my left arm to the elbow, brought out a bottle of whiskey, and gave me a drink. He began to look more like Napoleon. I began to like him better.

Then he put a tight compress on my upper arm, stopped my pulse with his fingers, and squeezed a rubber bulb connected with an apparatus on a stand that looked like a thermometer. The mercury jumped up and down without seeming to stop anywhere; but the doctor said it registered two hundred and thirty-seven or one hundred and sixty-five or some such number.

"Now," said he, "you see what alcohol does to the blood-pressure."

"It's marvelous," said I, "but do you think it a sufficient test? Have one on me, and let's try the other arm." But, no!

Then he grasped my hand. I thought I was doomed and he was saying good-bye. But all he wanted to do was to jab a needle into the end of a finger and compare the red drop with a lot of fifty-cent poker chips that he had fastened to a card.

"It's the hemoglobin test," he explained. "The color of your blood is wrong."

"Well," said I, "I know it should be blue; but this is a country of mix-ups. Some of my ancestors were cavaliers; but they got thick with some people on Nantucket Island, so—"

"I mean," said the doctor, "that the shade of red is too light."

"Oh," said I, "it's a case of matching instead of matches."

The doctor then pounded me severely in the region of the chest. When he did that I don't know whether he reminded me most of Napoleon or Battling or Lord Nelson. Then he looked grave and mentioned a string of grievances that the flesh is heir to—mostly ending in "itis." I immediately paid him fifteen dollars on account.

"Is or are it or some or any of them necessarily fatal?" I asked. I thought my connection with the matter justified my manifesting a certain amount of interest.

"All of them," he answered cheerfully. "But their progress may be arrested. With care and proper continuous treatment you may live to be eighty-five or ninety."

I began to think of the doctor's bill. "Eighty-five would be sufficient, I am sure," was my comment. I paid him ten dollars more on account.

"The first thing to do," he said, with renewed animation, "is to find a sanitarium where you will get a complete rest for a while, and allow your nerves to get into a better condition. I myself will go with you and select a suitable one."

So he took me to a mad-house in the Catskills. It was on a bare mountain frequented only by infrequent frequenters. You could see nothing but stones and boulders, some patches of snow, and scattered pine trees. The young physician in charge was most agreeable. He gave me a stimulant without applying a compress to the arm. It was luncheon time, and we were invited to partake. There were about twenty inmates at little tables in the dining room. The young physician in charge came to our table and said: "It is a custom with our guests not to regard themselves as patients, but merely as tired ladies and gentlemen taking a rest. Whatever slight maladies they may have are never alluded to in conversation."

My doctor called loudly to a waitress to bring some phosphoglycerate of lime hash, dog-bread, bromo-seltzer pancakes, and nux vomica tea for my repast. Then a sound arose like a sudden wind storm among pine trees. It was produced by every guest in the room whispering loudly, "Neurasthenia!"—except one man with a nose, whom I distinctly heard say, "Chronic alcoholism." I hope to meet him again. The physician in charge turned and walked away.

An hour or so after luncheon he conducted us to the workshop—say fifty yards from the house. Thither the guests had been conducted by the physician in charge's understudy and sponge-holder—a man with feet and a blue sweater. He was so tall that I was not sure he had a face; but the Armour Packing Company would have been delighted with his hands.

"Here," said the physician in charge, "our guests find relaxation from past mental worries by devoting themselves to physical labor—recreation, in reality."

There were turning-lathes, carpenters' outfits, clay-modeling tools, spinning-wheels, weaving-frames, treadmills, bass drums, enlarged-crayon-portrait apparatuses, blacksmith forges, and everything, seemingly, that could interest the paying lunatic guests of a first-rate sanitarium.

"The lady making mud pies in the corner," whispered the physician in charge, "is no other than—Lula Lulington, the authoress of the novel entitled 'Why Love Loves.' What she is doing now is simply to rest her mind after performing that piece of work."

I had seen the book. "Why doesn't she do it by writing another one instead?" I asked.

As you see, I wasn't as far gone as they thought I was.

"The gentleman pouring water through the funnel," continued the physician in charge, "is a Wall Street broker broken down from overwork."

I buttoned my coat.

Others he pointed out were architects playing with Noah's arks, ministers reading Darwin's "Theory of Evolution," lawyers sawing wood, tired-out society ladies talking Ibsen to the blue-sweatered sponge-holder, a neurotic millionaire lying asleep on the floor, and a prominent artist drawing a little red wagon around the room.

"You look pretty strong," said the physician in charge to me. "I think the best mental relaxation for you would be throwing small boulders over the mountainside and then bringing them up again."

I was a hundred yards away before my doctor overtook me.

"What's the matter?" he asked.

"The matter is," said I, "that there are no aeroplanes handy. So I am going to merrily and hastily jog the foot-pathway to yon station and catch the first unlimited-soft-coal express back to town."

"Well," said the doctor, "perhaps you are right. This seems hardly the suitable place for you. But what you need is rest—absolute rest and exercise."

That night I went to a hotel in the city, and said to the clerk: "What I need is absolute rest and exercise. Can you give me a room with one of those tall folding beds in it, and a relay of bellboys to work it up and down while I rest?"

The clerk rubbed a speck off one of his finger nails and glanced side-wise at a tall man in a white hat sitting in the lobby. That man came over and asked me politely if I had seen the shrubbery at the west entrance. I had not, so he showed it to me and then looked me over.

"I thought you had 'em," he said, not unkindly, "but I guess you're all right. You'd better go see a doctor, old man."

A week afterward my doctor tested my blood pressure again without the preliminary stimulant. He looked to me a little less like Napoleon. And his socks were of a shade of tan that did not appeal to me.

"What you need," he decided, "is sea air and companionship."

"Would a mermaid—" I began; but he slipped on his professional manner.

"I myself," he said, "will take you to the Hotel Bonair off the coast of Long Island and see that you get in good shape. It is a quiet, comfortable resort where you will soon recuperate."

The Hotel Bonair proved to be a nine-hundred-room fashionable hostelry on an island off the main shore. Everybody who did not dress for dinner was shoved into a side dining-room and given only a terrapin and champagne *table d'hôte*. The bay was a great stamping ground for wealthy yachtsmen. The *Corsair* anchored there the day we arrived. I saw Mr. Morgan standing on deck eating a cheese sandwich and gazing longingly at the hotel. Still, it was a very inexpensive place. Nobody could afford to pay their prices. When you went away you simply left your baggage, stole a skiff, and beat it for the mainland in the night.

When I had been there one day I got a pad of monogrammed telegraph blanks at the clerk's desk and began to wire to all my friends for get-away money. My doctor and I played one game of croquet on the golf links and went to sleep on the lawn.

When we got back to town a thought seemed to occur to him suddenly. "By the way," he asked, "how do you feel?"

"Relieved of very much," I replied.

Now a consulting physician is different. He isn't exactly sure whether he is to be paid or not, and this uncertainty insures you either the most careful or the most careless attention. My doctor took me to see a consulting physician. He made a poor guess and gave me careful attention. I liked him immensely. He put me through some coordination exercises.

"Have you a pain in the back of your head?" he asked. I told him I had not.

"Shut your eyes," he ordered, "put your feet close together, and jump backward as far as you can."

I always was a good backward jumper with my eyes shut, so I obeyed. My head struck the edge of the bathroom door, which had been left open and was only three feet away. The doctor was very sorry. He had overlooked the fact that the door was open. He closed it.

"Now touch your nose with your right forefinger," he said.

"Where is it?" I asked.

"On your face," said he.

"I mean my right forefinger," I explained.

"Oh, excuse me," said he. He reopened the bathroom door, and I took my finger out of the crack of it. After I had performed the marvelous digito-nasal feat I said:

"I do not wish to deceive you as to symptoms, Doctor; I really have something like a pain in the back of my head." He ignored the symptom and examined my heart carefully with a latest-popular-air-penny-in-the-slot ear-trumpet. I felt like a ballad.

"Now," he said, "gallop like a horse for about five minutes around the room."

I gave the best imitation I could of a disqualified Percheron being led out of Madison Square Garden. Then, without dropping in a penny, he listened to my chest again.

"No glanders in our family, Doc," I said.

The consulting physician held up his forefinger within three inches of my nose. "Look at my finger," he commanded.

"Did you ever try Pears'—" I began; but he went on with his test rapidly.

"Now look across the bay. At my finger. Across the bay. At my finger. At my finger. Across the bay. Across the bay. At my finger. Across the bay." This for about three minutes.

He explained that this was a test of the action of the brain. It seemed easy to me. I never once mistook his finger for the bay. I'll bet that if he had used the phrases: "Gaze, as it were, unpreoccupied, outward—or rather laterally—in the direction of the horizon, underlaid, so to speak, with the adjacent fluid inlet," and "Now, returning—or rather, in a manner, withdrawing your attention, bestow it upon my upraised digit"—I'll bet, I say, that Henry James himself could have passed the examination.

After asking me if I had ever had a grand uncle with curvature of the spine or a cousin with swelled ankles, the two doctors retired to the bathroom and sat on the edge of the bath tub for their consultation. I ate an apple, and gazed first at my finger and then across the bay.

The doctors came out looking grave. More: they looked tombstones and Tennessee-papers-please-copy. They wrote out a diet list to which I was to be restricted. It had everything that I had ever heard of to eat on it, except snails. And I never eat a snail unless it overtakes me and bites me first.

"You must follow this diet strictly," said the doctors.

"I'd follow it a mile if I could get one-tenth of what's on it," I answered.

"Of next importance," they went on, "is outdoor air and exercise. And here is a prescription that will be of great benefit to you."

Then all of us took something. They took their hats, and I took my departure.

I went to a druggist and showed him the prescription.

"It will be $2.87 for an ounce bottle," he said.

"Will you give me a piece of your wrapping cord?" said I.

I made a hole in the prescription, ran the cord through it, tied it around my neck, and tucked it inside. All of us have a little superstition, and mine runs to a confidence in amulets.

Of course there was nothing the matter with me, but I was very ill. I couldn't work, sleep, eat, or bowl. The only way I could get any sympathy was to go without shaving for four days. Even then somebody would say: "Old man, you look as hardy as a pine knot. Been up for a jaunt in the Maine woods, eh?"

Then, suddenly, I remembered that I must have outdoor air and exercise. So I went down South to John's. John is an approximate relative by verdict of a preacher standing with a little book in his hands in a bower of chrysanthemums while a hundred thousand people looked on. John has a country house seven miles from Pineville. It is at an altitude and on the Blue Ridge Mountains in a state too dignified to be dragged into this controversy. John is mica, which is more valuable and clearer than gold.

He met me at Pineville, and we took the trolley car to his home. It is a big, neighborless cottage on a hill surrounded by a hundred mountains. We got off at his little private station, where John's family and Amaryllis met and greeted us. Amaryllis looked at me a trifle anxiously.

A rabbit came bounding across the hill between us and the house. I threw down my suit-case and pursued it hotfoot. After I had run twenty yards and seen it disappear, I sat down on the grass and wept disconsolately.

"I can't catch a rabbit any more," I sobbed. "I'm of no further use in the world. I may as well be dead."

"Oh, what is it—what is it, Brother John?" I heard Amaryllis say.

"Nerves a little unstrung," said John, in his calm way. "Don't worry. Get up, you rabbit-chaser, and come on to the house before the biscuits get cold." It was about twilight, and the mountains came up nobly to Miss Murfree's descriptions of them.

Soon after dinner I announced that I believed I could sleep for a year or two, including legal holidays. So I was shown to a room as big and cool as a flower garden, where there was a bed as broad as a lawn. Soon afterward the remainder of the household retired, and then there fell upon the land a silence.

I had not heard a silence before in years. It was absolute. I raised myself on my elbow and listened to it. Sleep! I thought that if I only could hear a star twinkle or a blade of grass sharpen itself I could compose myself to rest. I thought once that I heard a sound like the sail of a catboat flapping as it veered about in a breeze, but I decided that it was probably only a tack in the carpet. Still I listened.

Suddenly some belated little bird alighted upon the window-sill, and, in what he no doubt considered sleepy tones, enunciated the noise generally translated as "cheep!"

I leaped into the air.

"Hey! What's the matter down there?" called John from his room above mine.

"Oh, nothing," I answered, "except that I accidentally bumped my head against the ceiling."

The next morning I went out on the porch and looked at the mountains. There were forty-seven of them in sight. I shuddered, went into the big hall sitting room of the house, selected "Pancoast's Family Practice of Medicine" from a bookcase, and began to read. John came in, took the book away from me, and led me outside. He has a farm of three hundred acres furnished with the usual complement of barns, mules, peasantry, and harrows with three front teeth broken off. I had seen such things in my childhood, and my heart began to sink.

Then John spoke of alfalfa, and I brightened at once. "Oh, yes," said I, "wasn't she in the chorus of—let's see—"

"Green, you know," said John, "and tender, and you plow it under after the first season."

"I know," said I, "and the grass grows over her."

"Right," said John. "You know something about farming, after all."

"I know something of some farmers," said I, "and a sure scythe will mow them down some day."

On the way back to the house a beautiful and inexplicable creature walked across our path. I stopped irresistibly fascinated, gazing at it. John waited patiently, smoking his cigarette. He is a modern farmer. After ten minutes he said: "Are you going to stand there looking at that chicken all day? Breakfast is nearly ready."

"A chicken?" said I.

"A White Orpington hen, if you want to particularize."

"A White Orpington hen?" I repeated, with intense interest. The fowl walked slowly away with graceful dignity, and I followed like a child after the Pied Piper. Five minutes more were allowed me by John, and then he took me by the sleeve and conducted me to breakfast.

After I had been there a week I began to grow alarmed. I was sleeping and eating well and actually beginning to enjoy life. For a man in my desperate condition that would never do. So I sneaked down to the trolley-car station, took the car for Pineville, and went to see one of the best physicians in town. By this time I knew exactly what to do when I needed medical treatment. I hung my hat on the back of a chair, and said rapidly:

"Doctor, I have cirrhosis of the heart, indurated arteries, neurasthenia, neuritis, acute indigestion, and convalescence. I am going to live on a strict diet. I shall also take a tepid bath at night and a cold one in the morning. I shall endeavor to be cheerful, and fix my mind on pleasant subjects. In the way of drugs I intend to take a phosphorous pill three times a day, preferably after meals, and a tonic composed of the tinctures of gentian, cinchona, calisaya, and cardamon compound. Into each teaspoonful of this I shall mix tincture of *nux vomica*, beginning with one drop and increasing it a drop each day until the maximum dose is reached. I shall drop this with a medicine-dropper, which can be procured at a trifling cost at any pharmacy. Good morning."

I took my hat and walked out. After I had closed the door I remembered something that I had forgotten to say. I opened it again. The doctor had not moved from where he had been sitting, but he gave a slightly nervous start when he saw me again.

"I forgot to mention," said I, "that I shall also take absolute rest and exercise."

After this consultation I felt much better. The reestablishing in my mind of the fact that I was hopelessly ill gave me so much satisfaction that I almost became gloomy again. There is nothing more alarming to a neurasthenic than to feel himself growing well and cheerful.

John looked after me carefully. After I had evinced so much interest in his White Orpington chicken he tried his best to divert my mind, and was particular to lock his hen house of nights. Gradually the tonic mountain air, the wholesome food, and the daily walks among the hills so alleviated my malady that I became utterly wretched and despondent. I heard of a country doctor who lived in the mountains nearby. I went to see him and told him the whole story. He was a gray-bearded man with clear, blue, wrinkled eyes, in a home-made suit of gray jeans.

In order to save time I diagnosed my case, touched my nose with my right forefinger, struck myself below the knee to make my foot kick, sounded my chest, stuck out my tongue, and asked him the price of cemetery lots in Pineville.

He lit his pipe and looked at me for about three minutes. "Brother," he said, after a while, "you are in a mighty bad way. There's a chance for you to pull through, but it's a mighty slim one."

"What can it be?" I asked eagerly. "I have taken arsenic and gold, phosphorus, exercise, *nux vomica*, hydrotherapeutic baths, rest, excitement, codein, and aromatic spirits of ammonia. Is there anything left in the *pharmacopœia*?"

"Somewhere in these mountains," said the doctor, "there's a plant growing—a flowering plant that'll cure you, and it's about the only thing that will. It's of a kind that's as old as the world; but of late it's powerful scarce and hard to find. You and I will have to hunt it up. I'm not engaged in active practice now: I'm getting along in years; but I'll take your case. You'll have to come every day in the afternoon and help me hunt for this plant till we find it. The city doctors may know a lot about new scientific things, but they don't know much about the cures that nature carries around in her saddlebags."

So every day the old doctor and I hunted the cure-all plant among the mountains and valleys of the Blue Ridge. Together we toiled up steep heights so slippery with fallen autumn leaves that we had to catch every sapling and branch within our reach to save us from falling. We waded through gorges and chasms, breast-deep with laurel and ferns; we followed the banks of mountain streams for miles; we wound our way like Indians through brakes of pine—road side, hill side, river side, mountain side we explored in our search for the miraculous plant.

As the old doctor said, it must have grown scarce and hard to find. But we followed our quest. Day by day we plumbed the valleys, scaled the heights, and tramped the plateaus in search of the miraculous plant. Mountain-bred, he never seemed to tire. I often reached home too fatigued to do anything except fall into bed and sleep until morning. This we kept up for a month.

One evening after I had returned from a six-mile tramp with the old doctor, Amaryllis and I took a little walk under the trees near the road. We looked at the mountains drawing their royal-purple robes around them for their night's repose.

"I'm glad you're well again," she said. "When you first came you frightened me. I thought you were really ill."

"Well again!" I almost shrieked. "Do you know that I have only one chance in a thousand to live?"

Amaryllis looked at me in surprise. "Why," said she, "you are as strong as one of the plough-mules, you sleep ten or twelve hours every night, and you are eating us out of house and home. What more do you want?"

"I tell you," said I, "that unless we find the magic—that is, the plant we are looking for—in time, nothing can save me. The doctor tells me so."

"What doctor?"

"Doctor Tatum—the old doctor who lives halfway up Black Oak Mountain. Do you know him?"

"I have known him since I was able to talk. And is that where you go every day—is it he who takes you on these long walks and climbs that have brought back your health and strength? God bless the old doctor."

Just then the old doctor himself drove slowly down the road in his rickety old buggy. I waved my hand at him and shouted that I would be on hand the next day at the usual time. He stopped his horse and called to Amaryllis to come out to him. They talked for five minutes while I waited. Then the old doctor drove on.

When we got to the house Amaryllis lugged out an encyclopedia and sought a word in it. "The doctor said," she told me, "that you needn't call any more as a patient, but he'd be glad to see you any time as a friend. And then he told me to look up my name in the encyclopedia and tell you what it means. It seems to be the name of a genus of flowering plants, and also the name of a country girl in Theocritus and Virgil. What do you suppose the doctor meant by that?"

"I know what he meant," said I. "I know now."

A word to a brother who may have come under the spell of the unquiet Lady Neurasthenia.

The formula was true. Even though gropingly at times, the physicians of the walled cities had put their fingers upon the specific medicament.

And so for the exercise one is referred to good Doctor Tatum on Black Oak Mountain—take the road to your right at the Methodist meeting house in the pine-grove.

Absolute rest and exercise!

What rest more remedial than to sit with Amaryllis in the shade, and, with a sixth sense, read the wordless Theocritan idyl of the gold-bannered blue mountains marching orderly into the dormitories of the night?

46

Makes the Whole World Kin

The burglar stepped inside the window quickly, and then he took his time. A burglar who respects his art always takes his time before taking anything else.

The house was a private residence. By its boarded front door and untrimmed Boston ivy the burglar knew that the mistress of it was sitting on some oceanside piazza telling a sympathetic man in a yachting cap that no one had ever understood her sensitive, lonely heart. He knew by the light in the third-story front windows, and by the lateness of the season, that the master of the house had come home, and would soon extinguish his light and retire. For it was September of the year and of the soul, in which season the house's good man comes to consider roof gardens and stenographers as vanities, and to desire the return of his mate and the more durable blessings of decorum and the moral excellencies.

The burglar lighted a cigarette. The guarded glow of the match illuminated his salient points for a moment. He belonged to the third type of burglars.

This third type has not yet been recognized and accepted. The police have made us familiar with the first and second. Their classification is simple. The collar is the distinguishing mark.

When a burglar is caught who does not wear a collar he is described as a degenerate of the lowest type, singularly vicious and depraved, and is suspected of being the desperate criminal who stole the handcuffs out of Patrolman Hennessy's pocket in 1878 and walked away to escape arrest.

The other well-known type is the burglar who wears a collar. He is always referred to as a Raffles in real life. He is invariably a gentleman by daylight, breakfasting in a dress suit, and posing as a paperhanger, while after dark he plies his nefarious occupation of burglary. His mother is an extremely wealthy and respected resident of Ocean Grove, and when he is conducted to his cell he asks at once for a nail file and the *Police Gazette*. He always has a wife in every State in the Union and fiancées in all the Territories, and the newspapers print his matrimonial gallery out of their stock of cuts of the ladies who were cured by only one bottle after having been given up by five doctors, experiencing great relief after the first dose.

The burglar wore a blue sweater. He was neither a Raffles nor one of the chefs from Hell's Kitchen. The police would have been baffled had they attempted to classify him. They have not yet heard of the respectable, unassuming burglar who is neither above nor below his station.

This burglar of the third class began to prowl. He wore no masks, dark lanterns, or gum shoes. He carried a 38-calibre revolver in his pocket, and he chewed peppermint gum thoughtfully.

The furniture of the house was swathed in its summer dust protectors. The silver was far away in safe-deposit vaults. The burglar expected no remarkable "haul." His objective point was that dimly lighted room where the master of the house should be sleeping heavily after whatever solace he had sought to lighten the burden of his loneliness. A "touch" might be made there to the extent of legitimate, fair professional profits—loose money, a watch, a jeweled stick-pin—nothing exorbitant or beyond reason. He had seen the window left open and had taken the chance.

The burglar softly opened the door of the lighted room. The gas was turned low. A man lay in the bed asleep. On the dresser lay many things in confusion—a crumpled roll of bills, a watch, keys, three poker chips, crushed cigars, a pink silk hair bow, and an unopened bottle of bromo-seltzer for a bulwark in the morning.

The burglar took three steps toward the dresser. The man in the bed suddenly uttered a squeaky groan and opened his eyes. His right hand slid under his pillow, but remained there.

"Lay still," said the burglar in conversational tone. Burglars of the third type do not hiss. The citizen in the bed looked at the round end of the burglar's pistol and lay still.

"Now hold up both your hands," commanded the burglar.

The citizen had a little, pointed, brown-and-gray beard, like that of a painless dentist. He looked solid, esteemed, irritable, and disgusted. He sat up in bed and raised his right hand above his head.

"Up with the other one," ordered the burglar. "You might be amphibious and shoot with your left. You can count two, can't you? Hurry up, now."

"Can't raise the other one," said the citizen, with a contortion of his lineaments.

"What's the matter with it?"

"Rheumatism in the shoulder."

"Inflammatory?"

"Was. The inflammation has gone down." The burglar stood for a moment or two, holding his gun on the afflicted one. He glanced at the plunder on the dresser and then, with a half-embarrassed air, back at the man in the bed. Then he, too, made a sudden grimace.

"Don't stand there making faces," snapped the citizen, bad-humoredly. "If you've come to burgle why don't you do it? There's some stuff lying around."

"'Scuse me," said the burglar, with a grin; "but it just socked me one, too. It's good for you that rheumatism and me happens to be old pals. I got it in my left arm, too. Most anybody but me would have popped you when you wouldn't hoist that left claw of yours."

"How long have you had it?" inquired the citizen.

"Four years. I guess that ain't all. Once you've got it, it's you for a rheumatic life—that's my judgment."

"Ever try rattlesnake oil?" asked the citizen, interestedly.

"Gallons," said the burglar. "If all the snakes I've used the oil of was strung out in a row they'd reach eight times as far as Saturn, and the rattles could be heard at Valparaiso, Indiana, and back."

"Some use Chiselum's Pills," remarked the citizen.

"Fudge!" said the burglar. "Took 'em five months. No good. I had some relief the year I tried Finkelham's Extract, Balm of Gilead poultices and Potts's Pain Pulverizer; but I think it was the buckeye I carried in my pocket what done the trick."

"Is yours worse in the morning or at night?" asked the citizen.

"Night," said the burglar; "just when I'm busiest. Say, take down that arm of yours—I guess you won't—Say! Did you ever try Blickerstaff's Blood Builder?"

"I never did. Does yours come in paroxysms or is it a steady pain?"

The burglar sat down on the foot of the bed and rested his gun on his crossed knee.

"It jumps," said he. "It strikes me when I ain't looking for it. I had to give up second-story work because I got stuck sometimes half-way up. Tell you what—I don't believe the bloomin' doctors know what is good for it."

"Same here. I've spent a thousand dollars without getting any relief. Yours swell any?"

"Of mornings. And when it's goin' to rain—great Christopher!"

"Me, too," said the citizen. "I can tell when a streak of humidity the size of a table-cloth starts from Florida on its way to New York. And if I pass a theatre where there's an 'East Lynne' matinée going on, the moisture starts my left arm jumping like a toothache."

"It's undiluted—hades!" said the burglar.

"You're dead right," said the citizen.

The burglar looked down at his pistol and thrust it into his pocket with an awkward attempt at ease.

"Say, old man," he said, constrainedly, "ever try opodeldoc?"

"Slop!" said the citizen angrily. "Might as well rub on restaurant butter."

"Sure," concurred the burglar. "It's a salve suitable for little Minnie when the kitty scratches her finger. I'll tell you what! We're up against it. I only find one thing that eases her up. Hey? Little old sanitary, ameliorating, lest-we-forget Booze. Say—this job's off—'scuse me—get on your clothes and let's go out and have some. 'Scuse the liberty, but—ouch! There she goes again!"

"For a week," said the citizen. "I haven't been able to dress myself without help. I'm afraid Thomas is in bed, and—"

"Climb out," said the burglar, "I'll help you get into your duds."

The conventional returned as a tidal wave and flooded the citizen. He stroked his brown-and-gray beard.

"It's very unusual—" he began.

"Here's your shirt," said the burglar, "fall out. I knew a man who said Omberry's Ointment fixed him in two weeks so he could use both hands in tying his four-in-hand."

As they were going out the door the citizen turned and started back.

"'Liked to forgot my money," he explained; "laid it on the dresser last night."

The burglar caught him by the right sleeve.

"Come on," he said bluffly. "I ask you. Leave it alone. I've got the price. Ever try witch hazel and oil of wintergreen?"

47

The Last of the Troubadours

Inexorably Sam Galloway saddled his pony. He was going away from the Rancho Altito at the end of a three-months' visit. It is not to be expected that a guest should put up with wheat coffee and biscuits yellow-streaked with saleratus for longer than that. Nick Napoleon, the big Negro man cook, had never been able to make good biscuits. Once before, when Nick was cooking at the Willow Ranch, Sam had been forced to fly from his *cuisine*, after only a six-weeks' sojourn.

On Sam's face was an expression of sorrow, deepened with regret and slightly tempered by the patient forgiveness of a connoisseur who cannot be understood. But very firmly and inexorably he buckled his saddle-cinches, looped his stake-rope and hung it to his saddle-horn, tied his slicker and coat on the cantle, and looped his quirt on his right wrist. The Merrydews (householders of the Rancho Altito), men, women, children, and servants, vassals, visitors, employés, dogs, and casual callers were grouped in the "gallery" of the ranch house, all with faces set to the tune of melancholy and grief. For, as the coming of Sam Galloway to any ranch, camp, or cabin between the rivers Frio or

Bravo del Norte aroused joy, so his departure caused mourning and distress.

And then, during absolute silence, except for the bumping of a hind elbow of a hound dog as he pursued a wicked flea, Sam tenderly and carefully tied his guitar across his saddle on top of his slicker and coat. The guitar was in a green duck bag; and if you catch the significance of it, it explains Sam.

Sam Galloway was the Last of the Troubadours. Of course you know about the troubadours. The encyclopedia says they flourished between the eleventh and the thirteenth centuries. What they flourished doesn't seem clear—you may be pretty sure it wasn't a sword: maybe it was a fiddlebow, or a forkful of spaghetti, or a lady's scarf. Anyhow, Sam Galloway was one of 'em.

Sam put on a martyred expression as he mounted his pony. But the expression on his face was hilarious compared with the one on his pony's. You see, a pony gets to know his rider mighty well, and it is not unlikely that cow ponies in pastures and at hitching racks had often guyed Sam's pony for being ridden by a guitar player instead of by a rollicking, cussing, all-wool cowboy. No man is a hero to his saddle-horse. And even an escalator in a department store might be excused for tripping up a troubadour.

Oh, I know I'm one; and so are you. You remember the stories you memorize and the card tricks you study and that little piece on the piano—how does it go?—ti-tum-te-tum-ti-tum—those little Arabian Ten Minute Entertainments that you furnish when you go up to call on your rich Aunt Jane. You should know that *omnæ personæ in tres partes divisæ sunt*. Namely: Barons, Troubadours, and Workers. Barons have no inclination to read such folderol as this; and Workers have no time: so I know you must be a Troubadour, and that you will understand Sam Galloway. Whether we sing, act, dance, write, lecture, or paint, we are only troubadours; so let us make the worst of it.

The pony with the Dante Alighieri face, guided by the pressure of Sam's knees, bore that wandering minstrel sixteen miles southeastward. Nature was in her most benignant mood. League after league of delicate, sweet flowerets made fragrant the gently undulating prairie. The east wind tempered the spring warmth; wool-white clouds flying in from the Mexican Gulf hindered the direct rays of the April sun. Sam sang songs as he rode. Under his pony's bridle he had tucked some sprigs of chaparral to keep away the deer flies. Thus crowned, the long-faced quadruped looked more Dantesque than before, and, judging by his countenance, seemed to think of Beatrice.

Straight as topography permitted, Sam rode to the sheep ranch of old man Ellison. A visit to a sheep ranch seemed to him desirable just then. There had been too many people, too much noise, argument, competition, confusion, at Rancho Altito. He had never conferred upon old man Ellison the favor of sojourning at his ranch; but he knew he would be welcome. The troubadour is his own passport everywhere. The Workers in the castle let down the drawbridge to him, and the Baron sets him at his left hand at table in the banquet hall. There ladies smile upon him and applaud his songs and stories, while the Workers bring boars' heads and flagons. If the Baron nods once or twice in his carved oaken chair, he does not do it maliciously.

Old man Ellison welcomed the troubadour flatteringly. He had often heard praises of Sam Galloway from other ranchmen who had been complimented by his visits, but had never aspired to such an honor for his own humble barony. I say barony because old man Ellison was the Last of the Barons. Of course, Mr. Bulwer-Lytton lived too early to know him, or he wouldn't have conferred that sobriquet upon Warwick. In life it is the duty and the function of the Baron to provide work for the Workers and lodging and shelter for the Troubadours.

Old man Ellison was a shrunken old man, with a short, yellow-white beard and a face lined and seamed by past-and-gone smiles. His ranch was a little two-room box house in a grove of hackberry trees in the lonesomest part of the sheep country. His household consisted of a Kiowa Indian man cook, four hounds, a pet sheep, and a half-tamed coyote chained to a fence-post. He owned 3,000 sheep, which he ran on two sections of leased land and many thousands of acres neither leased nor owned. Three or four times a year some one who spoke his language would ride up to his gate and exchange a few bald ideas with him. Those were red-letter days to old man Ellison. Then in what illuminated, embossed, and gorgeously decorated capitals must have been written the day on which a troubadour—a troubadour who, according to the encyclopædia, should have flourished between the eleventh and the thirteenth centuries—drew rein at the gates of his baronial castle!

Old man Ellison's smiles came back and filled his wrinkles when he saw Sam. He hurried out of the house in his shuffling, limping way to greet him.

"Hello, Mr. Ellison," called Sam cheerfully. "Thought I'd drop over and see you a while. Notice you've had fine rains on your range. They ought to make good grazing for your spring lambs."

"Well, well, well," said old man Ellison. "I'm mighty glad to see you, Sam. I never thought you'd take the trouble to ride over to as out-of-the-way an old ranch as this. But you're mighty welcome. 'Light. I've got a sack of new oats in the kitchen—shall I bring out a feed for your hoss?"

"Oats for him?" said Sam, derisively. "No, sir-ee. He's as fat as a pig now on grass. He don't get rode enough to keep him in condition. I'll just turn him in the horse pasture with a drag rope on if you don't mind."

I am positive that never during the eleventh and thirteenth centuries did Baron, Troubadour, and Worker amalgamate as harmoniously as their parallels did that evening at old man Ellison's sheep ranch. The Kiowa's biscuits were light and tasty and his coffee strong. Ineradicable hospitality and appreciation glowed on old man Ellison's weather-tanned face. As for the troubadour, he said to himself that he had stumbled upon pleasant places indeed. A well-cooked, abundant meal, a host whom his lightest attempt to entertain seemed to delight far beyond the merits of the exertion, and the reposeful atmosphere that his sensitive soul at that time craved united to confer upon him a satisfaction and luxurious ease that he had seldom found on his tours of the ranches.

After the delectable supper, Sam untied the green duck bag and took out his guitar. Not by way of payment, mind you—neither Sam Galloway nor any other of the true troubadours are lineal descendants of the late Tommy Tucker. You have read of Tommy Tucker in the works of the esteemed but often obscure

Mother Goose. Tommy Tucker sang for his supper. No true troubadour would do that. He would have his supper, and then sing for Art's sake.

Sam Galloway's repertoire comprised about fifty funny stories and between thirty and forty songs. He by no means stopped there. He could talk through twenty cigarettes on any topic that you brought up. And he never sat up when he could lie down; and never stood when he could sit. I am strongly disposed to linger with him, for I am drawing a portrait as well as a blunt pencil and a tattered thesaurus will allow.

I wish you could have seen him: he was small and tough and inactive beyond the power of imagination to conceive. He wore an ultramarine-blue woolen shirt laced down the front with a pearl-gray, exaggerated sort of shoestring, indestructible brown duck clothes, inevitable high-heeled boots with Mexican spurs, and a Mexican straw sombrero.

That evening Sam and old man Ellison dragged their chairs out under the hackberry trees. They lighted cigarettes; and the troubadour gaily touched his guitar. Many of the songs he sang were the weird, melancholy, minor-keyed *canciones* that he had learned from the Mexican sheep herders and *vaqueros*. One, in particular, charmed and soothed the soul of the lonely baron. It was a favourite song of the sheep herders, beginning: "*Huile, huile, palomita,*" which being translated means, "Fly, fly, little dove." Sam sang it for old man Ellison many times that evening.

The troubadour stayed on at the old man's ranch. There was peace and quiet and appreciation there, such as he had not found in the noisy camps of the cattle kings. No audience in the world could have crowned the work of poet, musician, or artist with more worshipful and unflagging approval than that bestowed upon his efforts by old man Ellison. No visit by a royal personage to a humble woodchopper or peasant could have been received with more flattering thankfulness and joy.

On a cool, canvas-covered cot in the shade of the hackberry trees Sam Galloway passed the greater part of his time. There he rolled his brown paper cigarettes, read such tedious literature as the ranch afforded, and added to his repertoire of improvisations that he played so expertly on his guitar. To him, as a slave ministering to a great lord, the Kiowa brought cool water from the red jar hanging under the brush shelter, and food when he called for it. The prairie zephyrs fanned him mildly; mockingbirds at morn and eve competed with but scarce equaled the sweet melodies of his lyre; a perfumed stillness seemed to fill all his world. While old man Ellison was pottering among his flocks of sheep on his mile-an-hour pony, and while the Kiowa took his siesta in the burning sunshine at the end of the kitchen, Sam would lie on his cot thinking what a happy world he lived in, and how kind it is to the ones whose mission in life it is to give entertainment and pleasure. Here he had food and lodging as good as he had ever longed for; absolute immunity from care or exertion or strife; an endless welcome, and a host whose delight at the sixteenth repetition of a song or a story was as keen as at its initial giving. Was there ever a troubadour of old who struck upon as royal a castle in his wanderings? While he lay thus, meditating upon his blessings, little brown cottontails would shyly frolic through the yard; a covey of white-topknotted blue quail would run past, in single file, twenty yards away; a *paisano* bird, out hunting for tarantulas, would hop upon the fence and salute him with sweeping flourishes of its long tail. In the eighty-acre horse pasture the pony with the Dantesque face grew fat and almost smiling. The troubadour was at the end of his wanderings.

Old man Ellison was his own *vaciero*. That means that he supplied his sheep camps with wood, water, and rations by his own labours instead of hiring a *vaciero*. On small ranches it is often done.

One morning he started for the camp of Incarnación Felipe de la Cruz y Monte Piedras (one of his sheep herders) with the week's usual rations of brown beans, coffee, meal, and sugar. Two miles away on the trail from old Fort Ewing he met, face to face, a terrible being called King James, mounted on a fiery, prancing, Kentucky-bred horse.

King James's real name was James King; but people reversed it because it seemed to fit him better, and also because it seemed to please his majesty. King James was the biggest cattleman between the Alamo plaza in San Antone and Bill Hopper's saloon in Brownsville. Also he was the loudest and most offensive bully and braggart and bad man in southwest Texas. And he always made good whenever he bragged; and the more noise he made the more dangerous he was. In the story papers it is always the quiet, mild-mannered man with light blue eyes and a low voice who turns out to be really dangerous; but in real life and in this story such is not the case. Give me my choice between assaulting a large, loudmouthed rough-houser and an inoffensive stranger with blue eyes sitting quietly in a corner, and you will see something doing in the corner every time.

King James, as I intended to say earlier, was a fierce, two-hundred-pound, sunburned, blond man, as pink as an October strawberry, and with two horizontal slits under shaggy red eyebrows for eyes. On that day he wore a flannel shirt that was tan-colored, with the exception of certain large areas which were darkened by transudations due to the summer sun. There seemed to be other clothing and garnishings about him, such as brown duck trousers stuffed into immense boots, and red handkerchiefs and revolvers; and a shotgun laid across his saddle and a leather belt with millions of cartridges shining in it—but your mind skidded off such accessories; what held your gaze was just the two little horizontal slits that he used for eyes.

This was the man that old man Ellison met on the trail; and when you count up in the baron's favor that he was sixty-five and weighed ninety-eight pounds and had heard of King James's record and that he (the baron) had a hankering for the *vita simplex* and had no gun with him and wouldn't have used it if he had, you can't censure him if I tell you that the smiles with which the troubadour had filled his wrinkles went out of them and left them plain wrinkles again. But he was not the kind of baron that flies from danger. He reined in the mile-an-hour pony (no difficult feat), and saluted the formidable monarch.

King James expressed himself with royal directness. "You're that old snoozer that's running sheep on this range, ain't you?" said he. "What right have you got to do it? Do you own any land, or lease any?"

"I have two sections leased from the state," said old man Ellison, mildly.

"Not by no means you haven't," said King James. "Your lease expired yesterday; and I had a man at the land office on the minute to take it up. You don't control a foot of grass in Texas. You sheep men have got to git. Your time's up. It's a cattle country, and there ain't any room in it for snoozers. This range you've got your sheep on is mine. I'm putting up a wire fence, forty by sixty miles; and if there's a sheep inside of it when it's done it'll be a dead one. I'll give you a week to move yours away. If they ain't gone by then, I'll send six men over here with Winchesters to make mutton out of the whole lot. And if I find you here at the same time this is what you'll get."

King James patted the breech of his shot-gun warningly.

Old man Ellison rode on to the camp of Incarnación. He sighed many times, and the wrinkles in his face grew deeper. Rumours that the old order was about to change had reached him before. The end of Free Grass was in sight. Other troubles, too, had been accumulating upon his shoulders. His flocks were decreasing instead of growing; the price of wool was declining at every clip; even Bradshaw, the storekeeper at Frio City, at whose store he bought his ranch supplies, was dunning him for his last six months' bill and threatening to cut him off. And so this last greatest calamity suddenly dealt out to him by the terrible King James was a crusher.

When the old man got back to the ranch at sunset he found Sam Galloway lying on his cot, propped against a roll of blankets and wool sacks, fingering his guitar.

"Hello, Uncle Ben," the troubadour called, cheerfully. "You rolled in early this evening. I been trying a new twist on the Spanish Fandango today. I just about got it. Here's how she goes—listen."

"That's fine, that's mighty fine," said old man Ellison, sitting on the kitchen step and rubbing his white, Scotch-terrier whiskers. "I reckon you've got all the musicians beat east and west, Sam, as far as the roads are cut out."

"Oh, I don't know," said Sam, reflectively. "But I certainly do get there on variations. I guess I can handle anything in five flats about as well as any of 'em. But you look kind of fagged out, Uncle Ben—ain't you feeling right well this evening?"

"Little tired; that's all, Sam. If you ain't played yourself out, let's have that Mexican piece that starts off with: '*Huile, huile, palomita.*' It seems that that song always kind of soothes and comforts me after I've been riding far or anything bothers me."

"Why, *seguramente, señor,*" said Sam. "I'll hit her up for you as often as you like. And before I forget about it, Uncle Ben, you want to jerk Bradshaw up about them last hams he sent us. They're just a little bit strong."

A man sixty-five years old, living on a sheep ranch and beset by a complication of disasters, cannot successfully and continuously dissemble. Moreover, a troubadour has eyes quick to see unhappiness in others around him—because it disturbs his own ease. So, on the next day, Sam again questioned the old man about his air of sadness and abstraction. Then old man Ellison told him the story of King James's threats and orders and that pale melancholy and red ruin appeared to have marked him for their own. The troubadour took the news thoughtfully. He had heard much about King James.

On the third day of the seven days of grace allowed him by the autocrat of the range, old man Ellison drove his buckboard to Frio City to fetch some necessary supplies for the ranch. Bradshaw was hard but not implacable. He divided the old man's order by two, and let him have a little more time. One article secured was a new, fine ham for the pleasure of the troubadour.

Five miles out of Frio City on his way home the old man met King James riding into town. His majesty could never look anything but fierce and menacing, but today his slits of eyes appeared to be a little wider than they usually were.

"Good day," said the king, gruffly. "I've been wanting to see you. I hear it said by a cowman from Sandy yesterday that you was from Jackson County, Mississippi, originally. I want to know if that's a fact."

"Born there," said old man Ellison, "and raised there till I was twenty-one."

"This man says," went on King James, "that he thinks you was related to the Jackson County Reeveses. Was he right?"

"Aunt Caroline Reeves," said the old man, "was my half-sister."

"She was my aunt," said King James. "I run away from home when I was sixteen. Now, let's re-talk over some things that we discussed a few days ago. They call me a bad man; and they're only half right. There's plenty of room in my pasture for your bunch of sheep and their increase for a long time to come. Aunt Caroline used to cut out sheep in cake dough and bake 'em for me. You keep your sheep where they are, and use all the range you want. How's your finances?"

The old man related his woes in detail, dignifiedly, with restraint and candor.

"She used to smuggle extra grub into my school basket—I'm speaking of Aunt Caroline," said King James. "I'm going over to Frio City today, and I'll ride back by your ranch tomorrow. I'll draw $2,000 out of the bank there and bring it over to you; and I'll tell Bradshaw to let you have everything you want on credit. You are bound to have heard the old saying at home, that the Jackson County Reeveses and Kings would stick closer by each other than chestnut burrs. Well, I'm a King yet whenever I run across a Reeves. So you look out for me along about sundown tomorrow, and don't worry about nothing. Shouldn't wonder if the dry spell don't kill out the young grass."

Old man Ellison drove happily ranch-ward. Once more the smiles filled out his wrinkles. Very suddenly, by the magic of kinship and the good that lies somewhere in all hearts, his troubles had been removed.

On reaching the ranch he found that Sam Galloway was not there. His guitar hung by its buckskin string to a hackberry limb, moaning as the gulf breeze blew across its masterless strings.

The Kiowa endeavored to explain.

"Sam, he catch pony," said he, "and say he ride to Frio City. What for no can damn sabe. Say he come back tonight. Maybe so. That all."

As the first stars came out the troubadour rode back to his haven. He pastured his pony and went into the house, his spurs jingling martially.

Old man Ellison sat at the kitchen table, having a tin cup of before-supper coffee. He looked contented and pleased.

"Hello, Sam," said he. "I'm darned glad to see ye back. I don't know how I managed to get along on this ranch, anyhow, before ye dropped in to cheer things up. I'll bet ye've been skylarking around with some of them Frio City gals, now, that's kept ye so late."

And then old man Ellison took another look at Sam's face and saw that the minstrel had changed to the man of action.

And while Sam is unbuckling from his waist old man Ellison's six-shooter, that the latter had left behind when he drove to town, we may well pause to remark that anywhere and whenever a troubadour lays down the guitar and takes up the sword trouble is sure to follow. It is not the expert thrust of Athos nor the cold skill of Aramis nor the iron wrist of Porthos that we have to fear—it is the Gascon's fury—the wild and unacademic attack of the troubadour—the sword of D'Artagnan.

"I done it," said Sam. "I went over to Frio City to do it. I couldn't let him put the skibunk on you, Uncle Ben. I met him in Summers's saloon. I knowed what to do. I said a few things to him that nobody else heard. He reached for his gun first—half a dozen fellows saw him do it—but I got mine unlimbered first. Three doses I gave him—right around the lungs, and a saucer could have covered up all of 'em. He won't bother you no more."

"This—is—King—James—you speak—of?" asked old man Ellison, while he sipped his coffee.

"You bet it was. And they took me before the county judge; and the witnesses what saw him draw his gun first was all there. Well, of course, they put me under $300 bond to appear before the court, but there was four or five boys on the spot ready to sign the bail. He won't bother you no more, Uncle Ben. You ought to have seen how close them bullet holes was together. I reckon playing a guitar as much as I do must kind of limber a fellow's trigger finger up a little, don't you think, Uncle Ben?"

Then there was a little silence in the castle except for the spluttering of a venison steak that the Kiowa was cooking.

"Sam," said old man Ellison, stroking his white whiskers with a tremulous hand, "would you mind getting the guitar and playing that '*Huile, huile, palomita*' piece once or twice? It always seems to be kind of soothing and comforting when a man's tired and fagged out."

There is no more to be said, except that the title of the story is wrong. It should have been called "The Last of the Barons." There never will be an end to the troubadours; and now and then it does seem that the jingle of their guitars will drown the sound of the muffled blows of the pickaxes and trip hammers of all the Workers in the world.

48

Witches' Loaves

Miss Martha Meacham kept the little bakery on the corner (the one where you go up three steps, and the bell tinkles when you open the door).

Miss Martha was forty, her bank-book showed a credit of two thousand dollars, and she possessed two false teeth and a sympathetic heart. Many people have married whose chances to do so were much inferior to Miss Martha's.

Two or three times a week a customer came in in whom she began to take an interest. He was a middle-aged man, wearing spectacles and a brown beard trimmed to a careful point.

He spoke English with a strong German accent. His clothes were worn and darned in places, and wrinkled and baggy in others. But he looked neat, and had very good manners.

He always bought two loaves of stale bread. Fresh bread was five cents a loaf. Stale ones were two for five. Never did he call for anything but stale bread.

Once Miss Martha saw a red and brown stain on his fingers. She was sure then that he was an artist and very poor. No doubt he lived in a garret, where he painted pictures and ate stale bread and thought of the good things to eat in Miss Martha's bakery.

Often when Miss Martha sat down to her chops and light rolls and jam and tea she would sigh, and wish that the gentle-mannered artist might share her tasty meal instead of eating his dry crust in that draughty attic. Miss Martha's heart, as you have been told, was a sympathetic one.

In order to test her theory as to his occupation, she brought from her room one day a painting that she had bought at a sale, and set it against the shelves behind the bread counter.

It was a Venetian scene. A splendid marble palazzio (so it said on the picture) stood in the foreground—or rather forewater. For the rest there were gondolas (with the lady trailing her hand in the water), clouds, sky, and chiaro-oscuro in plenty. No artist could fail to notice it.

Two days afterward the customer came in.

"Two loafs of stale bread, if you blease.

"You haf here a fine bicture, Madame," he said while she was wrapping up the bread.

"Yes?" says Miss Martha, revelling in her own cunning. "I do so admire art and" (no, it would not do to say "artists" thus early) "and paintings," she substituted. "You think it is a good picture?"

"Der balance," said the customer, "is not in good drawing. Der bairspective of it is not true. Goot morning, madame."

He took his bread, bowed, and hurried out.

Yes, he must be an artist. Miss Martha took the picture back to her room.

How gentle and kindly his eyes shone behind his spectacles! What a broad brow he had! To be able to judge perspective at a glance—and to live on stale bread! But genius often has to struggle before it is recognized.

What a thing it would be for art and perspective if genius were backed by two thousand dollars in bank, a bakery, and a sympathetic heart to—But these were day-dreams, Miss Martha.

Often now when he came he would chat for a while across the showcase. He seemed to crave Miss Martha's cheerful words.

He kept on buying stale bread. Never a cake, never a pie, never one of her delicious Sally Lunns.

She thought he began to look thinner and discouraged. Her heart ached to add something good to eat to his meager purchase, but her courage failed at the act. She did not dare affront him. She knew the pride of artists.

Miss Martha took to wearing her blue-dotted silk waist behind the counter. In the back room she cooked a mysterious compound of quince seeds and borax. Ever so many people use it for the complexion.

One day the customer came in as usual, laid his nickel on the showcase, and called for his stale loaves. While Miss Martha was reaching for them there was a great tooting and clanging, and a fire-engine came lumbering past.

The customer hurried to the door to look, as any one will. Suddenly inspired, Miss Martha seized the opportunity.

On the bottom shelf behind the counter was a pound of fresh butter that the dairyman had left ten minutes before. With a bread knife Miss Martha made a deep slash in each of the stale loaves, inserted a generous quantity of butter, and pressed the loaves tight again.

When the customer turned once more she was tying the paper around them.

When he had gone, after an unusually pleasant little chat, Miss Martha smiled to herself, but not without a slight fluttering of the heart.

Had she been too bold? Would he take offense? But surely not. There was no language of edibles. Butter was no emblem of unmaidenly forwardness.

For a long time that day her mind dwelt on the subject. She imagined the scene when he should discover her little deception.

He would lay down his brushes and palette. There would stand his easel with the picture he was painting in which the perspective was beyond criticism.

He would prepare for his luncheon of dry bread and water. He would slice into a loaf—ah!

Miss Martha blushed. Would he think of the hand that placed it there as he ate? Would he—

The front door bell jangled viciously. Somebody was coming in, making a great deal of noise.

Miss Martha hurried to the front. Two men were there. One was a young man smoking a pipe—a man she had never seen before. The other was her artist.

His face was very red, his hat was on the back of his head, his hair was wildly rumpled. He clinched his two fists and shook them ferociously at Miss Martha. *At Miss Martha.*

"*Dummkopf!*" he shouted with extreme loudness; and then "*Tausendonfer!*" or something like it in German.

The young man tried to draw him away.

"I vill not go," he said angrily, "else I shall told her."

He made a bass drum of Miss Martha's counter.

"You haf shpoilt me," he cried, his blue eyes blazing behind his spectacles. "I vill tell you. You vas von *meddingsome old cat!*"

Miss Martha leaned weakly against the shelves and laid one hand on her blue-dotted silk waist. The young man took the other by the collar.

"Come on," he said, "you've said enough." He dragged the angry one out at the door to the sidewalk, and then came back.

"Guess you ought to be told, ma'am," he said, "what the row is about. That's Blumberger. He's an architectural draftsman. I work in the same office with him.

"He's been working hard for three months drawing a plan for a new city hall. It was a prize competition. He finished inking the lines yesterday. You know, a draftsman always makes his drawing in pencil first. When it's done he rubs out the pencil lines with handfuls of stale bread crumbs. That's better than India rubber.

"Blumberger's been buying the bread here. Well, today—well, you know, ma'am, that butter isn't—well, Blumberger's plan isn't good for anything now except to cut up into railroad sandwiches."

Miss Martha went into the back room. She took off the blue-dotted silk waist and put on the old brown serge she used to wear. Then she poured the quince seed and borax mixture out of the window into the ash can.

49

The Marionettes

The policeman was standing at the corner of Twenty-fourth Street and a prodigiously dark alley near where the elevated railroad crosses the street. The time was two o'clock in the morning; the outlook a stretch of cold, drizzling, unsociable blackness until the dawn.

A man, wearing a long overcoat, with his hat tilted down in front, and carrying something in one hand, walked softly but rapidly out of the black alley. The policeman accosted him civilly, but with the assured air that is linked with conscious authority. The hour, the alley's musty reputation, the pedestrian's haste, the burden he carried—these easily combined into the "suspicious circumstances" that required illumination at the officer's hands.

The "suspect" halted readily and tilted back his hat, exposing, in the flicker of the electric lights, an emotionless, smooth countenance with a rather long nose and steady dark eyes. Thrusting his gloved hand into a side pocket of his overcoat, he drew out a card and handed it to the policeman. Holding it to catch the uncertain light, the officer read the name "Charles Spencer James, M. D." The street and number of the address were of a neighborhood so solid and respectable as to subdue even curiosity. The policeman's downward glance at the article carried in the doctor's hand—a handsome medicine case of black leather, with small silver mountings—further endorsed the guarantee of the card.

"All right, doctor," said the officer, stepping aside, with an air of bulky affability. "Orders are to be extra careful. Good many burglars and hold-ups lately. Bad night to be out. Not so cold, but—clammy."

With a formal inclination of his head, and a word or two corroborative of the officer's estimate of the weather, Doctor James continued his somewhat rapid progress. Three times that night had a patrolman accepted his professional card and the sight of his paragon of a medicine case as vouchers for his honesty of person and purpose. Had any one of those officers seen fit, on the morrow, to test the evidence of that card he would have found it borne out by the doctor's name on a handsome doorplate, his presence, calm and well dressed, in his well-equipped office—provided it were not too early, Doctor James being a late riser—and the testimony of the neighborhood to his good citizenship, his devotion to his family, and his success as a practitioner the two years he had lived among them.

Therefore, it would have much surprised any one of those zealous guardians of the peace could they have taken a peep into that immaculate medicine case. Upon opening it, the first article to be seen would have been an elegant set of the latest conceived tools used by the "box man," as the ingenious safe burglar now denominates himself. Specially designed and constructed were the implements—the short but powerful "jimmy," the collection of curiously fashioned keys, the blued drills and punches of the finest temper—capable of eating their way into chilled steel as a mouse eats into a cheese, and the clamps that fasten like a leech to the polished door of a safe and pull out the combination knob as a dentist extracts a tooth. In a little pouch in the inner side of the "medicine" case was a four-ounce vial of nitroglycerine, now half empty. Underneath the tools was a mass of crumpled banknotes and a few handfuls of gold coin, the money, altogether, amounting to eight hundred and thirty dollars.

To a very limited circle of friends Doctor James was known as "The Swell 'Greek.'" Half of the mysterious term was a tribute to his cool and gentleman-like manners; the other half denoted, in the argot of the brotherhood, the leader, the planner, the one who, by the power and prestige of his address and position, secured the information upon which they based their plans and desperate enterprises.

Of this elect circle the other members were Skitsie Morgan and Gum Decker, expert "box men," and Leopold Pretzfelder, a jeweler downtown, who manipulated the "sparklers" and other ornaments collected by the working trio. All good and loyal men, as loose-tongued as Memnon and as fickle as the North Star.

That night's work had not been considered by the firm to have yielded more than a moderate repayal for their pains. An old-style two-story side-bolt safe in the dingy office of a very wealthy old-style dry-goods firm on a Saturday night should have excreted more than twenty-five hundred dollars. But that was all they found, and they had divided it, the three of them, into equal shares upon the spot, as was their custom. Ten or twelve thousand was what they expected. But one of the proprietors had proved to be just a trifle too old-style. Just after dark he had carried home in a shirt box most of the funds on hand.

Doctor James proceeded up Twenty-fourth Street, which was, to all appearance, depopulated. Even the theatrical folk, who affect this district as a place of residence, were long since abed. The drizzle had accumulated upon the street; puddles of it among the stones received the fire of the arc lights, and returned it, shattered into a myriad liquid spangles. A captious wind, shower-soaked and chilling, coughed from the laryngeal flues between the houses.

As the practitioner's foot struck even with the corner of a tall brick residence of more pretension than its fellows the front door popped open, and a bawling negress clattered down the steps to the pavement. Some medley of words came from her mouth, addressed, like as not, to herself—the recourse of her race when alone and beset by evil. She looked to be one of that old vassal class of the South—voluble, familiar, loyal, irrepressible; her person pictured it—fat, neat, aproned, kerchiefed.

This sudden apparition, spewed from the silent house, reached the bottom of the steps as Doctor James came opposite. Her brain transferring its energies from sound to sight, she ceased her clamor and fixed her pop-eyes upon the case the doctor carried.

"Bress de Lawd!" was the benison the sight drew from her. "Is you a doctor, suh?"

"Yes, I am a physician," said Doctor James, pausing.

"Den fo' God's sake come and see Mister Chandler, suh. He done had a fit or sump'n. He layin' jist like he wuz dead. Miss Amy sont me to git a doctor. Lawd knows whar old Cindy'd a skeared one up from, if you, suh, hadn't come along. Ef old Mars' knowed one ten-hundredth part of dese doin's dey'd be shootin' gwine on, suh—pistol shootin'—leb'm feet marked off on de ground, and ev'ybody a-duellin'. And dat po' lamb, Miss Amy—"

"Lead the way," said Doctor James, setting his foot upon the step, "if you want me as a doctor. As an auditor I'm not open to engagements."

The negress preceded him into the house and up a flight of thickly carpeted stairs. Twice they came to dimly lighted branching hallways. At the second one the now panting conductress turned down a hall, stopping at a door and opening it.

"I done brought de doctor, Miss Amy."

Doctor James entered the room, and bowed slightly to a young lady standing by the side of a bed. He set his medicine case upon a chair, removed his overcoat, throwing it over the case and the back of the chair, and advanced with quiet self-possession to the bedside.

There lay a man, sprawling as he had fallen—a man dressed richly in the prevailing mode, with only his shoe removed; lying relaxed, and as still as the dead.

There emanated from Doctor James an aura of calm force and reserve strength that was as manna in the desert to the weak and desolate among his patrons. Always had women, especially, been attracted by something in his sick-room manner. It was not the indulgent suavity of the fashionable healer, but a manner of poise, of sureness, of ability to overcome fate, of deference and protection and devotion. There was an exploring magnetism in his steadfast, luminous brown eves; a latent authority in the impassive, even priestly, tranquility of his smooth countenance that outwardly fitted him for the part of confidant and consoler. Sometimes, at his first professional visit, women would tell him where they hid their diamonds at night from the burglars.

With the ease of much practice, Doctor James's unroving eyes estimated the order and quality of the room's furnishings. The appointments were rich and costly. The same glance had secured cognizance of the lady's appearance. She was small and scarcely past twenty. Her face possessed the title to a winsome prettiness, now obscured by (you would say) rather a fixed melancholy than the more violent imprint of a sudden sorrow. Upon her forehead, above one eyebrow, was a livid bruise, suffered, the physician's eye told him, within the past six hours.

Doctor James's fingers went to the man's wrist. His almost vocal eyes questioned the lady.

"I am Mrs. Chandler," she responded, speaking with the plaintive Southern slur and intonation. "My husband was taken suddenly ill about ten minutes before you came. He has had attacks of heart trouble before—some of them were very bad." His clothed state and the late hour seemed to prompt her to further explanation. "He had been out late; to—a supper, I believe."

Doctor James now turned his attention to his patient. In whichever of his "professions" he happened to be engaged he was wont to honor the "case" or the "job" with his whole interest.

The sick man appeared to be about thirty. His countenance bore a look of boldness and dissipation, but was not without a symmetry of feature and the fine lines drawn by a taste and indulgence in humor that gave the redeeming touch. There was an odor of spilled wine about his clothes.

The physician laid back his outer garments, and then, with a penknife, slit the shirt-front from collar to waist. The obstacles cleared, he laid his ear to the heart and listened intently.

"Mitral regurgitation?" he said, softly, when he rose. The words ended with the rising inflection of uncertainty. Again he listened long; and this time he said, "Mitral insufficiency," with the accent of an assured diagnosis.

"Madam," he began, in the reassuring tones that had so often allayed anxiety, "there is a probability—" As he slowly turned his head to face the lady, he saw her fall, white and swooning, into the arms of the old negress.

"Po' lamb! po' lamb! Has dey done killed Aunt Cindy's own blessed child? May de Lawd' stroy wid his wrath dem what stole her away; what break dat angel heart; what left—"

"Lift her feet," said Doctor James, assisting to support the drooping form. "Where is her room? She must be put to bed."

"In here, suh." The woman nodded her kerchiefed head toward a door. "Dat's Miss Amy's room."

They carried her in there, and laid her on the bed. Her pulse was faint, but regular. She passed from the swoon, without recovering consciousness, into a profound slumber.

"She is quite exhausted," said the physician. "Sleep is a good remedy. When she wakes, give her a toddy—with an egg in it, if she can take it. How did she get that bruise upon her forehead?"

"She done got a lick there, suh. De po' lamb fell—No, suh"—the old woman's racial mutability swept her into a sudden flare of indignation—"old Cindy ain't gwineter lie for dat debble. He done it, suh. May de Lawd wither de hand what—dar now! Cindy promise her sweet lamb she ain't gwine tell. Miss Amy got hurt, suh, on de head."

Doctor James stepped to a stand where a handsome lamp burned, and turned the flame low.

"Stay here with your mistress," he ordered, "and keep quiet so she will sleep. If she wakes, give her the toddy. If she grows any weaker, let me know. There is something strange about it."

"Dar's mo' strange t'ings dan dat 'round here," began the negress, but the physician hushed her in a seldom employed peremptory, concentrated voice with which he had often allayed hysteria itself. He returned to the other room, closing the door softly behind him. The man on the bed had not moved, but his eyes were open. His lips seemed to form words. Doctor James bent his head to listen. "The money! The money!" was what they were whispering.

"Can you understand what I say?" asked the doctor, speaking low, but distinctly.

The head nodded slightly.

"I am a physician, sent for by your wife. You are Mr. Chandler, I am told. You are quite ill. You must not excite or distress yourself at all."

The patient's eyes seemed to beckon to him. The doctor stooped to catch the same faint words.

"The money—the twenty thousand dollars."

"Where is this money?—in the bank?"

The eyes expressed a negative. "Tell her"—the whisper was growing fainter—"the twenty thousand dollars—her money"—his eyes wandered about the room.

"You have placed this money somewhere?"—Doctor James's voice was toiling like a siren's to conjure the secret from the man's failing intelligence—"Is it in this room?"

He thought he saw a fluttering assent in the dimming eyes. The pulse under his fingers was as fine and small as a silk thread.

There arose in Doctor James's brain and heart the instincts of his other profession. Promptly, as he acted in everything, he decided to learn the whereabouts of this money, and at the calculated and certain cost of a human life.

Drawing from his pocket a little pad of prescription blanks, he scribbled upon one of them a formula suited, according to the best practice, to the needs of the sufferer. Going to the door of the inner room, he softly called the old woman, gave her the prescription, and bade her take it to some drug store and fetch the medicine.

When she had gone, muttering to herself, the doctor stepped to the bedside of the lady. She still slept soundly; her pulse was a little stronger; her forehead was cool, save where the inflammation of the bruise extended, and a slight moisture covered it. Unless disturbed, she would yet sleep for hours. He found the key in the door, and locked it after him when he returned.

Doctor James looked at his watch. He could call half an hour his own, since before that time the old woman could scarcely return from her mission. Then he sought and found water in a pitcher and a glass tumbler. Opening his medicine case he took out the vial containing the nitroglycerine—"the oil," as his brethren of the brace-and-bit term it.

One drop of the faint yellow, thickish liquid he let fall in the tumbler. He took out his silver hypodermic syringe case, and screwed the needle into its place, Carefully measuring each modicum of water in the graduated glass barrel of the syringe, he diluted the one drop with nearly half a tumbler of water.

Two hours earlier that night Doctor James had, with that syringe, injected the undiluted liquid into a hole drilled in the lock of a safe, and had destroyed, with one dull explosion, the machinery that controlled the movement of the bolts. He now purposed, with the same means, to shiver the prime machinery of a human being—to rend its heart—and each shock was for the sake of the money to follow.

The same means, but in a different guise. Whereas, that was the giant in its rude, primary dynamic strength, this was the courtier, whose no less deadly arms were concealed by velvet and lace. For the liquid in the tumbler and in the syringe that the physician carefully filled was now a solution of glonoin, the most powerful heart stimulant known to medical science. Two ounces had riven the solid door of the iron safe; with one fiftieth part of a minim he was now about to still forever the intricate mechanism of a human life.

But not immediately. It was not so intended. First there would be a quick increase of vitality; a powerful impetus given to every organ and faculty. The heart would respond bravely to the fatal spur; the blood in the veins return more rapidly to its source.

But, as Doctor James well knew, over-stimulation in this form of heart disease means death, as sure as by a rifle shot. When the clogged arteries should suffer congestion from the increased flow of blood pumped into them by the power of the burglar's "oil," they would rapidly become "no thoroughfare," and the fountain of life would cease to flow.

The physician bared the chest of the unconscious Chandler. Easily and skilfully he injected, subcutaneously, the contents of the syringe into the muscles of the region over the heart. True to his neat habits in both professions, he next carefully dried his needle and re-inserted the fine wire that threaded it when not in use.

In three minutes Chandler opened his eyes, and spoke, in a voice faint but audible, inquiring who attended upon him. Doctor James again explained his presence there.

"Where is my wife?" asked the patient.

"She is asleep—from exhaustion and worry," said the doctor. "I would not awaken her, unless—"

"It isn't—necessary." Chandler spoke with spaces between his words caused by his short breath that some demon was driving too fast. "She wouldn't—thank you to disturb her—on my—account."

Doctor James drew a chair to the bedside. Conversation must not be squandered.

"A few minutes ago," he began, in the grave, candid tones of his other profession, "you were trying to tell me something regarding some money. I do not seek your confidence, but it is my duty to advise you that anxiety and worry will work against your recovery. If you have any communication to make about this—to relieve your mind about this—twenty thousand dollars, I think was the amount you mentioned—you would better do so."

Chandler could not turn his head, but he rolled his eyes in the direction of the speaker.

"Did I—say where this—money is?"

"No," answered the physician. "I only inferred, from your scarcely intelligible words, that you felt a solicitude concerning its safety. If it is in this room—"

Doctor James paused. Did he only seem to perceive a flicker of understanding, a gleam of suspicion upon the ironical features of his patient? Had he seemed too eager? Had he said too much? Chandler's next words restored his confidence.

"Where—should it be," he gasped, "but in—the safe—there?"

With his eyes he indicated a corner of the room, where now, for the first time, the doctor perceived a small iron safe, half-concealed by the trailing end of a window curtain.

Rising, he took the sick man's wrist. His pulse was beating in great throbs, with ominous intervals between.

"Lift your arm," said Doctor James.

"You know—I can't move, Doctor."

The physician stepped swiftly to the hall door, opened it, and listened. All was still. Without further circumvention he went to the safe, and examined it. Of a primitive make and simple design, it afforded little more security than protection against light-fingered servants. To his skill it was a mere toy, a thing of straw and pasteboard. The money was as good as in his hands. With his clamps he could draw the knob, punch the tumblers and open the door in two minutes. Perhaps, in another way, he might open it in one.

Kneeling upon the floor, he laid his ear to the combination plate, and slowly turned the knob. As he had surmised, it was locked at only a "day com"—upon one number. His keen ear caught the faint warning click as the tumbler was disturbed; he used the clue—the handle turned. He swung the door wide open.

The interior of the safe was bare—not even a scrap of paper rested within the hollow iron cube.

Doctor James rose to his feet and walked back to the bed.

A thick dew had formed upon the dying man's brow, but there was a mocking, grim smile on his lips and in his eyes.

"I never—saw it before," he said, painfully, "medicine and—burglary wedded! Do you—make the—combination pay—dear Doctor?"

Than that situation afforded, there was never a more rigorous test of Doctor James's greatness. Trapped by the diabolic humor of his victim into a position both ridiculous and unsafe, he maintained his dignity as well as his presence of mind. Taking out his watch, he waited for the man to die.

"You were—just a shade—too—anxious—about that money. But it never was—in any danger—from you, dear Doctor. It's safe. Perfectly safe. It's all—in the hands—of the bookmakers. Twenty—thousand—Amy's money. I played it at the races—lost every—cent of it. I've been a pretty bad boy, Burglar—excuse me—Doctor, but I've been a square sport. I don't think—I ever met—such an—eighteen-carat rascal as you are, Doctor—excuse me—Burglar, in all my rounds. Is it contrary—to the ethics—of your—gang, Burglar, to give a victim—excuse me—patient, a drink of water?"

Doctor James brought him a drink. He could scarcely swallow it. The reaction from the powerful drug was coming in regular, intensifying waves. But his moribund fancy must have one more grating fling.

"Gambler—drunkard—spendthrift—I've been those, but—a doctor-burglar!"

The physician indulged himself to but one reply to the other's caustic taunts. Bending low to catch Chandler's fast crystallizing gaze, he pointed to the sleeping lady's door with a gesture so stern and significant that the prostrate man half-lifted his head, with his remaining strength, to see. He saw nothing; but he caught the cold words of the doctor—the last sounds hie was to hear:

"I never yet—struck a woman."

It were vain to attempt to con such men. There is no curriculum that can reckon with them in its ken. They are offshoots from the types whereof men say, "He will do this," or "He will do that." We only know that they exist; and that we can observe them, and tell one another of their bare performances, as children watch and speak of the marionettes.

Yet it were a droll study in egoism to consider these two—one an assassin and a robber, standing above his victim; the other baser in his offenses, if a lesser law-breaker, lying, abhorred, in the house of the wife he had persecuted, spoiled, and smitten, one a tiger, the other a dog-wolf—to consider each of them sickening at the foulness of the other; and each flourishing out of the mire of his manifest guilt his own immaculate standard—of conduct, if not of honor.

The one retort of Doctor James must have struck home to the other's remaining shreds of shame and manhood, for it proved the *coup de grâce*. A deep blush suffused his face—an ignominious *rosa mortis*; the respiration ceased, and, with scarcely a tremor, Chandler expired.

Close following upon his last breath came the negress, bringing the medicine. With a hand gently pressing upon the closed eyelids, Doctor James told her of the end. Not grief, but a hereditary rapprochement with death in the abstract, moved her to a dismal, watery snuffling, accompanied by her usual jeremiad.

"Dar now! It's in de Lawd's hands. He am de jedge ob de transgressor, and de suppo't of dem in distress. He gwine hab suppo't us now. Cindy done paid out de last quarter fer dis bottle of physic, and it nebber come to no use."

"Do I understand," asked Doctor James, "that Mrs. Chandler has no money?"

"Money, suh? You know what make Miss Amy fall down and so weak? Stahvation, sub. Nothin' to eat in dis house but some crumbly crackers in three days. Dat angel sell her finger rings and watch mont's ago. Dis fine house, suh, wid de red cyarpets and shiny bureaus, it's all hired; and de man talkin' scan'lous about de rent. Dat debble—'scuse me, Lawd—he done in Yo' hands fer jedgment, now—he made way wid everything."

The physician's silence encouraged her to continue. The history that he gleaned from Cindy's disordered monologue was an old one, of illusion, willfulness, disaster, cruelty and pride. Standing out from the blurred panorama of her gabble were little clear pictures—an ideal home in the far South; a quickly repented marriage; an unhappy season, full of wrongs and abuse, and, of late, an inheritance of money that promised deliverance; its seizure and waste by the dog-wolf during a two months' absence, and his return in the midst of a scandalous carouse. Unobtruded, but visible between every line, ran a pure white thread through the smudged warp of the story—the simple, all-enduring, sublime love of the old negress, following her mistress unswervingly through everything to the end.

When at last she paused, the physician spoke, asking if the house contained whiskey or liquor of any sort. There was, the old woman informed him, half a bottle of brandy left in the sideboard by the dog-wolf.

"Prepare a toddy as I told you," said Doctor James. "Wake your mistress; have her drink it, and tell her what has happened."

Some ten minutes afterward, Mrs. Chandler entered, supported by old Cindy's arm. She appeared to be a little stronger since her sleep and the stimulant she had taken. Doctor James had covered, with a sheet, the form upon the bed.

The lady turned her mournful eyes once, with a half-frightened look, toward it, and pressed closer to her loyal protector. Her eyes were dry and bright. Sorrow seemed to have done its utmost with her. The fount of tears was dried; feeling itself paralyzed.

Doctor James was standing near the table, his overcoat donned, his hat and medicine case in his hand. His face was calm and impassive—practice had inured him to the sight of human suffering. His lambent brown eyes alone expressed a discreet professional sympathy.

He spoke kindly and briefly, stating that, as the hour was late, and assistance, no doubt, difficult to procure, he would himself send the proper persons to attend to the necessary finalities.

"One matter, in conclusion," said the doctor, pointing to the safe with its still wide-open door. "Your husband, Mrs. Chandler, toward the end, felt that he could not live; and directed me to open that safe, giving me the number upon which the combination is set. In case you may need to use it, you will remember that the number is forty-one. Turn several times to the right; then to the left once; stop at forty-one. He would not permit me to waken you, though he knew the end was near.

"In that safe he said he had placed a sum of money—not large—but enough to enable you to carry out his last request. That was that you should return to your old home, and, in after days, when time shall have made it easier, forgive his many sins against you."

He pointed to the table, where lay an orderly pile of banknotes, surmounted by two stacks of gold coins.

"The money is there—as he described it—eight hundred and thirty dollars. I beg to leave my card with you, in case I can be of any service later on."

So, he had thought of her—and kindly—at the last! So late! And yet the lie fanned into life one last spark of tenderness where she had thought all was turned to ashes and dust. She cried aloud "Rob! Rob!" She turned, and, upon the ready bosom of her true servitor, diluted her grief in relieving tears. It is well to think, also, that in the years to follow, the murderer's falsehood shone like a little star above the grave of love, comforting her, and gaining the forgiveness that is good in itself, whether asked for or no.

Hushed and soothed upon the dark bosom, like a child, by a crooning, babbling sympathy, at last she raised her head—but the doctor was gone.

50

Confessions of a Humorist

There was a painless stage of incubation that lasted twenty-five years, and then it broke out on me, and people said I was It.

But they called it humor instead of measles.

The employees in the store bought a silver inkstand for the senior partner on his fiftieth birthday. We crowded into his private office to present it. I had been selected for spokesman, and I made a little speech that I had been preparing for a week.

It made a hit. It was full of puns and epigrams and funny twists that brought down the house—which was a very solid one in the wholesale hardware line. Old Marlowe himself actually grinned, and the employees took their cue and roared.

My reputation as a humorist dates from half-past nine o'clock on that morning. For weeks afterward my fellow clerks fanned the flame of my self-esteem. One by one they came to me, saying what an awfully clever speech that was, old man, and carefully explained to me the point of each one of my jokes.

Gradually I found that I was expected to keep it up. Others might speak sanely on business matters and the day's topics, but from me something gamesome and airy was required.

I was expected to crack jokes about the crockery and lighten up the granite ware with persiflage. I was second bookkeeper, and if I failed to show up a balance sheet without something comic about the footings or could find no cause for laughter in an invoice of plows, the other clerks were disappointed. By degrees my fame spread, and I became a local "character." Our town was small enough to make this possible. The daily newspaper quoted me. At social gatherings I was indispensable.

I believe I did possess considerable wit and a facility for quick and spontaneous repartee. This gift I cultivated and improved by practice. And the nature of it was kindly and genial, not running to sarcasm or offending others. People began to smile when they saw me coming, and by the time we had met I generally had the word ready to broaden the smile into a laugh.

I had married early. We had a charming boy of three and a girl of five. Naturally, we lived in a vine-covered cottage, and were happy. My salary as bookkeeper in the hardware concern kept at a distance those ills attendant upon superfluous wealth.

At sundry times I had written out a few jokes and conceits that I considered peculiarly happy, and had sent them to certain periodicals that print such things. All of them had been instantly accepted. Several of the editors had written to request further contributions.

One day I received a letter from the editor of a famous weekly publication. He suggested that I submit to him a humorous composition to fill a column of space; hinting that he would make it a regular feature of each issue if the work proved satisfactory. I did so, and at the end of two weeks he offered to make a contract with me for a year at a figure that was considerably higher than the amount paid me by the hardware firm.

I was filled with delight. My wife already crowned me in her mind with the imperishable evergreens of literary success. We had lobster croquettes and a bottle of blackberry wine for supper that night. Here was the chance to liberate myself from drudgery. I talked over the matter very seriously with Louisa. We agreed that I must resign my place at the store and devote myself to humor.

I resigned. My fellow clerks gave me a farewell banquet. The speech I made there coruscated. It was printed in full by the Gazette. The next morning I awoke and looked at the clock.

"Late, by George!" I exclaimed, and grabbed for my clothes. Louisa reminded me that I was no longer a slave to hardware and contractors' supplies. I was now a professional humorist.

After breakfast she proudly led me to the little room off the kitchen. Dear girl! There was my table and chair, writing pad, ink, and pipe tray. And all the author's trappings—the celery stand full of fresh roses and honeysuckle, last year's calendar on the wall, the dictionary, and a little bag of chocolates to nibble between inspirations. Dear girl!

I sat me to work. The wall paper is patterned with arabesques or odalisques or—perhaps—it is trapezoids. Upon one of the figures I fixed my eyes. I bethought me of humor.

A voice startled me—Louisa's voice.

"If you aren't too busy, dear," it said, "come to dinner."

I looked at my watch. Yes, five hours had been gathered in by the grim scytheman. I went to dinner.

"You mustn't work too hard at first," said Louisa. "Goethe—or was it Napoleon?—said five hours a day is enough for mental labor. Couldn't you take me and the children to the woods this afternoon?"

"I am a little tired," I admitted. So we went to the woods.

But I soon got the swing of it. Within a month I was turning out copy as regular as shipments of hardware.

And I had success. My column in the weekly made some stir, and I was referred to in a gossipy way by the critics as something fresh in the line of humorists. I augmented my income considerably by contributing to other publications.

I picked up the tricks of the trade. I could take a funny idea and make a two-line joke of it, earning a dollar. With false whiskers on, it would serve up cold as a quatrain, doubling its producing value. By turning the skirt and adding a ruffle of rhyme you would hardly recognize it as *vers de societé* with neatly shod feet and a fashion-plate illustration.

I began to save up money, and we had new carpets, and a parlor organ. My townspeople began to look upon me as a citizen of some consequence instead of the merry trifler I had been when I clerked in the hardware store.

After five or six months the spontaneity seemed to depart from my humor. Quips and droll sayings no longer fell carelessly from my lips. I was sometimes hard run for material. I found myself listening to catch available ideas from the conversation of my friends. Sometimes I chewed my pencil and gazed at the wall paper for hours trying to build up some gay little bubble of unstudied fun.

And then I became a harpy, a Moloch, a Jonah, a vampire, to my acquaintances. Anxious, haggard, greedy, I stood among them like a veritable killjoy. Let a bright saying, a witty comparison, a piquant phrase fall from their lips and I was after it like a hound springing upon a bone. I dared not trust my memory; but, turning aside guiltily and meanly, I would make a note of it in my ever-present memorandum book or upon my cuff for my own future use.

My friends regarded me in sorrow and wonder. I was not the same man. Where once I had furnished them entertainment and jollity, I now preyed upon them. No jests from me ever bid for their smiles now. They were too precious. I could not afford to dispense gratuitously the means of my livelihood.

I was a lugubrious fox praising the singing of my friends, the crow's, that they might drop from their beaks the morsels of wit that I coveted.

Nearly every one began to avoid me. I even forgot how to smile, not even paying that much for the sayings I appropriated.

No persons, places, times, or subjects were exempt from my plundering in search of material. Even in church my demoralized fancy went hunting among the solemn aisles and pillars for spoil.

Did the minister give out the long-meter doxology, at once I began: "Doxology—sockdology—sockdolager—meter—meet her."

The sermon ran through my mental sieve, its precepts filtering unheeded, could I but glean a suggestion of a pun or a *bon mot*. The solemnest anthems of the choir were but an accompaniment to my thoughts as I conceived new changes to ring upon the ancient comicalities concerning the jealousies of soprano, tenor, and basso.

My own home became a hunting ground. My wife is a singularly feminine creature, candid, sympathetic, and impulsive. Once her conversation was my delight, and her ideas a source of unfailing pleasure. Now I worked her. She was a gold mine of those amusing but lovable inconsistencies that distinguish the female mind.

I began to market those pearls of unwisdom and humor that should have enriched only the sacred precincts of home. With devilish cunning I encouraged her to talk. Unsuspecting, she laid her heart bare. Upon the cold, conspicuous, common, printed page I offered it to the public gaze.

A literary Judas, I kissed her and betrayed her. For pieces of silver I dressed her sweet confidences in the pantalettes and frills of folly and made them dance in the market place.

Dear Louisa! Of nights I have bent over her cruel as a wolf above a tender lamb, hearkening even to her soft words murmured in sleep, hoping to catch an idea for my next day's grind. There is worse to come.

God help me! Next my fangs were buried deep in the neck of the fugitive sayings of my little children.

Guy and Viola were two bright fountains of childish, quaint thoughts and speeches. I found a ready sale for this kind of humor, and was furnishing a regular department in a magazine with "Funny Fancies of Childhood." I began to stalk them as an Indian stalks the antelope. I would hide behind sofas and doors, or crawl on my hands and knees among the bushes in the yard to eavesdrop while they were at play. I had all the qualities of a harpy except remorse.

Once, when I was barren of ideas, and my copy must leave in the next mail, I covered myself in a pile of autumn leaves in the yard, where I knew they intended to come to play. I cannot bring myself to believe that Guy was aware of my hiding place, but even if he was, I would be loath to blame him for his setting fire to the leaves, causing the destruction of my new suit of clothes, and nearly cremating a parent.

Soon my own children began to shun me as a pest. Often, when I was creeping upon them like a melancholy ghoul, I would hear them say to each other: "Here comes papa," and they would gather their toys and scurry away to some safer hiding place. Miserable wretch that I was!

And yet I was doing well financially. Before the first year had passed I had saved a thousand dollars, and we had lived in comfort.

But at what a cost! I am not quite clear as to what a pariah is, but I was everything that it sounds like. I had no friends, no amusements, no enjoyment of life. The happiness of my family had been sacrificed. I was a bee, sucking sordid honey from life's fairest flowers, dreaded and shunned on account of my stingo.

One day a man spoke to me, with a pleasant and friendly smile. Not in months had the thing happened. I was passing the undertaking establishment of Peter Heffelbower. Peter stood in the door and saluted me. I stopped, strangely wrung in my heart by his greeting. He asked me inside.

The day was chill and rainy. We went into the back room, where a fire burned, in a little stove. A customer came, and Peter left me alone for a while. Presently I felt a new feeling stealing over me—a sense of beautiful calm and content, I looked around the place. There were rows of shining rosewood caskets, black palls, trestles, hearse plumes, mourning streamers, and all the paraphernalia of the solemn trade. Here was peace, order, silence, the abode of grave and dignified reflections. Here, on the brink of life, was a little niche pervaded by the spirit of eternal rest.

When I entered it, the follies of the world abandoned me at the door. I felt no inclination to wrest a humorous idea from those sombre and stately trappings. My mind seemed to stretch itself to grateful repose upon a couch draped with gentle thoughts.

A quarter of an hour ago I was an abandoned humorist. Now I was a philosopher, full of serenity and ease. I had found a refuge from humor, from the hot chase of the shy quip, from the degrading pursuit of the panting joke, from the restless reach after the nimble repartee.

I had not known Heffelbower well. When he came back, I let him talk, fearful that he might prove to be a jarring note in the sweet, dirge-like harmony of his establishment.

But, no. He chimed truly. I gave a long sigh of happiness. Never have I known a man's talk to be as magnificently dull as

Peter's was. Compared with it the Dead Sea is a geyser. Never a sparkle or a glimmer of wit marred his words. Commonplaces as trite and as plentiful as blackberries flowed from his lips no more stirring in quality than a last week's tape running from a ticker. Quaking a little, I tried upon him one of my best pointed jokes. It fell back ineffectual, with the point broken. I loved that man from then on.

Two or three evenings each week I would steal down to Heffelbower's and revel in his back room. That was my only joy. I began to rise early and hurry through my work, that I might spend more time in my haven. In no other place could I throw off my habit of extracting humorous ideas from my surroundings. Peter's talk left me no opening had I besieged it ever so hard.

Under this influence I began to improve in spirits. It was the recreation from one's labor which every man needs. I surprised one or two of my former friends by throwing them a smile and a cheery word as I passed them on the streets. Several times I dumbfounded my family by relaxing long enough to make a jocose remark in their presence.

I had so long been ridden by the incubus of humor that I seized my hours of holiday with a schoolboy's zest.

Mv work began to suffer. It was not the pain and burden to me that it had been. I often whistled at my desk, and wrote with far more fluency than before. I accomplished my tasks impatiently, as anxious to be off to my helpful retreat as a drunkard is to get to his tavern.

My wife had some anxious hours in conjecturing where I spent my afternoons. I thought it best not to tell her; women do not understand these things. Poor girl!—She had one shock out of it.

One day I brought home a silver coffin handle for a paper weight and a fine, fluffy hearse plume to dust my papers with.

I loved to see them on my desk, and think of the beloved back room down at Heffelbower's. But Louisa found them, and she shrieked with horror. I had to console her with some lame excuse for having them, but I saw in her eyes that the prejudice was not removed. I had to remove the articles, though, at double-quick time.

One day Peter Heffelbower laid before me a temptation that swept me off my feet. In his sensible, uninspired way he showed me his books, and explained that his profits and his business were increasing rapidly. He had thought of taking in a partner with some cash. He would rather have me than any one he knew. When I left his place that afternoon Peter had my check for the thousand dollars I had in the bank, and I was a partner in his undertaking business.

I went home with feelings of delirious joy, mingled with a certain amount of doubt. I was dreading to tell my wife about it. But I walked on air. To give up the writing of humorous stuff, once more to enjoy the apples of life, instead of squeezing them to a pulp for a few drops of hard cider to make the pubic feel funny—what a boon that would be!

At the supper table Louisa handed me some letters that had come during my absence. Several of them contained rejected manuscript. Ever since I first began going to Heffelbower's my stuff had been coming back with alarming frequency. Lately I had been dashing off my jokes and articles with the greatest fluency. Previously I had labored like a bricklayer, slowly and with agony.

Presently I opened a letter from the editor of the weekly with which I had a regular contract. The checks for that weekly article were still our main dependence. The letter ran thus:

> DEAR SIR:
> As you are aware, our contract for the year expires with the present month. While regretting the necessity for so doing, we must say that we do not care to renew same for the coming year. We were quite pleased with your style of humor, which seems to have delighted quite a large proportion of our readers. But for the past two months we have noticed a decided falling off in its quality. Your earlier work showed a spontaneous, easy, natural flow of fun and wit. Of late it is labored, studied, and unconvincing, giving painful evidence of hard toil and drudging mechanism.
>
> Again regretting that we do not consider your contributions available any longer, we are, yours sincerely,
> THE EDITOR.

I handed this letter to my wife. After she had read it her face grew extremely long, and there were tears in her eyes.

"The mean old thing!" she exclaimed indignantly. "I'm sure your pieces are just as good as they ever were. And it doesn't take you half as long to write them as it did." And then, I suppose, Louisa thought of the checks that would cease coming. "Oh, John," she wailed, "what will you do now?"

For an answer I got up and began to do a polka step around the supper table. I am sure Louisa thought the trouble had driven me mad; and I think the children hoped it had, for they tore after me, yelling with glee and emulating my steps. I was now something like their old playmate as of yore.

"The theatre for us tonight!" I shouted; "nothing less. And a late, wild, disreputable supper for all of us at the Palace Restaurant. Lumpty-diddle-de-dee-de-dum!"

And then I explained my glee by declaring that I was now a partner in a prosperous undertaking establishment, and that written jokes might go hide their heads in sackcloth and ashes for all me.

With the editor's letter in her hand to justify the deed I had done, my wife could advance no objections save a few mild ones based on the feminine inability to appreciate a good thing such as the little back room of Peter Hef—no, of Heffelbower & Co's. undertaking establishment.

In conclusion, I will say that today you will find no man in our town as well liked, as jovial, and full of merry sayings as I. My jokes are again noised about and quoted; once more I take pleasure in my wife's confidential chatter without a mercenary thought, while Guy and Viola play at my feet distributing gems of childish humor without fear of the ghastly tormentor who used to dog their steps, notebook in hand.

Our business has prospered finely. I keep the books and look after the shop, while Peter attends to outside matters. He says that my levity and high spirits would simply turn any funeral into a regular Irish wake.

Other Titles In This Series

Other Titles In This Series